MW01516618

Gathering Thunder

Evan Burgess

Book Two

For my family and friends

who encouraged me to keep writing.

Prologue

His gift, it was his blessing.

As well as his curse.

From the beginning, he had been unloved, unwanted. They been repulsed by him, disgusted. They had pushed him away, neglected him from the day he was born. *He wasn't normal, he wasn't right.* Before he was even a year old, his parents had placed him in a blanket and left him on the steps of Saint Briggon's Monastery. They would have put him in a basket first, but that would be a waste of a perfectly good basket.

The women at the church had cooed over this *miracle* left at their doorsteps. They picked him up and hugged him close. That's when they had noticed what was different. Their love ceased, their concern halted, replaced with confusion and disgust. But still, they took the poor babe in. The nurtured him, they clothed him, they let him play with the other orphans.

But yet, he was always different.

He was set apart. The other orphans treated him different; the women that looked after them always seemed to give their love to the others just a little bit more. Why didn't they love him? Why wasn't he *normal?*

Normal.

He wanted to join in their games, he wanted to sit with them at dinner, he wanted to laugh, to play, to run around with them. But no, they would not allow it, neither the orphans nor the priestesses. For all his life, he was always the odd man out, the thorn in one's side, the rotten apple on the clean tree.

Day after day, month after month, he was tormented. They would tease him, they would pester him. There were two that were the worst, two brothers. It seemed their only goal in life was to make his a living hell. He had grown used to neglect, he had grown accustomed to the name calling, the ridicule, but the physical abuse he couldn't stand. There was no ignoring that.

They would beat him every chance they got, every time the priestesses weren't watching, making his eyes puff up and his lips bleed. They would strike him until he could hardly walk. He would hobble around, his knees scratched and elbows scuffed. But yet, the priestesses wouldn't do anything. Was it because they truly didn't notice, or because they didn't care?

He hated himself. He hated them, *all* of them.

It was in his nature to obey. *Why? Why was he like this?* He couldn't help it. Whoever held the highest authority, he had no other choice but to obey whatever they told him. He tried to disobey, but he simply just *couldn't*. It was agony.

His entire life he was subjected to this. As long as the priestesses weren't around, he was forced to listen to the brothers' idiotic, insulting demands. He would do things for them that would often end in pain, embarrassment or trouble with the priests of the church. His life was anguish.

Slowly, slowly, he began to notice something different with himself. As he reached his teenage years, his life rearing into adulthood, a new power, *ability* seemed to make itself present to him. Instead of being forced to obey, he found he could sway others with the cool of his voice. He found if he chose the *right* words, coupled with a certain tone, pitch, and body movement they would be convinced by what he was saying. This came to his advantage.

He found he could mould the priestesses into doing things they ordinarily wouldn't, like letting him out into the city at night, where he felt his mind unwind, or make another orphan give him their serving of food.

Over the years, he was even able to force the two boys that tormented him to keep away. With his new power, life was looking up.

But it didn't last long.

One dark night he stood under the stars, blood on his worn tunic. His fingers shook and he couldn't unclench his jaw. His thin, tall body was as taut as a wire, images flashing past his vision. *What had he done?*

3

Nothing, really. Yes, it wasn't him, they couldn't blame him. He hadn't done it, *they* had. He had only...*convinced* them to. That's right. They had done it to themselves.

He gawked at the body in front of him, the same body that he had stared at with pitiless contempt for his whole life when it was still alive. Now it was as still as a shadow, staring blankly up into the sky. The body's brother was still alive out there somewhere. But he was mortally wounded. He wouldn't live for much longer.

They had jumped him and he had reacted, using his power with more force than ever before. The one boy almost willingly stabbed his brother before stabbing himself and eventually running back into the night. With one boy gone and the other dead at his feet, he picked up the knife as the situation struck him. *What had he just done?*

A sound interrupted his thoughts. Before he could react, a chubby, richly adorned youth strutted out into the small alley he was standing in. The strong smell of whiskey clung to his breath.

They stared at each other for a moment, both registering confusion. The richly dressed young man spotted the body. His head snapped back up to the orphan still standing dazed.

"How did that man die?" he asked. There was no fear in his voice or anger, just...curiosity. And an inner cunning brewing behind his bloodshot eyes.

"I—I..."

"Was it you? I'll have you sent to the dungeons for this." His jutted his chin forward confidently, as if he was trying to prove something. "Speak up!"

"No, I didn't kill them," he said at last. "He killed himself, so to speak."

"Why would he do that?" The young man inspected him closer for a moment, as if he was looking for something in his pale features.

"I told him to. Well, his brother actually killed him."

The youth took a step back, startled. He raised his eyebrows. "You told him to kill his brother, and he obeyed, just like that?"

"Yes. But they were trying to attack me, I had no other... Well, you see I have a gift; I can manipulate people like that. I swear, I didn't mean to do it, I—I just..."

The man squinted at his eyes, bewildered. He put his whisky bottle down on a hay bale. "Come with me. If you can truly do what you speak, I have a great need of you, sir...?"

"Zeptus."

The young man took Zeptus's hand with a sly grin. "It's a pleasure to meet you, Zeptus. I am Prince Morrindale. I can promise you right now, you and I will go far together. Come with me and do as I say."

Zeptus frowned. He could remember it clearly. The first day he had met King Morrindale, the only man that hadn't been repulsed by his purple eyes. From then on in, everybody accepted him, they had to. For three years later he had become the king's advisor, a respectful position. He, Zeptus, orphan, neglected, outcast, had become one of the most important and influential men Vallenfend had ever seen.

It shamed him to think how the King was using him. But he had no choice, he had to obey.

Zeptus stepped out onto the balcony where half of Vallenfend was awaiting eagerly. A cheer erupted as he appeared, but he quickly waved it back down.

"People of Vallenfend," he declared, "Kael Rundown is a traitor to this city, a criminal. He alone is the one reason your safety, your peace is compromised. He has joined sides with the dragon and now plots to destroy us at this very moment. He is our enemy."

The crowd cheered even louder. Now, anger spread across their faces. For the first time in thirty years, people were fighting against the enlistment less and overall the city was more unified in their shared hatred towards this one individual.

Zeptus looked sideways at King Morrindale, who was smiling at the crowd sinisterly. All thanks to him, almost every man, woman and child was now against Kael, making the boy's plight even more impossible. King Morrindale's plot was nearly unstoppable now.

5

"Forgive me," Zeptus whispered to himself, "forgive me Kael Rundown. Forgive me, *Vallenfend.*"

Chapter 1

Kael Rundown was jerked rudely awake. He snorted and shook his head of disorientation. He looked around, quickly remember where he was and what was happening. He leaned forward, reflecting the dream he had just been plagued by.

He had been falling—no, flying? Floating? He had been weightless, suspended in the middle of no discernable mass or space. There was no down, there was no up, but yet *underneath* him were ships. Huge, massive ships. Their many sails, ropes and masts made them look like they were covered in a strange coat of mottled fur. The ships were travelling across dark water, towards a land that he couldn't recognize, travelling at a speed that was impossible. He could see people on the boats far below, little specks that clung to them like sticks or pieces of branches in the beast's fur. He squinted, trying to see their faces, but they were so dark...

Then it had stopped.

Another tremor ran through Shatterbreath's body. Kael patted the dragon's back and she looked back with one lazy eye.

"Sorry, Tiny," she mused, "did I wake you? I didn't mean to, I hit some turbulence."

"Why do I not believe you?"

Shatterbreath chuckled, sending another tremor underneath Kael. "You think I woke you on purpose?" she teased. "Why would I do that? That's just rude. Who do you think I am?"

Kael put his hands up. "Never mind, never mind," he countered, "that's just what it felt like."

Shatterbreath pointed her muzzle back forwards, huffing. "Yeah, I'm right, you're wrong. Again. What reason would I have to wake you anyway? It's not like you were snoring, gagging, wheezing, snorting, grunting..." She trailed off. Kael laughed.

They were travelling over a vast field of endless green, most of which was dappled with spots of Fall brown. Despite the change of seasons, it was still quite warm out. The mountains of Vallenfend were far behind them now, signifying that home was far away.

7

Kael looked back, staring at the backside of Shatterbreath's mountain. *Home,* it was no longer his. How strange that was. *Banished,* he was never allowed to get back in. His heart skipped a beat thinking that. It made him sad, so he tried to pry his mind away from his homesickness.

He had to force himself to remember why he and Shatterbreath were on this journey. *To save Vallenfend.* Months ago, Shatterbreath had befriended Kael in the hopes of finding the true reason soldiers were being sent in vain attempts to kill her. As Kael had discovered, Vallenfend's king was reducing the population in preparation for the city to be captured by an invading empire. Seeing his own city refuse him, Kael and Shatterbreath had decided their best chance to fend off the threat would be to convince other nations to assist them.

Kael turned his attention to the clouds passing by. He enjoyed his time in the air. He loved flying with Shatterbreath, and she loved flying with him as well. She had told him earlier that she liked it better than flying by herself. Being so high in the air gave Kael a sense of...empowerment as well. He felt invincible soaring hundreds of feet above the ground, even higher than the birds that would skirt around Vallenfend. Nothing could harm him up here, there wasn't anybody that sought to take his life, there was no dilemma he had to solve. All was peaceful.

He leaned back, wary of Shatterbreath's spines. Although he had placed sword caps on the ones around her shoulders, they could still give him a good bruise if he hit one a tad too hard. A strange feeling washed into his body as he watched the dragon's wings beat on either side of him. He was fond of Shatterbreath; there was no doubt about that. But it still seemed strange to him. They had formed such a strong friendship in the little time they had been together, one which Kael could sense would be inseparable. Although she didn't say anything, Kael knew Shatterbreath felt the same way.

He closed his eyes, letting out a content sigh.

A few minutes later, he was rocked awake again. This time, it felt different. Shatterbreath wasn't playing now.

Kael, his senses suddenly alert, rocked forward, leaning out over her shoulder.

"Shatterbreath, what was that, what's happening?"

The dragon didn't respond, instead keeping her muzzle set forward.

Kael tried again. "Shatterbreath?"

Her brows shot upwards and a chill ran up her back, which Kael watched as it ran over her body, ending at her tail. Her jaw clenched before she spoke. "Ripwind," she said ominously, voice low.

"What?"

"Kael, Ripwind!" She growled and began to beat her wings harder, making Kael's heartbeat quicken. What was happening? "Bah, I can't avoid it!"

Suddenly, Kael realized there was a massive black cloud approaching them at a surreal speed. How had he not noticed it? How had *she* not noticed it? It seemed to pulsate angrily, brief flashes escaping from its sinuous, frothing entity. It carrying with it a loud and terrible noise that like hundreds of Shatterbreaths, all roaring at once. It was frightening, yet strangely intriguing.

"Are—are we going into that?" Kael screamed, pushing himself back to the center of Shatterbreath's shoulders. "It doesn't look too friendly!"

Shatterbreath kept flapping. "It's too late, Tiny, I can't outrun it now, and it's far too big to avoid. We're going to have to fly right through this."

"Why didn't you see it earlier?"

"These types of storms, which our species call Ripwind, are very swift. They often appear out of nowhere and contain high wind speeds that are very deadly."

"There's lightning in it!"

Shatterbreath was yelling to talk to Kael now. "It's the wind you have to worry about." She gasped as the cloud finally reached them. "Oh, hang on tight, Kael! Try to wrap a blanket or something around—"

Her voice was cut out as the storm cloud hit them.

Immediately, the wind struck them with the force of fist. At once, his eyes were forced shut and he was blind to his surroundings. His hair slicked straight back and his clothes whipped in the wind, creating a deafening sound. He clambered desperately to find one of Shatterbreath's spines, clinging on for a frightening moment with only his legs.

He struggled to pull himself forwards, fighting the screeching wind every inch he moved closer. He finally tucked himself into the meagre cover of Shatterbreath's shoulders and the wind died down slightly around him.

It was cold! The wind was moving so fast, that it had become as cold as snow. Kael began to shiver, his whole body suddenly very tense. The gale was so fierce, Kael's skin was starting to prickle and sting. He needed to wrap himself up in something.

He tried to reach for his blanket, keeping one hand on Shatterbreath's spine. He leaned back and groped at his pack, which was tied onto the top of Shatterbreath's back. The wind pushed into him, only making his uncomfortable position worse. He opened the top of the pack with some effort. The wind was only intensifying as well, making Kael's grip falter. It felt as though there were three grown men pulling on him, trying to pry him off Shatterbreath's back. If that was to happen, he'd surely be dead. He finally snagged a blanket from his pack, tucked it under his arm and secured the bag tighter than before, worried that the wind would carry it away. He quickly wrapped the blanket around himself.

The wind seemed to be coming from every direction, blowing in Kael's face, pushing him from behind and rocking him back and forth violently. Fear began to rattle him. *How would they survive this?*

Kael couldn't tell if Shatterbreath was worse off than he, for she too was getting pummelled by the wind, even with her colossal size. She was furiously beating her wings, struggling to keep them oriented upright. Every once and a while, he could hear her roar and more or less feel a *whoosh* as her wings were snapped to an uncomfortable angle. She was doing her best, but her best was not good enough. How long would this last?

There seemed no end to the cloud. Kael chanced opening his eyes for a moment. Chaos was all around them, smothering. Rain endlessly swirled around them in torrents, weaving a strangely beautiful pattern that was only disturbed by Shatterbreath's body. It would have been unnervingly dark inside the cloud if it wasn't for the occasional flash of lightning within its depths. As they moved deeper into the Ripwind, the heavy, frothing clouds only grew darker.

Lightning cracked below them, followed directly by a sickening *boom* of thunder that shook Shatterbreath's body and made Kael deaf for a few terrifying seconds. For a moment, he thought he had lost his hearing entirely.

An exceptionally powerful gust of wind met them, blowing Kael's blanket out of his grip and sending it sprawling into the depths of the cloud. In less than a second, it was gone. A new noise greeted them as they pressed reluctantly forward. It sounded like pouring sand and the wash of waves on a beach.

"Hrmmc-ome-stheh-ail!" Shatterbreath called back at him, fright thick in her voice.

"What?" he screamed.

"Here comes the hail!" she roared over her shoulder, her eyes shut tight.

Kael was about to yell something back, but instead he got a mouthful of ice. Suddenly, a bombardment of hail began to rain over them, blocking out Kael's vision.

Kael usually liked hail. It was a thing he rarely experienced. As a boy, he had enjoyed the *plunking* sounds they made as they fell over his house. He used to love to go out and collect the biggest chunk he could find and watch it melt away in his palm. It had been a treat for him.

He no longer liked hail. Now he hated it.

The hail, propelled from the breakneck wind, was like getting stung by hundreds of bees all at once. The razor-sharp ice washed over him, stinging his face, slicing his clothes and cutting in more protrusive places. He cried out in pain as he felt his knuckles split open and begin to bleed. The warm blood did little to stop the hail that continued to widen the small cuts.

11

He hid his face from the stinging hail, but had no choice but to try and endure the rest that was rushing over his body. If he lightened his grip, ever so slightly, he could risk losing his position altogether. He doubted Shatterbreath would be able to find him in this storm before he hit the ground.

Kael had thought the small hail was bad, but it got even bigger.

Through his tightly-clenched eyes, he was aware of passing slivers of ice as big as gold coins. There was nothing he could do to stop the large chunks of hail. He screamed, feeling the cuts on his hands intensify and the stinging ice open the flesh on his knees and forearms.

Why hadn't he worn his armour? It was just behind him, rippling in the screaming wind, but he couldn't get to it safely now, it had been hard enough before. If he went for it now, there was no chance he would be able to strap it all on while being throttled like this.

Shatterbreath heard his scream and bravely, she reared upwards, becoming perpendicular to where Kael presumed the ground was, so that he was protected by the bulk of her body. The full brunt of the wind struck her, ceasing the shower of hail over Kael. He could feel her wince, but didn't say anything, grateful that she was protecting him.

The temporary shelter did not last long.

The wind changed and slammed into Shatterbreath's side, making her roll through the air and submitting Kael to the biting wind once again.

They fell freely for a spell before Shatterbreath was able to realign herself. When she did, she valiantly put herself in the same position, chest forward, underbelly directly exposed to the incoming wind.

That's when the worst of the storm hit.

Ice as large as his fist—and even bigger—began to soar by, literally *whizzing* as each piece did. A crack of lightning sounded overhead, followed by another deafening *boom*.

Shatterbreath roared as the projectiles struck her underside. She sounded as though she was in pain, but more than that, she was frustrated. No, she was downright enraged.

Kael felt her body become warmer from the pure rage. Instinct was cutting in, she was fighting for life. She roared again, this time more savage. Suddenly, Kael felt afraid to be riding on her back. He hadn't seen this part of her since the first day they met, when she killed his troupe.

She breathed a great jet of flame into the air ahead of her, still upright in the buffering wind. The flame washed back over her, making her backside light up as it flew past Kael. The heat was intense, but luckily he was far enough away from the blast to stay unharmed.

Shatterbreath quickly pitched forward, startling Kael.

Her back flexed underneath him as she beat her wings as hard as she could, propelling them into the awaiting wind.

The sudden speed from her, coupled with the storm's rage, was so powerful, Kael couldn't hold on much longer. Then, altogether, his legs gave out and he was picked up off of Shatterbreath's back. He cried out in alarm as he lost his grip with his left hand as well. Shatterbreath was unaware. Only his right hand was still holding on tightly to her spine. The unrelenting hail forced him to cover his eyes with the crook of his elbow.

His fingers slipped, just barely. He was holding on to the sword cap that he had placed on her spine. He gritted his teeth from the strain of holding on with just his fingers. His other arm was preoccupied with covering his eyes—he was worried if he brought it forward, the ice would blind him.

Time slowed to a crawl and the world disappeared as the sword cap slipped slightly. He couldn't see it, but he could tell the cap was barely fixed on her spine. If it came loose entirely, it would surely mean his death. With all his might, he willed it to stay on, squeezed harder to try and pinch it tighter to the ivory spine. It didn't obey him. With one last wrench from the wind, the sword cap came free altogether. Kael was suddenly airborne, completely free of Shatterbreath's back. His mind seemed to freeze. His body went numb.

Then, quite suddenly, all was still.

He slammed back down onto the dragon's back, at once going limp. His gut was jabbed sharply by her capped spine, knocking the wind out of him. He lay futilely on her back, watching the heinous thundercloud drift away.

Kael squinted at the bright sunlight overhead, dazed. Minutes passed by before he dared to move, his body quite sore. He lifted the sword cap, which was still in his grip, up to his eyes. He scowled at it and tried to let go, but his fingers wouldn't obey, they were still wrapped firmly around it. With his other hand, he pried his fingers off, wincing. When he did, they remained in the same position, looking like the crooked talons of a bird. He groaned as he clenched his fist, sending an explosion of pain up his arm.

It took an eternity for Shatterbreath to overcome her enragement and look back to see if he was okay. When she did, her pupils were dilated and she still wore a snarl on her muzzle.

"Are you okay?" she said, her voice full of disbelief towards what just happened.

Kael moaned. "Yeah, you?"

"More or less."

"Can—can we get ground under our feet—immediately?"

Shatterbreath nodded. "Yes," she said numbly, still dazed. "Let—let's rest."

She dipped downwards.

Kael took another bite of the venison. He wished there was some spice on it, but Shatterbreath had taken his can of spices again. He hated when she did that.

He repositioned himself on the log he was sitting on, trying to swallow the pain that erupted all when he did. All over his body, he had small gashes that resembled paper cuts and his nice blue tunic was shredded. The inside of his legs were raw from holding on so tight and almost every muscle was stiff now. His knuckles had suffered the most. They had been cut so badly, tendons had been showing and skin had been peeled back. They reminded Kael of the ground beef he often saw at Bunda's shop.

The dragon was as bad off as he. In fact, she was even worse. Her wings had gaping holes in some places in the membrane, big enough for Kael to put his hand through. Her legs were cut and her cheeks were slit neatly open, being the most protrusive parts of her body. Her underbelly was not as damaged as Kael would have first thought, but enough that she had to lie on her back when she rested. The front sides of her wings were the worst.

Kael glanced over at her. She winced and twitched as she moved one of her legs closer to her body. She was gazing up at the night sky, her chest pointing upwards. The tip of her tail danced thoughtfully.

"Ripwind? Is that what you called it?" Kael asked, breaking the silence.

For a time, she simply continued to stare at the sky, entranced by the twinkling lights. "Hmm?" She took notice of him and moved her head to the side to look at him. "What was that?"

"That cloud, you called it Ripwind."

"Yes, that's what our species calls it. I think you can guess why." She looked skywards again, but kept talking. "We should consider ourselves lucky. Those storms are deadly and unforgiving. Few dragons have enter those and survive. Younger, inexperienced ones always die."

Kael nodded. Maybe it was because they had overcome a death-defying challenge, or maybe it was just the serenity of the place they were in, but he felt good for some reason. They had landed immediately after the storm, picking a nice place situated in between a hill made of boulders and a small creek that ran through the centre of a desert of grass.

"I was thinking about this," Kael started, "about where to start, what to do... How are we—how am I—supposed to convince an entire kingdom to help us out? I couldn't even convince Vallenfend."

Shatterbreath sighed. "We'll start at the nearest city, and work out way across the continent, as easy as that. As for *what* to do, we'll deal with that when we get there. Every kingdom is different and as such there will be different ways to convince them. Don't worry about it."

"Yes, but—"

"You'll do fine. I believe you will."

Kael smiled. "Thanks."

Shatterbreath returned his smile. "Don't worry about it, Tiny. Now," she was interrupted by a huge yawn, one which curled her tongue and made her bare all her fearsome, pearl-white teeth. "Now I'm going to sleep. I am *so* tired. I ache all over, especially my wings. It will take us longer, but I'm afraid we're going to have to walk tomorrow."

"Really?" Kael groaned.

"Yes," she gave him a shove with her tail, "*really*. Stop complaining, you little hatchling. Once I'm feeling fit again, we'll be airborne again. It'll only be for a day."

Mollified, Kael leaned back. "Fine, so be it. Oh hey, wait, what's the name of the first kingdom we're going to visit? Do you even know?"

Shatterbreath eyed him. "I course I *know*, Tiny. It's called... Umm..."

"Yes?"

"Let me think. Oh yes, it's called Snailtown."

"Snailtown?"

"Yes, that's it." Shatterbreath smiled at his expression. "You don't believe me?"

Kael shook his head. "No, I do, it's just a strange name."

Shatterbreath shook her neck and with one last glance, rolled onto her side, turning away from Kael. "Whatever. I'm going to sleep now. Good night."

Kael stared at her back. "See you in the morning."

Shatterbreath's heavy breath echoed through the immediate area, signalling that she was fast asleep. However, Kael stayed awake, gazing up at the sky. There was no moon that night, but the stars shed a great amount of light. They were brighter here than in Vallenfend. As he admired the sparkling gems above him, he wondered what waited in the cities before him; he could only imagine what it would be like to be in a town that wasn't his. More than that though, he was deeply concerned with how he was going to convince thousands of people of the upcoming danger. He suddenly felt so small.

Chapter 2

Faerd stood in the middle of the market, staring up at the sky. The clouds above him slithered by, forming various shapes that reminded him of animals. He frowned.

Today was his day off, but he couldn't find anything exciting to do. He could visit his various friends, but he didn't really want to. He didn't want to look at their flowery, overzealous expressions. For once, he was tired of all the attention the girls gave him. It just didn't feel right to be doing so much flirting when such terrible things were happening all around him.

Once again, his thoughts turned back to Kael.

He began to stroll through the market, making his way steadily home. Where could his Kael be? What was he doing *right* now? It made Faerd feel even worse to know that he was safe and sound, doing essentially nothing, while his best friend was fighting for all their lives. The people of Vallenfend didn't even realize it.

His thoughts were so troubled, he decided to take the long way home to mull it over some more.

Faerd wished Kael had brought him with them, him and that dragon. It bothered him not being able to help. He groaned out loud. His heart ached for action, but he just *couldn't*. For a moment, he was actually angry with Kael. How dare he leave him behind to fester! Faerd could help, surely he could. Couldn't he?

Sure, Faerd, he thought, *you, help? Ha! What a prospect. How could* you *help? You don't know how to fight with a sword. You hardly know what's going on right now. All you could be is a burden on him.* You'd *probably get him killed if anything.*

As much as Faerd didn't want to listen to the mocking voice in his head, he had to admit, it was right. There really was no way he could help. What skill did he have that Kael could use?

Bah, curse this all.

He would just have to settle for sitting here, waiting.

Similar troubling thoughts plagued him as he walked home. Eventually, he was forced back into the real world as he bumped into some stranger.

"Sorry there," he mumbled to the man, whose face was hidden by a black cloak. Indeed, the man was wearing an entire outfit made of black.

The man put out his hands defensively. "Don't worry about it," he said throatily. His voice sounded familiar.

No matter.

Faerd walked the remaining distance to his house wondering about the man. Who was he? He had never seen that guy walking around this street before...

Once again, his thoughts were interrupted as he spotted his house. He loved his house dearly. Like Kael's it was little more than a shack with a bedroom, but it was home. It filled him with a familiar warm, nostalgic feeling when he set eyes on it.

His content was soon replaced by anxiety when he spotted the door. It was slightly ajar. Had he left it open? No, he remembered clearly locking it that morning. He had always had trouble with the door. It often took him several minutes to force the lock to work. Upon that, he had a sticky door, which made it hard to close it shut.

Somebody had definitely broken into his house.

He rushed up to the building, nestled in between two similar structures. He swung the door open, expecting to find the interior in shambles.

He was surprised to find there was nothing wrong at all.

His shelves containing all his things were still upright, his walls were intact. His table was still there, holding the two plates and matching cutlery. All was perfect, just how he left it. Then why had the door been broken into?

He walked into his room, which was also untouched. His shoulders sagged, his heart returning to its regular pace. And then he spotted it. There was a slip of paper resting on his bed.

At first, he thought it was a letter of drafting, which sent his heart beating wildly again. Putting a hand to his chest, Faerd growled to himself. It wasn't an enlistment letter. Those came in envelopes. This was just a plain white piece of paper.

He strolled over to it, curious. However, he was wary to pick it up. He could see that there was writing on the other side, but he feared what it would say. What was this all about?

With shaking fingers, he picked it up. It said:

Faerd Nedarb,

They know that you are friends with Kael Rundown. You are in danger. They are sending guards to apprehend you friends, the Stockwins. Go to them and get them out of the city at once. You will be drafted in a week; there is nothing here for you. Do NOT fight the guards, just run. You will die if you stay, and so will your friends. Get out of Vallenfend.

Sincerely, a Friend.

Faerd reread the note over and over, mouthing the words as he did. He had never liked reading, and now he liked it even less. Faerd placed the note back down on his bed and stared at it, one hand on his hip, the other rubbing his jaw absently. What should he do? Should he heed the note's warning? It could be a trap. Whoever had left it here *had* broken in to place it there to begin with. Plus they knew his last name. Nobody knew his last name, he had assured that. Whoever made this warning obviously had access to the castle's records.

Faerd picked the note back up and stared at it some more. He frowned at it and crumpled it into a ball, tossing it across his room. No, he wouldn't listen to its warning, he didn't trust it. But then again...

In a snap decision, he resolved that he would go to the Stockwin's and stay there for a while, just in case some guards did attack. Whatever happened though, he wasn't going to run away. That was just cowardly. If one thing was for certain, Faerd had never been a coward, he was one who would stay and fight. He had the scars on his face to prove that.

He rubbed his face, feeling the small grooves. He hoped he wasn't wrong about this.

A few hours later, Faerd sat on the Stockwin's front porch, leaning back in a wooden chair. Laura and Mrs. Stockwin were still inside. They had taken the message more seriously. In fact, they had been eager to heed its warning and leave. Faerd wouldn't allow it. The message was fake he reasoned. Somebody was just trying to scare them away, perhaps for the purpose of taking their homes.

Still, the two women had refused to go back to work and now here they all there, waiting for something to happen. Or in Faerd's case, waiting for *nothing* to happen.

He scanned the area around the Stockwin house. There was a chicken walking down the road, scratching at the gravel, otherwise all was unnervingly still. The Stockwin's neighbours were all gone. Except for one family.

A woman peered out her window, peeling back the curtains to get a view of Faerd, who scowled back at her through furrowed brows in return. She quickly withdrew back, letting the curtain fall back into place.

Faerd stared at their front door. What was that about?

He fingered the cloth in his hands, a grey napkin Mrs. Stockwin had given him to wipe his hands on. He flicked the apple core that was in his other hand away.

There came a shuffle from down the street. Faerd started.

He stood up and knocked on the door to the Stockwin's house. Laura and her mother came outside just in time as a small battalion of soldiers strolled into view from down the gently curved street.

Faerd held his breath as they approached, hoping they'd pass by without any fuss.

The soldiers hesitated in the middle of the street. There were five of them in total. One of them pulled a parchment from his tunic and studied it for a moment. After sharing some words among his peers, the apparent leader pointed towards the Stockwin's house.

"You there," the leader called, "we have come here to arrest the Stockwins."

Faerd scrutinized the group of soldiers, wearing a smirk. On the inside though, he was screaming. *The letter had been correct!*

"On what charge?" Faerd asked.

The group of boys shifted their weight. Some of them put their hands on the hilts of their swords. They probably hadn't been expecting resistance. "Fraternizing," the lead soldier said at last, "with the enemy. We were told that these two were seen in direct contact with an enemy of Vallenfend." He pointed up at them, taking a step forwards as he did. "They revealed vital information about our city. They must be brought into justice."

Faerd scoffed. "They shared no such information." The soldiers weren't particularly intimidating, dressed in nothing more than blue tunics and leather plates. Still, the weapons they carried were noteworthy. Two had swords, another two had spears and one boy had a large, two-handed hammer. That one didn't concern Faerd. The boy couldn't even hold it without one end dragging over the ground.

The soldier frowned. "What's your name?"

"Faerd."

The soldier pulled the parchment closer to his face and squinted. "I don't see your name here. Step aside, enough of this. Move out of our way or we'll be forced to—"

He didn't get to finish his sentence as Faerd leapt off the balcony, putting all his weight into one massive punch straight to the young man's jaw. Laura screamed.

The soldier dropped to the ground, knocked out almost instantly. Faerd clenched his fists tighter, bending his knees as he faced the rest of the soldiers.

Faerd didn't know how to fight with a weapon, no. But he had seen his fair share of fistfights. He knew how to dodge as well as take a hit.

The other soldiers froze for a moment, staring at their fallen comrade. One of the boys drew his sword, cursing loudly. "You'll pay for that!"

Sure, Faerd thought, *try.*

He quickly wrapped the grey napkin he had been holding around his left knuckles.

The boy raised his sword high and tried to bring it down on Faerd. He sidestepped the blade, spun around and smacked the boy across his cheek with the back of his hand with a satisfying *smack.*

Faerd would have followed through, but a different soldier took a lunge at him with his spear. The boy was stocky and had a big, flat forehead. Faerd wasn't intimidated. He dodged the spear nimbly grabbed the shaft. The soldier was stronger and succeeded in wrenching it from his grasp, but Faerd simply jumped forwards and knocked him out with one clean stroke.

A blade narrowly missed Faerd's flesh, glancing his backside and cutting his shirt. Faerd batted the flat side of the sword away, sweeping his feet underneath the boy as he did. This soldier fell as well. Seconds later, he too was unconscious.

A pain erupted across Faerd's back. He whipped around and seized the shaft of the spear that the soldier had swung at him. This time, he succeeded in the weapon away. Faerd cracked the spear against the side of its owner's head.

One last soldier remained. Faerd ducked as the hammed swung over his head. The boy holding it kept spinning as the head of the hammer swung passed Faerd, propelled by the momentum of the heavy thick piece of metal. How convenient.

Faerd wrapped his arm around the boy's neck, pinching the crook of his elbow around his trachea. He squeezed. The boy gasped and clawed at Faerd's arms, but it was all in vain. Faerd waiting for a short time until the soldier stopped thrashing. Once the boy was unconscious, he relaxed and let his limp body fall to the ground.

He turned back to Laura and her mother, who were still both standing on their porch, wearing absolutely dazed expressions.

Laura was the first to speak. "Are—did you kill them?"

Faerd laughed. "Of course not! I'm not a killer!" He smiled. "See, I told you there was nothing to worry about! In *danger,* psh. I knew that note was fake."

Laura gave him an angry look.

Chapter 3

Walking was far more gruelling that flying, that was for sure. Kael wished dearly that they hadn't passed through that Ripwind cloud. There was nothing he could do about it now though.

He rubbed his knuckles absently, which sent a spasm of pain shooting up his arm. Cursing as he stumbled over a rabbit hole, he turned to Shatterbreath.

"Are you feeling better yet?" he asked her.

She rose up on her hind legs and beat her wings twice, wincing as she did. "No," she said curtly, "for the millionth time *today*, I am not feeling better yet."

Kael groaned. "Really? You can't hurt that bad. This is taking *forever!* You could at least let me ride on your back or something."

The dragon released a jet of flame. "Huh, not likely." She smirked at him. "I am not a horse. You have legs, you can use them. I will only let you ride me when we are in the air. Or maybe if you were injured. Maybe."

Kael pursed his lips, aggravated by this all. They had been walking for two days now. *Two days!* Judging by the ground they had covered in the first day alone while in the air, they could have probably been there by now. Instead, they were walking at an agonizing pace, both of them limping from their wounds and becoming increasingly impatient. Kael wouldn't have minded the walking if there was something to look at. *This place was so barren!*

They were surrounded by brown in every direction. Fields and fields of prairie grass and weeds grew in vast amounts everywhere he looked, stretching off to infinity like the ocean. The grass even carried waves over it like the ocean, caused by the occasional wisp of wind that would rush by, carrying seeds with it that would stick to Kael's hair and make Shatterbreath sneeze. Kael recalled the beauty of Shatterbreath's mountain, which was long out of sight by now. He wouldn't have minded hiking in there as opposed to this.

At least it wasn't so hot out.

Shatterbreath suddenly perked up, stretching her neck out to its fullest length. She bobbed and licked her lips. Kael wanted to know what she found so interesting.

"Oh, nothing," she said when he inquired. "Just saw a coyote or something."

Kael sighed. This was all so *boring*. It gave him time to think about what he was going to do when he eventually reached the first city. More often than not, these thoughts were negative. He kept replaying situations that could quickly get awkward and possible ways the people could react to what he was doing.

He just wanted to get there already, so that his agony wouldn't be prolonged. He figured that the first city would be the shove to get the log rolling. Their reaction, in a way, would determine how he would talk, act or respond to the rest of the cities.

Kael screamed. "Are we there yet?"

"Yes."

"What, really?"

"Oh yeah. I just loved the way you were squirming with impatience. The city's been in view for quite some time now."

"That's not funny."

Shatterbreath laughed, bringing her muzzle close to Kael, nudging him roughly in the shoulder with her snout. He gave her a shove back. A small object fell out from behind her horn. He bent and picked it up.

"Hey, this is my can of spice!"

"Alright, Tiny, listen closely." Shatterbreath poked her head out from behind the massive rock she was crouched behind to check on the city off in the near distance. "You have to watch your back at all times. Are you listening?"

Kael nodded, bringing his attention away from the unfamiliar kingdom that loomed before them. "Yeah."

"Their behaviour might be different than you're used to, keep your mind open. Don't trust anybody. Stay in charge. Most of all, if things get out of hand, just run.

"Of course. Wish me luck."

"Kael..." There was longing in her voice.

"Yes?"

She stared at him for a moment, her soft eyes washing over him. "Just stay safe. And good luck."

He nodded, tightening a strap on his armour. "Sure. I'll see you later, alright?"

She nodded as well. "I'll be watching. If you're in danger I'll come."

Quiet as a shadow, she slunk away through the thick grass and out of sight. Kael took a deep breath and started walking towards the kingdom.

As he approached, it at once became apparent that Snailtown was very much different than Vallenfend. The first thing Kael noticed was the lack of walls surrounding the city itself. The border of the city started at no set line, but instead houses appeared around its edges gradually. Also unlike Vallenfend, the entire city was constructed on a visible grid, with almost every house sharing almost the exact same shape.

Indeed, the architecture of the city wasn't terribly exciting. The houses were rigidly square as to fit as tightly to the city's grid as possible. Though the houses grew in size as Kael moved deeper into the city—some ranging several stories high, with separate staircases leading to each floor—every building held the same colour scheme: a boring, nonchalant brown.

Kael took an extra-deep breath, hugging himself with one arm as he passed by a small crowd. He never considered himself a claustrophobic person until that moment. The city was built so tight! He felt as though at any moment, the buildings might come together and squeeze him flat.

Pushing those thoughts aside, Kael focussed instead on the tactical properties of the city. It didn't seem like it would be an easy place to defend at first, but thinking about it as he strolled through the streets, he guessed it probably would be. There were plenty of rooftops to fire arrows down from, making Kael guess that their main weapon would be bows. He was correct as he spotted a small group of soldiers strolling by, all with quivers strung to their backs.

Seeing them made Kael realize something. There was something odd about the people bustling around in this city. Kael couldn't figure out what it was at first. They seemed ordinary enough. Their clothing was slightly different. They wore brick-red tunics that resembled the colours of their houses—but that wasn't especially unordinary. Yet, there was something...different. They talked the same as he did, looked physically the same and went about their business like anybody else.

Then it struck him.

There were men.

A pang of sorrow plucked at Kael's heart.

He no longer felt so unique, a feeling he had carried throughout his life. He had grown up knowing that he was special, one of the few boys in the city. He had cherished this feeling, knowing that he was set apart. Now, he simply blended in. No women gave him a second glance, no girls stared at him. He fit in.

It...was nice in a way.

Right. Kael shook his head. Back to his task.

Kael finally made it to the centre of the city. He gasped as he saw what resided in the kingdom's centre. A vast marketplace opened up before him, filled with kiosks, huts, tables, and of course, people.

Whereas Vallenfend was built in different sections and often one would have to travel around to get all the necessities the needed, everything anyone would ever need was all located in this one convenient area. Kael had to admit, this was a clever way to do it. Although he liked walking around his city. He missed Vallenfend.

Kael strolled through the crowds, looking for nothing in particular. The merchants seemed to sense this and tried to goad him to come over to their tents and sell him trinkets. He hardly knew what to do. He waved his hands and shook his head, trying to yell back at them that he wasn't interested. Eventually, he just gave up and ignored them.

Perhaps this wasn't the best place to start.

Shatterbreath watched Kael meander around Snailtown. She was perched up on a boulder half a mile away, more than far enough for her to watch what was happening without fear of detection. Perhaps she should have informed him more about this place. It was based around merchandising and was one of the hubs for other cities to buy supplies and weapons. How she knew this, she couldn't remember.

Once again, it startled her how much she knew about this land, especially concern humans. She didn't deliberately try and learn these things, in fact, she couldn't think of a situation where she would learn things like this, but she was still thankful nonetheless. Perhaps being around for over two-thousand years had its advantages after all.

Earlier, Shatterbreath had told Kael that they would try the nearest city first. She had lied. This was perhaps the fourth nearest city, however, it was the most passive and she wanted to start Kael off with a place that wasn't dangerous. He needed to find his voice first. Besides, he had just escaped from a dangerous place. He didn't need any of that now.

She settled down some more, lying on her side lazily like a feline. She flexed her wings, which were still fiercely sore. Settling herself for a long wait, she yawned toothily. Kael was talking to somebody now. She hated waiting.

"What do you want?" a guard said as Kael grabbed his shoulder. The man hadn't heard him the first time, so Kael had to physically alert him. The market was loud.

"Yes, I—I am from another kingdom, I'd like to have a word with your king." Kael gulped, wishing he had put some more conviction into that sentence. He was unnerved by this man. Kael was so used to seeing boys as soldiers or guards. This older man was far different than any soldier in Vallenfend.

The guard raised his eyebrow. He rolled his shoulders, the quiver of arrows rattling on his back. He was wearing simple suit of light plate mail, with archery gauntlets and a helmet that covered the backside of his head, as well as either side of his face. His decent set of armour made him all the more intimidating.

"You...want to see the king?" he asked sceptically. "What for?"

He didn't seem to care that Kael was an outsider. That was good. "It's about..." How to word this... "I need to speak to him about *foreign* relations my city is having trouble with. It is urgent."

The man cast his gaze around, perhaps looking for some of his buddies. He apparently didn't see any. "Are you the leader of this city?"

Kael faltered. "No." Not even close.

"Listen," he said impatiently. He wasn't rude, but Kael didn't like his tone already. "Saultrion doesn't usually get mixed in with other kingdom's problems, okay? Whatever issue you have, you and your kingdom will have to settle it on your own."

"Saultrion?" Kael asked. "Is that your king?"

The guard frowned, taking a step forward. Now he really didn't trust Kael. Had he said something wrong?

"Saultrion," the guard spat, "is the name of the kingdom you're standing in right now. If you truly were an ambassador or messenger for your kingdom, I'd expect you to know a little more about the city your visiting."

"Oh, sorry," Kael spluttered apologetically. "It's been a long day, I hope you understand. Got things a little mixed up." The guard pursed his lips. The damage had already been done. *Thanks a lot, Shatterbreath,* he cursed in his mind.

The guard's frown intensified. He glanced over Kael's shoulder. "Here, even though I'm not sure about your little story, I'll help you out." He pointed through the crowd. Kael craned his neck to see. A group of soldiers were buying some food, they all had yellow stripes across their chests and held halberds as well as their standard bows.

"See them?"

"Yes."

"They are with the king's private guard. If you really want to see the king, you're going to have to do so under their supervision."

Kael stared down at the soldier blankly.

The man rolled his eyes. "Fine, I'll introduce you."

They walked over to the group of elite soldiers. The group scrutinized Kael as they approached. He felt childish and out of place under their gaze.

"What do you want?" demanded one of the men with an air of authority.

"This bloke wishes to see King Horz."

The soldiers shared wordless glances. The one closest to Kael sized him up some more. "Is that so?" he said apathetically. "What for?"

"Some sort of foreign problem with his kingdom. I don't really know."

The guard looked lazily from the soldier that led Kael over to Kael himself. "Does he have a voice?"

Kael cleared his throat. "Yes, sir."

The guard leaned on his halberd, his green eyes still lingering on Kael. "What is your purpose?"

"I'd rather discuss it with the king himself, thank you," Kael said, working up some courage. "I hope you understand."

The guard raised an eyebrow. His expression was unreadable. "Fine then, it is not my place to deny one an audience with the king. The public disserves to see their monarch."

Kael frowned, taken aback. "Really?"

"Yes. Are things run different where you come from?"

"No," Kael lied. In truth, things were much different. King Morrindale was a secluded person. The only time the king spoke to anybody, it was either his servants or Zeptus. The fact that this king was so open to ordinary people speaking with him was startling. Yet another thing that set Vallenfend apart from Saultrion.

Indeed, the difference between the two cities became even more significant when Kael finally reached the castle. A bridge led to the castle itself, one that rose high above a river that ran through the city, providing it with water. The castle, like the buildings surrounding, was built in the same pattern, with straight edges and tawny colourations. However, it was slightly more intricate than any other building, proving that *some* creativity had gone into building it.

Once they passed over the bridge, Kael and the soldier who was escorting him then entered the castle itself. The main hall was built tall and grand, with archways that supported the high roof. They seemed to stretch up the walls like arms reaching towards the heavens, only to grasp onto each other in the middle of the ceiling. Kael was amazed.

After the main hall, they entered another large room. Tapestries adorned the pillars in this room, portraying kings past and great deeds done. They seemed to lead up to the current king, who was sitting on his grand throne at the front of the room.

King Horz was not what Kael had been expecting. He had been expecting a crude ruler, one which was both stocky and thick with muscle. He didn't know why he had thought this, for when he set eyes on the man, he realized how wrong he had been.

The king had a small greying beard, matching his salt-and-pepper hair, which clung tightly to his head. He was of a normal stature, but thicker-looking due to the large robe he was wearing. He was leaning on his arm, with his jawbone cradled in his jewel-encrusted hand. He looked very bored.

Kael and the soldier stopped halfway through the large room, waiting as a man lamented to his king about some wrong deed that had been done by his neighbour. This was yet another thing Kael was surprised to discover. This king actually listened to people's problems. Strange. King Morrindale had *never* done that. If anybody wanted to complain, they would have to talk to Zeptus first. Nobody ever complained.

The man in front of the king finished his story. The king yawned and waved his hand. "Let it be known that this man's neighbour is a thief." Servants on either side of the king hastily scrawled down his declaration. "He will pay full recompense to this man for the goat that was slain. Off with you. Next."

Kael stepped forward, gulping as he did. Being in front of royalty—other than the aloof King Morrindale—was certainly unnerving.

"What is your problem, son?" King Horz asked.

Kael hesitated, struggling to find the right words. Why was he so worked up? "Hello. I have come to beg for your assistance."

"Yes, they all do. Speak freely."

Kael frowned. "No, that's not quite what I mean. You see, noble king, I am not from Saultrion." Kael stumbled on the name of the city, almost calling it *Snailtown* again. "I come from a kingdom far to the west. We are in need of your help, there is an invading army coming from overseas. We have no men to stand up and fight when it finally arrives. When it does, we'll be crushed."

The king sat up straight in his throne, his interest peaked. "So," he said, cocking his head, "what exactly are you here for, young messenger?"

Kael hid a smile, the king was listening! "As I said, we have no fighting force; I was hoping...that perhaps your army could assist in repelling the enemy forces as they come to our city. If all goes well, other kingdoms will join our cause and we'll be able to overcome this threat."

The king laughed shrilly. The guards on either side of him flinched. This must be a noise he didn't make often. "You come here asking for Saultrion's help? How rich!"

Kael blinked and looked at the floor. "Yes."

The king shifted his chair. "What makes you think we'll join your campaign against these so-called invaders?"

Kael took a step forward. "If we don't stand and fight against them, they will sweep across our land like a plague. My kingdom is only the first, a place to establish themselves on this land. Once they are through with my kingdom, they'll move onto yours."

The king's smile was gone. He thought about the situation for a moment, his shoulders hunched. "What city, young messenger, are you from? What nation requires our assistance?"

"Vallenfend."

A whisper ran through the room. The king's face twisted into a sneer. "Vallenfend?"

Kael nodded.

"Bah. You will have no assistance from us."

Kael's heart dropped. "What? Why?"

"Vallenfend, is unfriendly towards all other nations. They have made it abundantly clear that they are friends to no one. We've tried to make peace-agreements with them, but they always send out offerings away, leaving our messengers bleeding or on the verge of death. What you speak is surely a trick."

Kael could feel the blood drain from his face.

"We've given up hope on them. On you."

Blinking, Kael tired to think of something that would fix this situation. "But—but," he stammered.

"Enough. Be gone with you. If what you say is true, then let them destroy your city. I do not care."

Kael's temper flared. "But they'll destroy you too!"

The king crossed his arms defiantly. "I do not believe you. Guards, get this *boy* out of my sight. I have had enough of his lies. Do not resist, or I'll give the order to lop off your head. Consider yourself lucky to be leaving alive, unfortunate citizen of Vallenfend."

With that, the guards, including the soldier that had brought him there, seized Kael and roughly forced him out of the castle.

Shatterbreath watched with strained patience. They were leading her boy out of the city now, after ejecting him from their castle. He had been in there for hardly half the day and they had already rejected him. That was quick. Obviously, he had been unsuccessful with convincing them to help his city.

As he slowly walked back to her, his head and spirits low, she grieved for him. All this, just for a city that hated him. Was it all worth it for him? Was it worth it for her? She hated to see him this way.

She bounded from where she had been hiding, forgoing all stealth altogether. It didn't matter now. Let Snailtown see her, what would it affect now? A fleeting thought passed through her mind that perhaps he was just relaying what he had learned to her, and that he was in fact going back into the city. She pushed it away. They had forced him from the castle. That was very unlikely.

"How did it go?" she chirped, perhaps a tad bit cheerier than was needed. She coughed, as if her happy tone was caused by a bit of phlegm. Either way, Kael didn't care.

He stopped as she reached him, returning her anxious gaze with a shrug.

"Terrible," he grumbled. "I thought things were going good, but then I told him that I came from Vallenfend. As soon as I did, the king wasn't interested. King Morrindale, or perhaps Zeptus, has set up quite the reputation."

"To cut Vallenfend off, to make sure no help would come." Shatterbreath paused, trying to read his thoughts. "They planned this. Hopefully we'll have better luck elsewhere."

Kael sighed. "Yeah, hopefully. We better get going then, this place was a loss."

"I thought as much," Shatterbreath mumbled. She had said it quietly, so tiny Kael wouldn't hear. Apparently, he did.

"What do you mean by that?" he snapped.

Shatterbreath looked away and flexed her wing. "Hmm, I'm not so sore now; we can probably be in the air by tomorrow."

"No, what did you say just then? *You thought as much?* What does that mean?"

Shatterbreath kept her muzzle pointed away, but Kael continued to stare at her neck. She could *feel* his angry gaze. Curse her loud mouth. "It..." She decided to forgo the lies. She trusted Kael, he deserved to know. "Kael, I wasn't expecting you to succeed, I'm going to be honest."

Kael's face darkened. "What?" he said throatily.

"I didn't expect you to succeed. Simple as that." She looked him straight in the eye. It was his turn to feel uncomfortable. "I didn't take you to the closest city, no. I knew this place would be unlikely to agree to your terms. But they are passive, so I knew they wouldn't harm you either."

"You wanted me to fail?" he shouted. "Why? What could I possibly gain from all this? *Why did we bother?* I embarrassed myself for no reason! Arg!" He threw up his hands, frustrated.

Shatterbreath stood up and paced around to face him when he turned away. He avoided her eyes. "I needed to test you, Tiny. I needed to see how you would handle failure. I wanted to see if you would still be up to the fight." She put as much conviction in her voice as she could while wrapping a sore wing around him. "Tell me, are you still so convinced that this is the right thing to be doing?"

Kael's jaw clenched. He looked fleetingly into her eyes and for a moment looked as though he wanted to just run away from everything. He quickly inspected his boots, kicking a rock. He didn't answer.

"Kael," Shatterbreath said gently, "I needed to get you used to failure. It is only invariable that a kingdom would deny you. Why give you a false sense of confidence right away? That could lead to your downfall."

Sighing loudly, Kael nodded. "You're right. I suppose failure is inevitable."

"There you go. Now, do you still wish to continue? Keep in mind that there may *never* be a place that will agree to help you. Are you still willing to try? Are you willing to thrust yourself into potential danger for your city? How far will you go?"

"What other choice is there?"

"We could leave," Shatterbreath said calmly. "Fly away to safer lands and never return. This could be somebody else's problem and not ours. We could start a new life away from it all."

Kael looked back at the kingdom, crossing his arms thoughtfully. He seemed torn, Shatterbreath couldn't tell for sure. Was that a tear? No, impossible.

At last, he shook his head. "We will continue. I can't let my friends suffer such a fate. I couldn't live with that, knowing that I had a chance to save them, save *everyone* and that I gave up. What sort of man would I be?"

Shatterbreath nuzzled his shoulder. "I would still respect you, Kael."

He slowly put up a bandaged hand to pet her snout softly, still looking out at the castle, no, in the distance at the sunset. For a moment, everything was blissful, everything was peaceful. Shatterbreath was grieved to know that the tranquility wouldn't last.

Chapter 4

Jobra, leader of the King's Elite, bowed before King Morrindale. The king nodded and the man clad in black stood back up straight, his clothed helmet cradled in the crook of his arm.

"Sir, it seems the soldiers you sent to apprehend Kael Rundown's friends failed." He spoke in a tone which he knew pleased the king. He talked the same way his inferiors talked to him. The king didn't like patronizing, but you had to know just exactly *how* much to put in. He had learned how to speak in this tone a long time ago, which had landed him this position to begin with.

"I see." The king thought for a moment, pressing his fingers to his chin. Jobra waited like a patient guard dog for his orders. "I suppose *you'll* just have to go get them. That is your backup plan, yes?"

Jobra nodded. "That it is, sir."

The king leaned back in his chair, glancing lovingly at the fat ring on his plump fingers. "Good. Get going then."

Jobra stayed where he was. "We are not as expendable as you think, Basal."

The king froze, his lips pursing. "What does that mean?"

"Our services should not be taken for granted. Without us, you would have no protection."

The king actually laughed. "Jobra," he wheezed through a chortle, "what are you talking about? Taken for *granted*? Do you expect some resistance?"

Jobra shifted his weight. He knew it was unwise to get on King Morrindale's bad side, even though Jobra was the leader of his secret task force. "What I meant," he said delicately, "is that we shouldn't be ordered around like dogs. Perhaps sending another squad of regular soldiers would get the job done. It is just *one* boy after all."

The king frowned. "No. I want assurance that these people will get put behind bars. What other way can I get this assurance? You,

Jobra, will ensure I sleep happy tonight. I like success. Another failure cannot be tolerated."

Jobra bit his lip. He was about to say something else, but Zeptus entered the room, calmly walking past him. The advisor didn't say anything, but Jobra could tell this argument was over. Zeptus could make manipulate people like sculptors mould clay.

"I understand, sir." With that, he turned around, placing his helmet back on his head.

Jobra was not worried about his own safety, as the king had deduced. No, that wasn't it at all. He was just...bored. The secret life was not adventurous or wild as he had once thought. Most of the time, his job consisted of fetching rebellious civilians and bringing them to jail, like a dog catcher. This was a prime example.

When he exited the king's improvised throne room, four of his men were already waiting for him. They looked at him eagerly, waiting for their next orders.

"Alright," he droned. "Same drill as usual. Get out, get them, get back. All without being seen. Follow my lead."

They walked down to the second floor of the castle, which was the same height as the walls just outside. They walked wordlessly, for they all knew what do to. This was becoming all too routine. In some odd way, although it had been dangerous, it had been a great thrill when Kael Rundown had broken into the castle. He almost wished something like that would happen again.

Jobra paused at a certain tapestry. It depicted a goat staring at a chicken. He didn't like the picture. He glanced around to make sure that no *regulars* were watching, then picked at a fray in the bottom right corner. He tugged and the whole thing swung free.

Followed by his orderlies, Jobra crept through the secret tunnels that snaked through the castle's protective walls. They reached the bottom and pushed aside yet another door, hidden as a section of the wall itself. There was no real reason to take this route, other than speed.

As soon as Jobra stepped out, a feeling of bliss washed over him. He liked the city at night. At night, the kingdom was no longer King

Morrindale's, it was no longer under the sharp scrutiny of Zeptus. At night, Vallenfend was his. All his.

As silent as fluttering moths, they sprinted forward. Their boots were padded and there was no moon that night, covering the city with darkness. Even though they passed by several civilians along the way, their presence wasn't even close to detection. They were skilled at their art. It was their life. It's all any of them ever knew.

Jobra slowed down when they reached the alleyway near the target house. It surprised him to know that one boy had knocked out five soldiers by himself. In a dark way, he hoped that the boy would be a challenge.

He would love a challenge.

They crouched in the shadows, ready to pounce. No, Jobra didn't want to strike just yet, he wanted to toy with them first. He could see them now. The boy was sitting on the porch, rubbing his knuckles, staring at nothing in particular. And there was the target girl, watching the boy with concern at the other side of the porch.

"Gimoran, stay here," Jobra whispered. He gestured towards the house, nodding at one of his men. "You, go inside and secure anybody within. Rudoran, you're with me."

The men split off, knowing their jobs. Followed closely by Rudoran, Jobra made his way around the target house. With a muffled grunt, he pulled himself up onto the roof of an adjacent building and crept across the roof.

He paused at the edge of the roof to catch a glimpse at the target boy, a blonde-haired, scar-covered young man—Faerd was his name? Didn't look like there would be much of a challenge. Jobra flicked his finger, wordlessly telling Gimoran to make a distraction. Jobra then leapt across the roof, clinging to the side of the target building with some hooks hidden on his gauntlets and toes of his boots.

If his timing was right—which it always was—he would have to strike...now! Gimoran whistled loudly, turning the targets' attention towards the other side of the street. Meanwhile, Jobra pulled himself around the corner of the house and released his grip. He landed right behind the target girl with a muffled *whump*. While she was distracted, Jobra grabbed her around the throat, clapping his hand over her mouth. Unfortunately, the target boy heard him.

Faerd whipped around, bearing an expression of utter shock. Jobra chuckled in amusement. He could imagine the boy's mind racing, wondering *'where did he come from?'*

Rudoran was less graceful than his leader. He snuck across the roof of the target building, aiming to do the same as his leader had. His heavy landing startled the boy and in a matter of seconds, Faerd wheeled around and struck Rudoran in the gut. Faerd took advantage of the assassin's temporary reeling, reached out, grabbed Rudoran's head and cracked it down over his knee. Jobra's comrade fell to the ground, bleeding profusely from his forehead and clearly unconscious.

By then, Gimoran had snuck up behind Faerd. The boy whipped around, casting his head between Jobra and the newcomer. The girl—Laura was her name—squirmed in Jobra's arms as Gimoran protruded a sword from the depths of his sleeve. Jobra squeezed her tighter.

"Don't worry little missy," he hissed into her ear. "We'll take *real* good care of your friend."

She stopped squirming to let out a long sob. Jobra cracked a smile underneath his cloth faceguard, feeling her tears stream into the cloth of his gauntlets.

Faerd scowled at the assassins, flexing his fists. Jobra willed him to make the first move. Gimoran took a step towards him, spurring him into action. In a flash, Faerd spotted something at his feet then bent over the unconscious Rudoran, wrenching off the man's gauntlets. He shoved one hand into a gauntlet and thrust out the same arm.

There was a loud *ping* as a sword met the thick metal of the gauntlet. Jobra frowned. The gauntlets the King's Elite wore were thick and sturdy, meant for climbing walls and doing exactly what Faerd was doing right now—blocking swords. Going to retrieve a fist-fighter, they should have foreseen that something like this would happen. They had practically *given* him a form of attack and defence. That was just...unprofessional.

He didn't have the fluidity and grace of the King's Elite, but with both hands in the gauntlets, Faerd was able to block all of Gimoran's attacks. Jobra watched patiently, his respect growing for the boy. Standing his own like this against a trained assassin was impressive, even more so considering it was night out.

The battle lasted longer than it should have. Both of them were getting tired now. Gimoran kept looking towards Jobra, as if to plead for some assistance. Jobra stayed where he was, watching. The girl in his arms had stopped squirming and would twitch every time the blade came close to ending the duel. By then, the mother of the girl had been caught as well. Another assassin stood near Jobra, holding her in a similar position as her daughter.

Finally, Faerd made a move that surprised Gimoran. He ducked low and swept his foot underneath the man. The assassin didn't fall, but his temporary hesitation was just enough. Faerd struck him in the gut with his metal-plated fist and then following through with a massive uppercut to his jaw.

Gimoran was sent reeling, blood at once issuing from his mouth. Jobra wouldn't have been surprised if his jaw was broken. The assassin knew he was beat. Before Faerd could strike him anymore, Gimoran fetched a small glass vial from his pocket and threw it at the ground.

Faerd whipped around to face Jobra, an infuriated look on his face. Jobra smiled. This boy had spunk. It was a shame that he had to kill him. The assassin next to Jobra pulled the bow off his back and notched an arrow. The woman he had brought out of the house didn't move. She was white in the face. She was no threat.

Faerd stopped in his tracks, the white scars on his face sticking out against the red background of his face. He took a threatening step forward, brandishing his fists.

"Fight me!" Faerd hollered at Jobra. "No tricks, no weapons! Fist-to-fist combat, right now!"

Jobra cocked his head, amused by the boy's bravado. This one had mettle. He stood where he was, thoroughly contemplating what to do. It wasn't professional to engage the boy on his terms. What

41

he should do is tell his orderly to shoot him in the chest with an arrow. But that was unexciting.

"Come on!" Faerd yelled, his voice rising. Jobra swore. The whole neighbourhood was probably awake by now. Nobody was looking out their windows yet. Probably scared. "Are you a coward? Fight me!"

Jobra cast his hostage aside, making her fall to her knees. Keeping his eyes on the boy, he removed the sword from his hip as well as the two blades hidden in his sleeves. He pulled out a few more extra knives from various locations and then stepped forward. He still had one knife tucked in his boot, but he wouldn't tell the boy that.

Jobra whipped off his gloves. They clanged to the ground, the noise shortly followed by a similar sound as Faerd dropped his as well. Jobra's remaining assassin unsheathed a sword, and held the weapon out towards their captives, despite the fact that they would not dare intervene. On a whim, Jobra also removed his helmet, letting his clean-cut hair and intolerant features show. He wanted the boy to clearly see the one that would best him.

The two stepped closer, assassin and simple peasant boy. They stared at each other, hate resonating in Faerd's eyes, twisted humour in Jobra's. Faerd had a piece of cloth on his left hand, signifying that he was dominant with that one. Jobra had black clothes wrapping both fists. Then, in a blink of an eye, they were at it.

Faerd lashed out with bloody knuckles. Both his attacks missed, punching air instead. Jobra weaved under the second strike and struck him in the ribs. Faerd backed off and lunged again.

This attack was more coordinated. He faked a right punch, but instead of swinging left as Jobra was expected, actually followed through with his weaker right hand not a second later. The attack merely struck his shoulder, but it pushed him enough to set up another attack. Faerd hit him in the cheek, hard.

The world swirled in Jobra's vision, but nevertheless, he recovered. He grabbed the very hand that had just collided with his face, twisted it, and then kneed Faerd in his side, exactly where he had struck before.

Faerd yelled in pain, but managed to get one more strike to Jobra's face before they broke off. The boy winced for a moment and Jobra spat out blood, grinning between red teeth. Sharing a glance, they were back at it again.

The street echoed with the dull collisions of flesh against flesh. Blood began to splatter across the ground, issuing from knuckles and cheeks.

The boy was getting more and more savage with each punch he took, instinct pushing him further and further. This was getting out of hand. As much as Jobra enjoyed a good fist fight, he was getting far more hurt than he would have liked. It was time to end this.

Faerd surged towards him, but Jobra simply fell backwards as the boy's fist came towards his head. The boy's momentum carried him forward and he too began to fall towards the ground. Jobra rocked onto his back, tucked in his legs, letting Faerd fall overtop them. Then, using his shifting momentum, he picked up the boy and flung him over his head, headfirst.

Jobra kicked his feet and was back upright in a second. Faerd landed in a heap, gasping for air and blinking dizzily.

Jobra fetched the knife from his boot and jumped at Faerd, aiming to slice his jugular vein. Faerd took notice at the last moment and tried to stop the blade, attempting to push the incoming arm away. The blade went high instead of slitting Faerd's throat in one pass. Instead, it tore across Faerd's face. The boy howled in pain as he was blinded in his left eye and nearly the other.

Jobra backed off, relishing how the boy squirmed and clutched his ruined eye. He brought the blade up high, which flicked blood into the air as he did. It dripped as if it had just fed. It was hungry, he would appease its demand for sustenance. Nothing the boy could do would stop this final attack. He was finished. This would be an honourable death.

A noise made Jobra hesitate. He brought his knife out in front of him, an arrow glancing off the flat of the blade. The last remaining assassin notched another arrow, aiming that one at him as well.

"What is this?" Jobra demanded.

The assassin's face was grave. "Leave him alone."

Jobra laughed, but he was hardly amused. "Why would I do that? Stand down, Tooran."

Tooran pulled the string on the bow farther back. "Leave them alone," he repeated.

Jobra clenched his fists, anger brewing. "Explain, soldier. What is this about?"

"These are friends of Kael. They must survive." His face remained grave.

"I'll have your head for this."

"I don't think so."

With that, Tooran let his arrow fly. Jobra tried to doge, but the shaft still embedded itself into his shoulder, just above his chest and below his collarbone. He growled in pain and slunk off into the shadows. He was in no position to fight back.

Jobra watched where he was hiding as Tooran helped Faerd back to his feet, who was still writhing in pain, feeling like a cat stalking its prey. Tooran gathered the two members of the Stockwin family and made them hold tight to Faerd as they all began to walk off. Jobra was outraged, he was boiling with rage, but he was injured, so there was nothing he could do.

Except for one thing.

"Take this you—" He hurled his knife at Tooran's dark form as they all slunk away from the house. The blade lodged itself into Tooran's shoulder, just above his shoulder blade, almost exactly where he had shot Jobra with an arrow moments earlier. His injury would be much worse than Jobra's. The leader of the King's Elite smiled sinisterly as Tooran faltered, but continued to walk on.

He was still angry, oh yes, but there was no way Tooran was going to get away with this. He was personally going to hunt him down. He no longer cared about Faerd or the Stockwins, no, now he held a personal vendetta against that traitor.

But for now, let him run.

With the two men injured, it took Laura and her mother far too long to get to a safe place. They placed Faerd and their mysterious saviour against the wall of a merchant's hut.

"Wh—what do we do?" Laura asked her mother. Her heart was beating so fast it seemed as though it was a caged animal trying to escape from her chest.

Mrs. Stockwin was pale in the face. "I—I don't know!"

The mysterious assassin spoke up. "Put a cloth over his eye," he said wearily, "take this blade out of my shoulder and quickly apply pressure. I'd do it myself, but I can't move my arm. We'll have to stitch up these wounds later."

Laura didn't like the way he had said *these* wounds, but she obeyed his order. She took the cloth out of Faerd's hand, which was sweaty and already covered in blood. She ripped off a section of her skirt and wrapped that around it. She then placed it gently over Faerd's ruined eye. He winced furiously, which caused her to do the same as if she could feel exactly what he did. He was strangely quiet, staring at the ground with his good eye.

Mrs. Stockwin also obeyed what the black-clad man had ordered. She ripped off a huge section of her own dress. Her hands hovered above the embedded knife. She began to tremble furiously.

"I can't do this!"

The assassin grasped her hand tightly in his own. He stared at her with burning eyes. "I am going to die if you don't hurry up. You want that on your conscience?"

She shook her head, wordless.

"Then take this blasted thing out and push against the wound as hard as you can." She stayed where she was. "Now!"

Laura watched as without another hesitation, her mother pulled out the knife with a gut-wrenching *slick*. The wound began to squirt blood. She screamed but quickly placed a wad of clothing over the gash.

"Good," the assassin said, even more weary. He put a hand to the cloth as he instructed the flustered woman. "Now use the knife to cut a strip off your dress. Really long and thick."

Mrs. Stockwin reached for the knife, but this is when her wits collapsed. She placed her hands over her face and began to weep.

The assassin growled. "You," he said sharply at Laura, "cut a length of cloth."

Laura frowned. She was on the verge of tears also, barely hanging on. But yet, she managed to pull out some defiance. "How do I know I can trust you?"

The man roared. He flexed his hands as if grabbing an invisible throat in front of him. "I just saved your life! What do you mean, 'can I trust you?'"

Laura flinched. "You were one of them. You didn't intervene when your buddy cut Faerd's eye. That doesn't seem trustworthy to me."

The man looked her square in the eye. There was an intensity in his gaze that Laura recognized. "Truthfully, I thought he could hold his own." There was earnestness in his voice, his sudden flare of anger already subsiding. "I was wrong."

Laura was still unconvinced. The man squirmed in pain. "I need more than that. Why did you even save us to begin with? I need to *know* I can trust you. Otherwise you can do this with one arm."

The man looked as though he wanted to choke her again, but he took a deep breath. "I know all about you, Laura Stockwin, all of you. I've been watching you for quite some time now. I...I am Tooran. I am Korjan's son."

Laura's eyes shot wide open, Mrs. Stockwin stopped crying and even Faerd, who had been silent this whole time, looked up and sideways at him. Laura blinked a few times, her mouth moving as if to say something.

"Will you help me now?"

Still lost for words, Laura nodded.

She took the bloody knife and cut a long strip off her dress. *Korjan's son?* She handed the cloth to him. He took one end.

"Here, grab this and wrap it over the cloth on the wound. That's right. Now give it to me." Once the cloth was wrapped over the wound, he hefted up his injured arm and put it through the cloth. "One smaller cloth, please."

Laura cut him a small piece. He took that one and tied it to the middle of both sides of the long cloth. As he did, Mrs. Stockwin tied a bandage around Faerd's head to hold his wad of cloth to his eye. Korjan's son, Tooran, finished tying his bandage. It looked like a regular sling, except with another piece running across his chest and around his arm to hold the cloth against his wound tighter. He nodded at their work, glanced at Faerd, and then struggled to stand up.

"Whoa, whoa," Laura said, placing a hand on his good shoulder, "where are you going so soon? You need to keep still."

Tooran stretched. "I *do* need to keep still. Unfortunately, we have to keep moving. Vallenfend is no longer safe. We must get out of here immediately."

Laura's heart skipped a beat. "We have to leave?" she asked, her emotions flaring.

"Yes. The King's Elite won't stop until they've scoured every inch of this kingdom looking for you, *us*."

Mrs. Stockwin helped Faerd to his feet. "What about my house? Our home? What of our *lives,* Son of Korjan?"

Tooran turned his fierce gaze towards her. "What of your lives, Mrs. Stockwin?"

She opened her mouth but closed it again.

"We have no choice. They will kill us if we stay."

Laura threw up her arms. "And where," she screamed, "are we supposed to go?!"

Faerd grunted. The Stockwins and Tooran turned their attention towards him. He was staring off in the distance somewhere. They couldn't see it this late at night, but everybody knew that he was looking at the mountain range to the immediate east.

"Shatterbreath's cave," he said sullenly. "That's the only place we *can* go. Maybe Kael will be there as well. He could help."

Laura bit her lip. It was unlikely Kael was indeed there, but Faerd was right, that was the only safe place. The soldiers would never think to look for them there. Hopefully, they didn't even know the dragon was gone.

Nobody disagreed.

Laura sighed loudly, a part of her hope escaping with it. This is how it would be.

There would be no return.

"To Shatterbreath's cave," she said slowly, "to the lair of death itself."

"Where this all began," Faerd added.

Chapter 5

Shatterbreath was still sore, which mean they had to continue by foot. Kael didn't mind though. He realized that Shatterbreath had been wise to start them off at a city that would refuse him. It made him understand that failure was inevitable. With that new perspective, walking didn't seem so bad. Instead of imagining the horrible scenarios that could arise, he was contemplating the ways he could convince people to join him.

As they trekked, Kael's thoughts turned back to home. How were his friends doing? How was Laura? He felt a tug towards home and even the wind itself seemed to flow towards Vallenfend, whispering to him. It tried to push him gently, guide him back to the life he used to know. He couldn't turn back now.

They camped in a large grove of trees the first night. Shatterbreath lit a fire for Kael and together they sat watching the stars. The moon was hardly a sliver that night, barely visible at all.

"What's the next city we're going to visit?" Kael asked, poking at some embers with a stick. "The *real* name this time please."

Shatterbreath's eyes gleamed from the reflection of the fire. She looked so powerful, so mighty. In comparison, he was tiny and weak. He shook his head subtly. What a duo.

"The next town," she murmured, gazing deep into the fire. "I don't actually know."

"Unbelievable," Kael scoffed.

Shatterbreath frowned at him. "I honestly thought that place was called Snailtown, I swear. I haven't the faintest clue about this next city. You'll have to figure out while you're there I suppose."

Kael sighed. "Do you know anything about it at least?"

Shatterbreath nodded slowly, still peering into the depths of the fire. She was entranced by it. "It's placed by the ocean, even closer than Vallenfend. It's a fishing city, but has a sturdy enough fighting force. Its true strength is in its naval fleet. It could be a powerful ally."

"Hmm. I guess we'll find out."

Shatterbreath glanced over at him. "I suppose so."

For another day they travelled by foot. Kael had underestimated how sore Shatterbreath really was. He offered to take some of it away by taking it upon himself, but she refused. He, on the other hand, was fine. His forearms were no longer stiff and his knuckles had healed quite nicely. The smaller cuts on his face were also healed over, hardly noticeable now. Kael speculated Shatterbreath had something to do with his recovery—perhaps using a fraction of her magic—but she didn't mention anything.

The fields slowly transformed into mountainous terrain, rolling hills and low valleys. The scenery was breathtaking. The lakes that pitted the mountains provided hydration as well as a place for Kael to wash his clothes. Although the water was clean and refreshing, Shatterbreath insisted the lake on her mountain was far better. She wouldn't admit it, but Kael suspected she felt some homesickness. After being in her cave for so long, it was only fair for her to miss her home. Kael felt the same way, after all.

When they finally reached the top of one of the tallest mountains, Kael could see for miles in any direction. Way off to the north, the ocean gleamed, hardly anything but a blue sliver.

Shatterbreath had paused to enjoy her surroundings as well. Her jaws split into a grin. Without warning, she placed the tip of her tail on Kael's shoulder.

A second later, Kael's world swooned and disappeared. It reappeared a moment later. He quickly realized he had Shatterbreath's rich vision. His perspective was so high and he couldn't move his eyes on his own free will. He twitched as he realized that he was *in* Shatterbreath's vision. On cue, she turned her head to look down at him.

An extreme sense of disorientation struck him as he watched himself move his arm. He was still in his own body, but in Shatterbreath's perspective. It was very unnerving. Sensing this, Shatterbreath looked away, out towards the ocean, though it was no more a simple sliver. Individual waves could be picked out. The dragon scanned the horizon and stopped as an irregularity struck out.

She focussed on that irregularity. It took a moment, but eventually the fuzzy image cleared. It was a tiny city, pressed up against the line of blue.

Shatterbreath glanced over her shoulder, but saw nothing but more mountains and fields of prairie grass. She let go of her hold on Kael.

He landed back in his own perspective rudely, stumbling as he did. Once again, his vision was dull and blurred in comparison. He got his balance and stared out to where Shatterbreath had picked out the city. He couldn't see anything. Amazing.

"That," Shatterbreath said informatively, "is the next city."

"Fascinating." Kael chirped. His sense of interest was instantly replaced by annoyance. "That's a long way to walk."

She flexed her wings with curiosity in her eyes. "I think I'm good enough to fly again. Still a little stiff, but I can work that out."

Kael regarded her cautiously. "Are you sure? If you're not okay and your wings give out in mid-air..."

Shatterbreath nudged him. "We'll be fine. Besides, I'm not patient to walk all the way there. That's a long way."

Kael shrugged, still unsure, but nevertheless hopped on her forearm, climbed up her shoulder and plopped himself in between her shoulder blades. He quickly checked his gear, making sure his armour and shield were tied snugly to her back. He kept his sword at his hip at all times, so he didn't have to worry about that. She craned her neck and glanced back. He nodded at her.

She walked over to the edge of the mountain, which curved down far below them. Shatterbreath could push off the mountain with great force, but if she couldn't stay airborne, they would be in for a nasty fall. The pointed pine trees that skirted the mountain didn't look very welcoming either.

Kael could hear Shatterbreath's heart beating underneath him. Its tempo was slow compared to his, but still pumping at an accelerated pace. She was unsure of this also.

She licked her lips and bent lower, her whole body coiling like a spring. She paused for a slight moment. No, time was slowing for Kael. He watched in distorted time as Shatterbreath's powerful leap started at the front of her body and worked its way to her hind legs. Her legs flexed, deep lines etched on the surface, and then she pushed off.

A fist of wind struck against Kael, but after spending so much time with the dragon, he was used to it by then. They soared several feet out and the land dropped out from underneath them, so that the tops of the tallest trees were far below. Shatterbreath's wings were wide open, cupping the air. Her shoulders rippled as she pumped her wings downwards, creating lift. Still in slow motion, Kael witnesses as Shatterbreath's muscles shuddered, just for a moment. Would she hold?

Yes. She relentlessly pushed even harder until her wings were at the base of her wing beat. Then she brought them back up and pumped again, gaining significant altitude with each stride. Each time she beat her wings, she did so with more strength, the stiffness quickly leaving her.

Time returned to normal.

Shatterbreath laughed, her strong, female voice echoing over the rolling land below. Without telling Kael first, she pulled into a barrel roll, roaring as she did.

"Oh how I missed this!" she called back to him.

"You weren't even sore for a week," Kael lamented, holding on tightly.

"Yes, but a week is far too long to go without flying," Shatterbreath exclaimed. "I usually go flying every day. Besides, you must admit that you missed it too."

Kael shifted on her back. True, he *had* missed this. "You're right."

"Ha ha, as always! Now," she said, pointing her whole body northward, "to the city by the sea."

Even though they were in the air, it still took a good portion of the day to near the city. As the sun set in the west, the city twinkled down below. Shatterbreath circled high above like a hawk, peering down while Kael once again entered her perspective. This city was interesting.

The city was nestled in a mountain range shaped like a halo. Either tip of the mountainous ridge stretched around and sank into the ocean. A faint line ran along the ocean floor, completing the massive circle. The city itself took up the majority of the space in between the circular range and the ocean, with docks that reached out into the water like fronds.

Kael removed himself from Shatterbreath's perspective. He shook his head, trying to rid himself of the dizziness. He still wasn't used to the experience yet.

"What's with those mountains?" Kael asked Shatterbreath.

The dragon yawned. "It's a long-dormant volcano."

Kael cocked a brow. "Really?"

"Yes. By the looks of it, it's thousands of years older than me. It probably erupted once and then moved on."

"Volcanoes move?"

Shatterbreath yawned again. "Oh yes. It takes an unbelievable amount of time, but they do move around. I don't know how it works... I think the volcano that lived here moved on to form Icecrow Mountain. That's just speculating, mind you."

Kael put a hand to his head. This was all terribly confusing. How could volcanoes move? He had a vague understanding of how they created islands, but he was still unsure about that as well.

"Let's find somewhere to roost," Shatterbreath said, interrupting Kael's thoughts. "I'm tired."

"Sure."

She angled her wings and they soared downwards towards a hill not too far away from the city nestled in the volcano. She alighted about halfway up the mountain in a large, flat glade in the forest.

While she licked herself clean, Kael stared out at the volcano rim, which hid the city. Despite the fact he was going to go there tomorrow, he wasn't thinking about it. Instead, he was thinking of his friends. There was a burning in his gut. He couldn't say for sure, but it felt like he could sense they were...in *danger*. Suddenly, going into that city felt trivial. He wanted to see his friends again to make sure they were alright. But he couldn't. He was here and he had to do this first.

53

Kael hesitated, looking around. He was inside the city, wondering what to do next. Fishermen passed him, some carrying hooks, rods and even large fish. It was strange to stand inside a volcano, even though it was long dormant. Kael glanced over his shoulder at the one entrance to the city, a pass between the mountains. The gap appeared as though somebody had taken a giant knife and cut out a triangular piece of the crater wall.

The city itself held a warm, cheery disposition. The smell of the ocean was strong and a supple wind of mist washed over once and awhile. Kael already liked this place. To his surprise, there was no castle. He wondered at that. Who would he talk to? Who governed this place? He could just be wrong, perhaps there was a castle, but he couldn't see it.

The people wore interesting clothing. It was soft as down and clung to its wearer loosely, which meant it was light. Many of the people wore large hats, often decorated with large feathers that *swished* as they turned their heads.

"Excuse me," Kael asked, grasping a man by his shoulder. "I'm visiting here. Could you please help me?"

The man raised an eyebrow and placed his bucket of fish down on the ground. "Welcome to Farthu, stranger," the man said cheerily, shaking Kael's arm. He had a strange accent, one Kael had never heard before. It was difficult to understanding him at first. Kael sized him up, trying to get a feeling of what the city's populace was like. This man in particular had a greying beard that covered the majority of his chest. He considered Kael with one eye wide open and the other pinched tight in a strange squint that worked its way across his face, puckering one side of his jaw. His back was bent, his hands worn and he reeked of fish—obviously a fisherman for most of his life. He offered a crooked hand to Kael. "My name is Captain Kroako."

"It's a pleasure to meet you." Kael took his hand, feigning a smile. The captain's hand was sticky with fish blood. "I was wondering how I could get an audience with your king."

"Ye say ye want to speak with our king? Gyar! Farthu has no king, I'm sorry to disappoint."

Kael winced. No king? "Who rules over your city then?"

The man shrugged. "The Council of course. If ye want an audience with them, ye will have to make an appointment first."

Kael frowned. "How exactly would I do that—and how long would it take?"

Captain Kroako thought for a moment. "I'm not sure exactly how ye go about making an appointment," he declared truthfully, "but I do know it usually takes a few days from the time ye make the appointment to when e actually stand before them. There are a quite a few requests ye see..."

Kael thanked Captain Kroako. Tipping his hat, the fisherman picked up his bucket of fish and strolled off. Kael rubbed his chin, deep in thought. A few days? Kael couldn't spare that much time. He would have to discuss the issue with Shatterbreath. Yet he didn't want to go out to where she was patiently waiting. That would waste only more time.

Kael started towards the ocean, mulling over his choices. He couldn't waste any more time than was necessary. The faster he could get to another city, the better. A few days sounded like too much time.

He was considering turning around and going back to Shatterbreath when he noticed how close the ocean was. Sighing, he strode down to the beach to look around. There were several large docks protruding from the water's edge, jutting far out into the water. They branched off into smaller piers where an innumerable amount of sturdy wooden boats were tied up. Most were out at sea at that time of day, but the sheer amount was still astounding.

Then Kael spotted them. The warships. Great, massive crafts lined the western arm of the volcano crater. They were seemed small from where Kael was standing, but comparing them to the tiny slivers of trees in the background proved how truly grand they were. He strained to see the finer details of the ship.

That decided it for Kael. If there was a chance—any chance at all—he would try his hardest to convince this nation. Their navy was impressive to say the least, if he could convince them, they would be a powerful ally indeed.

He set back into the heart of the city. He hadn't made it very far when a guard stopped him. The man held a trident in his hand, more of a fishing spear than an actual weapon.

"Say, I haven't seen you around before," he said. "Your clothing is strange. You aren't from here, are you?"

Kael cleared his throat from the saltiness of the ocean air. "No. I come from a city far to the west. I wish to have an audience with your council. It is concerning matters of life and death."

The guard raised his eyebrows.

"How soon is your meeting?" Shatterbreath asked, a tinge of annoyance lacing her voice.

"Three days time. It would have been five, but they decided what I had to say is important."

Shatterbreath growled softly. "Are you sure you can afford this?"

"Like you said," Kael replied, "they have a strong navy. We could use these people on our side. Besides, I'm sure other cities will make us delay like this to meet with their leaders."

Shatterbreath rolled her eyes. "It's not that. I can understand the delay to meet with their Council. But what you don't understand is that there will be a delay *after* that. Unlike kings, councils take a long time to come to a firm solution. They bicker like angry birds until the majority of them rule out. And if they *are* interested," she continued, "that would most likely mean even more delegations." She groaned. "Oh, Tiny, this could take a long time."

Kael leaned back, resting against a bumpy rock. "How annoying. We might as well carry through with this. However, I don't think I can come to visit you every night. It might arouse suspicion."

"I agree," she said, crumbling a stone in her talons. Her lips curled in distaste. "It would be better if you stayed there for as long as this will take. You should leave tomorrow at dawn."

Kael frowned. "Where will I stay? I don't have money, Shatterbreath."

The dragon shrugged and rested her whole body on the ground with a *whump*. "So? Just steal some. I don't know. This is no longer my problem. Whatever you do in there, it's out of my league. I can only watch."

"Can't you do anything to help?"

Shatterbreath chuckled. "I'm flying you around, that should be good enough."

Kael scowled at her. She scowled back.

"Fine, I'll go inspect the next city on our agenda. I'll come back in a week and then wait for you to finish."

"Good. Hopefully you can find something of use." Kael put a little sarcasm in his voice, just to bother Shatterbreath. She flicked her tail in a certain way, telling Kael he had succeeded.

Kael's second day in Farthu wasn't any more exciting. He roamed around the city, mostly around the fish market, looking for any opportunities he could find to steal some money or something of value so he could buy himself a room for a few days. Nothing presented itself.

Kael chuckled to himself. He was trying to *steal*. Before he had met Shatterbreath, stealing wasn't even an option. Had he ever changed...

Movement caught his attention. Kael flicked his eyes towards a fat merchant. To his surprise, Kael had discovered not everybody in Farthu talked in the same surly fashion as Captain Kroako. In fact, it was as if only the older generation spoke in that fashion. Indeed, the younger populace preferred a different style of clothing as well— mostly tighter-fitting shirts and the lack of giant hats.

The merchant Kael was watching seemed to be caught between generations, with a shirt too small and hat too big. The merchant placed a small bag of gold down on his countertop and turned around to stick his face into a large wooden chest behind him.

Kael slunk off the bench in one fluid moment. Casually, he began to stroll towards the merchant's hut, keeping his face emotionless and avoiding looking at the small bag directly. He was nearly there. He reached out, keeping an even pace. *So close.*

57

"Hey!"

Kael flinched and whipped around, hands out, ready to defend. He expected to see a group of soldiers ready to pounce, but there wasn't anything there. He frowned, nerves still on edge. The crowd around him continued to throb as if nothing was wrong.

"Yeah, over here!" A stranger waved at him, poking his head above the crowd. The young man, roughly Kael's own age, stumbled over to him. "Hello!" the boy said cheerily. "Y—you aren't from here, are you?"

Kael shook his head, biting his lip. Did the boy see what he was going to do? "How'd you guess?" he scoffed.

"You're wearing unfamiliar armour," the boy said, pointing at Kael's chest.

"Yeah, I'm not from here. What about you?"

The boy shrugged. "I'm from here," he said, clicking his tongue directly after he finished his sentence. "Born and raised." Clearly. Although he seemed more caught up in the older generation's style, minus the hat and thicker accent.

They stared at each other for a moment. Kael was silently willing him to leave.

"Oh, yes. I'm Rooster," the boy said, thrusting out his hand.

Kael took it after a slight hesitation. "Rooster?" he scoffed. Now that he took a closer look, the name seemed appropriate. The boy's build and posture loosely reminded Kael of a rooster, and indeed, he had a birdlike nose and a certain twitch to the way he moved. Even his hair was stuck up in a way that would look normal on a bird. Still, Kael asked, "Is that your real name?"

The strange boy known as Rooster laughed. "No, no. My friends and even my parents call me that. It's better than my real name anyway."

"What's that?"

"Cleaud."

"Oh."

The boy shrugged. "Just call me Rooster."

"Alright, Rooster," Kael said, placing a hand on his shoulder. "I've got important business to attend to. I'd like to attend to it alone."

"I can give you a place to say," Rooster said as Kael turned around. He clicked his tongue again. "And food. For free."

Kael stopped, wheeling back around. "You can? Why?"

"I'm going to be honest. The Council is unsure about you. They want to know your motives first, and what type of person you are. They don't know if they can trust you."

"Do I seem trustworthy?" Kael said with some bite in his voice.

Rooster looked him in the eye. "I'm not sure yet. Judging by what you just tried to do, I wouldn't think so at first glance." Kael's eyes narrowed. Rooster didn't move away, or blink. "But I have been wrong before." His expression softened. Kael relaxed as well.

"You said the Council sent you?" Kael asked after a moment of thought.

"More or less, yes. You could also say that I'm a seasoned tour guide. I know quite a bit concerning this and other cities. I'm here to guide you as well as keep an eye on you."

"Really?" This peaked Kael's interest. A guide could come in handy. Kael could use this boy. But first he needed to make sure he could trust him. Unfortunately, it seemed the only way he could tell for certain would be to follow him. "Fine, Rooster. I'll stick to your lead then."

Rooster smiled warmly. "Alright. You can come live at my place and stay there as long as it takes."

"I'd appreciate that."

Rooster proceeded to lead Kael around the city. He took a winding route, going at a speed which Kael had trouble keeping up to. Rooster hadn't been lying, he really knew his way around the city. He led them through places Kael would usually stay away from, dipping through alleys and backstreets.

Once, Rooster had paused. He put his fingers to his lips and whistled shrilly. The noise was so loud and splitting, it startled Kael. Rooster waved at a group of young boys. Only one of them waved back.

59

With a click, Rooster started off again.

"That was amazing!" Kael exclaimed.

"What?"

"That whistle, it was so loud! Could you teach me?"

Rooster looked back over his shoulder with a grin. "Sure."

It wasn't much later until they arrived at their destination: a humble, two-story building with a rounded top. Warm light flooded from the windows of the house and a sweet smell could be detected out over the abundant stench of fish.

Rooster led Kael inside. Kael was expecting to see a large family, or at least a mother and a father, but to his surprise, there wasn't anybody home.

"Make yourself comfortable," Rooster said, stepping inside after unlocking the door. It was a simple house, but far more lavished than Kael's had been. There was a nice stove to the side that was providing a good source of heat, as well as furniture made of driftwood. Definitely cozy.

Kael sat down at a table as Rooster took two bowls and poured thick, creamy soup into them from a cauldron. He placed it down in front of Kael, clicking his tongue in his strange way again. He twitched his head, reminding Kael of the way his military trainer, Captain Terra had. The days under the Captain's scrutiny seemed so distant...

"So," Rooster said absently, taking a bite of soup, "where are you from?"

Kael hesitated. He suddenly felt like this was all a bad idea. Following a boy he didn't know to a house unfamiliar to him, eating food he didn't even know was safe. It could be poisoned for all he knew. He glanced up at Rooster and then slowly took a bite. It was delicious.

"Vallenfend," Kael stated through a mouth of soup. He was still wary, but chomped down the food, grateful to have something besides venison.

Rooster placed his spoon back into his bowl. He cocked his head, a look of disgust across his face, as if he had just bitten into a sour apple. "Vallenfend?" he repeated. For a moment, he was speechless. *"Vallenfend?"*

Kael swallowed. "Is that bad?"

"I guess not, it's just... What are you doing here then?"

Kael hesitated once again. He hadn't told anybody his story for a long time. He wasn't entirely sure Rooster was the one to share it with, but the young man had been so hospitable, Kael figured he owned him at least an explanation. But he couldn't tell Rooster about Shatterbreath yet. "I was banished," Kael stated truthfully.

Rooster's disapproving look quickly faded. "Oh." He leaned forward, as if Kael was telling a dirty secret. "What for?"

"I tried to kill the king's advisor, a man named Zeptus."

The bird-like boy clapped his hands. "Ha! That's amazing! I was worried about you, you know. Not anymore!"

Kael smiled as well. Obviously, Zeptus's reputation was far and wide.

Kael spent the next few days alongside Rooster. He liked the rambunctious—if not strange—boy. Rooster would lead him around the city, showing him various things of interest, as well as explaining how the Council worked and how Farthu was founded. Most of it was rather unexciting, but Kael couldn't get enough of walking around the oceanfront. He loved the ocean; he had forgotten that for a time.

Rooster also taught him how to perform his shrill whistle. It took Kael nearly three whole days to get it right, but once he did, he found he could whistle even louder than Rooster could. That made the young man jealous to no end.

Finally, the day came when he was to stand before the Council.

A knot formed in Kael's stomach as he strode up to the squat building where the Council held their meetings with two guards on either side of him. He imagined a shrewd group of people that would scowl down at him disapprovingly, as if he were just an ant. To his dismay, when he entered, he saw that he was exactly right.

The Council room was dimly lit and smelled of dust, parchment and authority. There were seven members of the Council in total, all

61

dressed in dark robes and with wrinkled, long faces. Despite being indoors, the men of the Council wore the hugest hats Kael had seen yet. They were a frightening, discerning lot; one Kael would not want be around them for very long. It made his heart sink lower to know he was going to have to spend time with them. If they were interested to begin with.

"Kael Rundown. That is your name, right?" The woman who spoke seemed to be in charge. Her gown was hemmed with red and she carried a small sceptre in her right hand.

"Aye." Kael wasn't sure what he would call her. He decided to avoid addressing any of them directly to be safe.

"You have come from a foreign land to deliver a message. Obviously it is of great importance." She placed her fingers down on the stone desk in front of her. Her long fingernails *clacked* as she did. She was elevated a foot above Kael, so she looked down at him.

"Aye," he repeated, still lost.

"Let's hear it then."

With some trouble, Kael proceeded to explain to her about the incoming empire. He was having trouble, so he decided to relay what he had told the first city, almost word for word. They listened patiently, never breaking eye contact with him.

When he had finished, the presiding Council member, the lady with the sceptre, leaned back in her chair and pursed her lips. Kael's beating heart was the only noise he could hear.

"You have given us much to think about, Kael Rundown. Be it known to you that your city is unfriendly to all others?"

It took Kael a few seconds to realize what she had said. "Yes, I fully realized this. I do not speak on my behalf of my kingdom. What I do is purely on my own. I fight on free will, to save the city and ones I love."

"So you want us to help a city that doesn't even know it needs help?"

"Yes, I suppose so."

"They have no idea what you are doing?"

"No."

The Council members murmured one to another for a moment. The presiding lady waved her sceptre and they were all quiet. "Ultimately, the decision for action cannot be made by one alone. This Council will continue to meet every day until a decision is met." She turned to a servant behind her. "Clear our schedule, I don't care about complaints." She faced Kael once again. "I hope you don't have anywhere to be, Kael Rundown, for we will need you to attend these meetings with us to inform us of any information you might have overlooked."

Kael blinked slowly. He kept his countenance straight, but yet he was screaming inside. He really didn't want to have to do this. He was hoping that the decision would be a snap one, but deep down, he knew it would end up like this. Shatterbreath was right.

"That is fine," he said emotionlessly.

This was going to be a long week...

Chapter 6

Helena was sick worried. She had heard talk that Faerd and the Stockwins had been taken away by soldiers. She had heard they had been killed because they had resisted. She had heard they had run away.

She dearly wished the first two rumours were false.

Her heart fluttered as she thought about the innocent Stockwin family and the charming boy Faerd being taken away. What would they do with them? Were they dead? Had they really escaped? Even if they had escaped, they would be fugitives. Where would they hide?

Her ox grunted as the cart she was sitting on rolled over a rock. She clutched onto the handrail near her even tighter. She hated worrying. It made her anxious and gave her a pit in her gut.

But this was a good reason to worry.

Kael had started this, that part was obvious. His picture had been posted all over the city and she had *been* there when he had been banished. Now the Faerd and the Stockwins were missing. There was a chain to all this. First the weed, then the roots.

Curse that boy Kael.

She didn't want to get angry at him, but she just couldn't help it. If he hadn't done...whatever it was that was accused of, she wouldn't have to spend all this energy concerned over what was probably nothing.

She glanced up at the sky through her wicker hat. She was late today. She needed to get these apples in town before sundown. She wasn't making good time. Her ox was getting old.

She spotted a few figures off in the distance, young men dressed in blue tunics. Soldiers? No! They couldn't be after her, she hadn't done anything. Kael hadn't even talked to her in months! *She hadn't done anything.*

But she kept calm. She kept quiet. She kept her fraying nerves and fright hidden as best as she could. They were getting close now.

They were walking down the path she was going up. There would be no other reason for them to hike out on this road. There was nothing of concern for them. Oh gods in heaven, this couldn't be happening to her.

The city was close, maybe they really were just strolling around, getting exercise. That's it. Just pure, innocent exercise. There was nothing wrong with that.

As if it was nothing special, she passed right by them. They simply waltzed on by, casting her not a second glance. She exhaled sharply. A ripple of gooseflesh ran over her body, giving her a chill. What had she been so worried about?

"Excuse me," a voice called out from behind.

Helena stopped her cart, turning around in her seat. "Y—yes?" she said innocently, failing to keep her fright out of her voice.

Four soldiers walked up to her cart. Two went on either side, one to the rear and one went right up near the head of her ox. The soldier patted the neck of the ox, a crooked smile on his lips.

"Are you Helena?" the soldier asked sharply.

Helena froze. She clenched her jaw, trying to keep tears from forming in her eyes. *She was so frightened.* The ox trotted in place impatiently, as if waiting for her answer as well.

"Why, of course not," she said through a fake smile. "Helena's still out in the field. She wanted to get some extra work done before she came inside tonight."

The soldier, an acne-covered hooligan, took his hand off the ox. "Oh, really?" he said sinisterly, pulling a sheet of paper from the depths of his tunic. He practically pressed his nose against the parchment to read it. "You fit this description so perfectly."

The blood rushed from Helena's face. She heard one of the young men chuckle behind her. "No, sorry. Helena's still out in the fields."

The soldier's eyes narrowed. "Get her, boys."

The young man who had just been talking to her unsheathed his sword and without any hesitation, slit the throat of Helena's ox. Helena screamed. The other soldiers quickly climbed up onto the cart.

Helena flailed, trying to keep their hands off of her. They reached out towards her, laughing and mocking her. Blood began to flow freely from the throat of her ox as it crumpled, painting the ground in dark red.

She kicked out, catching one of them in the jaw. He stopped laughing and tumbled backwards off her cart. The others cursed loudly and finally grabbed her.

They pulled her off her cart and thrust her to the ground, sending a choking cloud of dust sprawling over the scene. Helena tried to scramble away, but one of the soldiers kicked her in the side with his boot. She wheezed through a breath of dust, struggling to keep away from them. It was to no avail.

A pain erupted at the top of her head as one of the boys lifted her back to her feet by her hair. He then cut the lock off with his sword, smelling it before laughing to his pals.

They shoved her around, as if playing a twisted game of catch. She tried to sprint away, but the one who slew her ox grabbed stuck out his leg and tripped her. Helena stripped over his boot and fell hard. Before Helena knew it, there was a knife pressed against her neck and hot breath washing over her ear. She froze, feeling tears steam down her face.

"I don't know why, but Zeptus wants you locked up," the warm breath hissed. "I don't see why we can't a little fun with you first, eh guys?" They laughed. "Yeah. Let's make you pretty so you'll look acceptable in front royalty."

"Get away from her," a strong voice demanded.

The soldiers turned around, their attention pulled away from Helena. Weary, she lifted her head up to see Korjan standing a few metres away, hands clenched. He stared at them underneath his heavy brow, a feral intensity burning in his dark eyes.

The young man above Helena put his knife back into its holster at his waist and instead unsheathed his sword.

"Get lost, you commoner," he spat, "king's business."

"Leave her *alone,*" Korjan spat. The soldiers shifted their weight uneasily, casting unsure glances at each other. "Leave her alone or I will force you to."

"We've got weapons, if you haven't noticed. I think it would be wiser for you to leave."

Korjan's eyes narrowed even more. "You ignorant slug. If *you* haven't noticed, I have weapons as well." He reached over his shoulders and pulled a broadsword from his back. The boys' expressions were priceless. In ordinary circumstances, Helena would have laughed about it. "I'll give you one more chance. Leave."

The cocky soldier scoffed. "Enough of you. Get him!"

The first soldier to run at Korjan stopped short. Without relent, Korjan cut him down within seconds. The soldier was dead before he hit the ground. Korjan bent lower. "You give me no other choice."

He rushed forwards, so did the remaining soldiers.

Korjan dodged a sword, blocked a lunge from a spear with the flat of his blade, and then killed the attacker—the one Helena had kicked in the face. The soldier with the spear didn't stand a chance. Korjan swung his broadsword, the soldier tried to block with the shaft of his blade. It wasn't enough. His body joined the others littering the ground.

The only soldier remaining was the one who had slit the ox's throat. He brandished his sword out in front of him, the weapon visibly shaking in his grip. His eyes were wide and deep fright etched into his forehead. Korjan took a step towards him.

"No, please! I didn't mean it," the soldier yelped, "I was just following orders! Please, let me live! I want to live!" He turned the other way and began to sprint away, dropping his sword altogether.

Korjan reached behind his back and pulled one of two axes free. He wound up to throw the weapon, but Helena stopped him.

"Leave him," she sobbed. "Just leave him. Please, no more..."

Korjan watched the young man flee back towards the city. Once he was out of range, the blacksmith knelt beside Helena, putting out his hand welcomingly. Numb and white-faced, she took Korjan's strong hand. He helped her to her feet.

"Wh—what are you doing here?" she asked dully.

Korjan stared at his feet for a moment. "I was waiting for you to come home. When you didn't come on time, I decided to come find you."

"It was lucky you did," Helena stated blandly, recovering from her fright. "But why were you waiting for me?"

Korjan avoided her gaze by wiping his sword on the tunic of a dead soldier. "I wanted to invite you to dinner tonight. I guess that's not going to happen now."

Helena managed a dry laugh. "No, I don't feel like eating now." She spotted her faithful ox, now slain, and looked away.

Korjan wrapped his arm around her and they began walking slowly back towards Vallenfend, leaving the soldiers' bodies to rot out in the sun. Helena suddenly felt secure, safe. Korjan wasn't going to let anything happen to her now. She would stay with him.

"Why were you carrying those weapons?"

Korjan shrugged. "Since Kael left, I carry a weapon everywhere I go. It's a good thing too."

Helena barely heard was he said. She was so overwhelmed. Four young men had just *died*, and now she was cradled in the arm of the man who had done it. She buried her face in her hands. Korjan held her tighter.

"Don't worry," he whispered to her, "I've got you. I won't let anything happen to you."

Chapter 7

Shatterbreath angled her wings, letting the wind guide her. Kael had told her to go inspect other cities to find out anything she could. She huffed. She knew enough already. She wasn't going to do *that*. She didn't feel especially good disobeying what he had asked of her, but this was important. Important to her.

How long had it been? Her supreme vision washed over the painfully familiar landscape below her. Memories of her former self flitted through her thoughts. A smaller body soaring low over the forests, searching for prey. She had to bring back food for her young ones. They were waiting.

Shatterbreath opened her eyes. It was all coming back now. Clear as the looming mountain before her. When she saw it, her heart shuddered like the wings of a dying bird. Torment. Tears struggled to find their way to the surface of her eyes, but she forced them back down.

She wouldn't cry. Too long had she let this ravage her. Too long had she let her past twist her future. She needed to put her former life behind her and embrace the trials to come. Otherwise the pain would only be worse. She couldn't let this destroy her on the inside any longer.

But first, she needed to visit the place. The place where her life ended. The place where she used to roost with her family. Her mate, her *children*.

The mountain was closer now. It was still the same as she remembered: smothered by a dense forest and cut into ridges by deep crags and paths. It was on the inside of two parallel mountain ranges that formed a steep valley with a small city somewhere to the south. To her, that mountain had been the world. Her world, *their* world.

Sending up a thick cloud of dust and leaves, she alighted on a protruding crag that jutted out like an elbow. She surveyed the scene.   There was a river that lazily wound itself down the mountain, joining into a large lake far below. There was plenty of food, both vegetation and her preference, meat. The tall trees provided a place to hide and the warm air in this region was perfect for flying. Shatterbreath took a step away from the ledge. It was a perfect place to raise a family.

She pushed a few trees aside, feeling impatient. She spotted it. A ridge ran down the mountain, like the form of a rib poking out of an animal's side from under its skin. It was behind that rib that the cave resided.

Shatterbreath strolled up to it. It had seemed large those many, many years ago. But then again, so had everything else. She hadn't realized how much she had grown.

Shatterbreath paused at the mouth of the cave, as still as a boulder.   She stared into the depths of the cave, looking for something that wasn't there. She closed her eyes, imagining small, youthful forms running towards her gleefully as she carried home dinner.

Her tail pounded against the side of the cave, breaking free a massive rock imbedded near the mouth of the cave. She frowned at it. Ages ago, her and her mate had tried to move that same rock, worried it might fall free and crush one of their young. How trivial it all had seemed. She wanted those days back.

Shatterbreath walked inside, dragging her tail. She ducked her head as she entered, brining her wings in tighter. She remembered now, it was tight at the beginning, and then opened up wide into a yawning cavern.

She cast her head to and fro. It was dark, but she could see clearly. She cocked her head and pointed it towards the ceiling. She let a burst of flame free, hundreds of rocks flaring light back at her. Even after she stopped the fire, they continued to glow brightly. She scowled at them.

At the back of the cave was a pile of rocks, formed in a rough circle. Shatterbreath's neck became taut. Her jaws clenched and her tail swished across the floor, making the only sound that disrupted the painful silence.

The air was so still, so dead. It hurt her throat to breathe.

Shatterbreath craned her neck down towards the rocky nest. She sniffed it. Her children's scent was long gone, erased by centuries of bareness. Oh, what she would give to smell her family's familiar scent, to nuzzle her children and feel their smoother scales touch her rougher ones.

Black scorch marks surrounded her. On the walls, the ground, even the ceiling. She could still recall the day the young dragons had learned how to breathe fire. Once they mastered it, there was hardly a time they weren't spewing flame over everything.

Tiny scratch marks covered the floor, as well as much larger ones. Her muzzle wrinkled in a snarl. Those marks weren't created from glee or play fighting. They were distinctly created from small talons scrambling to get free from the soldiers' stinging weapons.

Five long marks were etched in the ground, carved as if by a sword. They were Shatterbreath's, from long ago. She lifted her front paw, paused for the slightest moment, then rested it back down on her former claw mark. The size of her paw now easily overwhelmed the marks.

Her body went slack, her wings drooped and her tail stopped moving completely. If only she had been stronger, as big as she now was. The soldiers wouldn't have stood a chance. If only...

She roared. Roared as loud as she could. It was not the smartest thing to do, for the echoing nearly burst her eardrums, but it made her feel somewhat better. Somewhat. She felt her fury, her pain, and her defeat, rush out of her along with her breath. She felt her sorrows drift away, laying to rest on the cold hard ground.

She pounded her paw on the stone. Her fury wasn't sated and she did it again, and again. She stomped the ground as if it were an enemy, a prey, a soldier, a silly boy holding a club. She broke the solid stone; she ground it into little bits and didn't stop until her claws were covered by pulverized rock. She breathed heavily and withdrew her paw, staring at the indent she had made.

Shatterbreath lifted her head, shivered and rolled up into a tight ball. She gazed around, feeling small and unbearably alone. She wished she had her family. She wished she had Kael.

After several agonizing hours she reluctantly surrendered herself to the deep, chaotic state of a troubled sleep.

A shuffle disturbed her slumber. She thought at first she was back in her cave above Vallenfend, and that they had sent another insolent wave of useless soldiers at her. She shrugged off the muddled thought.

She heard the noise again. She picked herself up off the ground, shaking her body to rid herself of the stiffness still clinging to her body. Then, she strained to hear what she had before.

It came again, echoing off the walls of her cave and making it impossible to determine where it originated. For the first time, she noticed a few tucked-away crevices, paths created after she had left. She didn't like this.

The sound came, more steady this time, as if it was approaching. The noise sounded like a vast forest being pummelled by a strong gust of wind. She had heard it before, only much, much smaller. Her heart pumped a beat faster than normal.

What was this folly? What did she, Shatterbreath, have to worry about? She was a dragon! She could easily kill any mere animal that stood in her way.

She sat on her haunches patiently waiting for whatever animal that dared to disturb her peace to emerge. She wanted to kill it, whatever it was. Perhaps that would make her feel better.

A tip of a snout appeared. It hesitated at the entrance of the crevice, a black forked tongue lancing out to taste the air. Slowly, the beast revealed itself. Deep down somewhere, Shatterbreath had been hoping that perhaps the blunt snout had belonged to a dragon. She was very wrong.

72

A gargantuan snake slithered out of one of the crevices. It peered at her with brilliant orange eyes that seemed to glow against it black, shiny body. It raised its head to her level, the rest of its long body still pouring through the crevice. Its head hovered where it was, perfectly still, suspended by its powerful body. It looked at her impatiently, a mild intelligence showing behind its predator eyes.

The snake was huge! Its body was as thick as a deer, nearly twice as long as Shatterbreath. Red stripes ran under its neck— appearing as though some bigger animal had slit its throat multiple times—following through underneath its great, coiled body.

Shatterbreath rose to all fours, bending lower as the snake bobbed its head. It continued to flick its tongue, a flash of lightning spiking from its mouth and retreated back in just as fast. Shatterbreath's body was tense as she waited for the snake to make the first move. Hopefully, it would simply decide she was too much of a threat and move on. But she got the distinct feeling she was on its territory now. This was its home now. Not hers. She had surrendered it a long time ago.

The snake struck.

Fast as an arrow, its bulky head whizzed past Shatterbreath. She only just managed to dodge as it clamped its mouth down. She caught a glimpse of a pink mouth, rimmed with jagged teeth and two massive fangs.

It reared back; pupils dilated a tongue flitting out furiously. It was fighting to the death now.

Shatterbreath whipped around right before it struck, catching it across its face with her tail. It shrieked, startling the dragon. It was a terrible noise, long, shrill and unnatural. Shatterbreath didn't even know snakes *could* shriek.

It hissed and struck again, as quick as a normal sized snake would. It may have been big, but by no means was it any slower. It might have been even faster if anything.

Poison ejected from its fangs as once again it missed. The liquid spattered on the wall behind Shatterbreath. She doubted she would live for long if some of that entered her bloodstream. She may have been at an advantage, having limbs and wings, but if she got hit even once by its bite, she'd be dead for sure.

She tackled into the side of the snake, biting down into its thick body and sinking her claws into its flesh. It shrieked again and began to writhe. It attempted to wrap its body around Shatterbreath, who thrashed wildly to try and deter it. If she let it get a good grip on her, it would certainly crush her. This was quite the enemy.

She leapt as a coil of its long body tried to wrap itself around her neck. It only succeeded in catching her tail. As soon as the coil constricted, Shatterbreath felt the blood cut off from her tail. She roared in pain as the snake squeezed even tighter.

The snake tried to bite her again, but she brought her wing forwards. It clamped down on the membrane, its fangs penetrating straight through the soft tissue. More venom squirted from its fangs, luckily splashing against Shatterbreath scales instead of going into her body.

She jumped hard off the ground, the coil still wrapped around her tail. She snatched onto the snake's neck as it tried to retreat its head. She got a solid grip at the base of its neck, but it was too thick, too strong, she couldn't simply break its spine. Blood issued freely into her mouth, but she swallowed it grimly. She would not let go until it was dead.

She struggled to find the ground through the squirming coils of the snake. It managed to grab onto one of her forearms with its body and began to squeeze there as well. It hurt furiously, but freed up some space for Shatterbreath to place her hind legs down on. With a snarl, she pushed off the ground with all her might.

Both intertwined bodies slid towards the entrance. Shatterbreath landed on the snake, which yelped. She growled through a mouth of blood and did it again, sending them even closer to the entrance.

Just one...more time... Shatterbreath, muscles aching, tail numb, forearm burning, forced them both that extra distance. They stopped just on the edge of the hill that lead up to the cave. The snake wiggled slightly, tipping their balance and sending them both sliding down the mountain.

They tumbled and rolled, colliding with trees and uprooting them. The noise and debris was immense. Shatterbreath lost her grip on its neck, taking a mouthful of flesh with her. The snake lost its grip on her also, sending a painful rush of blood back into her tail and paw.

Once they both stopped tumbling Shatterbreath coughed, winded. The snake wasn't any better. It stayed motionless for a time, its loathsome head resting on the ground.

It stirred and Shatterbreath was ready at once. In a heartbeat, they collided with each other. They twisted, uprooting more trees. Shatterbreath managed to take advantage of the situation and lunged at the snake. She clamped her jaws down on the base of its neck again, this time just below its head.

She took a deep breath through another mouthful of blood. She felt the fire crawling up her neck, eager to engulf this new prey. It stopped—the snake had its body wrapped around Shatterbreath's neck. Only a small burst of flame escaped, burning a patch of the beast's hide, but not even close enough to kill it.

She succeeded in squeezing one paw in between its body and her throat, but it was still strangling her. She pulled as hard as she could with her paw, keeping the snake from collapsing her throat, but not enough to halt the strangulation. This was it. It was either her, or the snake.

She repositioned her jaws on its throat and bit down furiously. She could feel her teeth contract the snake's throat. It gasped for air, but couldn't get any.

They stayed pinned like that, both thirsty for air, both disallowing the other to drink it in. Shatterbreath's lungs ached and her body was getting weak. Desperation crawled all over her body,

75

but she couldn't do anything. Blackness fringed her vision and she saw white spots.

The snake's body was writhing, trying to do anything to get Shatterbreath off of it. All it was doing was wasting precious oxygen in its body. Shatterbreath remained as still as she could. The only muscles she used were the ones in her jaw and her arm.

The snake was slowing down. It stopped convulsion furiously, it stopped opening and closing its jaw and Shatterbreath could feel its heart slowing down. Slightly, just slightly, it loosened its grip on her. It was more than enough.

She pried open the coil around her neck, taking a huge breath through her nostrils. It felt good to breathe once again! And then, she finished it.

She released the pent-up burst of fire she had been keeping, still holding on to its neck. The snake would have shrieked, but Shatterbreath still held it firmly. A terrible smell of burning flesh filled the air, bringing tears to Shatterbreath's eyes. The blackened head of the snake went completely limp. Its body stopped moving altogether, all its coils falling to the ground.

Shatterbreath finally let go and roared loudly in triumph, placing one paw on the twitching body of her foe.

She flopped down on her side, still breathing haggardly and very worn out. The snake's head still smouldered and crackled from the heat. Shatterbreath looked away. It was a shame to kill the creature like that; judging by how large it was, she wouldn't have been surprised if it was as old as she was—perhaps older.

It didn't taste half-bad either.

After she had eaten her fill, she moped back up to the cave, shaking her neck, trying to get rid of the pain that still resided there.

The recent battle gave her something to think about. She sat down in the middle of the cave, staring at the floor as she pondered. Hopefully, there was only one of those monsters...

After a few minutes, Shatterbreath lifted up her head, as if to face somebody floating up in the air.

"I can't do this anymore," she wailed. "I can't dwell on the past. You must understand—there are more important things to worry about." She listened for a moment. There was no response. "I need to move on—focus on what fate has set before me. I'm helping a young man, Kael. He is strong-hearted and brave. He has an impossible task set before him and I feel it is my duty to assist him." She paused again. "So please, please understand, I must move on. I must let go. *You* must let me go."

There was no response, but deep down, Shatterbreath felt as though she had been released by the ghosts of her past. She no longer felt a strong tie to this cave; it was just another rock formation. She was still grieved about the loss of her beloved family, but no longer would it occupy a majority of her mind every waking moment. Now, at last, she could focus on more important things. At last, she had been forgiven. *She was free.*

A warm feeling crept over her scales. She closed her eyes and drank it in. For a moment, she felt as though she was with her family again. She could feel her mate nudging her neck and her children nuzzling her legs. When she opened her lids, there was nothing. Just the cave. Just her.

Shatterbreath walked to the entrance. She cast her head back, surveying every little detail of the derelict cave. "Farewell," she muttered as she walked out for the last time.

She was airborne at once. She didn't look back. She felt fulfilled, free! She did a barrel roll and twisted into a back flip. She glided on a thermal, searching over her mental map of the land. The nearest city was behind her now. She didn't want to go to that place. The next closest was only a few dozen wing beats from where she was. She would go there and see what she could find. Yes. She would help Kael, as she had originally intended.

Chapter 8

Delegations...yuck. Kael wished he could be anywhere else. Strolling the streets of a peaceful Vallenfend, soaring on Shatterbreath's back. Heck, he'd even prefer to be sneaking around Vallenfend's castle again. Anything was better than this.

After the second day, Kael was wondering if this had been the right decision after all. They'd bicker among themselves, the Council, displaying what they thought about, for or against Kael's suggestions. It seemed to get nowhere. He would simply sit there, head on hand, listening half-heartedly to their boring conversations. Every once and a while, they would go to him for more information, but besides that, he did little more than spectate.

It seemed, for the most part, that the Council was divided in half concerning the matter. Little more than half of them didn't agree, the lesser half did. This only made the delegations last longer.

They would argue for a good four hours of the day before they decided that was enough. After that, Kael would spend more time with Rooster exploring the city. Eventually, Kael even grew weary of the city and that became rather boring as well. Farthu wasn't quite as exciting as Vallenfend—in his opinion anyway. Although it was a lot more striking visually.

By the fourth day of delegations, a rough decision was finally made.

The head of the Council, Raniro was her name, put up her hands. "Enough!" she declared. The Council room fell silent. Kael sat up in his chair. She turned to him. "I apologize for all this," she said, "but it appears we are split on this decision, with no member willing to change their mind. We're at a standoff. I'm sorry we've wasted so much of your time, Kael Rundown, but this is a decision that we will have to continue pondering in the future."

Kael placed his hands down on the stone table of the Council room, controlling his emotions. "But we don't have any time. I don't know exactly when the empire will arrive. It could be today for all I know. They could have already arrived! I need a decision at once so I may plan accordingly."

Raniro shook her head. "This is too important of a decision to make so quickly. There are many things to consider. Borrowing our army could leave us defenceless to attack. There would be the injured to attend for and compensate... The list goes on, Rundown. I'm afraid we'll have to get in touch with you later to relay our final decision."

Kael pounded the flat of his palm on the table, the scars on his knuckles from the Ripwind still clearly visible. "How do you plan to do that? I'm not going to be readily available like this after I leave here. And I don't intend to stay."

Raniro's eyes softened. "I'm sorry," she said again.

Kael stood up. "Is that it then?" he growled. "Are we done here?"

Raniro stood up as well, along with the rest of the Council. "Yes, Rundown," she sighed. "You are done here."

Kael turned to leave. "I will return. I don't know when or even if I can, but I will try to come back. And when I do, I expect a decision."

Raniro clasped his shoulder. "Don't bother, young knight. I do not wish to spend anymore of your time than necessary. Don't come back. I assume you'll be disappointed with our decision."

Kael looked her straight in the eye. That was it. She had basically given him the answer he had been waiting for, and fearing. He couldn't rely on these people. They weren't going to help him. He had just wasted effort. Inside, he was furious, he was angry; he wanted to stab his sword into something. But he smiled instead and took each council member's hand in turn.

"That you for your trouble," he said warmly. He rolled his shoulders, his armour which he wore everyday squeaking slightly. "Goodbye." Without a second glance, Kael strolled out of the council building.

Rooster was waiting for him. He was smiling, but when he spotted Kael's disapproving frown, he dropped it. "Didn't go well?" he ventured.

Kael shook his head. "They've decided to continue their delegations without me. Raniro basically said no though. Rooster, I'm done here, I'm going to leave."

Rooster shook his head. "Just like that?"

Kael shrugged. "Thank you for your hospitality, Rooster." With that, he turned away, leaving Rooster dumbfounded. Solemnly, Kael headed to the entrance of Farthu, head bent and shoulders heavy.

He was close to the craggy entrance when Rooster's voice called out to him. Confused, Kael impatiently turned around, eager to get out of Farthu. Rooster ran up to him, carrying a sword at his hip. He carried a backpack as well.

Kael couldn't help but to smile as the eager young man approached. "Where are you going?" he asked jocularly.

"I'm coming with you!" he said cheerily.

Kael winced. "What? No, you're not."

Rooster scoffed. "Yes, I am. The Council demands it. They want to see what you do after this."

"I don't care what the Council demands," Kael growled. "They basically refused me, so I have no tie to them anymore. Besides, I tread alone."

Rooster crossed his arms. "I'm still coming with you, on my own preference."

"We'll see." Kael doubted Shatterbreath would approve. "I just hope she isn't hungry," he added quietly under his breath.

"Pardon?"

Kael waved his hand. "Nothing. You can't come with me. Just...stay here."

Rooster walked along side Kael, holding onto the strap of his backpack tightly. "No, I want to see how you're going about this. I can help, trust me! You need a guide, and I'm just that."

Kael shrugged. It was true, a guide would help. Shatterbreath's insight alone wasn't enough. "Fine, alright. You can come if my partner decides this is okay."

"Your partner? You just said you work alone."

"I lied."

They walked through the fields together. The dormant volcano became smaller as they strolled away from it, and soon they left the outskirts of Farthu entirely. They eventually reached the foot of the mountain where Shatterbreath had said she would wait for him. Kael looked up eagerly, trying to catch the rough blue outline of the dragon.

He whistled loudly, surprising Rooster.

"I'm still angry about that, you know."

Kael laughed. "That I'm better at this whistle than you? It'll probably serve me better. I'm going to try and teach my partner to come to it."

Rooster tripped, but kept walking. "Ah, so your partner is a horse?"

Kael laughed again. "Not in the least."

A shadow passed overhead. Rooster glanced upwards, but the figure was already gone. Kael smiled. Shatterbreath would have just landed right in front of him, but she was obviously worried about this stranger.

"Don't worry!" Kael called out, "he's a friend."

"Who are you talking—?"

Shatterbreath swooped in seemingly appearing out of thin air. She brought her wings forward to cushion her fall, but she the ground still rattled as she landed. Rooster was bucked from his feet, his backpack's contents sprawling across the ground. He stared wide-eyed up at Shatterbreath in absolute fright.

"A friend?" Shatterbreath snorted. "What did I tell you, Tiny? Don't trust anybody. How do you know he's truly a friend?"

Kael placed a hand on her forearm. "What happened to your neck?"

"A long story, don't worry about it. How do you know he can be trusted?"

"He's a guide," Kael explained, "he knows a lot about cities."

Rooster scrambled to his feet, his eyes lingering on Shatterbreath's imposing form. She considered him with one wise eye. She wrapped her tail around him as he tried to run then dragged him forward and placed her massive paws on either side of him, peering down at him with interest.

"Oh my..." Rooster's eyes went even wider.

"Aren't you a funny one," Shatterbreath commented. She sniffed him, ruffling his lightweight clothing. He flinched but otherwise couldn't move because Shatterbreath's tail was still wrapped around his legs. "He looks like a bird."

Kael gave her a shove. "His name is Rooster. Be nice, let him go."

She unravelled her tail, backing off. "Hello, *Rooster,*" she snarled.

Rooster stood up uncertainly. He took a few steps backwards, glancing at Kael. "Uh...hello?"

Kael clapped his hand on Rooster's shoulder. "Now that you know each other..."

"He's not coming," Shatterbreath interjected. "I don't like him."

Rooster spoke up before Kael could. "A dragon?" It took a moment, but his surprised expression turned into amazement. "A real-life dragon! I've never seen one before, only pictures! Wow, you're dazzling! Pictures don't even begin to do your species justice. You're magnificent. So strong, so noble. Wondrous!"

Shatterbreath puffed out her chest. "Oh, why thank you. I may have been a tad hasty. I like this bird."

Kael frowned. "Prideful dragon," he muttered. "Okay. Does that mean he's coming?"

Shatterbreath swished her tail through the grass, considering them both. "No."

"But he's a guide!" Kael retorted. "He can help us in our cause! He can help us avoid another *Snailtown.*"

Rooster nodded rigorously, reaching into his pack to pull out some parchment. "Yes, yes! Look, I have maps too! Don't want to get lost, do you?"

"Lost? Hardly." Shatterbreath curled her lips in disgust. After some consideration, she sighed. "Fine. He can come to the next city with us to prove his worth. If he turns out to be useless or gives us a reason to distrust him, he's gone."

Kael nodded, turning to Rooster. "I guess you're part of this odd group now. A duo is now a trio."

Rooster gazed back up at Shatterbreath. "Wonderful!

Chapter 9

A warm pot of tea steamed on the middle of the table in Korjan's house. Helena reached out and poured herself a cup. Korjan watched patiently.

"Are you feeling better now?" he asked.

She nodded. "Much better, thank you."

Korjan scratched his head. "Don't worry about it."

"Korjan, I'm worried about all this," Helena stated, gripping her cup tighter. "Not about me, but just...this situation. Kael is banished, but his influence is spreading. The Stockwins are missing and so is Faerd."

Korjan nodded wordlessly.

"But we haven't done anything!"

"It's not that. They're probably trying to make a point. They don't want what Kael was saying to take root. They want to scare people. Anybody that agrees with what he had to say will be too frightened to do anything about it."

A tear formed in Helena's eye. "That's terrible! Can people be that evil?"

Korjan's expression was grave. "They can be a lot worse than that."

They both stayed silent for a long time. Korjan sat down on a wooden chair across from Helena, hands resting on his knees. He stared at the table, lost in his thoughts.

"Oh, Korjan, what's happening to Vallenfend?" Helena asked through a quavering voice.

The blacksmith sighed deeply, which sounded more like a growl than anything. "This has been happening for thirty years, only Kael has figured it out and survived to tell anybody about it."

"You've heard what he said, right?" Helena asked. "About the empire? Do you think it can be true? Is Vallenfend truly in danger?"

The blacksmith rolled his neck. "I heard what he said. I'm not sure if I believe it or not. I trust Kael. I've always suspected some sort of plot but it's...it's just..."

"Too much?"

Korjan nodded. "Exactly. It's just so impossible."

"It fits together though. With our men gone, our army next to nothing, it would be all too easy for an invading army to conquer us."

The blacksmith clenched his fists. "It makes perfect sense. I just don't want to believe."

Another moment of silence passed over them.

Helena perked up. "All the people that have been attacked...we're all friends of Kael. He had spoken to us before he disappeared, right?"

"Yes."

"Well, who else does he usually speak to?" she asked, dumbfounded. "Who else does he visit often with? His friends could all be in trouble. Who would they go after next?"

Korjan considered her for a moment. He blinked a couple times as he realized what Helena was saying.

They looked at each other, fright in their eyes. In unison, they said, "Bunda."

Bunda brought her meat clever down, hacking a slab of meat off of a carcass. It was nearing closing time, but she felt the urge to keep working. She needed something else to think about besides Kael. She growled to herself. *Kael, where are you?*

The sound of her front door opening shook her of her thoughts. She wiped the bloody knife on her apron and stepped into the front of her shop. Hmm, nobody was there. She fingered the cleaver in her hand for a moment, confused. She shrugged and walked into the back.

She was picking at a chip in her blade when a dark, impatient voice startled her.

"Hello."

She screamed and backed away from a black-clad figure that was standing among the hanging carcasses. The man scrutinized her through a black face mask before taking a step towards her.

"Bunda the butcher, you are under arrest."

Bunda barely managed to find her voice. "Who are you? What are you doing in my shop? Get out! Get out at once before I cleave your face like a piece of steak!"

"That would be unwise," the man said coldly. "Come quietly and I'll make sure your suffering is lessened."

Bunda put her hands on her hips. She had overcome her shock, but her heart was still thrumming. "Oh yeah? You and what army, sweet stuff?"

On cue, three more men wearing black appeared from the depths of her shop. *Assassins?* A chill ran up her spine. She took a few more steps backwards. Reversely, they stepped towards her.

"Back, stay back," she yelled, waving her cleaver at them. They pulled swords from sheaths at their waists, waving the weapons musingly back at her. Her face twisted in terror. "Leave me alone!"

The leader pointed at her sharply and the assassins descended on her. She tried to fight them off, swinging her cleaver. One of the men slipped past the knife and grabbed her, pinning her arm behind her head in a painful way, causing her to drop her weapon.

Bunda still had fight in her though. As the second assassin—a man with a swollen and crooked nose—approached to detain her, she lashed out at him with her other hand. To her surprise, her fist collided with his face. The *crack* of his already-broken nose was shortly followed by his scream.

"Arg!" he hollered, "you stupid, fat woman!" Bunda was blinded by the back of the assassin's hand. Stars danced across her vision as it slowly returned. Her cheek had never stung so hard. Nostrils flaring, the assassin reached back to strike her again. His fist was caught by his leader's hand.

"Stow it, Gimoran," the leader hissed. He turned to Bunda, all sorts of confident. "Look at you. You've got mettle, that's for sure. Still, I was expecting a half-decent fight. The other friends of Kael had. I suppose you're an exception."

Bunda spat in his face. She tried to kick him in his crotch as well, but he back away and her foot missed.

"I ought to cut *you* up and feed you to the pigs." He wiped the spit from his face and smiled like a demon. "Wouldn't that be sweet irony for you?"

Tears began to streak Bunda's round face. She squirmed, but the man holding her only tightened his grip. Where were they going to take her, what were they going to do with her? What had she done? They mentioned something about Kael's friends. This was all Kael's fault! Curse that boy.

"Alright boys," the main figure said, in a tone that suggested he was disappointed. "Let's get her to the dungeons."

Suddenly, the tip of a blade sprouted Gimoran's neck. Before anybody realized what happened, the other person holding Bunda went limp as well. She squirmed and freed herself from his dying grasp. She cocked her head at her saviour. "Korjan? What are you doing here?"

Korjan, broadsword in his hands and two thin swords strapped to his back, nodded in reply. "Saving you. Get out of the way, please."

Bunda jumped out of his way. Korjan bent lower, holding the broadsword out in front of him. The lead assassin studied Korjan for a while, mischief gleaming in his loathsome eyes. As Korjan stepped forward, the assassin snapped his fingers.

Out of nowhere, a black-clad figure lunged at Korjan. The blacksmith spun around, dodged the attack and used his momentum to cut down the foe. He couldn't stop there, however, as another hidden assassin attacked.

Korjan blocked the attack with the flat of his blade, but at the cost of his balance. The force of the strike made him take a step back. A clean kick from the assassin knocked Korjan's broadsword from his grip.

That didn't bother the blacksmith though.

In a flash, Korjan pulled the thinner swords from their sheathes, holding them both in either hand. Bunda could hardly keep up as Korjan fell upon his attacker. So swift was the blacksmith with his blades, the assassin was dead within minutes.

Bunda watched in fright as Korjan turned to face the three assassins. But by then, *two* more had appeared. Once again, the

87

leader snapped his fingers and his two orderlies jumped to engage Korjan.

Swords clanged together as the blacksmith held his own against the two assassins. He spun, parried and moved his swords at a wicked speed. Bunda had never known Korjan was *that* skilled. She was impressed and simultaneously frightened for his life at the same time.

At last, Korjan found an opening in one of the assassin's attack and ran his sword through the man's chest. The other soldier took advantage and knocked that sword from Korjan's grasp.

Korjan gripped his remaining sword with less confidence, but still was still more than a match for the assassin. With his attention set on only one man, the black-clad soldier didn't stand a chance and soon, he too was dispatched. Catching his breath, Korjan fetched his second sword and brandished the weapons, facing the remaining assassin.

The leader clapped his hands.

"Impressive. You are, beyond a doubt, the best swordsman I have ever seen."

Korjan wiping his brow on his sleeve. "Flattery will get you nowhere."

"Hmm. It is quite a shame I'll have to kill you. We could use more soldiers like you."

"I'd like you see you try," Korjan chuckled.

The black-clad man cocked his head. "Very well."

The leader of the black soldiers pulled a sword from his waist. He held it out at the ready, facing Korjan. They stared each other down for what seemed like hours. Bunda could hardly take the tension. She was choking on it. She whimpered, spurring Korjan into action.

The two men's blades collided. Korjan tried to hack at the assassin with both his swords, but the leader was quick and managed to block all attacks with his one blade. They locked swords over and over, Korjan with his two, the enemy with his one broader weapon.

The assassin kicked Korjan in the chest, but he quickly shook the attack off, twisting his hands to capture the black-clad figure's blade between his two.

Their faces were just a hand's breadth away. "By the way," the leader snarled, "my name is Jobra."

They wrestled over the weapons for a moment, Korjan trying to wrench the sword from his grasp, the other man trying to pull it free. Eventually, the leader's won and he pulled free.

Korjan backed up. "Why bother telling me your name?"

The one known as Jobra kicked Korjan in the shin. He slapped the flat of his blade against Korjan's hand, making him drop a weapon. "I thought you should know the name of the one who kills you. That way you'll remember me in the afterlife."

Korjan struggled to fend off all Jobra's attacks with only one blade. Desperation was spread across his face. "You're wrong," he said, pushing Jobra's sword away zealously. "It is my name *you* will have to remember. It's Korjan!"

With that, Korjan threw his sword to the side. He reached behind his back and pulled two axes free. Jobra laughed and tore his cloth helmet off, showing his face.

They engaged in their battle again.

The fight lasted far longer than Korjan would have liked. With each passing second, with each blow he blocked, he was getting more and more tired. He may have been the better fighter, but Jobra had superior stamina.

At last, Jobra slipped an attack in. He slashed Korjan across the chest. The wound was non-fatal, but it was enough to stun Korjan for a second.

Jobra struck him hard across his face, making him reel to one side. Before Korjan could recover, Jobra kicked him in the chest. Korjan crashed to the ground, losing both weapons at once.

Jobra hovered above Korjan, the tip of his blade inches away from his neck. The insidious man stomped down on Korjan's hand as he tried to grasp one of his swords that lay nearby.

"As fun as that battle was," Jobra hissed through his teeth, "it will be my honour to kill you, mighty warrior." He raised his sword high above his head, readying for the final blow. Korjan shielded his eyes as if that would stop the darkness to come.

"Guh!"

Nothing came. No pain, no darkness, no end. Korjan opened his eyes in confusion.

Jobra cursed loudly as he tried to grab something on his back. He wasn't succeeding. When he turned around, still grasping, Korjan noticed that there was a meat cleaver lodged in his back. Bunda stood on the other side of Jobra, anger spread across her face.

The black-clad assassin finally wrenched the knife free. He wheeled around to face Bunda, exposing his gouged back to Korjan. Blood issued from the wound, staining his black clothes and dripping to the floor.

"You bedraggled wretch!" the man screamed, a vein sticking out from his temple. He brought his sword back in attempt to decapitate the butcher. He didn't succeed.

Korjan quickly snatched his sword and from where he lay hacked off Jobra's right hand with one clean sweep.

The black-clad man clutched his bloody stomp, howling. Jobra managed to take control of himself enough to pull a dagger from his clothes with his good hand and tried to jump at Korjan. Before he could, Bunda tackled him, sending them both sprawling towards where Korjan still lay.

Thinking fast, Korjan put his sword up. Jobra spun around as he fell, but it did little to stop the blade from piercing through his chest.

Bunda landed beside them, face first.

Jobra stopped. He blinked several times, staring at the red piece of metal protruding indifferently from his chest. He tried to clasp the end of the blade with shaking fingers, as if to try and pry it out. Korjan pushed the blade in even farther with a snarl.

"That's for my family," he hissed.

The assassin's breath left him and his heart fluttered uselessly until it stopped. Just like that, Jobra, leader of the King's Elite, died.

Korjan caught his breath. He waited for what seemed an eternity for the body of the black-clad soldier to finally stop moving before shoving it off in disgust, removing his sword as he did. He picked himself back onto his feet, helping Bunda up as well. He stared down at the dead assassin grimly.

"Rot in hell," Korjan said, spitting on the corpse. "Thanks for the help, Bunda."

"Don't worry about it." Bunda sighed. "Look at this place."

Bunda's shop had always smelled of blood, but never was the metallic stench so profound. Bodies littered the floor and it was no longer possible for Korjan or Bunda to step anywhere without their shoes sticking in the fresh blood.

Bunda sighed again. "This is the end, isn't it Korjan?" she asked, her voice laced with melancholy. "The end of our normal lives."

Korjan shrugged, rubbing his forearms. "Yes, I suppose it is."

A tear came to Bunda's eye, perhaps the first Korjan had ever seen from her. "What has this kingdom come to?"

"I don't think I'm the one to answer that." He wrapped her in his arm. "We must get to my place at once, before more soldiers come. We have much to talk about."

Bunda tried to push him away. "I don't want to," she wailed. "I just want things to be how they used to be, with everyone safe."

Korjan held her tighter. "We've never been safe, Bunda. Something like this was bound to happen sooner or later. The king and his advisor have been planning all this for years."

Her eyes darkened. "Blast that man."

"Agreed. Now, please come with me."

"Fine," she whispered, defeated.

They made it through the streets easily, avoiding anyone along the way, which was good, considering they were both covered in blood. Bunda had her cleaver tight in her hand, carrying it with white knuckles. The moon was just a faint sliver that night.

Helena was waiting eagerly for them. She embraced them both when they arrived. "Thank the gods, you're both fine! My word, look how much blood you've got on you."

Korjan inspected himself. His brown tunic was now red and crusty. "Whatever."

Bunda sat herself down on a chair, her eyes going vacant for a moment. Helena looked from her to Korjan with concern. "What do we do now?" she asked, directing the question at no one in particular.

The room stayed silent. Bunda was hunched over, staring at her bloody cleaver. Korjan was leaning up against the wall, brooding, and Helena was standing in between them both, her brows raised expectantly.

The blacksmith was the first to talk. "There's really only one place where we can go. The place where they'll never find us."

Bunda scoffed. "Oh and where's that? It can't certainly be in Vallenfend."

"No," Korjan replied patiently. "You're right. As direful as it may sound, I'm afraid it's the only option we've got."

"Where?"

Korjan closed his eyes. He truly wished there was another choice, but he could see no other. He looked at them both in turn, trying to read what they were thinking. He placed his hand on a vertical column in his house, feeling the rough wood beneath his fingers. He would dearly miss this place. He wasn't usually an emotional person, but a knot was forming in his stomach.

"We must go..." He faltered. "We must go to the dragon's cave."

Helena and Bunda both gasped, their expressions identical.

"Shatterbreath's lair?!" Bunda shrieked. "You must have hit your head back there—we can't go to where the dragon lives! It's better to hide from death here rather than seeking for it up there."

Helena, softer, agreed. "That would be suicidal."

Korjan shook his head. "No, Kael is friends with the dragon, that's what he said, right?"

Helena rolled her shoulders. "More or less. I think he mentioned it more like."

Bunda sat up. "Did I miss something? That seems very unlikely to me."

"Zeptus accused him of joining the dragon's side. He didn't deny it," Helena told her.

"Unbelievable," Bunda whispered. "Our boy Kael...friends with a dragon." Her expression went blank. "How can this be?"

Korjan continued. "See? It is our only hope. He can make sure the dragon spares us. We can hide up in there until—"

"Until what, blacksmith?" Bunda cried, throwing up her arms. "When exactly do you think we'd be getting our lives back? When do you think we'd be able to leave? What if the dragon decides it doesn't want to let us leave? What if we become its servants, like Kael has?"

"Is that better than what awaits us here?" Korjan asked, raising his eyebrow. "What's to say he's a servant? For all we know, they could be mutual friends."

It was Helena's turn to interrupt. "I have to agree with Korjan on this, Bunda."

Bunda scowled at her. "This is ludicrous." He folded her arms in frustration.

Korjan sighed again. He was tired, he needed sleep. Plus had lost quite a bit of blood. The wound had stopped bleeding by then, but it had still taken its toll. "So, what'll it be, Bunda? Will you come with us, or stay and wait for more soldiers? I doubt they will be seeking to just imprison you next time. They're out for revenge now."

Bunda bit her lip, refusing to meet either's gaze. At last, she faced them. "As much as I don't want to...I'll come."

Korjan smiled faintly. "Good. It is settled. Tomorrow, at the crack of dawn, we'll pack everything we can afford to bring and be off."

With that, he strolled groggily into his bedroom, aiming to catch as much sleep as possible. He paused in the doorway to catch a glance at the two women. Bunda was already settling down on one of his couches and Helena was walking towards his spare bedroom. Korjan patted the sturdy doorframe which he had personally built. He bent his head. More than any physical pain could, it was going to hurt to leave.

He walked the last few feet and threw himself onto his bed.

Chapter 10

"I hope you know I'm making an exception," Shatterbreath whispered at him. Kael was sitting behind her head, where her neck met the back of her skull, just behind her great horns. He didn't usually sit there, but Shatterbreath wanted to talk to him while they flew—without Rooster hearing.

"I know."

"But you seem sure of this boy. I think you mostly just want company. I imagine it's hard for you to convince an entire city to join your side."

Kael sighed, fitting his hand into a crag in her horn. "It can be, yes. It will help to have a second voice corroborating what I say. It wasn't really my choice though, he insisted to come. I mostly want his guidance in the cities. If what he says is true, he will be an invaluable resource to me. Because, let's face it, your knowledge isn't complete."

Shatterbreath huffed. "I swear that city was called Snailtown."

Kael chuckled, patting her neck. "Sure you did." He turned around to see what Rooster was doing. The boy had his arms spread, an expression of absolute glee spread across his birdlike features. "How's it going?"

"This is great!" Rooster yelled. "I feel like a bird!"

Kael cocked his head. "You look like one too."

"Ha ha, you're so funny..."

Kael felt Shatterbreath grumble. "What happened to you anyway?" he asked her, "your scales are all discoloured around your neck and there are large puncture marks on your wing. You didn't inspect cities, did you?"

Shatterbreath yawned. "I did. I just took a short detour."

"What did that detour involve?"

Shatterbreath tried to look back at him, but she couldn't see him because of where he was sitting. "I visited an old cave, a place where I used to live."

Kael detected the pain in her voice. She wasn't very good at hiding it when she was thinking about her old family.

"Oh, sorry."

Shatterbreath grinned. "Don't worry about it, Tiny. I am done living in the past. You are my future now. I ran into some trouble in the cave, that's all. I dealt with it then left and actually surveyed some kingdoms."

"Find anything useful?"

"Not especially. It's not easy to learn something from a book by staring at its cover."

"Fine." Kael stretched his back, staring down at the landscape below. A few round hills speckled on the ground here and there but otherwise all was flat. Although, off in the distance, loomed a wall of mountains, running on a diagonal angle, reminding Kael of Shatterbreath's range.

After an hour or so, the mountains were still pretty far off in the distance, but close enough to pick some detail. They were truly magnificent, towering high above the rest of the landscape. Rivers flowed over their surfaces, appearing like veins on a large, dormant monster. Snow capped the tops of the mountains and most of the peaks were shrouded by clouds.

"We make camp at the base of those mountains," Shatterbreath called back to Kael and Rooster.

"Why?" asked Kael.

"The only way I see past those mountains is to go over. And if you can see with your pitiful vision, it's cold up there."

Kael shivered already. He didn't have any warm clothing. He doubted spending a night at its base would help any. But still, he agreed with Shatterbreath. He would rather get a good night's sleep before tackling those behemoths.

They alighted near a cheery creek about a quarter of the way up the mountain. As soon as they landed, darkness seemed to fall as they were enveloped by the thick pine canopy. It was a miracle Shatterbreath had found a place to land to begin with.

The ground was moist and moss covered almost everything. The trees were lush and despite how pine obviously dominated, there was a huge variety of other green life. Strange birds called out through the trees and dazzling flowers shone in small packs, like small animals.

Kael marvelled at the beauty of the forest. He was beginning to enjoy witnessing the differences between landscapes and cultures, it was all so fascinating! It still amazing him how dissimilar things were from what seemed a short distance from home. Then again, he reasoned, he had travelled on a dragon's back. He had no idea how far he truly was.

Rooster, on the other hand, seemed less impressed. He came from a relatively beautiful area to begin with and was accustomed to the ocean. How different this must be for him.

Shatterbreath furrowed her brow. "I suppose it's nice," she commented, surveying the forest with an upturned lip, "but it's nothing compared to my mountain."

Within half an hour, the sun was already setting over the horizon. Once it did, the forest was plunged into breathtaking darkness. Kael had decided quickly that he didn't want to sleep on the ground. The forest was so lush and full of life. Who knew what type of things would find their way on him in the night? It was a squeamish thing to think, but he couldn't shake it from his mind.

"Shatterbreath," he ventured, sitting by the fire she had made. "Do you think I could sleep on your back tonight?"

The dragon smiled toothily. "Oh? And why's that?"

Rooster clicked his tongue. "Afraid of the creepy-crawlies?" he scoffed with a smile.

Kael shot him a look. "No," he retorted. "The ground is wet; I don't want to catch a chill before we head up the mountain."

"Sure, yeah."

"I'm serious!"

Shatterbreath growled. "Stop, both of you. I thought one hatchling was bad enough! You two bicker like angry squirrels. Kael, you can sleep on my wing and share my warmth."

Kael sidled closer to her. "Thank you." He turned to Rooster, who was unravelling a bedroll from his huge backpack. "Have fun on the ground."

The dragon growled again.

Kael was awoken with a start. The wing he was sleeping on moved, sliding across the ground. The noise, right beside his ear, was terrible. The other noise that had awoken him was worse.

Rooster was screaming. The boy was clawing at the ground, trying to pull himself free from the grasp of a shadowy form. Shatterbreath's fire had burned out long ago, so Kael couldn't see what it was.

A flame erupted from Shatterbreath's maw, lighting up the area. Kael gasped, springing fully to his feet. There was a wolf tugging on Rooster's foot, snarling furiously. The beast looked no other wolf Kael had ever seen.

Its fur was dark grey, almost black and each strand was tipped with golden yellow, blazing orange and sinister red, making appear as if it were on fire. The creature's muzzle was sharp and wrinkled as it snarled, half-hiding the leering blue eyes embedded deep within its skull. It was big, it was burly, and it wanted Rooster.

Kael quickly fetched his sword which he had left on the ground. Shatterbreath took a step forward and roared at the beast, her wings flaring and tail arching. The wolf caught sight of her and its eyes shot open, but the dragon's threat only made it pull on Rooster harder.

Kael was about to take a step forward, but a flash from the corner of his eye made him stop. Time slowed down as he faced another wolf soaring towards him, claws outstretched, teeth bared. Before the beast could tear him to pieces, he slowly brought his sword forward with wicked speed. Agonizingly real, Kael witness in altered time as his sword bit into the creature. The tip sank in and cut across its chest, leaving a gash that widened as the sword progressed. The wolf's face slowly twisted in pain. Kael ducked.

Time returned its usual pace.

The wolf fell to the ground, whimpering. With a *thud,* Shatterbreath cut off its head with one slice of her claws. Kael ran towards Rooster. He was stopped again from a noise that sounded off behind him. A wolf had latched itself to Shatterbreath's neck

97

while she was distracted. It was gnawing away, but having a hard time penetrating her thick scales. Kael hesitated, wondering whether to help Rooster or Shatterbreath.

Shatterbreath was bigger and could hold her own. He needed to help his other friend.

He cleared the distance between him and where Rooster was being reluctantly dragged away from the wolf. It had managed to bring him several feet before Kael reached it. He stabbed the angry beast in between its eyes, releasing its grip on Rooster.

Kael helped Rooster hobble back to where Shatterbreath was standing. She had killed the wolf on her neck already, but two more had grabbed on during the process. Before Kael's eyes, another slammed into her shoulder, knocking her onto her side. Before she could remove any of them, an entire horde of wolves erupted out of the trees, all leaping at her. They were roughly the size of her paw, but the sheer number of them was overwhelming, even for Shatterbreath. She roared again, biting down and killing a wolf instantly. Kael ducked as yet again another wolf jumped at him, pushing Rooster out of the way. He slit open the beast's stomach as it soared past and it fell in a heap, as good as dead.

Kael quickly rummaged through Rooster's things, which were scattered where he had been sleeping. Where was it...? There! He passed Rooster's sword to him, then brandished his own.

Kael dodged Shatterbreath's flailing limb, hacked off a wolf that was biting at her forearm then jumped up on her chest. One by one, Kael and Rooster removed the creatures from Shatterbreath's body. It took several minutes, but at long last the wolves were all dead.

Shatterbreath rolled herself back onto her feet, letting Kael slide off first.

Shatterbreath craned her neck, her jaw clenching. Kael went still as well, listening. Howling in the distance.

"There are more of these things," the dragon declared urgently. "Two more packs if I'm correct. Hurry, gather your things!"

Kael snatched up his pack and armour and Shatterbreath helped him up onto her back. In only a few seconds, his equipment was secured to her back. Rooster, unfortunately, was having a harder time. Kael cursed. The boy's pack was far too large!

A wolf leapt from the depths of the trees. Before it reached Rooster, who was struggling to stuff all his things into his pack, Shatterbreath let loose a jet of flame. The wolf was instantly engulfed, far too close to where Rooster was standing. The boy screamed but continued.

More wolves were bearing down. Their howls could be clearly heard. They'd be on them in a matter of seconds.

Kael jumped off and Shatterbreath winced. "Tiny!" she yelped. Kael fell backwards as the dragon slammed her tail down on a wolf right in front of him. "What are you doing?"

He scrambled over her tail and hit the ground in a sprint. "I have to help Rooster!"

The dragon groaned as Kael hurried over to Rooster. He wasn't fast enough. Before he could even start to help Rooster with his things, the second pack of wolves was on them. Time slowed down, but it was already too late. Kael was bent over, holding some pots and pans, as a wolf soared towards him.

Suddenly, he was lifted upwards. He moaned in discomfort as a pressure squeezed around his midsection. He glanced over to see Rooster dangling in the air next to him, clutched by a massive paw. Shatterbreath had them both.

Before she took off, she scooped up all of Rooster's belongings into her mouth in one great chomp, taking part of the ground with it. With her paws tucked in tight to protect her precious cargo, Shatterbreath reared up, her wings opening wide. She pointed her long neck upwards, body coiling, and leapt into the air.

The rush of air was immense, but they managed to get away from the wolves. Kael watched as they pounced up, trying to reach the airborne dragon, but they didn't even come close, Shatterbreath was already too high. One, however, managed to succeed.

The dragon yelped in pain. Kael craned his neck to see underneath her body. It was disorienting because he was looking upside-down, but he spotted a wolf with its jaws sunken into Shatterbreath's ankle.

Shatterbreath winced as the wolf bit down harder. It clawed with its sharp nails as well, penetrating the flesh around her anklebone. She was trying to kick it off with her other hind leg, but it was on the back of her ankle and she couldn't reach it. Kael fit his fingers around a few of Shatterbreath's scales haphazardly, getting a better grip.

"Shatterbreath, let go, I can get it!" he screamed up at her. She cocked her head down at him. Her mouth was full but her eyes said *no*. "Trust me! I can get it!"

Shatterbreath lifted him up to her neck and slowly, her claws unclenched. He climbed up onto her shoulder, almost losing his balance as she beat her wings. He carefully ran along her spine, her muscles flexing underneath his boots. This was a strange experience...

He lost his attention for a moment and tripped, falling flat on his stomach. He collided with her hip, face-first. He shook his head, disoriented and spitting out blood. Kael picked himself up and continued.

Shatterbreath lifted up her hind leg, making it as flat as possible for Kael. Her tail was whipping in the wind and it was nearly impossible to keep his balance, so Kael went on his hands and knees.

He crawled down the back of her thigh and over her muscular calf. The wolf peered at him with angry eyes, setting its jaw deeper into her ankle.

Kael, holding on with one hand, started hacking at the wolf with his sword. It wasn't working. On a whim, he swung underneath Shatterbreath's leg, which twitched in alarm as he did. He inched closer and finally, with one powerful swing, decapitated the wolf. Its body plummeted far below. Its jaw, however, stayed clamped down on the dragon's ankle. Gross.

With some trouble, Kael stuck his sword into its mouth and pried its head free, which also fell down into the swallowing depths of the forest.

Grabbing onto Shatterbreath's tail for a moment, he swung himself back onto the top of her leg and worked his way onto the safety of her upper back. He heaved, struggling to catch his breath as the wind rushed relentlessly by. Leaning up against the base of her neck, he flopped his arms down limply on either side of him.

Kael didn't like cats, they weren't nice. Now, he wasn't too fond of wolves either.

Shatterbreath glanced back at him. He smiled wearily, giving her a thumbs-up. She nodded, silently grateful. Kael couldn't see, but he assumed Rooster was alright.

Shatterbreath levelled out for a moment, curled her body and pitched down towards the ground, this time aiming them towards the fields beside the mountains. Kael sighed and closed his eyes, ready for a good night's rest. Hopefully, they would find it in the fields, unlike in the mountains.

Kael peered over Shatterbreath's shoulder down at Rooster, who was clutching the foot that the wolf had grabbed.

"You okay?" he called.

Rooster wiggled his foot. "Yeah. Luckily these boots are thick. The wolf hardly got me at all."

Kael was relieved. "Who didn't want to sleep on the ground?" he chuckled.

Rooster shot him a scowl.

Chapter 11

Zeptus stood out on the balcony, waving slowly at the crowd far below. They were still cheering about what he had just said about Kael. He had told them more lies about Kael being a traitor, a spy, an evildoer towards the kingdom. He blamed the kingdom's problems on him. He told them that Kael's friends were in jail, where they were punished accordingly for fraternizing with the kingdom's new sworn enemy. The crowd loved it. They truly hated him. They truly hated the only person who knew the truth and was fighting against it.

And Zeptus could do nothing about it.

It was his curse.

For King Morrindale, this was all too perfect. The city had grown weary sending their boys off to fight against the dragon. Not even Zeptus's silver tongue could resurrect that. But now that Kael had joined her side, now that they had a *human* to hate, they drank in all the lies.

Still, even still, their men were enlisted into the army. As Zeptus spoke, more young men were training to die. More were being recruited. They would still send them off. As long as the dragon was still in her cave, they would go, and they would die. If it wasn't home, the situation didn't change. King Morrindale had other ways to deal with them. He *assured* nobody came home. In all his years, Zeptus had only seen five men escape. Aside from Rundown and Captain Terra, the others probably perished in the desert.

Zeptus continued to wave, his fake smile long washed away. He stood there confidently, one hand draped behind his back, chest jutting out, chin raised. This was a lot different than the first time he had stood before a crowd. Much, much different.

He could still remember it...

Zeptus rubbed his hands together. He wasn't cold, but a chill ran down his spine. He was younger by thirty years then, hardly a man. He couldn't shake this stress.

Prince Morrindale clapped him on the shoulder. The pudgy young man beamed up at him. "Don't worry about it, Zeptus," he said warmly. "You'll do fine."

Zeptus was unconvinced. "But why me? Why does this burden have to fall on me?" He rolled his thin shoulders, as if there was a weight on them. It felt odd wearing lavishing clothing. It didn't feel right. Poor and lowly was all he had ever known. "I'm too young for this!"

Prince Morrindale scrunched up his face. "Nah, don't worry about it. All kingly figures need an advisor. My father has Malaricus, and I have you."

"Kings are meant to have advisors, not princes." Morrindale frowned at him. "Sir," Zeptus added quickly.

Prince Morrindale batted his hand. "No matter. If anybody complains, I'll have them locked in the dungeon."

"You can't do that."

Morrindale waved a finger at him. "No, of course not, my friend. But there will be changes, mark my words. You'll see. One day, I'll be king, and everybody will obey me. And when that comes, I want you by my side, Zeptus. You and your amazing...talent!"

Zeptus furrowed his brows, sceptical. His stomach twisted, but he didn't say anything further. What could he say? *I'm honoured. I'm looking forward to that.* No, that would be lying.

But the Prince was staring at him with expectant eyes. As distasteful as it was, Zeptus nodded his head. "Thank you, Sire," he said quietly.

Morrindale's goofy smile broadened. "There you go!" he exclaimed, clapping his shoulder once again. "Now, enough wait. Our subjects are eager to see their Prince's new advisor, and one day, the kingdoms."

"Yes, Sire." Zeptus swallowed. Prince Morrindale pushed aside the red cloth that was hanging in the doorframe. He strutted out onto the balcony, throwing his arms out. A small roar ran out from below.

Zeptus hesitated at the mouth of the doorway. His heart seemed going at a million beats per second, but he worked up his courage and strutted out the door.

"People of Vallenfend!" Morrindale declared as Zeptus strode into view. "I give you my new advisor, Lord Zeptus!"

Zeptus shot him a glance. What was with the 'Lord' business? He stopped at the edge of the wall, his knees inches away from the brick guardrail. He gasped.

The citizens of Vallenfend, young, old, male, female were lined up below him. The mass stared up at him with wide eyes. They had been rowdy a moment ago, but as soon as Zeptus came into view, they went dead silent.

Babies stopped crying, dogs stopped barking and off in the distance, roosters halted their crowing. Prince Morrindale stared up at Zeptus, as if he suddenly realized he was in the presence of a god.

Zeptus scanned over the crowd. His fear, his anxiousness quickly melted away. He could feel his weave of power over these people, even before he had started talking.

It was his blessing.

A grin played at the corner of his lips. He lifted his arms and a small susurrus ran through the crowd, as if he had just done something amazing. With a flick of his wrists, he twisted his palms upwards, drinking in the experience. They gazed up at him as if expecting a grand speech, a memorable start to his new position. They were expecting something great, something brilliant.

"Ladies and gentlemen," he said with an amused voice. "I am Lord Zeptus."

The throng burst out in applaud as if he had just something unimaginably amazing. A few cheers broke out, whistles and voices crying out in triumph. Zeptus's heart was thrumming harder, this time in elation. They loved him! Perhaps he had been wrong; perhaps he was fit perfectly for this job. Perhaps this was his life's purpose.

Yes, he could do this. Once Prince Morrindale succeeded his king, once Zeptus truly was the kingdom's advisor, he would be able to do magnificent things. Once it was his chance, he could lead the city into an age of posterity that was unheard of. He was their advisor, and they were his people. For the first time, life was looking good in Zeptus's purple eyes.

Wearing a broad smile, Zeptus left the stand, saying nothing else to the crowd. He spun around and calmly walked back into the entrance to the wall. Once he was behind the safety of the red curtain, he clutched his chest, glee flowing through his body.

After saying a few more words, Prince Morrindale followed. He too, was wearing a huge grin.

"Wow," he said simply, shaking his head. "Wow. I've never seen a crowd react like that. Not even for my father. All that," he gestured out at the crowd still howling outside, "and you only said...seven words." Morrindale's impossibly wide smile transformed into a mischievous smirk. "That makes it certain. You and I, Zeptus, are going to go a long way."

Zeptus chuckled. "Yeah. Maybe we will."

They clasped hands.

Zeptus opened his eyes, back in the present, back where he stood, sneering down at the crowd with little amusement. They held the vigour they had that day thirty years ago, but there was so much different. All he could see were women and children. The men were gone along with the kingdom's happiness. Hate radiated like light from a terrible flame down below. Zeptus's heart felt like someone was stepping on it. He clenched his jaw, his cheeks pitted with deep lines.

He turned away, putting his arms behind his back. He strode past King Morrindale and into the doorway. He paused on the inside, leaning up against the cold stone wall. His position mimicked his very same thirty years ago, just before this had all started. But now he was sullen and hunched over.

If only he had known. If only he could have seen what was coming. If only he had been strong enough. If he had realized what terrors he was going to bring, what pain and death would be declared because of him, maybe things would have been different.

But he hadn't.

105

The rush of the moment, feeling that respect that he had searched for his entire childhood had made him blind and arrogant.

King Morrindale entered. He shot Zeptus a triumphant look before passing by. No words were shared.

Zeptus placed a hand on his forehead, grieving at his situation. He couldn't escape, he couldn't refuse. He was Morrindale's voice, his motivator, his scapegoat.

And he could do *nothing* about it.

It was his curse.

Chapter 12

Shatterbreath sighed loudly, waking Kael. He couldn't fall asleep for the majority of the night, wary that more wolves might attack them. When he did managed to get some rest, the fire-tinged beasts flashed across his dreams, slashing the faces of those he loved. It was terrible.

Kael sat up, peering questioningly towards Shatterbreath. The dragon was inspecting her right rear ankle carefully, pausing to lick it. Kael rubbed his eyes.

"How is it?" he grumbled.

"I'll be fine," she said through a frown. "I have to keep pressure off of it, in case it did any damage to my tendon."

Kael nodded. "Anything else?"

She shook her head. "My skin is tough. I'm surprised it even did any damage at all. Its grip was ferocious."

That was no lie. Kael recalled how its head remained clamped tight even after he decapitated it. He shivered. "Let's stay away from that mountain. Sound good?"

Rooster perked up. "Sounds like a plan to me." The boy also sat up, blinking several times. He stared up at the sky. "Couldn't you two let me get some sleep? The sun's not even up yet!"

Shatterbreath cast her head to the east. "It's up, silly bird-boy. The mountains hide it. That is all."

"Fantastic."

Shatterbreath growled. "You watch your tone with me."

Kael was surprised by her sudden curtness, but didn't say anything, curious to see how Rooster would act.

The boy put his hands forward. "Sorry, I'm just tired."

"Aren't we all?" Shatterbreath stood up, flaring her wings as she did. "You should consider yourself lucky to be alive. You nearly cost us all our lives. And for what? What's in that pack that's so important?"

"Survival necessities!" Rooster countered. "Food and supplies!"

Shatterbreath huffed. "What use those will have."

"Please!" Kael interrupted, putting a hand to his temple. "Can we just get going? I would like to get to a new city today. We are getting behind schedule."

Shatterbreath licked her lips. "Yes." She took a flustered breath. "Yes, we will. Good thinking, Tiny."

Kael hopped onto Shatterbreath's back, in his usual spot in between her shoulders. Rooster quickly collected up his things, all of which were still damp from being in Shatterbreath's mouth. The boy didn't say anything, but he was utterly disgusted by the layer of saliva. Shatterbreath wore a smug grin, pleased by the boy's discontent. Kael wiggled the spine in front of her to silently chastise as Rooster hopped aboard.

Rooster sat a few spines behind Kael. Shatterbreath made one check to see if they were ready and took off explosively.

In minutes, they were nearing the mountain. Shatterbreath slowed her pace, pondering.

Kael leaned forward. "What are you thinking?"

"I was wondering," she voiced, "if we should just go around it. It will take several hours but then you won't have to sit through the cold."

Kael yawned. "Sure, why not? As long as you can stay awake, it sounds like a good idea to me. I can catch a short nap while you're doing it."

Shatterbreath took a deep breath. Kael could feel the air rushing into her lungs through her thick layer of muscle and skin. "Of course. Sit back and relax. I'll tell you when we arrive. The city is just on the other side of it."

"Perfect."

Turning himself around, Kael stretched out on his back. He listened to the dragon's wings beating the air and felt the rise and fall of her shoulders. After only a few minutes, he fell asleep.

Kael was bumped rudely awake. He snapped to attention at once, fearing another wolf attack. He shoved the thought away when he realized they were in there air.

"You like to do that, don't you?" Kael said snidely, putting a hand to his head.

Shatterbreath kept her muzzle forward, but Kael could see the corners of her jaws rise in a smiled. "Do what?"

"Ha, funny. Are we there?"

"Yes."

"Let me see."

Kael was taken away from his vision and thrust into Shatterbreath's. Through her rich eyesight, he could see a city far below, out on the plains. It appeared like a giant circle with a line going diagonally through the middle. A large stone structure branched off from the upper part of the city, most likely the castle. The building was built up on a hill overlooking the city. A large bridge crossed a gap from the city to the front of the castle.

"Interesting design," Kael stated as Shatterbreath inspected the city. "Those walls surrounding the city are even bigger than Vallenfend's. That place is heavily fortified. If we can get them to help, I'm sure they'd be an excellent ally."

"I was thinking the same thing," Shatterbreath replied.

"What're you two talking about?" Rooster complained, "I don't see anything." Kael forgot about Rooster. The boy had no idea that Kael was looking through Shatterbreath's eyes.

"There's a city down there," Kael pointed out, removing himself from the dragon's vision. "If Shatterbreath's nice enough..."

A puff of smoke escaped her jaws. "Never."

Kael turned around and shrugged. "You'll have to wait until we're closer."

It wasn't until they nearly landed Rooster spotted the city. The mountains weren't safe, so Shatterbreath had to land in a field relatively far away so that she didn't arouse suspicion.

"Oh, *that* city," he remarked as Kael jumped off Shatterbreath. His armour clanked as he landed solidly. "How could you see that? What did you mean about Shatterbreath letting me see?"

"Never mind," Kael said dismissively as he double-checked his sword. "Let's get going. Shatterbreath, any last advice?"

The dragon thought for a moment. "No. Nothing. I didn't know much about this city to begin with, to add upon that, they've changed a whole lot since I last remember."

Kael raised his eyebrows. "You're not tricking me again, are you?"

Shatterbreath rolled her eyes. "Just can't live it down, can you?"

Kael huffed. "Rooster?"

"No, she's right." Rooster squinted at the city. "I've heard a lot about this city—none of it entirely pleasant. It looks like it's changed a lot."

"Meaning?"

"Well..." Rooster clicked his tongue. "The most well-known part of this city is the treatment of its lower classes. There is a huge barrier between the classes. Poor people can barely afford food to begin with without the massive tax the king introduced. The noblemen treat the poor worse than swine. It was at the point where the poor refused to work at all, reasoning that all their income would be taken away anyway. As such, the city fell into a horrible state of disrepair. Like I said though, it looks as though the city is better-off than before. Look at the walls."

Kael studied the city from where he was. The walls appeared in perfect condition.

"Terribly fascinating," Shatterbreath snorted. "Would you get going all ready?"

"Fine. Wait here, I'll try to be back soon. Come on, Rooster." Kael started walking, waving goodbye to Shatterbreath. The dragon nodded and took off.

After a while of walking, Rooster clicked his tongue. Kael glanced sideways at him, carefully stepping over a boulder. "Are you any good with a sword?"

Rooster smiled mischievously. "I could probably teach you a few things."

Kael raised an eyebrow. "Oh yeah? That seems like a challenge to me."

"Uh-oh. We'll have to later." Rooster pointed forward, drawing his sword. "We have company."

A troupe of mounted soldiers was riding towards them. Their spears weren't lowered and their swords were sheathed, but Kael still slipped his arm into his shield strap. One of the men was clearly wearing a chainmail hauberk underneath his gold and green tunic. He also wore a helmet that covered most of his face. To Kael, the man looked like a true knight, one which Kael had once dreamed of becoming.

The soldiers approached and slowed their horses down. The animals chewed their bits and paced eagerly as the troupe inspected Kael and Rooster.

Kael lowered his shield. "I am Kael Rundown. This is my friend...Rooster."

"Rooster?" the knight interjected.

"Yes, sir."

The knight pulled on the reigns of his horse, trying to mollify the beast. "What is your business out here?" he asked with authority. "A dragon was spotted nearby. You should be in town."

"We're not from here," Kael stated. He didn't get a chance to elaborate.

A soldier gasped and pointed at Kael's shield. "He bares the symbol of the BlackHound!"

Kael was confused. He wiggled his arm in the straps of his shield. "Excuse me?"

The first knight leaned forward. "Let me see that."

Lifting his arm, Kael couldn't help but to wonder what they were all spooked about. Did they not like wolves or something? Last time he had checked, that's what was on the shield's surface. Kael had to admit, he didn't really like wolves anymore because of what happened the night before, but he still thought his shield was amazing.

They didn't think so.

The sergeant's eyes went wide. "Greggin's Ghost, it's true." His voice went dark. "He's one of *them*."

Kael cocked his head. "Who?"

The knight spurred his horse, raising his sword in the air. "Bind him! We will take him to our general. He will know what to do with these accursed swine."

Something slammed into Kael's back, making him fall to his hands and knees. Before he could react, two feet landed near him, and a moment later, another set on his other side. They seized his arms rudely and twisted them behind his back, tying them together.

Kael tried to struggle, but it was no use. They had him bound tight. They took his sword and shield away from him too. As he fought against them, he noticed they had Rooster tied up as well.

Kael's feet were wrenched from underneath him as a soldier tripped him with his spear. The world swooned before Kael's eyes as he hit the ground. He was dimly aware of being picked up and flopped on the back of a horse like a slab of old meat.

The soldiers set off, back towards the kingdom they had come from. With every step the horse took, Kael bobbed up and down. After only a few seconds, he was feeling dizzy, after several minutes, he was just about ready to vomit.

When they finally took him off the horse and set him roughly back onto his feet, it felt just about ready to vomit. If they had travelled any further, there was a good chance he would have. They gave him a shove forwards, making him stumble.

"Walk!" they barked.

He did as they ordered, solemnly placing one foot in front of the other. He wished he still had his sword. With his armour on, he posed more than enough of a threat against the soldiers off of their horses. Unfortunately, his weapon was in the grasp of the knight, who was two men ahead of him.

Kael was suddenly aware of a large shape near him. He lifted his eyes in awe. Before him, casting an equally huge shadow was the biggest gate he had ever seen in his life. The gate was tall and flat, stretching so high that even Shatterbreath wouldn't have been able to see over standing on her hind legs. Two round cylinders stood on either side of the large, spike iron doors. Windows yawned halfway up the structures, as well as near the top. Archers were posted at the very top of the towers, peering down at the small battalion that approached.

The knight that held Kael's sword reached through the iron gate and used a giant knocker on the thick, inner door. He waited a moment, tapping his foot. A small window opened above the knocker and a face peered through.

"We're back. And look what we found." He held up Kael's shield so the small face on the other side could see.

The rat-like face nodded feverishly. "Come in, come in. Open her up!"

The small portal closed. There came the sound of wood scraping against wood from the other side. The iron spikes slowly receded up into the depths of the wall as the inner wooden doors opened inwardly at the same speed. Overall, Kael was greatly impressed by this kingdom's security.

They passed through the massive gates and into the city itself. Once inside, Kael was slightly less impressed. The houses were all dishevelled and the ground surrounding the path was all muddy. The houses, which were made of a rich-coloured brick, were faded and chipped away. People wearing rags roamed around. There weren't especially many of them, but by first glance, Kael could tell that they were poor. Or at least he hoped these were the poor people, and not the commoners. Was it possible that the entire city was in the same state as this?

Even though the buildings were dishevelled, most being no more than simple shacks, it was all organized. Messy but neat, this area almost reminded Kael of a stable. Speaking of which, to the left, hugging tight to the wall and relatively close to the front gate were the real stables. From what Kael could see of it, the stables were huge, as orderly as everything else and extremely well kept. Obviously enough, this city cared a lot for their horses.

They walked through the streets, which became tidier as they went, as if the further in one got, the higher on the social line they were. And then, as if a physical line was drawn, the poor section of the city abruptly ended. Regular buildings replaced the shanties, two stories tall and comprised of the same rich-coloured brown brick.

113

The houses had clay shingles on the roofs, somewhat reminding Kael of Shatterbreath's scales. The buildings were plain, square but efficient. There were just enough windows and they were lined up as straight as an arrow, following an invisible grid. And even though everything was placed with intricate care, no two buildings were the same. Detailed corners, designs cut into the brick and many other smaller or grander differences set each building different from the next.

Kael was getting more and more impressed with the city every step they took.

That area proved out to be larger than the poor section had been. By the way people carried themselves and hustled about, Kael guessed this was the living area for the commoners. Stone arches appeared in front of them, supported by high columns. They strolled under these columns and into the city's market, which was thriving with activity. People wearing robes were strutting around, obviously of a higher status, while the commoners hurried from one place to the next, eager to buy their week's provisions. Even the market was orderly! Everything was planned out to be as effective as possible. Kiosks selling similar or related things were placed close to each other, so that everything anybody wanted could be acquired through one sweep around the rectangular market.

Kael hesitated for the slightest moment as he breathed in the wonderful smells and comforting atmosphere. He received a sharp shove from behind.

"Move your carcass!" the soldier barked.

Rooster and Kael exchanged glances. What was going to happen to them? Why were they being treated this way? Perhaps their answers would come soon. Hopefully, this would all just be a misunderstanding...

They passed through the market. People cast mixed expressions at them, some giving blank looks, others more of a flouting sneer than anything. Kael lowered his head and stared at his feet.

They soon left the fascinating sounds and smell of the market, delving back into the dwellings of the common folk. They followed the main road, a wide, cobblestone path that seemed act as the spine of the city. They passed by more people on the way to the market, as well as ox-drawn carts and countless amounts of men riding horses.

A wall came into view up ahead, as well as the soothing sound of calmly rushing water. The wall was short and had half-moon windows cut all along its low surface.

They travelled underneath another gate, through a wide arch and onto a bridge. Kael gasped. The bridge rolled over the width of the river, wide, long and structurally strong. The river seemed to cut through the city, for there was another similar wall on the other side of its bank. The opposing wall was more lavished, with wonderful care and details etched all over its surface. Similarly, smaller bridges could be seen crossing the gaps on either side.

They galumphed into the second part of the city, Rooster tripping halfway across the bridge. Once they entered the second half the city, Kael couldn't believe his eyes. The difference over several feet across the river was profound—he now understood Rooster's earlier words concerning the city's classes. The lower classes were *literally* separated by a river and wall. The houses on the other side of the river were massive, garnished with large yards, several stories and all the richest furniture Kael had ever seen. Each mansion was so lavished; it seemed each one could hold a king within their depths.

And although the shapes of the houses were very different from others, some rising high above the ground, others wide and squat, they all seemed to fit perfectly in a well-organized grid, as if simple puzzle pieces that were *meant* to fit together.

From first glance, the second half of the city seemed as large as the area they had just left, but because of the larger houses, probably held fewer inhabitants.

Just then, the castle came into view.

At once, it was apparent the castle was built in the same sturdy, easy-to-defend status as the rest of the kingdom. From where he stood, Kael could see the walls of the castle itself rising high above the ground an impossible height. As they walked further, Kael could see that the castle was actually perched on a verdant, round hill. Even still, the structure was massive and stolid. Upon that, the sun was shining directly over it, giving it a holy, almost refulgent

115

appearance. The castle could only be compared to Vallenfend's for brilliance.

As they strolled up the gently-elevating path, getting closer to the castle, the guards leading Kael suddenly strengthened their grasp on him. They grabbed him around his shoulders, making him panic. He squirmed and struggled to get free as the knight holding his sword and shield turned around. In one hand, he held Kael's weapon, in the other were two black cloths.

"Here, scum. Put this on," he spat. "It would be disgracing for you to see the inside of our beautiful castle, or the General's face for that matter."

Kael pursed his lips, his muscles straining to break free of their grasp.

"I take it you're not happy about this," the knight flouted. "Well, you shouldn't have come back here."

Kael lost his composure. "But I haven't been here before! I have no idea what this is all about? What is BlackHound? What is this injustice? Why are you doing this?"

The knight squinted. "Maybe you haven't been here before as an individual, no. It was your people that came here and tried to break our strong society. We are not the ones giving injustice; it was you who tried to thrust it on us. Consider this payment for all your people tried to do."

Rooster had more control of his emotions, though he was clearly terrified. "What are you going to do with us?" he asked as the knight took a step towards Kael.

The knight shrugged. He passed one of the dark cloths to another soldier. "Flog you, behead you, drop you off a cliff... It's really up to the General to decide. You better hope he's in a good mood. Maybe he'll give you a quick death."

The colour drained from Rooster's face. Kael writhed some more, but it didn't help. Wordlessly, the knight slipped the black cloth over his head, plunging Kael's world in darkness. He could sense them doing the same to Rooster. He could see his feet through the bottom of the shroud and part of the ground as well, but he wasn't going to admit that to them.

They pushed them forwards, hands tied behind their backs, heads covered. It was difficult and awkward to walk like that, but Kael didn't say anything. Every once and a while, he could hear Rooster puling, whether he was afraid or stumbling, Kael couldn't tell.

Suddenly, a step up on a ramp caught him off guard. Unable to put out his hands to stop his fall, Kael could do little more than try and keep his head up as he dropped to the ground. His cheek smashed against the ground and his right shoulder and knee throbbed in pain.

"Get up," someone growled. Kael felt a sharp pain in his ribs as the soldier kicked him. "Get up, get up, you swine!"

Kael tried, but it was nearly impossible without using his hands. He succeeded in straddling himself up on his knees, but the guards kicked him back down.

"Hurry up!"

Kael's temper flared again. Through the bottom crack of his blinding cloth, he could see the soldier's feet. One of the feet kicked at him again. He curled up to try and block the strike, which did little. As soon as the kick struck, Kael swept his legs underneath the one standing foot. He was satisfied as he heard the soldier fall solidly to the ground with a loud curse.

As quick as he could, Kael coiled his body, and somewhat awkwardly, sprang back up to his feet. He lunged, shoulder-first at where he thought the nearest man was and succeeded in hitting him, sending the soldier reeling. Blindly, he sprinted off. He didn't know if this would accomplish anything, but he had to try.

His left foot met empty space. Deeply confused, Kael brought his foot back, planting both on the edge of an unknown abyss. Through the gap in the cloth, Kael could see a long drop waiting for him. Far below him was a lush green valley.

Kael teetered on the edge, both feet now planted. But it was too late, his momentum had carried him too far forward. He tried to lean back to balance him back, but he was already going forward. His heart dropped into his stomach as he imagined what would come next. He was going to fall. Time slowed to a standstill.

Suddenly, he stopped. Everything returned to normal. He felt something holding on tightly to the back of his breastplate. Kael turned his head to try and see who had caught him, but realized foolishly that he was still wearing the cloth over his head.

"Whoa now," the voice of the knight said. "Where are you trying to go? I should just let you fall..." He let go for a moment, making Kael yelp in fright. He caught Kael right away. "But it's up to the General to decide your fate. You may want to kill yourself dearly, but it is up to him to decide your appropriate fate."

Kael wasn't sure if he should thank the man. Instead, he took a shaky breath and decided that cooperating would be his best option at the moment.

The knight pulled him away from the edge. Kael's knees gave out and he fell on his back.

"Pick him up." At once, two soldiers put their arms under Kael's and hefted him back onto his feet. Without any further delay, the set forward again.

The bridge they were apparently on gave way to a gravel path. They walked along the winding path in silence, brushing against bushes once and a while. Finally that path turned back into cobblestone and Kael could sense they were nearing a large structure. It could only be the castle.

Their footsteps echoed back at them, telling Kael they had entered another large gate. Their echoes became weaker, but did not diminish entirely. New sounds met them as well—people walking about, armour clanking and swords clashing and a strange new sound that Kael interpreted as horse hooves clomping against cobblestone.

They walked across a courtyard full of people and animals alike, through an inner gate and onto another pathway. That path was shorter than the other and they arrived at their destination quickly. The busy sounds of the castle's inner courtyard died down. Suddenly, Kael felt as if he was inside a church.

Large double-doors gave way, letting them inside a room that echoed, signifying that it was quite large. Kael watched his feet pass by one another over a dark green carpet.

He fell to his knees when he was struck in the back. Setting his jaw, he stayed silent as another blow was delivered across his face. Rooster yelped in pain.

"Keep them here, I shall go inform the General," the knight informed his comrades.

They kept Kael there, but they didn't leave him alone.

They began to mock him, corroborating the harsh things they were saying by giving him equally sharp jabs and kicks. Kael sat there, breathing heavily, unable to do anything more than brood. He wasn't listening to what they were saying; he was ignoring the physical pain they were giving him.

All he could think about was whether or not he was going to see Shatterbreath again, and if he would ever get to talk to his friends again. His heart longed to see Laura's serene face, to touch her skin one last time...

The sharp sound of a door opening echoed through the room. Kael lifted his head, trying to peer underneath his cloth. He wanted to know who this General was.

The knight was still talking to the man, but Kael couldn't hear what he was saying. The soldiers around him backed away, their voices going silent. Whoever this guy was, he demanded respect.

The knight's voice also cut off.

Kael's heart began to pump wildly. He cursed it. He was straining to hear what was happening, but the sound of it was making him nearly deaf.

A shuffle came from across the hall. A step forward, the sound of heavy armour and chainmail rattling as the General approached. It felt like Kael was in the presence of a saint. All was quiet, except for the noise of the man approaching. He could sense Rooster stiffen beside him as the General came ever closer.

Kael closed his eyes, trying to calm the wild animal in his chest. He struggled to stay in control of his frantic emotions, his tight-as-a-bowstring body. He wasn't doing a good job. He shivered.

When Kael opened his eyes, the sound of the man walking had stopped. His heart skipped a beat as he saw two heavy metal boots waiting patiently in front of them. He couldn't see any more of the man, but just his boots alone were highly intimidating and daunting.

The boots stayed where they were. The General didn't speak, didn't move. It felt like Kael was being judged for what he had done. He felt guilty, even though he had indeed done nothing to offend. Then, as if the judge had made his decision, Kael heard the ruffle of clothing, the painful sound of metal sliding against metal. A knee appeared in his shaking vision as the man crouched lower.

Then, the General spoke.

Kael winced as if he had suddenly been stabbed through the chest with a sword. His eyes opened wide and a chill ran through his spine. The sentence was simple, yet more profound than any other Kael had ever heard.

"Do I know you?" the voice said jocularly.

Chapter 13

Laura took a deep breath and swallowed. She braced herself for what was about to come. She had to be brave; she had to act as if nothing was wrong. She grieved at the fact this had to be done in the first place.

Gently and slowly, she peeled back the scarlet cloth over Faerd's ruined eye. She gasped and just barely managed to keep her scant lunch down. Her mother wasn't even watching. She had stood up and moved to the other end of the dragon's cave.

Had her experience with the cavern been the same as Kael's? When she first stepped up to the gaping black expanse, she felt as though she was treading into hell itself. In a strange reverse, the inside of the cave was cold and moist. And a ghostly hue of blue. It was as though the spirits of thousands were trapped in the walls of the cavern. Their voices were in the echoing *plunking* of water droplets that accentuated the yawning silence and again. Their faces were in the strange glowing stones providing a degree of light. Their arms reached out to each other from the ceiling to the floor, as if trying to hold onto each other for comfort. But in the cave, there was no comfort.

How sad the situation was. Laura, her mother, Faerd and Korjan's son were taking refuge like rats in another creature's home. She felt no better than a parasite, a bother. The dragon wasn't home, but Laura's demeanour had hit an all-time low.

She didn't want to do this. She didn't want to look at the resulting gashes from when the group of black-clad assassins attacked them. She didn't want to see her friend like this. Least of all, she didn't want to be the one who had to look after him. But she had to.

Faerd didn't wince. He didn't make any noise. He didn't even move. It was like he was suddenly empty, void of emotion and cause. Her chest felt hollow as she tended to him. Once such an energetic boy was now reduced to this lifeless shell. It was heart-wrenching.

121

She hesitated as the cloth caught on the dried blood of his wound. Faerd didn't flinch.

"Doesn't that hurt?" Laura asked, peeling away some more of the cloth.

Faerd's good eye moved slightly, as if he had just emerged back into the real world. Just for a moment. "I am used to pain," he said morosely, pulling on another heartstring.

Laura wanted to cry. She wanted to take revenge. She wanted to scream and put her hands over her ears and run away forever. *She wanted things to return to normal.* But none of these would happen. She wasn't strong enough to exact revenge, Faerd and Korjan's son needed her and running away was not an option. She would have to persevere.

Tooran, the son of Korjan, bent closer to inspect Faerd's eye. His arm was still bandaged and they had burned his wound closed (which had been disgusting), but it had left his right arm useless until it healed further.

Tooran nodded. "The wound will heal, but I'm afraid that eye is useless now." He paused. "I...I'm sorry."

Laura's emotions flared. She stayed silent.

She supposed she should be thankful. They were alive and they were thriving. Every day, Laura and her mother would gather anything edible off the mountain and bring it back for the two men. They would eat what they had in silence. It was a terrible way to survive and her mother had lost weight already, but they were alive. *Alive.* Was that even a good thing?

By the sixth day, it was obvious the dragon and Kael weren't coming back, so Laura stopped hoping for them. She had been hoping in the back of her mind that they would come back and save them. She didn't know what would happen if they did, but she wished dearly for it. Sometimes, her dreams would plague her with visions of Kael in his gleaming armour coming and taking her away to a peaceful land. In the waking world, she imagined the opposite. She didn't want him to come. He was the cause of all this.

Because of Kael, her life was ruined. Their lives were ruined. There was no turning back.

Laura's mother perked up from where she sat several metres away. She hustled over to where Laura, Faerd and Korjan were sitting.

"I hear something!" she warned, clinging onto her daughter's weak arm.

No, this couldn't happen! Were there soldiers? Was there something worse coming? Faerd jumped to his feet, picking up thick black gauntlets he had found in the pile of armour stashed in the cave. When they had first arrived, Faerd had refused to settle down until he found a pair of suitable gloves. Laura had tried to force him to stop, but now she was glad he had ignored her.

Faerd slipped his pale hands into the heavy gauntlets and Tooran drew his sword. The two women slunk behind them, holding tightly onto one another as they waited for whatever was making the noise to appear. Laura stood dead still, staring at the mouth of the cave.

If it was soldiers, they'd be dead. Neither Tooran nor Faerd could hold off in their state.

Ages seemed to pass before silhouette appeared in the light that radiated through the mouth of the cave. It was large and oddly shaped. Laura strained her eyes, trying to decipher what it was. Tooran bent lower, holding his blade with one hand. Faerd didn't move.

"Oh my," a familiar voice echoed out, "put those away! It's me, Malaricus!"

Laura caught her breath. "Malaricus? Thank goodness it's only you!"

Malaricus's frail form neared them as he exited the beam of light. The reason he had been oddly shaped was because he was riding a donkey.

Even under the dire mood of all that had happened, Laura managed to laugh as she ran up to the scholar. Malaricus dismounted and wrapped his arm around her shoulders and she hugged him tightly. Mrs. Stockwin also hugged the scholar in turn, her features relaxing. Faerd slumped back to the ground and Tooran cocked his head questioningly.

123

"He's an old friend," Laura reassured him. She turned back to Malaricus. "What are you doing here? Where'd you get that donkey and—whoa! What all did you bring?"

Malaricus chuckled. "Slow down!" His face turned grave. "I heard soldiers had tried to arrest you, but you managed to flee. I figured the only place you could go was up here. So I bought this donkey and two weeks of food and supplies and came up here."

Laura considered the old man for a moment. Although he hadn't gone through quite as much as they had, she could see the torment in his eyes. They all showed it. It was the effect of Kael's gallivanting. She remembered when his library had been partially destroyed. She thought he had died that day. It was good to see him again.

She squeezed him again. "Thank you, thank you!"

Malaricus nodded. "I needed to do something to help." Just then, he caught sight of Faerd. "Oh my." He shivered. "Faerd, my boy, what happened to you?"

Faerd didn't answer, so Tooran stepped forward. "Jobra, the leader of the King's Elite, did this to him. He managed to wound me as well. We are lucky to still be breathing. Few escape from that man."

Malaricus peered at Tooran through his spectacles. He held up a hand as if Tooran was randomly going to hit him at any moment. "I'm sorry, who are you?"

Mrs. Stockwin was the first to respond. She always had enjoyed gossip. All the women did. "He's the long-lost son of Korjan, Tooran," she said matter-of-factly.

Malaricus's eyes shot wide open. "Really?" He stood up on his toes to inspect the man closer. "By my books, the resemblance is astounding!" He took Tooran's hand and shook it warmly. "It is truly an honour to meet you then!"

Tooran smiled. "As with you, Malaricus the Wise."

Laura turned her attention to Malaricus's donkey, which was watching them all with little patience. She opened one of the packs attached to its back. "So," she ventured, "what all did you bring?"

"Well..." Malaricus didn't get to finish his sentence.

"Wait!" Tooran interjected, "what is that sound?"

Laura strained her ears. Voices! Many of them. Every person craned their neck to the entrance immediately. Faerd sprang to his feet again. As silhouettes appeared, it was at once evident that these shadows were in fact soldiers.

Korjan hefted his pack. He was carrying easily double what the two ladies were, but that was quite alright. He could handle it. Besides, it lessened their complaining.

They kept to the backstreets to get to the exit of Vallenfend. They left late at night, so there was hardly anything to worry about. Even still, Korjan's heart was beating furiously. They had left in such a hurry; he hadn't even had time to take one last look backwards at his house, the life he was leaving. In a way, he was glad.

Korjan was a fighter. He always had been. He would have definitely stayed and fought off soldiers until they eventually killed him if that's what it took, but he had made a promise to Helena. He would keep her safe. As unfortunate as it was, the only way he was going to do that was to take her away from the city and up into that cave. He couldn't leave Bunda either.

He placed his huge, rough hands on either woman's shoulder. They both gazed up at him. They were now a family. Danger had brought them together.

It was a simple thing to bypass the guard watching the gate. Although she was a woman, Korjan had not refrained from knocking her unconscious. Helena had frowned at him while Bunda seemed unaffected. It was even simpler to break open the gates. One swing from an axe was all it took.

In no time at all, they were already scaling the mountain. They went at a lofty pace, which was difficult for Bunda because she was so plump, but also for Korjan. After only a few minutes, he had already grown tired of her complaining.

It was easy travelling however. A worn path twisted up the mountain. With a pang of disgust, Korjan realized it was the very same countless soldiers had taken to their deaths. Would they be doing the same thing? Was this all in vain? He didn't want to think about it. Such thoughts were for the weak.

125

The trail, Helena and Bunda pointed out several times, was beautiful though narrow and bushy. Korjan didn't really care for the view. He kept his head low, eager to just get to where they were going. The two women stopped once or twice to look at the view, and the blacksmith would eventually have to usher them onwards.

Much to Bunda's dismay, they had to sleep in the forest. Korjan was getting the impression Bunda hadn't ever been outside Vallenfend. Helena was much better. The butcher had no idea how to set up her bedroll and Korjan had to help her.

Once they did get settled in, the two women close together and Korjan farther off, he could hear the butcher muttering in fear and Helena trying to comfort her. Sometime during the night, he woke up to hear somebody crying. He thought at first it was Bunda, but realized it was Helena. He remained still for a while, pondering whether or not he should try and comfort her. He wasn't good at that sort of stuff, so he forced himself to go back to sleep.

The next day was worse than the previous, as unimaginable as that seemed. The trio was all tired and groggy from their hurried, wary sleep. To make things worse, the path narrowed and became slippery as they passed under waterfalls. Even Korjan had to admit at one point, the scenery was astounding. Vallenfend was no larger than the pommel of a dagger from up there. The gap in the trees gave them a perfect view. He didn't like the way his heart seemed to cry as he looked the city, so he forced them on.

With only a few stumbles, they finally got passed the worst part of the waterfalls. The path widened out as well, but there was still a breathtaking cliff next to them. Korjan paused and peered over the edge. He whistled. Now *that* was a drop. He swore he could see a skeleton far below.

The rest of the trip was uneventful. Once the path veered away from the cliffs, they were once again devoured by the forest's canopy again and Korjan settled into a thoughtless state, letting his body carry him onwards. He was dimly aware that the two women behind him were talking, but didn't bother to listen to what was being said.

It took another two and a half days, but finally, they made it to the top of the mountain in one piece.

The trio stopped in front of the cave. Korjan stared into its depths, wondering what it would hold. It yawned in front of them so simply, as if nothing was out of the ordinary with it. He marvelled at its size. From Vallenfend, it was no more than a black line. Standing in front of it, he got a true feeling of how large the dragon was.

Before they took more than two steps in, they heard noises. Korjan furrowed his brow. Helena looked up at him questioningly. "Sounds like..." Korjan's eyes shot wide open. "Swords!"

He quickly threw his pack off his back and unsheathed his broadsword, directed Helena and Bunda to stay quiet before running inside.

His footsteps echoed dryly back at him. Adrenaline began to course through his veins. He gritted his teeth, body tense with the anticipation of battle.

What he saw made his jaw drop.

It was Faerd, Malaricus and the two Stockwins. What in the world were they doing there? He shook his stupor and ran towards Faerd, who was fighting off a soldier with nothing more than gauntlets as a weapon. As Korjan approached, Faerd knocked the soldier unconscious then moved on to the next. There were about seven soldiers wearing blue tunics, and about five more wearing black outfits. Korjan's heart skipped a beat. The soldiers in blue posed little to no threat, but the ones in black would be trouble.

Two soldiers in blue didn't even realize what hit them. Korjan slashed them both in the back with one clean stroke. They both fell to the ground, as good as dead. Before an assassin even realized what happened to his comrade, Korjan decapitated him. The other soldiers finally became aware of him.

Korjan engaged two black-clad assassins at once, ducking just in time as the both lunged for his chest. As he did, he spotted a form behind him. He whipped around to stab the blue-tunic soldier through the chest, slit an assassin's stomach by ducking underneath the man's blade and finished the remaining assassin with a savage horizontal backslash.

He blocked an attack aimed for his head then proceeded to lock blades with a black-clad soldier who lacked a mask. Korjan stopped

127

immediately. So did the other man. A shiver ran through his spine. It was as if he was gazing into a mirror.

One of the women screamed. Korjan and his look-alike both rushed towards the scream, cutting down three blue soldiers along their way. Assassin had knocked Mrs. Stockwin down. Even as Korjan watched, Malaricus tackled into the man who remained standing. With a chuckle, the assassin pushed the scholar aside and raised his weapon, aiming to kill Mrs. Stockwin. Both Korjan and his look-alike slashed at the assassin at once. He fell down, hardly in one piece.

A gurgle came from behind. Korjan whipped around to face a scowling soldier. But the man's eyes rolled to the back of his head and he went limp. Bunda came into view. She wrenched her cleaver from the corpse, where several gashes were spread across his back. Korjan nodded at her.

With Korjan, the strange soldier, Faerd and Bunda all counterattacking, the soldiers stood little chance. Soon, the cave was littered with corpses and the floor drenched in blood. Despite the addition of gore, the overlaying stench of the cave was still overwhelming.

Helena rushed in and exhaled in relief. Everybody else seemed okay, although Faerd's eye was terribly damaged. It didn't seem recent though.

Korjan turned to the man who looked just like him. He stepped up right in front of him, pointing his finger at the man's chest. "Who are you?" he yelled. "Why were you helping us and not them?" He pointed to a dead assassin on the ground.

The look-alike couldn't find his voice. He stuttered and tried to say something, but no words came out. Korjan grabbed him, in a fury. "Who are you?!"

Laura ran up, her hair wild from the recent activity. She had quickly shaken her fear of the soldiers and surprise to see Korjan, Bunda and Helena come to their rescue. She grabbed onto Korjan's arm and tried to pull him away.

"Stop, Korjan!" she pleaded. "Stop!"

Korjan clenched his jaw and pushed her away.

"Stop! Please! Can't you see? He is your son!"

Korjan gasped. His grip faltered and the man extricated himself from the blacksmith's grasp. Korjan stared from Laura to the man in front of him. His lip began to tremble.

"S...son?" he said, barely a whisper.

The other man nodded, tears forming in his eyes.

The embraced each other.

For the first time since Korjan's wife had been taken away all those years, Korjan began to cry. He sobbed loudly and tears streamed down his face. His knees went weak but his son, *his son*, held him up. For what seemed an eternity they stayed that way. Korjan cried against his son's shoulder. The other closed his eyes and held his father tighter.

Laura watched with a weak smile. Tears were forming in her eyes. Korjan and Tooran, father and son, were finally reunited, after all those agonizing years. She could only imagine torment Korjan had gone through because he had believed his son was dead. Now... She could only imagine what joy, what relief he was feeling. Laura was moved deeply from the display.

Helena began to cry, as well as Mrs. Stockwin. Even Faerd, who had been lifeless moment ago, was struggling to hold back tears. Laura eventually began to cry herself. With the coming of Korjan, Helena and Bunda, she could feel hope returning to her. With their added strength and support, they stood a chance.

They were the once who had escaped from the city. They were the ones who had suffered from Kael's influence, but lived to come together as one. They were a family of outcasts.

They were Kael's friends, all of them. And now—now they were together.

Chapter 14

The cloth around Kael's head was suddenly pulled off. He squinted because of the sudden change of light, but the face he met was recognizable at once. For before him, wearing the same goofy expression he had when they first met was none other than Vert Bowman.

Kael's relief and surprise were at the same levels. Vert was *alive?*

"But...how...you...live?" was all he could muster.

Vert laughed boisterously. "I would say the same thing about you—if it made sense."

Vert helped Kael to his feet and undid the cords binding his hands. Kael and Vert gave each other a half-hug. It was absolutely mind-blowing to see Vert alive and well and even more shocking to see him in such a place of power.

Kael stared at the young man for a moment. So many thoughts were flowing through his mind, it was smothering. "How did you survive?" Kael asked with wonder. The memory of Vert getting kicked by Shatterbreath replayed in his mind. "How in the *world* did you get here? General? How?!"

Vert batted at the air. "That doesn't matter. That's a story I'd rather share later." He leaned forward. "What I want to know is how *you* survived and what *you're* doing in my city, Arnoth."

"I..." Before Kael could say anything else, Vert interrupted him.

"You..." He pointed at Kael's breastplate, raising his eyebrows.

"Uh, me?"

A wide grin slowly spread across Vert's face. "You teamed up with the dragon, didn't you?"

Kael was barely able to keep his face straight. He winced, aware of everyone watching them. The knight who had brought him in was standing slightly off to the side, holding his sword and shield.

His worked his jaw for a moment. He managed a dry laugh. "What are you talking about?"

Vert kept is scrutinizing expression on Kael. "Well, for one, you are *alive*. For another, a colossal blue dragon just *happens* to be spotted near Arnoth and they drag you in shortly afterwards."

Kael's grin faded. "Just a coincidence, I'm sure." Vert's eyebrows went even higher. "Okay, fine," he growled, "yes, Shatterbreath and I are friends now, if that's what you consider 'teaming up'."

Vert chortled. "I knew it!"

Still bound and kneeling on the floor, Rooster whimpered. Kael had completely forgotten about him. "What's happening?" the boy called out, trying to peek underneath the cloth. "Are we dead?"

"No," Kael replied. "Quite the opposite." He turned to Vert. "He's a friend," he said with a shrug.

Vert walked over and pulled the cloth of Rooster's face. He looked the boy top from bottom. After a minute or so, he turned to Kael. "I don't like him," he stated.

Rooster looked hurt. "Pleased to meet you as well."

Vert turned his attention back towards Kael, stepping into a sunbeam that was pouring through an adjacent window. The bright light made him look like a saint. He had changed since Kael had last seen him, but the differences were difficult to point out. "So you became friends with the dragon," he thought out loud. "Neat. In that case, what brings you here?"

"An invading army is coming, Vert," Kael explained. Rooster strolled over to join the conversation. "I've been travelling across the land with Shatterbreath and now my friend here, Rooster, trying to convince cities to join us."

Vert scoffed. "I knew there was something up!"

"Yeah, you were just a bit off though."

The boy shrugged. "Close enough."

Kael had told him his part, now he wanted an explanation. "Shatterbreath...spared me because she needed my help, but how did you escape?"

The knight standing beside them cleared his throat. He had been shuffling closer to the trio, trying to catch Vert's attention, but had been unsuccessful until then.

Vert scowled at the knight. "What?"

"I don't know what this is about, General, but this boy is from BlackHound."

At hearing this, Vert cast a sideways glance at Kael. "Why do you think that?"

The knight showed Vert Kael's shield. "It holds their mark."

Vert took the shield in his hands. Kael reached for his sword, but the knight drew away, giving Kael a cold stare. Vert rubbed his thumb on the shield.

"Where'd you get this?" he asked quietly, his brow furrowed and jocular tone gone.

"I got it from Shatterbreath's cave. Why, what's BlackHound?"

Vert exhaled sharply. "Oh, okay. You got this from... I thought you had joined *them,* Kael. BlackHound. We aren't sure if there's any hidden meaning behind the name or much about them for that matter, but we do know they're very influential. And not very good."

"Not very good?" Kael echoed. "Can I have an explanation?"

"Only for you," Vert said sarcastically. It was good to hear his voice again. "When I arrived here, the king was trying to do terrible things. Apparently, he had been forced or goaded into doing so by a group named BlackHound."

Kael rubbed his bruised cheek. "Aren't—aren't you in charge? Where's the king now?"

Vert chuckled. "Gone, disposed of, no longer a threat. That doesn't matter. BlackHound is not a good thing; my experiences here have proven that over and over."

Rooster piped up. "I don't understand. What do you mean by a group? What did these people look like?"

Vert frowned at the boy. Even though they had known each other for a total of three minutes, Vert seemed to really dislike him. "The original members of the group came to Arnoth long, long ago, dressed in heavy armour and brandishing fearsome weapons. Nobody can remember what they came for, but they organized a cult of sorts, left some armour and junk, then just left. According to what I've heard, they were black as midnight."

"What do you mean?"

Vert shrugged. "That's where it's unclear. It was just said that they were like shadows in appearance. As trustworthy and secretive too. After they left, the king had been acting all strange ever since. None of that matters now, for we've completely wiped their existence from Arnoth."

Something clicked in Kael's head. "A king acting strange... Sound familiar?"

Vert nodded. "I was thinking the same thing. Your appearance only strengthens it."

"I know clearly that there is an invading army coming to sack Vallenfend. I had only assumed that they had no set name. Now I finally know their true name," Kael said, looking between Rooster and Vert. He suddenly recalled the time he had intruded into Vallenfend's castle. "I broke into Zeptus's study once," Kael thought aloud, "there was a letter from the empire. Signed BH."

Vert Bowman shifted his weight. "BlackHound."

Rooster threw his hands in the air. "Oh joy, we know their name! What does this effect?"

With grunt, Vert hit Rooster in the arm

After it was decided by Vert that Kael and Rooster, were not hostile, the knight gave Kael his things back and people stopped scowling at them. The knight still glared at him, but walked away.

Vert wanted an audience in a more private location, so he started to lead them out onto the castle grounds.

"This is where I go to think," Vert said with glee. He was excited to see Kael again, that was for certain.

Kael was hardly listening. He was staring at his shield. He had always thought it was a wolf. Now that he looked closer, it did look like a shaggy hound. Knowing that the shield had once belonged to a soldier from the invading army, it suddenly seemed tainted, as if it was covered with diseases. He held it loosely with the tips of his fingers.

"All this time...I didn't even know. Are you sure this from the BlackHound empire?"

Vert took the shield from Kael's hands. He propped it up against his knee and pulled a dagger from his waist. He tapped the head of the hound with the tip of his blade. A single, sweet note resounded.

"What does that sound like to you?"

Kael listened harder. He bent closer. "Somebody whistling?"

Vert frowned. "Here, give me a second." He tried again, striking the shield harder. This time, the noise was definite. It sounded like a wolf howling. As he listened a few seconds longer, Kael realized it sounded nothing like a wolf's call, but more like the baleful laments of a dog. A hound.

The noise faltered and petered out, just as a regular howl would. It stopped entirely, leaving Kael shaken. That confirmed it.

Vert handed back Kael's shield. He was reluctant to take it. "I don't know if I want this now..." he said uncertainly, lips curling in distaste.

Vert pressed the shield closer. "It's a sturdy shield and I'm sure it has or will do you well. You should take it."

"But it's the embodiment of everything I strive against. Because of what it stands for, all this torment has befallen all of us. Now that I know the truth about it, it would feel hypocritical for me to use it. I'd only be denying what I'm trying to prove."

Rooster craned his neck and clicked his tongue. With Vert around, he was getting less attention. "I don't see what the big deal is. It's just a shield. It's not like you'll become evil just by wearing it."

Vert shifted his weight. "Feather-for-brains is right. Image does not define who you are. Take, for example, a weapon. Where did you get that sword?"

Kael unsheathed his weapon, reading the inscription on the handle. "From Shatterbreath's cave."

Vert paused. "Really? It's nice. Anyway, whatever blacksmith made that weapon, nothing about him is rubbing off on you is it? You aren't feeling the urge to make a weapon, are you?"

"Well, kind of. I used to be a blacksmith's apprentice. I miss the trade."

Vert rolled his eyes. "Whatever. The *point* is, it doesn't matter who that belonged to. It's yours now and *you* chose to use it for good. Besides, I think there's a little irony in there somewhere. Using BlackHound's weapons for good."

Kael smiled. "I suppose so."

"There you go," Vert said with a sigh. He beamed knowing he had won that argument. His expression seemed to say *I told you so.*

They reached a point on the mountain that was surrounded by a small guardrail. It overlooked part of the castle's inner courtyard. The outer wall was in front of them a ways while the city shimmered to the left. Kael leaned over the edge. It was a solid drop until the ground.

Now that he was at a higher advantage, Kael could see the route he had taken to get to the castle to begin with. There was a bridge leading up to the castle, the very same he had nearly fallen off of.

Vert inspected Arnoth for a moment. "Euch, *nobles,*" he spat. "I hate the lot of them. They think they're so wonderful and have special privileges because they're so rich. I'm glad I introduced the new tax system."

Kael had to smile. Vert loved technical stuff like that, whereas Kael had never really cared. Arnoth was all too fitting for him. Or he was for the city... Either way, they were perfect for each other.

Vert's tone was hinting for Kael to inquire. "You introduced a tax system?" Kael asked, taking the bait. Beside him, Rooster rolled his eyes.

"Yes," Vert declared, beaming. "Instead of a flat rate, as the old king had set up, I decided that the tax should be different for every person. Before, everybody was charged the same amount, which was nothing for nobles and a lot for the people who live in the poor stables."

"Wait," Kael interrupted. "You call the poor district stables?"

"Ha, yeah." He cocked his head, amused by his own humour. "Because quite frankly, they stink. Anyway, I introduced a new tax system once I became General. Everybody is charged ten percent of their income now."

"That's fairer."

"Uh, yeah."

Rooster stretched and yawned. "That's terribly interesting," he stated, leaning out on the guardrail. "But don't you think we should be getting back to business here, Kael? You're only going to get behind schedule again."

Both Kael and Vert shot him a look. "I haven't seen Vert for months, Rooster. I just discovered he's even still *alive*. I think we deserve some time to catch up."

Rooster put out his hands. "Fine, alright!" he said defensively. "Sorry." Kael was beginning to get sick of Rooster.

"Which brings up the question," Kael began, turning to Vert, "you *have* to tell me how you escaped and came here."

Vert shrugged. "Alright. So the last time I saw you, Kael, we were heading up the mountain to the dragon's cave..."

Chapter 15

The cave was silent. There was a ruffling sound, scales against stone. Everything seemed to be spinning, twisting. His eyes were closed, which only made things worse. What happened?

Everything came rushing back. A glaive in his hand, ducking underneath a thick blue tail... It was becoming clear to him. Vert Bowman was alive. He was lying face down, sprawled out like a rug on a floor. He caught his breath but refrained from sucking in too much air. The noise at the base of his skull continued, but as reality came rushing rudely back in, he quickly realized that the sound was not a figment of his pain, but actually real.

He opened his eyes, just a crack. It took an immense amount of willpower. He wanted nothing more than to just sit and wait. Every inch of his body seemed to be in pain. His right leg throbbed and his chest felt smaller than normal. When he flexed slightly, things shifted inside him. He felt broken.

A blue mass slowly slid across the ground. It moved away, out towards a light off in the distance. With a whoosh and a roar, whatever the shape had been was gone. It had been big, so Vert could only assume it was the dragon.

If he hadn't been in such agony, he would have laughed at himself. Of *course* it was the dragon, what else could it be? He was, of course, still lying in the dragon's cave.

Vert twitched his fingers. They seemed to work. Next, he moved his wrists. All okay. Arms, shoulders. All fine. His midsection was aching. A few ribs were undoubtedly broken. The last thing he could remember was slamming into a craggy wall. Hard. Legs...more or less okay. Around his shin spiked with pain, perhaps from a fracture. That could pose a problem.

Vert stayed motionless for a few more minutes. He debated what he should do. If he stayed there, the dragon would surely come back and finish him off. But it would take *effort* to get up, something he didn't think he could muster at that moment.

Eventually, his impatience towards his own lazy attitude won over. He *needed* to get up and moving. Otherwise surviving would be pointless.

He pulled his hands closer, braced his palms against the cold ground and gritted his teeth. Pushing himself up was the hardest thing he had ever done. His muscles shrieked at him and he winced mentally, pleading for his body to forgive him.

Alright, he was this far. Now for the other half.

Favouring his hurt leg, he brought his other forward. And then the next. Both feet were underneath him, complaining in silence. Finally, he pushed off and balanced in a low crouch. There rested, feeling his head throb.

Very slowly, Vert stood up, feeling the blood rush to his head. He clenched his hand and realized his glaive was no longer in his grip. He groaned as he spotted it on the ground. Wrapping his fingers around the shaft, he balanced on the weapon, grateful for the support. Warily, he hobbled over to the front of the cave. The light struck against his face and he put a hand out to block his stinging eyes. The smells of the mountainside—pine and earth—were a relief from the mephitic, bloody stench of the cave.

Vert looked to and fro. Everybody was gone. They were all dead. He could only presume that he was the only one who had survived. Standing there at the mouth of the cave, he considered what options he had. There was *no* way he was going back to Vallenfend. If he returned, they'd just send him right back. And if they didn't, well, the outcome would be the same.

Which left Vert in a precarious situation. One thing was for certain: he had to get away from that cave. Rubbing his neck, Vert set off down the mountain, aiming to put as much distance between him and the cave as possible. He did not want to be there when the dragon returned.

A few hours later, Vert chuckled to himself. He was a comfortable distance from the cave by then and feeling more flexible. A stream trickled nearby and a small alcove near a cliff provided him with adequate protection, which was vital, considering his injured state. Absently, he munched on some berries he had found a while back, replaying the carnage that had transpired a while ago. He was grieved that his friends, especially Kael Rundown, were all dead, but there was nothing that could be done to reverse that. What he found funny, however, was the damage he had done to the dragon before the accursed beast had kicked him. He would have preferred not to hurt it, but the fact that it had hurt him right back made his actions justified. In his eyes anyway.

Vert ate another handful of berries, brooding. He had no family in Vallenfend. His father had suffered the same fate as all men in the city do, and his mother had come to peace with Vert's departure.

The reality of the situation suddenly struck him. There was nothing for left for him. *Nothing.* He was utterly alone. Vert smiled. Goosebumps ran rampant over his skin. He could start a new life. Yes, that's perfect! That's what he would do. Everything he cared for was gone. A new city would hold a new life for him.

He could see it now. The man he wanted to be. And now, finally, it was within reach for him. Such opportunities were never easy to grasp. Vert was going to seize it. It was odd and perhaps poetic how this chance came to being. Only by stepping through the passage of death could this come. Vert had survived what no man had before. Great rewards were in store. But first, Vert needed a way to get to a new city. Every other city he knew about was too far away to get there by foot; he would perish on the way there.

Despite the flaw in his plan, Vert was feeling optimistic. Deep down, he felt that it would all turn out right. He didn't know how such a feat would come to pass, but that the solution would present itself, with time.

Vert glanced at the sky. Religion was never too strong in his life, but he felt like there was a greater force in play. He reconsidered what he knew. No, this was too great. Only the grace of some cosmic entity could ensure this. A second chance at life, a new slate.

Unsure at first, Vert bent to his knees, feeling humbled. There, for the first time in his life, he uttered a prayer of thanks. He didn't know to whom he owed his gratitude, but he let his voice carry the prayer out over the mountain and into the awaiting wind.

Awkwardly, Vert stood back up and remained there for what seemed an eternity, dead silent, letting the sounds of the forest overwhelm him. For that brief moment, he felt utter bliss.

The stars smiled down at him as Vert slipped into his bedroll. He didn't set up a perimeter to warn him of predators that night. He felt one with the forest. Nothing would harm him out here. Vert's prayer would ensure that.

A snap somewhere out in the bushes forced Vert awake. At once, his mind was racing, coming up with various ways to defend against an attacking predator. His glaive was already in hand, and he brandished it out in front of him, springing to his feet. His body relaxed as he saw what it was. A beautiful doe stood at the edge of his glade, both ears forward and neck taut. With wide eyes, it stared at him, but it did not bolt.

Vert lowered his weapon. He cocked his head and watched the deer. It stared right back for a moment longer, then lowered its head and nibbled on a few blades of grass. Vert smiled. Seconds later, the deer perked up, swivelling its neck around away from Vert. Something was disturbing the trees nearby. The deer bolted.

Vert's heart began to race. Whatever was lumbering through the trees was large. There were only a few things in this forest that could make such a noise. He tightened his grip on his glaive and crouched lower. His body protested, but he did his best to ignore it. Pain was something he had a tolerance for.

As he suspected, a bear roamed into view. It was massive, its shoulders at least a foot above Vert's head. He gazed up at it, gritting his teeth. All the stories he had ever heard about Vallenfend's bears flashed through his mind. They were bigger than normal bears, fiercer and were known to follow a particular scent for miles. It must have smelled something of Vert's, perhaps the berries he ate the day before.

Whatever its cause to find Vert, it inspected him with beady eyes. Its nose twitched as it snuffled at him and it took an eager step forward. Vert held his ground. He wasn't sure what he should do. Should he attack it? Should he stand his ground?

He decided to back away, moving very slowly. Keeping his eyes on it, Vert shuffled away from his pack. If it came to it, he would gladly lose his bag and everything in it if that meant his survival. The bear must have deciphered his movement as something else, for it reared onto its hind legs. Whatever interest it had for berries was lost and it growled at Vert, letting him know that it was a threat.

Holding out his hand, Vert continued to back away. He bumped into some thick bushes from behind, reminding him that he didn't have much room to manoeuvre. In his decision to make camp in a spot that was protected from almost all angles, he had successfully trapped himself. There was only one clear way out of his the glade, which the bear was blocking at that moment.

So, Vert did the only thing he could think of. He bolted, trying to run around the bear. It roared and took a swing at him. Long black claws raked against his pauldron, knocking him to the side. Vert cursed as he lost his balance and stumbled.

With a growl, the bear took another swing, aiming for his chest. Vert recovered and leaned back, dodging the claws. He decided to send the bear a message of his own and slashed its paw with his glaive. The bear roared louder than before. Its fur did well to protect it, but blood was still drawn from the attack—which only seemed to enrage the animal.

The bear charged. Vert was only just able to step aside as it careened towards him. It missed, claws coming within inches of his face, and crashed into the cliff behind. Rocks were shaken loose and Vert jumped to avoid them. The bear whipped around ready to battle.

Vert was ready as well.

He lunged towards the great beast, driven by an unfamiliar cause. The bear swung at him, but he rolled underneath the paw. He sprang up and thrust his glaive towards its hulking chest.

The blade sunk into the bear's chest. Vert withdrew it and plunged it in again. And again. Three more stabs killed the beast. With a rumbling sigh, the beast's legs gave out and it slumped onto its belly. Vert held the tip of the glaive above the bear's muzzle for a moment, wary. It was finished.

141

Vert slumped to the ground. He caught his breath, staring the dead animal over. There was enough meat on the beast to last him a week. He exhaled. As fatigued as he was, Vert picked himself up and began to skin the still-twitching animal. His body ached for rest already, but he needed to strip the carcass of meat and move on before another predator came.

Once he was done, Vert quickly packed up his things. It was already mid-day by the time he had taken off enough meat from the bear to last him a comfortable time. Leaving the carcass as it was, he set off, heading in no discernable direction.

His plans were still set. He make his way to another city, but in due time. He still had no clue how to get there, but he trusted there would be a way. He chuckled to himself. Perhaps he shouldn't have killed that bear, he could have ridden on its back. He laughed even louder. What a silly concept.

A week later, Vert was still stuck on the side of the mountain. He had set up a comfortable shelter overlooking a waterfall. There was a perimeter around his makeshift camp and he had devised a way to hide his things up in a tall tree. He was being uncharacteristically patient, despite his eagerness to get off the mountain.

His patience finally paid off. He was cooking some meat when he heard a rattle. The wire he set up as his perimeter had been disturbed, shaking a can filled with small rocks. Vert snatched his glaive and threw himself behind the safety of a boulder. A gentle breeze rustled through the bushes. Taking a breath, he peered over and squinted, trying to see what had disturbed his perimeter. Was it another pesky rabbit?

"Yah!" Vert screamed, waving his arms. "Shoo!"

The creature in the trees was quick to give a response. Instead of frightened rustling, Vert heard a noise that made his heart leap forward. It was a deep snort. Flinging himself over the boulder, Vert hurled himself towards the noise.

A dark brown horse threw back its head as Vert approached. It whinnied, but Vert thrust his arms forward, trying to mollify the animal.

"Whoa," he whispered, inching closer. He couldn't believe it. A horse! Way up in the mountains? What a stroke of luck! This is what he was waiting for. But he had to play it safe. The horse was spooked as it was, and Vert's yelling had only frightened the beast further.

The horse saw him and after several minutes of coaxing, calmed down enough for Vert to touch its side. It muscles were taut but as Vert stroked its coat it relaxed. He drew closer, rubbing its neck with both hands. It snorted and pawed the ground, still wary.

Vert espied a bridle. He grabbed onto it and looked over the horse. There was a saddle on its back as well. Smiling, he stroked its black mane. This was far too good to be true!

As comforting as he could, Vert led the horse back to his makeshift camp. He stopped it near a patch of grass and petted it some more. He backed off and sat down on the same rock he had been hiding behind before, watching the horse. It began to munch away at the grass, comforted by Vert's presence. He also felt comforted. This was his way off the mountain. He had no idea why a fully-saddled horse was way up in the mountains, but he was overjoyed by its appearance. Now he had a companion. Now he had a way to leave.

The path down the mountain was much quicker on the back of a horse. Vert was already grateful for his new companion. Together, they went up and over the mountain, as to avoid any conflict with Vallenfend. Vert would miss the city, but not its corruption.

Without any trouble, Vert and his new companion reached the rolling hills that rested on the other side of the mountain. Vert marvelled at everything. He had never been this far away from his home, except that for that one time he had gone to the coast—but that was in the opposite direction.

They travelled at a satisfying gate, moving fast enough to cover good ground while not wearying out Vert's horse too soon. He wasn't quite sure where to go. Somewhere in his mind a voice told him that he would be led to a safe place to go, but Vert decided that perhaps he should rely on a little more than divine revelation—if it

143

was indeed that. He had been a religious person for less than a week; he wasn't quite ready to put his entire life in the hands of an unseen deity, even if doing so had worked for him thus far.

He tried to recall everything he had heard about other cities. There wasn't much to remember. There were only bits and pieces, snippets of conversations he had overheard. Nothing more than strange cultural ways other places held. He distinctly recalled somebody once mentioning to him that there were wonderful cities to the east of Vallenfend. He had considered it trivial news at the time. Now, it seemed the directions the person had given him would play an important part.

Drawing an invisible map in his mind, Vert pulled on the reins, pointing his horse towards the city the old man had been talking about. It occurred to him that perhaps there was indeed no city there, but Vert wasn't concerned. If he headed in one direction, chances were he'd find a city sooner or later.

Vert opened his bag and cursed loudly. That's all the food he had left? He had travelled for four straight days, although he could have sworn he had enough for six. Shrugging, he closed the bag and placed it behind him on the back of his horse.

The sun was beating down on him relentlessly, as if it was angered that he was still alive and wanted to kill him itself. Vert cursed at it. Why did it have to be so bright? And around *all* day long? It was too much. He was beginning to like night better and better every day. His sunburnt arms agreed.

Every once and a while, one of the mountains on other side of him would snuff out the sun's light, providing temporary shade. Vert would stop his horse, which he had affectionately named Shadowmane, and basked in the shadows. His stomach ached, reminding him of how important it was for him to continue onwards.

Vert would have thought that such frequent mountain ranges as these would be vivid with life, but he was wrong. There was the occasional stream of water to drink from, but otherwise, all was bare. He was travelling through a mild desert.

For a time, Vert didn't think he would make it. He was optimistic person, so when that thought arose, it was a hard one to shake. He had accepted death before, but now was different. He couldn't die now! Not after all he had been through. He hadn't climbed out of the monster's lair and travelled so far for nothing.

As they rounded the base of a hill, something appeared on the horizon. At first, Vert thought it was just his mind playing tricks on him. He continued onwards though, hoping in the back of his mind that it was some sort of relief.

The hazy shape on the horizon waved from the heat radiating from the ground, but otherwise stayed in the same spot. Vert stopped Shadowmane and stared long and hard at it. A single cloud swept in front of the sun, giving Vert a better view of the shape off in the distance. Precipices rose up and the distinct outline of city walls could be seen. Vert's optimism returned. Energy flowed out of the core of his being, filling his limbs with excitement. A city! He made it!

The rest of the journey seemed to fly by. Before Vert knew it, he was standing at the front gates of the kingdom, looking up in awe at the stone pillars. A guard leaned out.

"Oi, you down there!" he called out. "What's your business here?"

Vert lowered himself off of Shadowmane. "I am a weary traveller, looking for a new home. Can I come in?"

The guard scratched his chin. "We don't usually accept strangers here, but you look famished and weary. I will see what I can do." He disappeared, leaving Vert feeling disheartened. *Don't usually accept strangers?*

The doors lurched and swung open. A battalion of soldiers marched out and surrounded him. Vert hugged close to Shadowmane. He wasn't worried for his own safety, but for his horse's. He had become attached to his companion over the time they had been together.

A guard spoke. He sounded like the same that had peered down from the battlements. "What exactly are you here for?"

145

"As I already said," Vert explained, trying to hold his patience, "I have come from another city, seeking help and a new home."

"Why did you leave your old kingdom?" a different soldier asked.

Vert shrugged. "Banishment," he lied. "Or close enough anyway."

"Why were you banished?"

"You ask too many questions, you know that?" Vert sighed. "Does it *really* matter?"

"Yes, it does matter," a soldier scoffed. "Our city is...exclusive. We will harbour neither thieves nor outlaws."

Vert clenched his jaw, but held his peace. "Then what are you worried about? I am neither of those. They sent me away for unjust reasons. I am more of a refugee than anything else."

The soldiers exchanged glances and shifted their weight. A few of them were staring at Vert's glaive, which was held tightly in his hand. If it came to it, he wouldn't hesitate to use it. They all stayed silent for a spell, until Vert's horse snorted. That seemed to spur them into action.

"You may not stay here, but," the soldier speaking paused, "we will supply you with temporary lodgings, food and any other comforts you may require."

"Much obliged," Vert said through his teeth.

"But be known, you won't be tolerated for long. We do this out of hospitality. Once you have replenished your strength, you will leave, or we will be obligated to make you leave."

Vert nodded, knowing he was pushing it as it was. "That's fair, I suppose. I appreciate your kindness."

"Quite so." The battalion turned as to face the gates. They still surrounded Vert. "Come, we will show you to your housing."

Vert didn't stay long. He didn't want to. The people of the city neglected him, pretending as if he didn't even exist as he strolled through the markets. They all looked the same, pale-skinned and with bright hair. They wore the same style of clothing and every building in the city was the same. When the soldiers had mentioned their city was exclusive, they had made a serious understatement. To

146

Vert, it seemed as though the only way somebody was allowed to live there was for them to be born into their society.

And they were all so pompous. Vert couldn't stand their arrogant manner. They referred to other people as if they were nothing more than swine, and insulted other cities for no apparent reason. As Vert would stroll around, they would turn their noses at him. Vert would mirror their expressions. He hated these people.

So, as soon as he felt recovered, Vert borrowed enough supplies to last him a week, packed them onto Shadowmane's back, and departed. Nobody said goodbye as he left.

Vert pulled the map he had borrowed. It wasn't very detailed. He spotted the kingdom he had just left. It was detailed in fine gold, whereas every other landmark on the map was done in a simple ink. Vert swore and shook his head, muttering rude things about the elitist kingdom. He was glad to be gone. Those were not his kind of people.

Something disturbed his thoughts and Vert looked up. He was at the base a massive mountain. Looking to and fro, Vert observed that the mountain before him was the first in a long chain, stretching in a southern direction as far as he could see. He checked the map again. There was a city near the tail end of this range. Inspecting the map closer, he spotted the name of the city. Arnoth. Hmm. It had a nice ring to it. Plus it wasn't that far away. All he needed to do was follow the mountains.

"I'll head to Arnoth," Vert told Shadowmane. "That seems like a good place, eh?"

The horse snorted.

"Well, anything's better than *that* place," Vert said, referring to the kingdom he had just left. "Even if it's built on a mound of feces." Vert chuckled.

"You take that back."

Vert flinched. He leaned over Shadowmane's shoulder. No, the horse hadn't just spoken, had it?

Movement caught his attention. A pale-skinned soldier appeared from behind a rock, holding a notched bow in his hands. He pointed the arrow at Vert.

"You take that back and I promise to give you a quick death," the soldier snarled. He was clearly from the posh city Vert left.

"Why are you following me?" Vert snapped.

"Nobody enters our city." Another soldier stepped out from the cover of a different rock. Two more followed suit. "And *nobody* speaks ill about it."

"I can say what I want!" Vert yelled. He reached down and seized his glaive from Shadowmane's side.

"Our laws state we cannot harm you as our guest," the soldier holding the bow said. "But you are no longer our guest. I know quite a few people that would pay quite a sum to see your head hanging from the battlements."

"This is folly!" Vert screamed. "You want me dead because I don't belong to your society? You are more foolish than I had thought. Who demanded of this? Your king?"

"There is a reward for your head," a soldier declared. "Just as you left, we got word of a wanted man fitting your description. It seems *Vallenfend* is looking for you, Vert Bowman."

Vert cursed. How did Vallenfend know? Had somebody seen him? Had somebody survived and witnessed as he escaped the cave? He couldn't worry about that now. The soldiers were closing in.

The soldier holding the bow let his arrow fly. Vert pulled his leg up in time and the arrow struck Shadowmane's shoulder instead. The horse reared, throwing Vert off its back. He landed on the ground, winded. Reacting quickly, Vert rolled back over his shoulder and popped to his feet, just as one of the soldiers attacked.

He deflected the blade with the shaft of his glaive. Another soldier lunged and he dodged it. All at once, the small group of soldiers bore down on him. Vert struggled to dodge or block all of their attacks. There was too many of them.

But he had gone too far to be defeated by these pompous buffoons. Letting his anger take over, Vert lashed out with his weapon, using speed he didn't know he had. He swung his glaive, sweeping their swords away and taking advantage of a soldier's stupor and to cut the man down.

The fallen man's comrades faltered, seeing how enraged Vert had become. Once again, Vert took advantage. He lunged at a man, slamming the blunt end of his glaive into his temple, deftly killing the soldier. Another he stabbed through the chest. Blood covered the field as Vert slashed his way through each and every one of the soldiers, finishing off with the archer.

Vert exhaled, suddenly wearing, and looked around himself. Eight men were lying, either dead or wounded. He scrutinized a moaning soldier without pity. Stepping over the wounded man, Vert gently reached for Shadowmane's reigns. He cooed to his horse, which had become quite frantic. It was a good thing it hadn't ran off. That would have left him stranded and vulnerable to another attack.

Vert inspected Shadowmane's shoulder where the arrow had hit. He removed the arrow, which made the horse bray loudly in protest. The wound wasn't life-threatening, but it would slow down their pace. Vert was anxious to get moving at once, but first he had to tend to his injured companion.

Casting a glance back at the soldiers, Vert walked Shadowmane away. He didn't stop until he thought he was a safe distance away. There, surrounded by a scant amount of trees, Vert attended to Shadowmane. He built a fire and stuck the end of the arrow in the coals, the very same which had hurt his companion to begin with. Once the tip was glowing red hot, Vert fished it out with two sticks and placed it on a cloth he had soaked in water. Gingerly, he picked it up, feeling the warmth flood through the cloth.

He held the glowing arrowhead right up to Shadowmane's shoulder, gripping the reigns tightly as well.

"I'm sorry," he whispered. He pressed the arrowhead to the wound.

It was a miracle Vert was able to keep Shadowmane from running away. The horse thrashed and its muscle rippled underneath the arrowhead. Vert spoke calming words to it as he sealed the cut closed.

Once it was done, he threw the arrowhead back into the fire and held Shadowmane's head up close.

Another city was in view. Vert stood up in the stirrups, trying to get a better view. Shadowmane kept walking. The wound on its shoulder was just a scar now. It had healed nicely.

Vert pulled out his map and put a finger down on it. Yes, there it was. He had arrived at last. The gods had heard his nightly prayers after all. He stopped Shadowmane, a tear forming in his eyes. He uttered a small prayer right there, thanking his guardian angel.

The gates to the city, Arnoth, were wide open and unprotected. Vert was unimpressed that they weren't guarded better. He strolled right inside. The first thing he noticed were large stables to his left. He smiled. He liked this place already.

Dismounting, Vert looked around in awe. He tied Shadowmane to a pole near the stables and decided to orient himself. Somebody walked by, but Vert clapped his hand down on the person's shoulder. The young man roughly his age stopped and stared at Vert.

"Yes?"

"I'm new here. Do you think you can show me around or something?"

The young man inspected him top to bottom. Vert inspected him as well. He was built similarly to him, but with thick sideburns and a more-noticeable nose.

"Sure," he said with a grin.

Vert smiled as well. He could tell they were going to be friends. "Thanks."

"You bet. Welcome to Arnoth. My name's Clodde."

Vert took his hand. "Vert Bowman." He paused, drinking in the experience of a new city. "I think I am going to like this place."

Chapter 16

"...In the end," Vert said, taking a breath, "I showed Arnoth how corrupt their king was and mentioned it to Clodde. Together, we led a revolution and after much bloodshed the king and BlackHound were eliminated. Unsure what to do from there, the people elected me to be their new leader."

As Vert explained his story, they had set back towards the castle. By the time he finished, they were sitting down around a long, sturdy wooden table in a room adjacent to the where Vert and Kael had been reunited. At one end of the room, opposite the main doors was a smaller entrance and Kael guessed correctly that it lead to a kitchen. Though it now appeared disused—with dust collecting in the corners—the room must have been the former king's dinner hall.

There were half a dozen other soldiers in the room, including a thick man hardly older than Kael. He had heavy brow that made his eyes appear sunken and his hair rested flat on his head. The most prominent feature about him was his thick sideburns, which came all the way down to the corner of his jaw.

"Wow," Kael remarked, taking note of how his voice echoed back at him due to the size of the dinner hall.

"Oh yeah," Vert said proudly. "I've been busy."

Kael smiled mischievously. "So have I."

He proceeded to relay his story to Vert, who interrupted less often than Kael had. He nodded every once and a while as Kael explained some things concerning the empire and Zeptus's clandestine plans.

"Huh. You *have* been busy," Vert said with a chuckle.

"Yeah," Rooster agreed. It occurred to Kael that he hadn't told the boy his story yet. It felt relieving to get it all off his chest, just as it had when he had told Faerd, Laura and her mother. His thoughts turned to them again. How were they doing?

They all stayed quiet for a moment. Vert suddenly broke the silence. "So I suppose that's why you're here."

"Exactly."

Vert bit his lip for a moment. "We have a lot to talk about in that case. Tell me everything you know about BlackHound."

"Like what?"

Vert smiled, thinking it was a joke, but Kael's serious expression made him drop his smile. "You're kidding right? Tactics, weapons, anything! Well, first of all, how many of them are there?"

Kael blushed. Now that he thought of it, he really knew next to nothing about them. "Well," he said, rubbing his hands over the knotted wood. "I assume they are coming with a large force. They are coming to take over a whole new continent."

Vert's eyebrows furrowed. "Kael, that's not good enough. I need numbers."

Rooster clicked his tongue, but didn't say anything. Kael looked around the room awkwardly, feeling the soldiers' eyes bore into him. "I don't know how many are coming. Have I told you that I know next to nothing about them?"

Vert rubbed his face. "I deduced that much, thank you. What *do* you know?"

Kael leaned in closer. "Can we get these guys out of here?"

Vert sighed. "Fine. Leave us."

All but one of the soldiers left the room. The one that remained was the one with the thick sideburns. Instead of leaving, he moved closer to Vert until he was standing directly beside him, emotionless.

"And him?" Kael nodded.

"He's my second-in-command, Clodde." Vert punched him in the arm. The soldier's lips twitched, a faint semblance of a smile, but otherwise he remained steady. "He's my loyal friend and bodyguard. He stays."

Rooster leaned back on his chair. "Back to business, gentlemen," he said, folding his arms behind his head.

Vert continued, ignoring the comment. "So, what do you know?" he repeated.

"I know they are coming to Vallenfend first. I know their name, thanks to you. They have a lot of riches, or *did*. It seems the king has all a lot of their gold now."

"Is that it?"

"Oh, and they have a rudimentary control over magic."

"Magic?" Vert scoffed. "I hardly believe they can do that. Magic, as far as I know, is chaotic and uncontrollable."

Kael shook his head. "No, it can be tamed, Shatterbreath has shown me that. But you're right, it is still spontaneous. I'm not sure anybody can control it by willpower alone. But when I escaped from the prison, the man who set me free told me about some items the empire had given them that were magical."

"Items? Like swords or shields that have been enchanted?"

"I'm not sure. I didn't exactly get to see one. But the way he described it, I imagine something smaller, something that can be fit into a pocket."

"That could pose a problem."

Rooster interrupted again. "Wait a minute, would you? Magic is nothing but a folktale, yet you two speak of it as if it were real."

Kael rubbed the bridge of his nose. "How do you think dragons breathe fire?"

"I always assumed they had chemicals inside their jaws that, when combined, would—"

"I always assumed," Vert said curtly, "that you were dumb. Looks like I was right. Stop interrupting."

Rooster shut his mouth, looking hurt.

Vert sighed again. "You've given me a lot to think about, Kael. I see a lot of flaws in what you're asking." He counted the ways on his fingers. "You don't know the size of the empire, you don't know *any* of their tactics, and you don't even know what weapons they'll be using. I'm going to take a wild guess and say you don't even know when they arrive. Am I right?"

Slowly, Kael nodded, a pit forming in his stomach.

Vert stared at the ceiling for a moment, lost. His second-in-command, the soft-spoken Clodde, leaned in.

"I think we should help them, Vert," he said.

"Really?" Vert, Kael and Rooster exclaimed at once.

"Well, sure. These guys are your friends, right General?"

Vert was quick to respond. "One of them is."

Clodde continued. "That should be good enough. From what I've heard, you two have been through a lot. And if we choose to let his city fall, the BlackHound will invariably sweep across our land and get to us."

Vert scratched his chin. "This is true. I love Arnoth even more than Vallenfend. I would hate to see either city destroyed or enslaved."

Kael saw an opportunity and took it. "Then help us, Vert. Make a stand at Vallenfend. You know how easily defendable it is."

Vert was thinking hard, Kael could see it in his eyes. There was a pained expression on his face.

"My intuition tells me this is a bad idea," Vert said at last. "But I have to look at the bigger picture. You two are right; we must make a stand at Vallenfend, despite the...indeterminate factors."

Kael's heart jumped. He chose his words delicately, feeling this was a precarious situation. "So," he ventured lightly, "does this mean I have your support?"

Vert grinned from ear to ear. He stood up and leaned over the table, thrusting out his hand. "It's a deal." Kael bent to take his hand, but he pulled it back. "On one condition. You let me do all the organizing, alright?"

Kael laughed. "I wouldn't have it any other way."

"It is agreed then. Arnoth's army is at your disposal, Kael Rundown," Vert declared. "However, whatever forces you muster are under my direction."

Kael's smile widened. They took hands and shook. "It's a deal."

"Are you sure you want to leave so quick?" Vert Bowman asked.

Kael nodded. "Yes. I am eager to get back to Shatterbreath." He had stayed two extra days in Arnoth on Vert's request. In that time, Kael and Rooster had seen most of the sights in the city. What he loved most though was spending time around the soldiers. It gave him hope that his plan would succeed. "We have tarried here long enough."

They were standing just outside the walls of Arnoth, with the gate yawning behind them. Vert had his hands clasped behind his back, with a thoughtful frown spread across his features. It was amazing to know how he had got to Arnoth to begin with. This whole time, Kael had thought only he and the Captain had survived... What other secrets would the future hold?

"Your hospitality was quite kind," Kael continued, "and I would like to stay longer but something tells me we are going to need more than one city's assistance to defend against the BlackHound Empire." The name of the empire tasted dirty on Kael's lips.

"Time *is* of the essence," Rooster added.

"Yes," Vert sighed. "You're right. As much as I enjoyed seeing you alive and well, Kael, I suppose I should let you go."

Kael snickered. "Unless you want to take me prisoner."

Vert laughed as well. "For fraternizing with the enemy? No. I'd have to find something else to arrest you for. Vallenfend may rage war on that dragon, but *we* have no conflict with it. Speaking of which..."

There was a lingering in Vert's tone. "What is it?"

"Can I see it?"

The question caught Kael by surprise. Rooster found his voice first. "Aren't you upset that she kicked you?" he asked.

"Of course not!" Vert scoffed, "I was only doing as instructed. If anything, I like dragons."

"I doubt she'll be happy to see you," Kael thought aloud.

"Come on," Vert goaded, "I just want a moment to appreciate her when she *isn't* trying to kill me."

Kael turned to Rooster for advice. The boy simply shrugged. "You know her far better than me. It's up to you."

"It's the least you can do," Vert said, crossing his arms.

"Let's go then." Kael caved it. Vert was right. Certainly Shatterbreath would understand that letting Vert *look* at her would be payment enough for their agreement. Without any further deliberation, they started out into the fields, where Shatterbreath was planning to pick Kael and Rooster up. Kael wondered if she'd even come with Vert there.

As they walked, Kael voiced a question. "How are you going to convince your troupes to fight in this war?"

Vert laughed heartily. "I know things don't work properly in Vallenfend, Kael, but they are *my* men and they *will* listen to me. Besides, it's for their own good. Even if they don't realize it at first."

Kael shook his head. "How do you have so much confidence, Vert? I don't get it, what drives you?" A similar question had been plaguing Kael's mind for the last view days he had stayed in Arnoth. "What's your motivation?"

Vert's smile broadened. "I wouldn't expect you to understand," he said. "But I have found peace, Kael. I have a guardian angel watching over me."

Kael paused, stunned. "Are you talking religious terms here? I wouldn't take you for a religious person, Vert."

"I wasn't. My adventures after the dragon's cave caused me to change my way of...thinking."

By then, they had walked a fair distance away from the city, which was now hidden from view by a wall of trees that snaked down from the mountains and partway into the fields. Kael stopped the small procession and turned his eyes skyward. Would Shatterbreath even come with Vert there? Thunder crackled the sky. Though Kael couldn't see her, he knew the dragon was watching.

Rooster hummed a tuneless song as they waited in silence. After several minutes, it was evident that Shatterbreath wasn't going to come down. Sighing, Kael put his fingers to his lips and whistled. As the shrill sound echoed over the fields, Kael waved up towards the mountainside, hoping she was there.

A buffet of wind suddenly pummelled them from behind. Kael stood his ground whereas Rooster was completely thrown from his feet. Though startled, Vert managed to stay standing as well.

Bearing a snarl, Shatterbreath considered them all. "Who is this?" she demanded.

"A friend."

Vert's mouth was open and his eyes were wide. Shatterbreath inspected him for a moment, as if he was nothing more than a morsel of food. Her eyes narrowed and she cocked her head. "Hey, I know you!" she declared, a small flicker of flame escaping her jaws. "You're that blasted boy who cut me!"

"Yeah, that was me..." Vert shook himself. "Um, so sorry." He turned to Kael and mouthed *she's great!*

Shatterbreath huffed. "Sure I bet. Tiny, I'm guessing you called me here to eat him, right? Is he bothering you?"

Kael waved his hand. "No, not at all. He just wanted to see you before we left."

She perked up. "Leaving? This one is *not* coming with us. One tagalong is enough."

"Now that you're not trying to kill me, you're amazing!" Vert exclaimed.

"Flattery fooled me once," Shatterbreath countered, voice boiling. "I will not be fooled again." She craned her neck down towards Vert, narrowing her eyes. "Have you had your fill of gawking, foolish mortal?"

Vert took a step back. After some thought, he slowly nodded his head, mouth agape.

Shatterbreath growled. "We're leaving, Tiny. Hop on. Now."

Kael clambered on her back, closely followed by Rooster. As she considered Vert once more, her spines bristled. Kael felt the vibrations in her body as she growled again.

"Thanks for everything, Vert," Kael called out, waving.

Without waiting for a reply, Shatterbreath took off explosively. In only a few seconds, Vert disappeared into the landscape below and Arnoth was nothing more than a jewel shimmering in the midday sun.

"I take it you had success?" Shatterbreath asked after several minutes of tense silence. Her voice was calm and patient. Kael saw through her. Her body betrayed her true emotions. Her shoulders were taut, her tail thrashed and she blinked more frequently than normal. Clearly she was agitated, though trying her best not to show it.

"Yes. Vert promised to assist us. Not only that, we have a name to our enemy now: BlackHound."

"Hmm, BlackHound..." Shatterbreath repeated, tasting the word. She paused. "Now that you had a taste of success, Tiny, you cannot slow your pace. One kingdom alone won't stop the empire."

157

"I told Vert the same thing."

Shatterbreath hummed. "We think the same. I will set a course towards the next city on our agenda. If we are to find a suitable ally, I think this place will be it."

"Who is it?" Rooster asked.

"Fallenfeld, the sister city of Vallenfend."

"Then to Fallenfeld," Kael declared. "And let's see how fast you can get there, Shatterbreath."

She hummed. "Hold on tight."

Chapter 17

Laura hesitated as she took a bite of stew. She looked around at her family. Faerd's energetic manner was returning, although she doubted it would ever return to its fullest. He wore an eye-patch over his ruined eye. It stood for a symbol of his pain, the anguish they all felt. And, although Laura would be embarrassed to admit, it made him look tougher.

Korjan and Tooran were sitting beside each other on the stone floor, devouring the soup. Together, it was hard to feed the two, although they were both quick to let somebody else eat before them. Bunda, Helena and Laura's mother were all talking to each other. Laura could only guess at what gossip they were discussing now. What was there to talk about anymore?

Malaricus would come and visit in spurts. For whatever reason, he was the only one who hadn't been targeted by soldiers. Perhaps it was his crucial role as the kingdom's scholar that kept him exempt. Whenever he arrived, riding his donkey, he would bring more food and supplies for them. He had never told them how he came across so much food in the first place. Laura speculated that he paid for all of it himself. It saddened her to see the sacrifice he was putting forth. Then she remembered the sacrifices they had paid as well.

Yes, they were all getting along well. They gave each other strength. They were unified. They had spent many nights talking about Kael and everything they had learned. Overall, they accepted what he had to say. Perhaps it was a crutch to lean on, an excuse for their torment, but they believed what he strived for. They believed in his words.

All except Laura.

She sniffed and wiped away a tear. How could they be so blind? Their lives had been so perfect. *Her* life had been perfect. Until Kael Rundown had gotten into trouble. Never before had one individual been so influential in her life. Because of him, because of one *boy,* her life was ruined. *Ruined.* He was the cause of all this.

He was the reason they were living like rodents in that cave. Why did the rest of them trust him?

The more Laura thought about it, the more her anger towards her *friend* escalated. She sniffed again, louder this time. They had been best friends. How could he have done this to them? Why did he have to run around, acting a fool and getting them tangled up in his mess? And for what? He wasn't even there to back them up! He was gone, running amuck, trying to pull others into his web!

No. She wouldn't have any part in this. She wouldn't have any part in Kael.

She sobbed, dropping her bowl. Clapping her hands over her face, she turned away from her ramshackle family. What did they think of her?

The glowing stones twinkled down at her. She stopped sobbing and stared at them, dazzled. They were losing their shine. Every day they provided less light. For some reason, that made her sob even more. How was that fair?

A shuffle made her cringe. She held herself tighter. Out of the corner of her eye, she could see Faerd sit down beside her. He stared at his bowl with his good eye, chewing. He placed the bowl down. Gently, he placed his hand on her shoulder. She didn't shy away.

He didn't say anything, but she couldn't hold back her laments any longer.

"How can he do this to us, Faerd?" she asked through swollen eyes. "How can he just leave us like this? Do we not matter to him?"

Faerd's jaw worked. He took a deep breath, taking his time to answer. "I don't know, Laura," he whispered. "Maybe he's busy. Maybe there's a place out there that needs him more than we do."

"But we're his family!" she shouted. "What could be more important than family?"

Faerd shrugged, keeping his voice calm. "I don't know, Laura. I don't know."

That only made her more frustrated. "Then why do you trust him so much, Faerd? You don't even know where he is or what he's doing! What evidence has he brought us to prove his words are true?

All we have to rely on is his words and the words of a dragon! I don't trust either."

Faerd looked sideways at her. His lip was set in a blank frown. Laura stared into his eye, trying to read what he was thinking. She couldn't help but to look at the cloth covering his ruined eye. A shiver ran through her spine.

"Well I trust him," Faerd said gently, "and whether or not you do too..." He wrapped his arm around her shoulders. "I promise, I *promise* you, I will protect you."

She blinked, trying to hold back another sob. A warm feeling welled up in her chest. "Thank you," she muttered. Slowly, she leaned into him and placed her head against his shoulder. They stayed like that for several minutes, silent, still.

"What was that?" Bunda shot to her feet, staring at the mouth of the cave.

"What was what?" Mrs. Stockwin asked, also rising.

A noise seemed to slither through the cave. Laura could hardly hear it. Faerd gave her a reassuring look and then stood up. He slipped on his gauntlets which were lying nearby. Korjan, Tooran and Faerd all put on breastplates that they had left in a convenient spot for easy access. They stood at the ready, several feet in front of the women huddled together. All eyes were set on the entrance of the cave. More soldiers? So soon?

The sun managed to break through the blanket of fog outside, sending a beam of light reaching into the cave. A ruffled clink of armour could be heard, followed by a strained grunt. Laura hugged close to her mother, eyes wide and heart fluttering.

Something disturbed the light. A shadow rose up. It grew in size until it stood tall at the mouth of the cave. Laura's breath caught in her throat. The shadow stood up straight, arms slightly out to the side, chest thrust forward. It appeared garbed in armour and holding a sword.

No. It couldn't be. "K—Kael?" Laura called out. Yes. It was him. The figure fit him perfectly. He had come after all! He did care about them!

161

She pushed past Faerd and Korjan, running up to the shadow. She could feel tears streaking down her face as she ran towards him. She could feel her doubts starting to melt away. He had come back!

The fog outside returned. The sun's light subsided to its regular dull strength. The shadow that had befallen the figure melted away, revealing who it truly was. Laura faltered. She skidded to a halt, her arms falling limp to her side.

He wasn't Kael.

A soldier garbed in blue sheathed his sword. His hair was cut short and he had a smattering of freckles spread across his face. He waved hesitantly. His eyes were sincere and he didn't hold a hostile posture. He meant no harm. "Hello?"

Laura tried to hide her disappointment behind anger. "Who are you, what do you want?"

The boy flinched. "I...I heard there are people staying here. Friends of Kael. Is that true?"

Laura frowned. "More or less." Korjan and Faerd stepped up beside her. The boy peered at them all in turn and then looked past them to the women still in the back.

"Oh, thank goodness," he sighed. "What a relief. You are all alive!" He waved to somebody out of sight. Another, thinner boy came into view. He sheathed his sword also.

"The lady asked you a question," Korjan rumbled. "Who are you and what are you doing here?"

"We are soldiers," the thinner of the two piped up. He seemed eager to speak. "We decided rather than fighting you, we would like to help you."

"What are you talking about?" Bunda yelled from behind.

The freckled boy coughed. "We ran away from our troupe, the very same you seemed to have...slaughtered."

"You know Kael?" Laura interjected.

"Yes. We've met Kael before," the thinner boy announced. "We went through training with him. You have no idea what that's like, training inside the castle. We've heard the rumours of what he spoke of. The empire, what the king's doing... We believe him. We want to help him. We want to help you guys."

Korjan scratched his chin, looking quite unconvinced. "You said you went through training with Kael?" he thought out loud.

"Yeah," the freckled boy said. "I duelled him once. He was good."

Korjan and Tooran exchanged glances. The blacksmith took a deep breath. "What do you think?"

Helena, Bunda and Laura's mother all walked up. They considered the two boys for a moment. Bunda was the first to speak.

"I'm not sure. I don't know if I believe their story."

"I think we should let them stay with us," Mrs. Stockwin announced.

"What?" Laura hissed through clenched teeth. She whipped around, facing her mother.

"Well, sure. They escaped alive. They are both like us. Outcasts, survivors. They are like family, aren't they?"

The mention of family struck everybody.

"Well, I'm against this," Laura said, crossing her arms. "All of it. I don't trust them, and I don't want them here. Kael's influence has got to them too. I don't anybody else to get caught up in this mess."

"Please," the taller boy said, "let us stay. We've got nowhere else to go. We want to help! I believe in Kael. All I want to is to help my city. Just like him."

"He's helping no one!" Laura snapped. "He's gone! Never returning! Don't any of you get it?"

Korjan bit his lip. "Whether or not that is true," he said, ignoring Laura's scowl. "You may prove to be of assistance to us. Any extra numbers we gain will be a benefit to our cause. And our plan."

The two young soldier's eyes lit up. Laura was fuming now. "What plan?" she demanded. "What are you talking about?!"

Korjan met her fierce gaze. He stared at her with such calm, dull eyes. Despite her anger, Laura faltered. He turned away from her and towards the newcomers.

"You may stay with us," Korjan announced. "But you are not part of our family quite yet. Not until you've proven yourselves." He gestured towards one side of the cave. "You may sleep over there."

163

"Away from us, for the time being," Tooran added. "If we see any small reason not to trust you, I won't hesitate to kill either of you."

Despite Tooran's last comment, the two boys smiled. The small one clapped his hands together in joy and the other shook Korjan's hand vigorously. Laura threw her hands up in the air and walked away. She kicked her cold bowl of stew as hard as she could, sending the contents scattering across the floor.

Why wouldn't they listen to her? How many people had Kael managed to siphon into his madness, anyway? How many more would feel the sting of his foolishness? This was all too much.

She turned her head slightly, curious to what the group was talking about.

"My name's Bruce Nendara," the taller boy was saying.

"And I'm Horan," the thinner boy told them.

She huffed and shook her head. Faerd came over and tried to comfort her, but she pushed him away and hustled towards the mouth of the cave, giving the chatting group a wide berth. She didn't want to be in there anymore. Not right then, not for a while. She needed to get outside for a breath of fresh air.

The mist surrounded her, as if it was trying to consume her. For a moment, Laura wanted it to. She wanted to embrace the simplicity of the fog. Life would be so much easier that way. Just hanging there, watching over the mountain's side. She sighed, staring into the endless miasma. Somewhere down there, she deduced, Vallenfend was waiting. Would she ever return? Would they ever accept her again? She shook her head.

She climbed partway up the mountain and found a massive rock overlooking a breathtaking cliff. She sat down on it and pulled her knees closer, chewing her lip. How conflicted Laura's heart was. Somewhere, deep in the back of her mind, she wanted to believe Kael. She just wanted to let go of her anger towards him and embrace the old, familiar feeling of warmth she used to get when she thought of him. She wanted him to press her in his arms again. But the reasoning part of her mind told her that would never happen again. The old Kael Rundown was dead.

Eventually, Faerd found her up on the rock. He checked to see if she was okay, his eyebrows slanted in concern. She reassured him, saying she just needed to be alone for a moment. As he walked away, the familiar feeling returned. She remembered it all too clearly. It had used to belong to Kael's presence. And his alone. Not anymore.

Korjan placed his hands down on the improvised table they had made. It was little more than a boulder with a tower shield placed on top, but it did the trick.

"So you all understand the plan, right?" he asked.

Everybody nodded. "I don't want you to go," Helena said, her voice full of longing. "But if this is something you must do..."

"I'm opposed to it," Laura stated, folding her arms.

"As am I. Korjan, you will be leaving us unprotected," Bunda pointed out. "We cannot defend ourselves without you men. This is foolishness. If we get attacked again..."

"You won't," Bruce assured her. "We only attack every month or so. When my troupe came up here, it was a rare exception. They lost too many men that day. They cannot afford to lose any more."

"Even still, if there's a chance something could go awry, I prefer not to take that chance, son." She scowled at him. "And I still don't trust you. Tooran, you must see the logic in this, you are one of them. What if these two little snots are planning something terrible? Think about it, while you men are gallivanting around in the kingdom, they could easily slip a dagger into your ribs while nobody's paying attention."

Tooran considered them all. "Then that would be unwise for them. Trust me, Bunda. I have trained for this sort of business all my life." He paused. "I know how to watch my back. Nothing is getting past me concerning these two."

Bruce smiled. Horan's expression didn't change. Korjan noticed as Laura frowned at them both.

Korjan sighed. "What's the final verdict then? Who's for this?"

"I am," Tooran said confidently.

"Me too," Horan exclaimed.

165

"Anything to help," Bruce said.

Helena was more conflicted. "I don't know if this is a good idea." She looked at Korjan. "I don't want you to go." There was longing in her voice. "But we all must help Kael. I can think of no better way."

Bunda crossed her arms. "I'm against this."

"As am I," Laura said softly. "There is *always* another way. But that's not going to change your mind."

Korjan gave Laura a look. She had made it apparent to all of them that she did not trust Kael anymore. As far as Korjan had ever known, Kael and Laura had been the best of friends, inseparable. Perhaps even more than that. It caused his hardened heart to grieve, but he didn't say anything.

"Then it is settled then," Tooran declared.

Korjan nodded, placing his calloused hands down on their improvised table. He rubbed them over the map they had placed there. It was a rough outline of Vallenfend Malaricus had given them. "Yes, it is. When the sun sets tomorrow, we will go back into Vallenfend. We succeed in what Kael tried to do. We will kill Zeptus."

Chapter 18

Kael leaned on Shatterbreath's forearm. She inhaled deeply, and he felt warmth flood from her into him. They had just landed from flying, after finding a suitable grove that would provide enough cover. A fracture of light spread across her face as she bent closer to him. Similar beams of light poured through various gaps in the thick forest canopy. He glanced out over the ledge they had slept on for the night. There were trees in the way, but somewhere in that wide valley was the next city on their list. He was anticipating this one the most.

"Fallenfeld," he said aloud, tasting the name on his lips. "What do you know about it?"

"A lot," Shatterbreath and Rooster said in unison. They frowned at each other.

Kael adjusted his pauldron. He was going into the city with his armour on. He didn't want to take any more chances. He raised his eyebrows, looking between Shatterbreath and Rooster.

Rooster spoke first. "Fallenfeld was established five-hundred years ago, by King Irgo. It was said that he and his brother travelled across the lands with their families, searching for hospitable land. However, they got in an argument and separated. He came here whereas his brother went further west to establish Vallenfend."

"Yes, all terribly interesting stuff," Shatterbreath said through a yawn. "But utterly useless for Kael." She nudged him with her snout.

"I find it interesting," Kael countered.

"Fallenfeld is built similarly to your city, I believe," Rooster went on to explain. "With the castle as the focal point and the city itself built in a ring-like fashion around it."

Kael sighed. "Okay, yeah, that's enough." He turned his attention to Shatterbreath. "What do you know?"

Shatterbreath scratched at her neck for a moment. "The king's a pretty calm person. Try to stay on his good side though. Don't patronize him, but don't be afraid to throw in a little praise once in a while. After all, he's a *normal* king, unlike yours."

"Is that it?"

"Not entirely," Shatterbreath said with a twitch of her tail. "There is strange little custom they have."

"You mean what they do at their banquets?" Rooster remarked.

Shatterbreath perked up. "You know about it? How would you know?"

Rooster looked sideways at her, clicking his tongue. "*Everybody* knows about that. Well, anyone who is interested in other cities, anyway." His tone quickly adopted some pride. "They abolished that silly trial three kingships ago."

Shatterbreath growled. Her tail smashed against a tree, uprooting it. "What are you talking about, hatchling? They still practise it. Maybe if you weren't so ignorant, you would know."

Kael placed a hand at her side. "Shatterbreath, what are you talking about?"

Flames licked around Shatterbreath's nostrils. "This fool knows nothing."

Rooster chuckled. "You call me the fool? They stopped practicing that barbaric custom long ago. You might have been around longer than I, but you don't stay up-to-date with what's going on, do you? I'm telling you, if they hold a banquet, there will be nothing to fear."

Shatterbreath shoved him to the ground with her forehead and placed her paws on either side of him, glowering down at him. "You dare to try me?"

"Kael's going to regret listening to you if it comes to that!" Rooster exclaimed, cowering underneath her. "For you are wrong. If he refuses their offering, they will surely slay him on the spot!"

"Stop!" Kael demanded. "What is this all about?"

With a huff, Shatterbreath pulled away from the thin boy and sat down on her haunches, her tail flittering angrily. "Whenever a visitor requests an audience with the king, they will sit him down for dinner after he has delivered his message. They are kind and their words are as innocent as a calm river, when in reality, snakes hide under the surface. If they believe their visitor's words to be true, they will offer him wine. However, if the king doesn't trust the visitor or his message, they will serve him ale, in which case, it is poisoned."

The blood drained from Kael's face. "Oh."

"Ah, ah, that's not true," Rooster intervened, waving a finger. Shatterbreath growled, but he clicked his tongue and continued. "They no longer do this. Whether they serve you ale or wine is redundant. If they sit you down for a feast at all, it means they trust you. Why would they be so devious? If they don't like what you're saying, they'll just politely tell you to leave. Fallenfeld isn't as barbaric as it once was."

Kael sat down on Shatterbreath's tail. "You're saying opposite things here. How sure are either of you?"

Shatterbreath leaned in close, setting her emerald eyes on him. "I know what I speak is the truth. Absolutely."

Rooster smirked. "I'm hardly ever wrong."

Kael scratched at the back of his neck, conflicted. He considered asking them when and where they discovered this, but he decided that would not resolve the conflict. He shrugged. "Hopefully this problem won't arise."

"Tiny, this is no solution. I am confident this problem will arise, although there is the chance they will serve you wine and you won't have to worry about it, but how can we know for certain? It is better to come up with a definite solution now than regret it later."

"And what if they do server me ale?" Kael wondered aloud. "Then it will be your word against Rooster's. If I choose to trust you, Shatterbreath, they will distrust me. If I choose your word, Rooster and you're indeed wrong, death will be my reward."

Rooster could only shrug.

"It would seem," Shatterbreath rumbled. "That one consequence outweighs the other."

"But this is more than that. I could lose a potential ally. Right now, that's all that's important to me. The odds aren't looking good for Vallenfend. We need more help."

Shatterbreath studied him. They all stayed silent for a time. Nobody could think of anything else to sway the argument. Kael trusted Shatterbreath, but Rooster had better knowledge of this.

Finally, Kael broke the silence. "I suppose I'll just go and see where this takes me—and hope for the best."

"I would like for you to come to a decision before you depart. This is strange for you not to dwell on this further. You are usually more cautious."

Kael rubbed her tail with his gauntlet. He searched for the right words for a long time, but they didn't present themselves to him. He brought his fingers to his lips for a moment, feeling the metal of his gauntlets on his face. He sighed. "I don't have time to be cautious. Rooster, let's just get going. We'll return as soon as possible, alright?"

Shatterbreath looked pained. The side of her jaw rippled as she clenched her teeth. "Trust your judgment. Whatever happens, just return to me, Tiny."

He nodded. "I promise."

Rooster clapped his hands together. "Let's be off then!"

Kael and Shatterbreath exchanged glances. Without further talk, he and Rooster set off down the hillside.

Even from up on the hill, it struck Kael how truly similar Fallenfeld was to Vallenfend. When he first saw the cozy city nestle in the valley, he thought somebody had picked up his city and placed it there. Seeing Fallenfeld brought fond memories to his mind of the better days. He could see himself playing with his friends when they were younger, and of his birthday dinner he had at the Stockwins only a few months ago. How things had changed...

Kael kept his eyes on that shimmering city as they descended. He couldn't tear his eyes away from it. As they approached, it felt more and more like he was returning to home. He stayed silent, dazzle by the prospect. Rooster stayed quiet as well, trying to read what Kael was thinking.

They passed by some houses skirting the outside of the city. There were some people out and about, but none seemed to give the newcomers a second glance. Kael shielded his eyes with his hand. The sun was shimmering just at the peak of the mountain, making it seem as if there was a large piece of gold situated up there.

The familiar feeling intensified as they strolled up to the gates. The walls of the city were exactly the same as Vallenfend's, thick and high, perfect for defence. There were soldiers guarding the entrance. It was strange to Kael that they were male, considering the guards in Vallenfend were almost all women.

"Halt," one of the soldiers declared, putting up his hand. Kael looked him top to bottom. He was wearing a suit of armour, although it wasn't nearly as dazzling as Kael's. "Who's this? You're not a regular to this gate."

It took Kael a moment to find his voice. "No, sir. We're from another city. We come seeking your help."

"Help," the guard echoed. "What kind of help?"

"I'd rather have this conversation with the king."

The man shifted his weight. "The king's a busy man, I hope you know. Where'd you say you were from?"

Kael clenched his jaw for a moment, wondering if he should lie or not. "I'm from Vallenfend, he's from Farthu," he said, pointing at Rooster.

"Vallenfend, eh?" The guard shook his head. There was more to his tone. "However busy the king is, I'm sure he'll make time for this. We'll escort you to him."

Kael smiled, his fears vanishing. "Thank you."

The streets were shaped the same as those in Vallenfend, but as they passed by crowds of people, it became apparent Vallenfend and its sister city were very much dissimilar. The architecture was very different. The houses here were packed in tighter, and stood taller than what Kael was used to. It seemed as people had added attachments to their houses. An extra level on the top, another room off to the side. Kael guessed that this was because of their steadily growing population. Vallenfend's population stayed level. There was no reason to upgrade.

A group of soldiers passed by them, each one of them wearing a full suit of armour. Kael marvelled at them. Over top of their breastplate, they wore a sky-blue tunic, brighter than Vallenfend's traditional colour. He couldn't help but to smile. This was what Vallenfend was supposed to be like, alive and thriving. After all this was over, he could see his city being like this. A warm feeling washed over him.

They took the most direct route to the castle. After weaving through the streets and crowds, the castle finally came into view— looming over the rest of the city, gray against the blue of the sky. It didn't hold the same hubris feeling as Vallenfend's castle, but more authority and power than anything. Just from looking at it, Kael could tell a true ruler lived in there, and not some greedy, selfish oaf, like Morrindale. Perhaps the king had a real advisor as well.

The gates to the castle were wide open and soldiers flooded in and out. As they squeezed through, Kael noticed some soldiers carrying a bloody body. The dead man was garbed in tattered brown clothing. Kael grasped the guard's shoulder who was leading them.

"What happened to that man?" he asked.

They paused. "Bandit," he said calmly. "One of many who perished in a failed attempt to raid our kingdom yesterday afternoon. He was one of the lucky ones. Any we take alive are hanged."

"That sounds civilized," Rooster remarked.

The soldier huffed. "We don't tolerate bandits. We've given them plenty of warning to leave us alone. Still, they don't understand our message, no matter how clear we make it. How did your city solve the problem, skinny?"

Rooster crossed his arms. "We don't have bandits."

The soldier laughed, incredulous. "Where do you come from again? Every kingdom has bandits, just to a lesser or greater degree. Do you have thieves? Murderers?"

"Well, yes."

"Then you have bandits, in a way. The difference between a petty thief and a bandit, however, is that these guys are organized. They plan their crimes."

"Is their influence profound?" Kael asked. "Can they be bartered with?"

The question caught the soldier off-guard. He hesitated, passing through a crowd of men-at-arms. "Uh, well, they keep us soldiers on our toes—but we've never tried to barter with them. It would prove pointless. They are mindless, savage brutes."

"But yet you mentioned they were organized," Kael remarked, keeping his tone casual, as if he was commenting on the weather. He didn't want to offend his escort. "Organization takes some sort of intelligence."

"Yes...well...I did say that, didn't I? What I *should* have said, was that they reside together in a colony somewhere to the southeast in the mountains. They are not as organized as I gave credit for. Just...keeping together, like dogs."

"Hmm... A colony? How many of these men are there?"

The soldier shrugged. "I don't know. Nobody has ever seen the bandits' camp except for bandits. As far as we can tell, there could be thousands of them. But they know what's best for them; they wouldn't all attack at once. Instead, they send smaller parties to try and steal things. A merchant's worth in gold, some weapons... Once, they even tried to ransack the castle."

"That didn't go over well, did it?"

The soldier grinned. "Not at all."

Kael rubbed his chin, deep in though. Bandits... He wondered if they would be a deterrent. A wild idea was forming in his head though. What if he could convince them to help him? Perhaps he could find a way to pay them... But no matter, he would have to think on that later. They reached the castle's entrance by then.

Upon seeing Kael's escort, the guards let them in without hesitation. The walls surrounding the inner courtyard weren't nearly as imposing as Vallenfend's. Built low and with evenly-spaced gasp, they served little more than to keep common folk out of the luscious garden surrounding the castle itself. It seemed Fallenfeld's training grounds were located somewhere else, unlike Vallenfend. Still, there was a strong sense of military within the courtyard; soldiers paced through the rows of plants here and there while royal gardeners tended to the flowers.

They left the inner courtyard to submit to the semi-darkness of the castle. It took Kael's eyes a moment to adjust. Torches lined the walls, giving the halls a warm and welcoming glow. Kael liked this castle already. A few servants passed by them as well as a guard here and there, but otherwise, the castle had a hushed feeling about it. Everybody was reverent.

Kael was pleased with how simple this trip was going. So far he hadn't run into any trouble at all. He could only wonder if his luck would continue, if the king would truly hear him out. His thoughts turned to the argument Shatterbreath and Rooster had earlier. *Ale or wine.* Which would he choose? He didn't want to think about it.

After two flights of stairs, they stopped in front of a large set of double doors. There was a crest set on each rosy door, the kingdom's symbol, if he had to guess. Kael glanced sideways at his guard. The same crest was adorned on his shoulder. It seemed to be a bird of some sort—perhaps a local eagle or hawk.

The guard paused, as if unsure. He clenched his jaw and ran a hand through his dark hair. Taking a breath, he knocked three times on the door and then gently pushed both open, revealing a room decorated with the same blue that the soldiers were wearing. Pictures line the walls, each depicting different richly adorned men. If Kael had to guess, he would say they depicted Fallenfeld's past kings. As they walked along, each portrait seemed grander than the last, as if each man was trying to outdo the last. Some of them were holding their sword into the light, others riding on a rearing war charger, and one held a gigantic skull with both hands. Every man's eyes were directed straight outwards, so that every portrait's eyes seemed to follow Kael as he walked deeper into the room. It was a fascinating and eerie effect.

Then Kael caught sight of the king. At once, he was impressed. The king sat on a throne of marble, wearing rich robes. But he didn't look comfortable. He was leaning to one side, his head on his hand as he listened to a thin man give a report of some kind. The king was a middle-aged man, with traces of gray dotting his beard and sideburns. When he spotted Kael, Rooster and the guard, he stood up with a flourish of his clothes.

"What's the meaning of this?" he asked in a strong, demanding voice, pointing his sharp grey beard at the newcomers. He puffed out his chest, which, Kael realized, was garbed with a breastplate. A sword hilt laced with gold rested at his hip. "Do you not understand that I am never to be interrupted at this hour?"

"I apologize, King Henedral, most sincerely. But I think something of more importance has come up."

The king stepped down from his throne to their level. "More important than my advisor's report on the bandit attack? What could be more important? Speak."

The soldier gave a hesitant bow. Evidently, he had never spoken to the king face-to-face before. "Th—these two here," he gestured at Kael. "This one comes from Vallenfend."

"Vallenfend?" the king echoed. "You were right, this is much important. Thank you, knight. You may take your leave."

"Good luck." The soldier nodded at Kael before he left.

"Thank you for your help," Kael said back to him. Then he was gone.

"So," the king barked, breaking the silence of the throne room. "You're from Vallenfend."

"Yes."

"What is your purpose here?" He didn't let Kael answer. "Let me guess... You're here to make sure your city still holds ire towards us, aren't you? You're here to spit on our crest again, to mock us. You're here to make sure we stay enemies. Am I right?"

Kael shook his head. "No, not at—"

"Then what happened to Zeptus? Where is that coward? I do dearly miss his visits, his *mocking* words. Why are you here in his stead?"

"Please," Kael interjected, putting up his palms, "I don't know what you're talking about."

The king huffed. He folded his arms behind his back and walked towards Kael, scrutinizing him. "I seriously doubt that. Do you know *Lord* Zeptus? Yes? And you come from Vallenfend, correct? Then that makes us enemies already. You're a brave fellow to come here like this, I'll give you that."

It dawned on Kael what the king was talking about. He remembered when Saultrion's king had been angry at him just because he was from Vallenfend. *Curse that Zeptus,* he thought bitterly.

Rooster leaned over to him. "Tell him what you told me," he whispered. "How well you and Zeptus get along. That convinced me."

"Perfect! Thank you." Kael turned back towards the king. "I'm sorry," he said, "but I have no affiliation with Zeptus. We've crossed blades more than once, rhetorically speaking. I do not represent my city, but rather a force fighting to save my city and this continent from a greater evil."

The king looked sideways at Kael. "Elaborate."

Kael was quick to stifle a smile. *He had the king's attention.* "An empire is coming to invade Vallenfend. They plan to make base in Vallenfend, then sweep across this land, conquering all."

The king rubbed his beard. "How do you know this?"

"King Morrindale and Zeptus have kept Vallenfend's population as low as they could in preparation for the empire's landing. They've sent our men to die under the might of a savage dragon." Now that he knew the true story about Shatterbreath, it was strange to Kael to utter those words. "They did this because the BlackHound Empire has bribed them richly. I searched through Vallenfend's castle to prove these things. In Zeptus's study I discovered a letter to King Morrindale as well as payment. Also, I have been proven correct by one of the king's personal guards. What I say is true. Your kingdom is in serious peril, Great King."

The king nodded. "Speak more on your disagreements with Zeptus."

Kael faltered. The king was more interested in Kael trouble with Zeptus than the threat of invasion. "He is a key part to this plot, so I decided to eliminate him. I personally tried to assassinate him. I'm sorry to say, I failed. This is why I was banished."

A huge grin spread across King Henedral's face. "Ah. I may have been wrong about you boy. What did you say your name was?"

Kael thrust out his hand. "Kael Rundown."

King Henedral coughed into his own hand. "A pleasure to meet you then," he said, staring at Kael's outstretched hand. "But if not a warning, what other purpose do you have here?"

Rooster spoke up now, surprising Kael. "We've gone around to a few cities, trying to get support. It's going to take a quite a fighting force to repel these guys. With your help, I'm sure we'll be that much closer to success."

The king inspected Rooster for a moment. He frowned and began to pace once again. Kael scowled at his friend.

"You ask for a lot. Taking our army away from Fallenfeld to fight in a massive war far away from here poses serious risks. We'd be almost defenceless to bandit raids."

"I'm sure," Kael ventured, "that in your wisdom, you can think of a solution."

The king's frown intensified. Kael cursed silently. Perhaps he had gone too far.

"You've given me too much to think about. Understand that we must discuss this further."

"I would have it no other way."

The king strolled over to his throne and sat down with a sigh. He ushered his frail advisor over. "If your schedule permits, you are free to enjoy are hospitality, Rundown. I will call for you later, when I have more time for discussion."

Rooster bowed and Kael followed suit, in a more awkward fashion. He wasn't used to bowing.

"I can spare a few days. Thank you, King Henedral." With that, he and Rooster left the throne room. Kael put a hand to his chest, relieved. He smirked at Rooster.

"That didn't start off well," Rooster remarked.

"Yeah, but I think King Henedral might be convinced."

Rooster shrugged. "I guess we'll have to wait and see."

A few guards met them and gestured for them to follow. Kael set forward. "Wait," Kael hissed. There was something more to the boy's tone. "What do you mean?"

"Well," he said innocently. "We'll have to wait for dinner, of course. According to your dragon, the king's going to agree with whatever we say."

Kael hesitated. "Right. I suppose we will see who is correct if it comes to that."

Rooster stared at something in the distance. "I guess we will."

Chapter 19

Kael yawned, cupping his hand over his mouth. He had slept well, but his dreams had been frightening and disturbing. And now he was tired because of it. It was like as if his efforts in his dreams had been real, taking their tolls on his body.

He had dreamed that terrible things were happening to his friends. They had been all huddled together in fright as darkness crept towards them. Blood was spattered across their faces, gleaming red under an unknown light source. Kael had watched helplessly as malicious forms stretched forth out of the darkness with pointed fingers. He thrashed and cried out to them from wherever he was watching, but was helpless.

And then the blackness consumed them.

Kael shook his head, stumbling as he did so. He looked back, as if he had tripped on something. Rooster scrutinized him.

"Are you alright? You gotta be in top shape for this."

Kael blinked. "Yeah, I'm fine. Just bad dreams," he said. "Just dreams..." His statement wasn't too convincing. Somewhere, Kael felt as though his dream was a warning. Although he hoped his friends were okay, Kael couldn't help but to wonder what was happening back home. Was life continuing for them without him? Kael wondered if they were as worried for him as he was for them.

A soldier strolled past them, giving Kael and Rooster a dirty look. Kael ignored him. They were on their way to the king's throne room, working their way through the halls. Kael had refused to let a guard show them the way, but he was regretting that now. Somewhere along the line, they must have made a wrong turn.

Finally, Kael recognized a hallway. "We're nearly there."

"Yeah," Rooster muttered.

Kael stopped him. "Listen, I understand that you're here to help me, Rooster. And you've been a great support. But that's all I want you to be, okay? Don't be offended, but I need to you just stay by my side and stay...quiet."

Rooster furrowed his brow. "Alright..."

"I want your opinions and advice, of course, just don't speak out of turn or unless asked a question."

He was indignant for a moment, but his features relaxed. "I understand. I'm here for moral support, right?"

Kael smiled warmly. "More or less. This is almost too much to handle alone. I think I might go crazy without another person to talk to."

Rooster took his time to reply. "Let's just...do this."

Kael nodded and pushed open the door. The king stood up at once and waved his hand. "Welcome. Come in, come in. You're late I see."

Kael nodded. "I was lost."

King Henedral laughed. "It's a tricky place at first, yes." He stepped down from the elevated platform on which his throne sat. His scrawny advisor stayed where he was, avoiding Kael's gaze. "Now, let's discuss your problem further, won't we?"

"Of course. What do you want to know first?"

The king scratched at his beard. "First off, I want you to tell us everything you know about this invading empire, Kael Rundown." King Henedral's advisor slunk up beside him. The thin man seemed to stick very close to him. The advisor didn't strike Kael as a very confident person.

"Us? He's staying for this?" Kael gestured at the king's advisor.

"Of course he is. Yseph *is* my official advisor after all." King Henedral crossed his arms. "Unless you have a problem with that."

Kael scoffed. "Yseph?" What a strange name. "Oh, yes, of course. The concept of a trustworthy advisor is a foreign thing to me. My apologies."

"Bah, don't worry about it." King Henedral spoke to him as if they were old friends. After the previous day's rough start, Kael was surprised at how straightforward he was. "Let's just get back to my question."

Kael shifted his weight. "They are known as the BlackHound Empire. From what I've gathered, they are aggressive and their influence is profound. They have not just come to Vallenfend seeking to bribe kings and leaders for no insignificant reason."

"What about their ranks?" Yseph startled Kael when he spoke. His voice was shrill and uncertain, as if he didn't speak often. "Do you know how large their invading force will be?"

"I think it's safe to assume they'll be coming with a large force, Yseph," the king said.

Yseph bowed his head. "I understand that, Sire, but how large exactly? It could require our assistance alone to defend against them, or the combined might of every city on this continent. Large is a broad spectrum."

The king pursed his lips. Kael blinked a few times. He was taken aback by Yseph's statement. "I'm not quite sure," he said honestly. "But the bigger the force I can rally, the better. Any assistance at all will help."

"Then we will offer two-hundred men-at-arms to assist you," Yseph stated. His hesitant, shy manner was fading away, as if he was thawing. "And you can be off."

Kael looked at the man for a moment, then at King Henedral, lastly Rooster. "That won't be good enough. We need troops, not...not just a handful of men. We are defending an entire continent here, not a simple bandit raid."

Yseph crossed his arms. "You said yourself, any assistance will help. To be frank, I don't trust you. I am offering assistance, and you can either accept or leave."

"I don't think you understand the magnitude of what this is about. I'm not just talking about Fallenfeld, I'm talking about all of us. I need your full support and cooperation if we are to withstand—"

"I don't care about anybody else," Yseph interrupted. "I just care about Fallenfeld and its wellbeing. If we indeed comply, we'll lose are entire army to a slack-jawed youngster that just appeared out of the forest itself, asking for the impossible. How can I even be sure you're from Vallenfend? What proof do we have? Empty words and a partner that hasn't said more than twenty words since he's been here."

Kael clenched his jaw.

"We have more evidence," Rooster said.

"Rooster," Kael hissed, trying to silence him.

181

"Kael, we have proof!" He turned to Yseph. "Listen, I know what he's saying is true, we came here riding—"

Kael stomped on his foot. "That's enough out of you," he snarled through his teeth. He addressed Yseph again. "He was, of course, referring to my shield," he said, thinking fast. Kael removed his shield from his back and held it at chest level so the king and his advisor could inspect it. "It used to belong to a member of the BlackHound Empire. This is your proof."

Yseph leaned closer, his pointed nose hovering inches away from the shield's surface. King Henedral stayed where he was, watching his advisor closely.

"This craftsmanship is like nothing I've ever seen," Yseph stated, straightening. "Where did you get it?"

"It's a long story," Kael replied. Yseph raised an eyebrow. "One that I would like to share later," he added.

"Hmm. I have never seen a shield like this before... I am conflicted. Your proposition poses many threats to our kingdom, but so does the opposite. If we choose to follow you, Fallenfeld's safety is compromised. If we don't, and you are right, it seems we could be destroyed all the same. Ultimately, the decision is yours, Your Majesty."

King Henedral rubbed chin, debating Kael's words. A tendon in his neck flared for a moment. He took a deep breath. Kael held his. What was King Henedral going to do? Would Fallenfeld join the resistance?

At last, the king spoke. "Yseph, take this young man to inspect our army. I would like to speak with Kael Rundown by myself."

Yseph bowed low. "Aye, Your Majesty. Come," he said, ushering Rooster towards the door. With a nod towards Kael, Rooster left with Yseph.

Kael turned his attention towards the king.

King Henedral sighed and rubbed his temple. He thrust out his arms, looking to either side of the room. "You see these pictures on my walls? Each one of these men was a noble king before me. Every man was grand in his own way." King Henedral paced down the hall, staring at each painting in turn. "He was the first; the one to found Fallenfeld. He was the one who ordered this castle to be built. Defending Fallenfeld from a massive attack, leading Fallenfeld safely through a drought, abolishing poverty, settling foreign disputes, slaying a dragon...these are just some of the great accomplishments of my predecessors. They were all great men in their own ways, whether in their intellect or strength."

"Slaying a dragon?" Kael echoed, cocking his head. He stared at the portrait of the king with the giant white skull. It must have been a dragon's.

"Yes, but as *you* said before, that's a story for another time." King Henedral had made it over to his throne. With a groan, he sat down, making sure not to sit on the haft of his sword. "All great men... Now it has come to me. I have done nothing to set myself apart. I succeed a long heritage of successful, powerful men. What have I done? Nothing."

Kael listened with interest. He kept his face straight, letting the king finish his thought.

"I have solved no great dilemma," the king continued, "I've had no opposition to overcome. As far as leading a kingdom goes, I have had it the easiest. I have this beautiful blade at my hip, but have never once risen up to use it. Do you understand what I'm saying?"

Rubbing the toe of his boot on the floor, Kael nodded. "You are looking for something more than what you already have. I remember a time when I wished for the same thing. Now I want the opposite."

"Hmm, indeed."

"Although," Kael thought aloud, "wouldn't leading Fallenfeld without incident—good or bad—be a memorable thing?"

King Henedral placed his elbow on the armrest of his chair. He cradled his chin in his palm, lost in thought. "Yes, I suppose it is."

An idea struck Kael. "Fighting off an invading empire for the sake of your continent would be a grand thing," he said, trying to hold off the excitement in his voice. This was almost too perfect of an opportunity. "People all over will know of the king who helped save this land. Not just for Fallenfeld alone, but everywhere."

"I have already thought of this. However, if this goes wrong, if what you say does not come to fruition, I would be known for the exact opposite. I would be remembered as the most foolish king Fallenfeld has ever seen. I would be known for the man who crippled this fine city. I cannot have that tarnishing my name forever more."

So much for my perfect opportunity, Kael thought bitterly. "What more can I do to convince you, King Henedral? What I fight for is just. I seek no self-gratification. This is not for me, but for all I care about."

"Why?" King Henedral asked, shaking his head, "why go through all this trouble? You said yourself that you are banished. Do your people hate you? Do they even know what you do for their sake? What are you truly seeking for?"

Shivers ran up Kael's spine. A strange emotion welled up in his chest. He furrowed his brow and looked deep into the king's brown eyes. "I'm..." he faltered, searching for the correct answer. He searched deep, but couldn't quite find the right words. He tried to speak again. "I'm seeking your help."

King Henedral lifted his head off of his hand. He stared at Kael for the longest time, wordless. Kael tried to read his expression but he couldn't decipher what the king was thinking.

King Henedral took a deep breath. "If only we didn't have such a great bandit problem..." He squinted at the paintings lining his halls. "We'll just have to hope for the best. Kael Rundown, you have my support, and with that, Fallenfeld's."

A huge smile spread across Kael's face. The answer was sudden, but nevertheless held a great amount of power. His spirits were lifted and elation filled his soul. "Thank you, thank you!"

King Henedral grinned. He stood up off of his chair. "Yes, this is a joyous occasion, isn't it?" He strolled over and placed his hands on Kael's shoulders. "This calls for celebration."

"Excellent! I have to warn you though, I cannot stay for long."

"Of course, of course." King Henedral backed off. "Stay for one more day, and I promise you, tomorrow we'll have a grand feast with all my generals!"

Kael's smile faltered. "A feast?"

"Yes! It has been a long time since we've had a grand feast! Why, I think the last banquet we had was during the reign of King Vad, who ruled three terms before me. We don't often get such an occasion to hold a banquet."

The blood drained form Kael's face. He did his best to stay cheery. "I'm...looking forward to it."

King Henedral beamed through his beard. He clapped Kael across the back. "Very good! You're free to explore the castle and the city if you want. I will see you tomorrow for dinner then." With that, he walked out of the room with a skip in his step.

Leaving Kael feeling numb.

Chapter 20

"Listen up!" Tooran shouted. "I'm in charge." Bruce and Horan stopped talking. Korjan sheathed his sword which he had been polishing. "This mission is going to be fast and very dangerous. Please try not to fall behind."

Korjan inspected his son. He could still remember when Tooran was but just a lad. He was so grown up now. Hardly his son at all... Tooran was trained for these sorts of missions so naturally he was taking control.

"Let's leave at once. It should be nightfall when we arrive, which is what I am aiming for. We will further discuss the plan as we head down." He leaned towards the two newcomers, Bruce and Horan. "You better not slow us down."

Bruce's face was very grave. "I'll keep up, I promise."

Tooran caught Laura's disapproving scowl for a moment. He quickly looked away. "Are you sure you want to do this? You can still stay behind if you want."

"No, we want to help."

"Then," Tooran chirped. "We leave now." He hefted a small backpack and threw it over his shoulder. "Let's go."

Korjan said his quick goodbyes to Helena, Bunda and Laura. Helena looked especially torn from his departure. Then he, Tooran, the two newcomers and Faerd walked out of the cave and into the twilight of a setting sun. Korjan had stayed up most of the previous night thinking about what was to come. *They were going to assassinate Zeptus.* He never would have thought the day would come...

He had discussed the situation with his son earlier. It would take a date to climb down the mountain. Once they arrived at the city, everything would be smooth from there, Tooran had stated. He knew all the secret entrances and tunnels interlacing the city. Getting to Zeptus would be easy.

Korjan wasn't quite so sure.

He couldn't help but to be pessimistic. It was in his nature. The whole idea, although he was the one who had thought of it to begin with, was looking like a bad idea brewing. So many things could go wrong. Korjan sighed. *Too late to second guess now.*

As they exited the mouth of the cave, their little party of five, the mist surrounded them, reminding Korjan where he was. *Shatterbreath's cave.* He longed to be home. He longed for this to all be better. As he imagined the life he could have had, his hatred surged towards Zeptus. This was all that man's fault. The more he brooded, the more he decided what they were doing was for the best. Killing Zeptus would be the best thing they could do for Vallenfend.

The gravel path was just as foreboding and hostile as it had been on the way up. Going down it instead of up didn't change that situation. If anything, it was even more dangerous. But they were making good time already. Tooran had set a lofty pace, walking with his back erect and squinting into the faded sunlight. Horan and Bruce were having more trouble, but they managed to keep up well enough. Behind them, Faerd walked along silently and behind him, bringing up the rear, Korjan resided.

As the scenery around him grew repetitive, Korjan delved into his memories. He recalled all the best weapons he had ever made, as well as the shoddiest. He remembered working beside Kael and showing the smiling young boy how to work a bellows properly. Kael had been like a replacement son for him. In a way, perhaps Kael had seen him as a father figure as well. Once again, Korjan stared at his son leading their ranks.

It was so wonderful to have his son back again.

Would he lose him again?

Faerd watched his feet as they passed each other. Every footstep brought him that much closer to the ultimate goal. *Zeptus.* They were finally going to put an end to this. He relished the thought of exacting revenge on that despicable man. Sweet vengeance for what Zeptus did to him, to his family. To Laura.

Laura...

Faerd turned his gaze upwards, blinking through a heavy lid at the pitiless sky far above. There was a pang of remorse in his heart for becoming close with Laura. Laura was Kael's friend. They had been friends for all their lives. For a time, they had been more than friends, with Faerd watching in the background. All his life, he had watched their close relationship with envy. He had tried to find a girl that would give him the same love Laura and Kael had shared. He had tried many times. But no relationship could amount to theirs.

Now that relationship was dead.

Kael had let her down. She no longer trusted him. She trusted Faerd.

Would he return to her safely?

They made camp about halfway down the mountain. They had no fire because Tooran had warned that people might see it from the city. They couldn't do anything to compromise their secrecy.

Tooran ushered them closer when they had all set up their bedrolls. Korjan shivered. It was chilly outside without the shelter of the cave.

"Tomorrow we strike. There's no turning back now. This won't be easy. Necks will have to be slit and blood will have to be spilt." Tooran paused, trying to read their expressions in the dark. "Can you do this? Can you take a life to protect your own?"

Faerd nodded, furrowing his brow over his eye-patch. "I'm ready," he said with conviction, "to do anything it takes."

"Me too," Korjan declared.

"I—I suppose so," Horan whimpered. "It's just...I've never taken a life before."

"No. I need a solid answer. *Can you do this?*"

"Yes, I can," Bruce said, pounding his fist against his knee through his bedroll.

"Good. How about you?"

Horan bit his lip. "Yeah. I'll do what it takes."

"Very well. I'll keep watch tonight. The rest of you, get some sleep."

Halfway through the night, Tooran woke Korjan so that he could get some sleep. Korjan agreed with a nod and stayed up the rest of the night, struggling to stay awake. When someone stirred in their sleep, he would watch them with interest, wondering how many of them would return to the cave alive.

When morning hit, Korjan woke the party. They needed to get going at once. It was better to arrive earlier than later.

Korjan wasn't feeling particularly talkative after his meagre sleep, nor was Tooran, but Bruce and Horan were. The two boys began chatting away, sharing their experiences during their time spent training and swapping embarrassing stories. Korjan listened half-heartedly. He could tell they were just trying to avoid the main topic pressing on everybody's mind. While they chattered away like squirrels, Korjan checked all his equipment to make sure all was accounted for.

On his back was his broadsword, the hilt just above his left shoulder. The hilts of his smaller dual swords were also at either shoulder so he could access them easy. His dual axes were hidden up against his lower back, pressing up against his waist. It was the same setup he had used when he had saved Bunda. Bringing so many weapons seemed excessive, and altogether weighed more than was comfortable, but Korjan was glad to have them. Besides, if anybody else lost their weapon for some reason, he would have enough to share.

Korjan was more concerned for Bruce and Horan. Tooran had no small amount of weapons hidden beneath his black clothing and Faerd would suffice with no weapon at all, but the two other boys only had standard-issue military swords—and rudimentary training. If one of them lost their sword, Korjan hoped they would know how to use a different weapon adequately.

The roar of the waterfalls could be heard through the trees and soon, they were in view. They all stopped for a moment to catch a breath. Korjan sidled up to the nearest waterfall and cupped his hands underneath. The water was cold and refreshing. It gave him a small boost of energy. After splashing the chilly water against his face a few more times, Korjan shook himself and blinked a few times, ready to continue.

They resumed their hike once again, but had to slow down their pace. This was the most frightening part of the path. They had to tread on extremely narrow paths slick with moisture. Even Tooran had to agree that taking that part quickly would be a bad idea.

The biggest waterfall loomed ahead. Korjan bit his lip as he concentrated on his foothold. The scenery was beautiful and the waterfall was grand, but he couldn't lose his concentration now.

Just then, Faerd's foot slipped. He yelped and stumbled, losing his balance altogether. Korjan rushed forwards and caught the front of his tunic with three fingers. But Faerd's weight pulled Korjan along as well. They both fell over the edge of the cliff. With one hand still clutching Faerd's tunic, Korjan reached out wildly for something—anything—to grasp. His hand wrapped around a root protruding from the face of the cliff. Faerd continued falling away from the path and plunged into the heart of the waterfall, nearly tearing Korjan's arm from its socket. For a moment, it seemed as though the force of the pounding water was going to wrench Faerd free of Korjan's grasp, but Faerd swung out of the waterfall, slamming into the cliff's face.

Korjan groaned from the strain. Somehow, the root held his and Faerd's weight. Lip twisted in a pained sneer, Korjan looked down at Faerd, who was soaked with water.

"You alright?" he managed to grumble.

"Yeah," Faerd said, coughing. He struggled to find a footing against the smooth surface of the cliff face, but couldn't find one. Instead, he reached up and grabbed onto Korjan's arm.

"They're alive!" Bruce's voice chimed from above. Korjan could just barely hear it over the roar of the waterfall. "Tooran..." His voice trailed off and he disappeared from sight. Not a moment later, Tooran's poked his head over the ledge.

"By the shadows, Father, you—you're fine!"

"Not for long. Do something, Tooran!"

Tooran shook his head, fear ravaging his face. "I cannot! I have rope, but there's not a secure enough anchor to pull you up!"

"I can't hold on forever!"

Tooran put his hands to his head at a loss. "Uh...uh... Okay! I have an idea, listen carefully!" He said something, but Korjan couldn't hear him.

"What?" he yelled.

"Try and swing Faerd that direction!" Tooran hollered, pointing to Korjan's left. "We can pull you up from there."

Korjan nodded. His shoulders were burning in pain and he was losing his grip, but he summed up enough strength to swing Faerd a little bit. But not near enough.

"Faerd, help me!" he screamed.

Korjan tried to swing him again. Faerd scrambled against the face of the cliff, easily doubling the distance he had swung before. As he rocked back, Korjan swung him just as hard the other direction, picking up momentum. This time he came up almost level with Korjan and he grasped a protruding rock. He faltered, but his grip stayed.

Faerd adjusted himself for a moment to make sure that he had a suitable grasp. He nodded at Korjan. Unsure at first, he relaxed his grip and let go of Faerd's tunic entirely. Then, they clasped each other's wrists. Korjan's heart skipped a beat as he lowered himself, let go of the root he was holding onto and then began to fall. Faerd pulled him up and Korjan swung underneath in a reverse of what had just happened. Korjan did his best to shuffle along the side of the cliff, succeeding in achieving momentum and receiving gashes along his one side.

Korjan reached the peak of his swing and found a footing. Still holding each other's wrists, both Korjan and Faerd looked upwards. Horan and Bruce were leaning over the edge of the cliff, where the path had widened out. Tooran was standing behind them, watching with concerned eyes. The path had also declined as well, so Korjan and Faerd were closer to it than they had been before.

Bruce thrust out his hand. "Jump up, we'll catch you!"

"Okay," Korjan replied. "Faerd will come up first."

"Gotcha. Alright, we're ready."

191

Faerd took a moment to get a better footing. He scrutinized Korjan with his one eye.

"Time to see if these two really are spies or not," Faerd said with a dry laugh.

"I suppose so." Korjan braced himself. "Ready?"

"No," Faerd said tentatively. "But it's now or never."

"Then here you *go!*" Korjan yanked on Faerd's arm as hard as he could, aiming to propel him up to where Bruce and Horan's hands were waiting. As he did, Faerd jumped upwards as best as he could on the small ledge he had been on.

Korjan released his grasp as Faerd shot upwards. Korjan held his breath as he watched Bruce and Horan grab onto Faerd. With no small amount of effort, they managed to pull Faerd up and over the lip of the path's edge. They scooted away from the edge for a moment before coming back for Korjan.

"Okay, now your turn!" Horan called out.

"One moment!" Korjan was losing his grip. One hand was holding a small clump of dishevelled grass while the other was braced up against the wet rock. His feet were resting on nothing more than indents in the cliff. "I...can't find a better—"

Just then, the clump of grass Korjan was holding onto ripped free from the cliff's surface, spurring up a cloud of wet earth that spattered in his face. Korjan began to fall backwards. He swung his arms in a vain attempt to try and stop his fall, but his feet left the cliff's surface all the same.

Somehow, Korjan spun around in the air before he truly began to fall. Far, far below, he could see the churning pool which the waterfall fed into. Surrounding it were hundreds of pointed rocks, all reaching up towards him as if waiting to feast on him. When he hit the bottom, it would surely mean death.

Something wrapped around Korjan's stomach and his torso and legs lurched forwards, nearly folding him in half as he came to an abrupt halt. He heard a strong voice groan behind him.

Disbelieving, Korjan clutched onto the arm holding tight to his midsection. He turned his head as beast as he could. Still dressed in black, face red from strain, was Tooran, his son. Tooran was stretched out, with both feet planted against the side of the cliff. It took Korjan a moment to realize, but he was holding a thick rope in his other hand, one that seemed to be tied around his waist.

"Hey, Father," he said through a grunt, "let's play catch."

Korjan managed a dry laugh. "Uh, you win... *Very* good catch."

"Yeah. Grab onto my tunic and hold tight. I'll pull us back up."

Relieved, Korjan spun himself around and did as he was told. He threw an arm around Tooran's shoulder and grabbed a fistful of his black clothing. With a nod, Tooran twisted his body and pulled himself around. Making it seem easy, he climbed back up the rope. Bruce, Horan and Faerd all pulled them up once they were close enough.

Korjan flopped down on the path, winded. Faerd lay on his back beside him, clutching his chest. Then, all at once, somebody began to laugh. For some reason, they all followed suit.

After Korjan had his fill, he leaned up. "Wow," was all he could say.

"Sorry I didn't get you earlier," Tooran said through a huff. "I had to tie off that rope first. I thought you would last longer than that."

Korjan clasped his son's shoulder. "There's nothing to be sorry about. If you *didn't* catch me, though, I would have been a bit upset. Don't worry about it."

Tooran smiled, still taking deep breaths. "Thanks."

"Ah," Faerd spoke up, "sorry about that. I lost my footing. Uh...is there anything I can do to make up for it? Seriously, you saved my life right then, Korjan. I owe you everything."

Korjan scratched the back of his neck. "Forget it, Faerd. Just promise me you won't do anything like that again. *Especially* when we're in Vallenfend. Got that?"

"Of course!"

Korjan looked out towards the city, which was in view through the forest canopy. Faerd shivered, his clothes now soaking wet. "Well, that was a pretty good break," he said, getting to his feet, "but we should continue."

"Aye," Tooran agreed. "I'm sure Zeptus is eagerly waiting our visit."

"I hope not," Horan commented, also standing up. "He shouldn't anyway."

Tooran chuckled heartily. His booming laugh surprised Korjan. It had been a long time since he himself had laughed like that. "Ah, let's just get going, skinny." He gave Horan a rough shove.

Korjan smiled. Their spirits were all lifted after that sudden fit of adventure. They all continued forward, resuming their regular positions. Korjan was once again bringing up the rear. After only a few steps, however, his smile faded. He gritted his teeth and rubbed his left shoulder, which was burning with terrible pain. He glanced forwards at Tooran, his noble son. Korjan bit his lip. No, he wouldn't tell them about his arm. It would only worry them.

Their elation eventually wore off as they resumed their hasty trek down the mountain. The terrain posed no further threat once the roaring waterfalls were gone from view. Every once and while, somebody would stumble, but otherwise their progress was smooth. Tooran, Korjan noted, never tripped at all.

The sun was flooding the horizon with brilliant orange as they reached the foot of the mountain. Vallenfend was just ahead of them, dark and foreboding in the waning light. Korjan forgot how high the walls of the city were. Vallenfend was truly built solid.

They stopped for a short break, but were on their way again in less than ten minutes. They ducked low and moved through the taller grasses, which was a slight detour, but necessary to keep out of sight from sentries.

Korjan could feel his heart pounding as the sun finally set, throwing the land into darkness. They were here.

Tooran pressed himself up against the outer wall, looking both directions. He motioned for the rest of the party to follow. Korjan rushed to the wall beside him. They were just north of the easternmost entrance to the city. They all exchanged glances. Faerd rubbed the knuckles of his gauntlets, malice in his face.

"The secret entrance is this way," Tooran whispered, "follow me."

They crept along the wall of the city, heading in a northern direction. At last, Tooran stopped. He placed both hands against the base of the wall, searching for something. Korjan turned away, surveying their surroundings. He listened as Tooran dragged his clothed gauntlets across the wall. With a *click,* a new sound presented itself: stone sliding against stone.

When Korjan turned back a rectangular section of the wall was open, bearing a yawning tunnel. Korjan leaned forward, taking a deep breath. A deep aroma of earth and secrecy wafted out of it. All the years he lived in Vallenfend, and he had no idea anything like this existed.

"How many more entrances like this are there?" Korjan asked, furrowing his brow.

Tooran hesitated, still holding onto the edge of the trapdoor. "Too many to count," he said sullenly. "Most of them were created during the reign of King Morrindale. How do you think people disappeared so fast if they were disobedient?"

Korjan shook his head. "The...King's Elite. All this time, he had this. He had *you.* This goes exactly against his own decree."

"Yes," Tooran agreed. "Instead of sending able-bodied young men, Zeptus and King Morrindale chose the best of the best to do their bidding."

"All the more reason to kill Zeptus," Faerd piped up. "So let's get going while we still have night left to spend."

Without another word, Tooran slipped into the dark tunnel, with Faerd close behind. Bruce climbed in as well. Horan was less reluctant, but Korjan tapped his foot impatiently as he held the door to the tunnel open. The young man scrambled in after them. Then Korjan followed, closing the door behind.

Compared to the choking darkness of the passageway, what little light had been left outside seemed welcoming. Korjan blinked several times, unsure whether his eyes were indeed open. There was a strange scratching noise from up ahead. Korjan bumped into somebody ahead of him.

"Oof!"

"Sorry, Horan," Korjan said, placing his palms on the young man's back. Korjan seized as the boy went limp in his hands. "Tooran?" he called out in alarm.

"One moment," Tooran grunted. Suddenly, there was a blinding light as Tooran lit a strange torch of sorts.

Bruce cried out in alarm as with the light came the appearance of several soldiers dressed in black. King's Elite! They were waiting for them! How did they know?

At once, Korjan had pulled one of the thinner swords from his back, stepping away from the limp Horan. Bruce also drew his sword just in time as one of the soldiers lunged at him. Korjan blocked an attack by a taller soldier.

The room was instantly filled with noise.

The sounds of ringing metal and angry shouts reverberated through the confined space, hurting Korjan's ears. But right then, he was more concerned with the blade glinting dangerously in the harsh light of the dropped torch.

The assassin was skilled and fighting in semi-darkness only made it harder for Korjan. He managed to take the upper hand as he kneed his foe's elbow. Involuntarily, the assassin dropped his sword. Korjan quickly finished him off, piercing his sword through the man's heart.

Korjan kicked the corpse off of his blade and turned to the assassin fighting against Faerd. With the assassin distracted, Korjan made quick work of him, pulling his second blade from his back. Carrying through with momentum, Korjan tried to attack another assassin, but his shoulder seized. Before the soldier could take advantage, Faerd intervened, blocking the attack with his gauntlets. It was just enough time Korjan needed to run the assassin through. Korjan gave a silent nod to Faerd before moving on to the next enemy.

Korjan heard Bruce gasp as an assassin struck him across the face. Before the soldier could carry through, however, Korjan hurled one of his axes at the man.

Two King's Elite were fighting against Tooran but evidently Tooran was the better fighter. With only a curved dagger in each hand, he ducked underneath both of their attacks and exploded upwards, driving his blades into the bass of their necks.

As fast as it began, the battle was over.

Suddenly, Korjan remembered Horan and rushed over to where the boy had fallen. Korjan propped him up against the soft wall of the tunnel and touched his face. "Horan," he said sharply, "Horan?"

Horan gurgled, his eyelids fluttering.

"Faerd, get me some light!" Korjan demanded.

"Got it." A moment later, Faerd was holding the torch over Korjan's shoulder.

The sight of red blood spattered across Horan's light blue tunic sent shivers up Korjan's spine. His stomach twisted and his throat clenched. Korjan couldn't see the wound well, but it was easy to tell it was life-threatening.

"Horan?" Bruce's voice sounded so young, so scared. "Buddy? Speak to me!" His voice cracked.

Tooran pushed Bruce out of his way and bent over Horan, scanning over his body. Without hesitation, he ripped a great hole in Horan's tunic and backed off, inspecting the wound.

Tooran shook his head. "The wound is deep, but the blade missed his organs. These soldiers were amateurs—ordered to guard this spot as their first assignment. They did not know how to kill properly. Had they been expecting us..."

Perhaps it was the scant light, but Bruce's face was going ghostly pale.

"If he is to survive, we must get him to a healer, fast." Tooran's words struck each of them hard as he scrunched up Horan's torn tunic and pressed it against the wound.

"What about the mission?" Faerd asked.

Tooran glanced at him sideways. "Do we sacrifice the life of one to continue? One of us could take him to a healer, but even one more loss to our numbers will be detrimental." Tooran's tone was flat and his expression unreadable.

"Tooran, can you be so heartless?" Bruce cried. "We must get him help immediately!"

Korjan furrowed his brow, staring at Horan's pale face. This was his fault.

"I'm not being heartless," Tooran countered, "I'm being practical. We need our numbers. His wound is significant. Even if one of us leaves the mission to get him help, it could spell failure to this entire ordeal. Which, might I remind you, is of the upmost—"

"I'll take him," Korjan interrupted.

"What?" Bruce asked.

"Excuse me?" Tooran demanded. "You, Father? No."

"It is my fault Horan was injured," Korjan explained, feeling the blood dribble down his arm. "I told him not to wear any heavy armour because he isn't strong enough to handle it. If he would have been wearing something to protect him..."

"That wouldn't have mattered," Tooran barked. "Even with light armour, this wound would still be just as bad. In fact, any protection would have encouraged his attacker to strike at a more vulnerable spot. Say, his head or neck."

"You didn't tell him not to wear armour at all," Faerd said, "he must have misinterpreted your advice."

"It doesn't matter," Korjan yelled, "whether he understood me or not! It doesn't matter what *could* have happened. This is what happened, and it is my fault. I can move fast and I am strong. Carrying him will be no problem for me. I will take him to Malaricus and hurry afterwards to the castle. This shouldn't delay us more than twenty minutes."

Tooran scratched his chin, deep in thought.

Horan coughed, spitting up blood.

"Either way, can we get out of here?" Bruce asked, voice quavering.

They all exited the dark tunnels. Night had fallen quickly and with the added shelter of the city's walls, it was thick.

"We will wait fifteen minutes at the castle's front gate," Tooran told his father. "That's all we can afford."

"I understand."

Tooran sighed. "If you aren't with us by that time, we will continue. I'll go slow and try to leave noticeable signs for you to follow, a trail."

Korjan nodded. "Thank you, son. I will hurry as fast as I can."

"Go if you must. And don't dawdle." Tooran leaned closer to the blacksmith. "Aside from me, you are the most vital asset to this team."

Korjan nodded solemnly. It was strange to hear those words, but he knew Tooran was right. "I'll be swift."

"Then go."

Without further hesitation, Korjan picked Horan up and cradled him in his arms as gently as he could. Horan groaned and tried to reach up at something. Korjan's heart sank lower. The boy had lost so much blood already...

Korjan hurried off towards the centre of the city, leaving his family behind. They slunk into the shadows as he left. It took Korjan some time to orient himself—it had been so long since he had been in Vallenfend—but eventually, he found his way. There were still people out in the streets, mostly poor women and the occasional drunk drowning his troubles. Korjan avoided them all. Carrying a bloody young man in his hands while in a hurry would draw too much unwanted attention. It cost him a few more minutes, but he figured it was worth it.

Korjan worked his way southward and in towards the centre of the city, aiming for the Royal Athenaeum. The thought flitted through his mind that perhaps Malaricus wouldn't be there. Perhaps the scholar had already left up the mountain to bring them supplies. Oh, the surprise he would get when he discovered the men weren't there.

"Please be home, Malaricus," Korjan muttered, glancing at the pale boy in his arms. He shook all other thoughts away.

The Athenaeum rolled into view. The section of the upper wall where the dragon had crashed through was still unrepaired, although most of the debris on street level had been cleared away. Korjan recalled the memory of when he had heard what had happened to Malaricus the day the library was damaged. Shatterbreath herself

199

had come down to fetch him. Everybody thought she had devoured him. When Malaricus returned to the city, unscathed, it was considered a miracle. It now occurred to him that the scholar most likely survived because of Kael. He was probably kidnapped in the first place because of Kael as well. How could people not see that the dragon was no harm?

From where Korjan stood, it looked as though there was a candle burning up there. That was a good sign. Malaricus wouldn't leave a candle unattended with his books. Korjan shifted Horan in his arms and walked up to the entrance to the Athenaeum. Malaricus's personal study was on one of the topmost floors. It was said that ancient books and records of the kingdom were kept in the lower levels. Korjan shook his head, amazed that books alone could take up so much space.

The stairwell was tight and Korjan had to walk sideways so he and Horan could fit. It was difficult business, and took longer than Korjan would have wished, but at last, he reached the door to Malaricus's study. With some effort, he knocked on the door, trying to ignore the burning in his thighs the stairs had induced.

There came multiple voices from the other side. Whispers and *shushes*. Korjan's brow furrowed. A lock grinded in the door and it cracked open, just enough for Malaricus to poke his narrow face through. He was wearing a frightened expression, but once he realized who it was, he was relieved.

"Korjan!" he cried. His smile was replaced by bemusement as he spotted Horan in the blacksmith's grasp. "Korjan?"

"Hello, Malaricus," Korjan grunted. "Haven't seen you for a few days. Can I come in?"

Malaricus threw the door open. "Of course...but...what are you doing here? Who is that boy in your arms?" He gasped. "And what *happened* to him?"

Korjan stepped into the room. He stopped at once. There were other people in Malaricus's study. All of his bookshelves were pushed tight to the walls, giving more space for the many blankets and bedrolls scattered across the floor. There were women, children and even a few men filling the room, either sitting on their beds, leaning against something or draped across Malaricus's lavished furniture.

Malaricus rushed past him, breaking Korjan's trance. He shooed two little boys off of his largest couch to allow Korjan to place Horan gently down there. Korjan backed off to let Malaricus inspect him.

The scholar leaned in close, pulling the cloth over Horan's wound away. Korjan turned his attention to the people in Malaricus's room who all stared back at him as if they were scared of him.

"Who are these people, Malaricus?" Korjan asked. "Why are they in here?"

"Not everybody believes in what Zeptus is telling the city," Malaricus explained. He frowned at Horan's still-bleeding wound for a moment, then pushed his way to the other end of the study. He disappeared for a moment into a closet of sorts. When he returned, he was carrying a couple bottles and a bag. He placed the bag on the couch beside Horan and unfolded it. It was full of medical supplies. "These people came to me when they heard rumours of what I was doing. They want to help. But they can't do that apart. The only way we'll stand a chance is if we stand together."

"But why here?" Korjan asked.

Malaricus shrugged. He put his glasses on, fingering the gold chain attached to the wire frame. "Where else? I'm not too happy about it," he whispered, "but this is the best place we've got. And if somebody *does* come to get us, we'll be able to resist."

"Hmm..." Korjan was glad there were others who believe in Kael, or at least *didn't* believe in the king and his advisor, but they couldn't keep staying at Malaricus's study. The room was wide open to the elements, thanks to the damage the dragon caused, and the scholar was getting worn out. There were bags under his eyes and he kept rubbing his temple. It must have cost him quite a bit to keep all those mouths fed, for his study was less adorned than Korjan remembered.

"You didn't answer my question," Malaricus said. He wetted a cloth with the liquid from one of the bottles. Gently, he tapped Horan's wound with it. The boy grimaced, but stayed unconscious. "What are you doing here, Korjan? And what happened to this boy?"

201

"Assassin got him," Korjan said numbly, "while we were in the dark. Can he be saved?"

Malaricus sighed. "It's too soon to tell. His wounds are grievous indeed. I will need assistance from others in here." Malaricus stopped and grabbed Korjan's arm. "Now tell me, what are you doing here?"

Korjan sighed, suddenly feeling awkward. He twitched, realizing that he needed to get back to the mission in question. "We came here," he said, "to kill Zeptus."

Those that overhead clapped their hands and their expressions brightened. Malaricus stood up and clasped his shoulder. "What did you say?"

"Tooran, Faerd, Bruce, Horan and I came to kill Zeptus."

"Who's Bruce and Horan? Oh, never mind. Korjan, you must listen to me!" Malaricus's eyes were wide in concern and his voice was high. He let his glasses fall to his chest, hanging from the gold chain around his neck. "Zeptus is not who you think. He is not the core of this problem. It is the king. He is the grandmaster of this plot, not Zeptus. The king is using Zeptus as his backup in case something like this happened. He is *using* Zeptus."

Korjan hesitated, confused. "The king? No. That is impossible, the king is too stupid."

"That's exactly what he wants people to think! You cannot kill Zeptus! He's been trying to help us and Kael all along! It is his influence alone that has kept all of our presence secret." Malaricus waved his arms around the room, referring to everybody occupying it. All their attention was suddenly turned to them.

Korjan shifted his weight uneasily, aware their eyes. He didn't like so much attention. Taking a deep breath, he turned away from the frightened eyes of the children and their mothers. "I must get going," he said. "Are you sure of this?"

Malaricus nodded. "Zeptus told me this himself."

Korjan bit his lip. "Then we are wrong. However, I stay unconvinced."

Malaricus's shoulders fell. "You must believe me."

"I've wasted too much time already," Korjan said with a frown. "For all I know, Zeptus could be dead already. The others went on without me. They won't wait forever."

Malaricus shivered. "Korjan, you can't let this happen!"

Korjan was already moving towards the door. "I pray that you are incorrect, Malaricus," he said over his shoulder. "Otherwise we are making a big mistake indeed."

Malaricus pushed his way through the room and grasped Korjan's sore shoulder before he had a chance to leave. Korjan pursed his lips. He didn't have time for this.

"You cannot kill Zeptus. Promise me, Korjan, you will not spill his blood tonight." Malaricus's concerned gaze bored into the blacksmith. Korjan tried to avoid his eyes, but anywhere he looked, he was met with the frightened expressions of the children and their mothers.

"Fine," Korjan said through a dry throat. "Unless he gives us a reason to do so, I give my word we will not kill Zeptus if I reach the others in time. But by no means does this mean our mission is over."

Korjan flung the door open. Malaricus inhaled through his teeth. "What does that mean? What will you do instead?"

Korjan gave him a nod goodbye before taking a step down the stairs.

"What are you going to do?" Malaricus's voice followed him.

Closing his eyes, there was only one reply Korjan could think of. "I don't know."

When Korjan reached the bottom of the stairs, he cursed. That had taken far longer than he would have liked. He was behind schedule. Doubtless, Tooran and the others wouldn't have waited that long.

Disregarding stealth, Korjan broke out in a sprint, taking long strides. He took the most direct route to the castle as he could while wondering how he would find his way inside. Tooran had told him they would leave something to guide him. But what exactly did that mean?

After only a few minutes, Korjan had made it to the south end of the castle grounds. He pressed up against the walls, searching for

203

any telltale sign that Tooran might have left. It was so dark out, he could hardly see. He turned his neck to throw a curse up at the moon. It was nothing more than a sliver. It did nothing to help his situation.

Wary, Korjan sprinted along beside the wall until he met the side of the castle itself. He crouched low as he spotted a shape in the dark. Korjan pulled an axe from behind his back, holding it at the ready. He sidled closer to the shape. It was a guard slumped against the base of the wall. There was an empty bottle of whisky beside him and the stench of the heavy drink permeated the air around him.

Korjan rushed over to the passed out guard and placed two fingers to his neck. The man was dead. Korjan shoved him aside, searching the wall. This must have been one of the signs Tooran had left him. It wasn't very subtle.

A twinkle caught his eye. A spot of blood glimmered in the faint moonlight. Korjan put a hand to the small cross drawn in blood. He pressed against it. A trapdoor set perfectly into the bricks opened up.

Korjan crawled inside. To his surprise, there was a torch already burning, filling the tight space with a heavy muskiness that made it feel more confined than it really was. The torch burned with a strange light, as if it were reluctant to burn at all. Korjan stifled a cough as he passed by it. Just up ahead he could see a faint sliver of light and a whisper of air met his stubbly chin. He wiped his brow with his gauntlet, feeling the tension rising in his chest.

He gently pushed on the exit, but it didn't budge. Korjan frowned in the dark, running his hands over the smooth surface. It felt like a wooden board. The must be *some* way to open it. Losing patience, Korjan back up and braced his legs against the wood surface. He had no time to figure out how to open it.

He kicked the trapdoor, shattering the hinges. Korjan cringed as it clattered to the ground. Stifling a curse, he peered into the halls, curious. He had never been inside the castle before. Torches lined the halls, bathing the smooth. He crawled out of the secret tunnel and into the halls of the castle, brandishing his axe, ready to defend against any guards who may have heard the noise. There were none. Wary nevertheless, Korjan picked up the trapdoor—a portrait on the outside—and placed it back over the entrance to the tunnel. It hung crooked and a corner was cracked, but Korjan was hopeful that no guards would notice in the darkness. With a shrug, he moved down the hallway.

Hopefully, Tooran had taken out the guards on his way up to Zeptus's study. Doing so quietly and without detection would take time, which would allow Korjan to catch up. He would have to sacrifice some of his own stealth for speed, but at that point, it would be worth it.

Walking around the corner, Korjan wondered what he would do next. He knew that Zeptus's study was located in a tall spire, but he had no idea where that was—or where he was for that matter. If he went in the wrong direction, he could miss any signs Tooran might have left behind.

A noise came from down his hallway. Korjan stiffened. Somebody was coming. He rounded a corner and watched with one eye as a guard dressed in a blue tunic and light leather armour came into view. Korjan watched as the guard frowned and crouched, inspecting something on the wall. Korjan took a deep breath as he left the cover of his corner to slink towards the young guard.

The guard cocked his head and touched something protruding from the wall. "What's this?" he remarked, his voice piercing in the quiet. "A dagger?"

Korjan rushed forwards, his equipment clinking together. The guard twist around, face screwed up in alarm.

"Who are you?" he cried. "Halt at once!"

Korjan struck him across the face. The young man reeled for a second, eyelids fluttering, then fell unconscious to the ground. Curious, Korjan stooped over to see what the guard had been inspecting. Indeed, there was a dagger set deep into the wall. Korjan pulled it free and leaned closer. There was a line drawn leading away from the dagger. Korjan put the tip of the knife into the line, tracing it.

He smiled, realizing that Tooran must have left it as a sign. He ran his finger over the line, following it through the hallways. He went at a lofty pace, aiming to catch up. He had no idea how far behind he was.

The long scratch in the wall led to a set of spiralled stairs. Unsure, Korjan followed it up. Luckily, no one met him on the stairs. It was late at night, he reasoned. Not even the castle's servants would be up at this hour.

Korjan slunk to the top of the stairs, staying as quiet as he could. He had heard a person coughing on his way up. He positioned himself on the steps so he could just barely see the guard standing at a window near the top of the stairs. The guard, this time wearing dark clothing, had either palm braced on the ledge of the window, staring outside. He coughed again, shaking his head.

Korjan surged forwards. "I'm not feeling too well," the man declared, seemingly to nobody. Korjan caught the man's head and slammed it against the side of the window, knocking him out cold.

"Have you tried—hey, what the...? You there!" So the guard *had* been talking to somebody. Another guard down the hallway drew his sword, rushing towards Korjan.

Korjan drew his own sword and they locked blades. This man was also a member of the King's Elite, and it was harder to fight in the confines of the hallway, but after a few strokes, Korjan dispatched him.

He probably should have hid the body, but right then, Korjan simply had no time. He left both bodies where they lay and continued on his way, once again following the dagger's trail.

After two more flights of stairs and one more knocked-out guard, the trail stopped. Korjan hesitated, staring at the spot on the wall where the line in the wall just disappeared. He looked around hastily. There was a strange smell to the air. He took a deep breath.

Then he spotted it. There was a puddle of blood on the ground. He knelt over it, cocking his head. Further down the hall, there was a door. He crept up to it and pressed an ear against it. He couldn't hear a thing. Throat tight, he cranked the handle. It swung free. It was dark inside, but even from the faint glow of the torches in the hallway, he could see a body crammed underneath a fancy desk.

Korjan locked his jaw and gently touched the dead man's hand. The corpse was still warm. He had not died long ago.

Korjan released his breath. For a moment, he had thought that the blood had belonged to one of his friends, or even his son. He realized how foolish the notion was and continued on his way. But without the dagger's trail to guide him, he quickly became lost.

After a few minutes of futile turns, Korjan stuck his head out a window. To his left, he spotted the tallest spire. His eyes shot wide. He was close.

He oriented himself towards where he believed Zeptus's study to be and set off in a mad sprint. Suddenly, a soldier rounded the corner. It was too late, Korjan couldn't stop himself. Full tilt, he ran into the man. Somehow, he managed to pull one of his thin swords and slit the man's throat as they tumbled. Picking himself up, Korjan gawked at the man for a moment before continuing on his way.

With one last turn, a rounded hallway presented itself to Korjan. The torches were snuffed in the hallways but a light shone through an open doorway not very far away. On either side of the doorway, there were two dark shapes slumped over. At once he knew he had made it.

Korjan rushed towards the doorway. The two rosewood doors were leaning at awkward angles, smashed free from their hinges. As Korjan entered, his heart jumped for joy as he spotted his son. A second later, it lurched.

In Tooran's hand was Zeptus's pale neck.

Tooran had a dagger raised with his other hand, preparing to strike.

Chapter 21

Kael left the city at once when morning hit. First, he had told Rooster that if anybody was looking for him, to tell them that he was exploring the city. Rooster had inquired where he should tell them Kael would be, but Kael could only shrug as he turned around. "Just tell the truth," he had said, "say you don't know."

Stepping over a pothole in the field, Kael's mind began to wonder. He ignored the people tending to the fields and the caravan of cattle that trampled past. His thoughts were busy swirling with questions about the banquet. He should be honoured that they would host one just for him, but Shatterbreath's words were echoing in his mind. *Poisoned ale.*

Kael whistled, the echoes coming back to him a moment later. His calves were getting sore and he realized he was already a fair distance up the mountain, although he had not ventured into the thick of the forests yet.

Kael turned on his heel and lowered himself down on a boulder, marvelling at how beautiful Fallenfeld was, nestled in the cozy valley. A gust of wind buffeted him, and without turning around, Kael greeted Shatterbreath.

"How goes it, Tiny?" the dragon asked. Kael drank in the comforting sound of her strong voice.

Kael turned to her. She exhaled, sending a warm wave rushing over him. Her breath smelled strongly of raw meat and blood was smeared on her lips. She must have been eating when he interrupted her.

Kael sighed. "They're holding a banquet for me."

Shatterbreath cocked her head, her emerald eyes shimmering in the sunlight. "Your tone suggests this is a bad thing."

"King Henedral told me I have Fallenfeld's support. He's holding a banquet tonight to celebrate his decision. I can't decide whether or not he truly believes me."

Shatterbreath slumped down beside Kael, sending seeds flying into the wind. "I knew you'd be dwelling on this. Just because he has declared a feast doesn't mean he distrusts you, Tiny. You will not be able to tell if his words are genuine or not until you are served."

"Wine means trust, ale spells death," Kael said morosely. He took off his gauntlet and rubbed his face. Even though the king promised safety, he wore is armour at all times now.

Shatterbreath rolled onto her back. Right then, Kael was envious of her carefree attitude. She didn't have to worry about the political matters of gathering a defending army. She didn't even have to talk to anybody but him. All she had to do was wait. For a split second, Kael was angry, but he calmed himself. There was nothing he could do to change the situation. It wasn't like Shatterbreath could to the talking for him. Plus, he knew how much agony it was for Shatterbreath to wait for him. She hated waiting.

For a time, Kael and Shatterbreath stayed silent, him sitting there, conflicted and her lying on her back, carefree. There they stayed in perfect harmony with the breathtaking beauty of the early day. Kael took a deep breath and not a second later, so did Shatterbreath. His sigh was drowned out by her rumbling exhalation.

"This is a problem indeed," she said at last, rubbing the top of her head on the ground, her intact horn digging up great clods of earth. She snorted and a small flame burst from her nostril, burning a small patch of ground.

"Do you have any ideas?"

Shatterbreath turned over onto her belly again. She stretched her wings and yawned, showing her array of gleaming teeth. "It seems to me," she said, "that your only option right now is to go. Do they know we are partners?"

Kael frowned. "No. Rooster nearly told them that we came riding a dragon, but I was able to stop them. As far as I know, they don't even know you're near Fallenfeld."

Shatterbreath shook her neck. She was particularly restless today. That or she was just happy to see him. Tail twitching, she hummed. "Then I will stay close," she said calmly, as if that alone was the

209

solution. "But not too close. If you get in any trouble, just whistle. I'll come and get you right away, no matter where you are."

Kael nodded. "Sounds good." He paused. "By the way, have you seen any bandits nearby?"

Shatterbreath yawned again. "Bandits? Grubby little humans? They are thieves, am I right?"

"Yes. They are giving Fallenfeld no end of trouble."

"I've seen them. More or less." She wrapped her tail around Kael and he was thrust into her vision. "They live over there," her eyes focussed on a hill across the valley. "Somewhere in that forest. I flew by overhead and could smell them from the sky. They must have a colony of sorts there."

Kael was taken out of Shatterbreath's vision. He rubbed his chin, blinking away disorientation. "Hmm..."

"Why? Why are bandits so important?"

Kael shook his head. "They aren't. I should be getting back now." He stood up, brushing dirt off of the backside of his armour. He put his hands on his hips, stretching his back. Shatterbreath watched him closely. There was a yearning in her eyes. Kael could tell she wasn't happy about him being away from her for so long. "Listen," he said, placing both hands on her paw, "when I get back, we'll have a day to ourselves. No cities, no delegations. Just you and I alone, soaring through the sky."

Shatterbreath nodded. "I look forward to it." She stopped him as he started down the hill. "Tiny," she said, her nostrils flaring, "don't take any chances. If they *do* offer you ale, just run. No second thoughts, no hesitation."

Kael nodded and gently pushed her tail aside, heading back down the hill towards Fallenfeld. She took off, temporarily flattening the grass surrounding with her powerful wing beat. Kael stumbled as she soared over him. She angled her wings and doubled back, heading to the top of the mountain. He watched her go and resumed his hike.

It didn't take long for him to reach the gate of Fallenfeld. The guard let him in without question. Although Kael had never met the man, almost everybody now knew Kael's face in the city. He was the foreigner from their hostile sister city. People gave him strange looks and mothers pulled their children away. He did his best to ignore them.

His visit with Shatterbreath had burned a lot of time. It was nearly midday by then. Kael was relieved, but at the same time mortified. He wanted to get going as soon as possible, but he was dreading the banquet that he would inevitably be attending. The two emotions conflicted with each other, waging a silent war inside Kael's mind, with him taking the toll. He was tired already. His recurring nightmares didn't help diminish the fatigue either.

Taking his time, Kael strolled to the castle. He walked through the front gates, which were wide open and made his way through the busy streets. Whenever Kael went inside the castle walls, he was always so impressed. In the wide courtyard, soldiers marched as their instructors yelled commands at them. Some sparred, some practiced their archery and some were taking horses outside to practice with them. Everybody was doing something.

Kael made his way around the outside, trying to stay out of the way. The guards let him inside the castle without a fuss. Before he entered, Kael checked the sky. It was getting closer to dinnertime. His stomach rumbled. He hadn't had lunch—or breakfast for that matter. Hopefully they would give him something to eat before they offered him a drink. He chuckled to himself, receiving a strange look from the guard nearest to him.

Blushing, Kael slipped inside.

The next few hours seemed to drag by. After stopping by the kitchen to grab a quick snack, Kael headed to the room the king had let him stay in. It had two comfortable beds and a good view of the castle's courtyard down below, but Kael usually preferred to be out and about doing something. Rooster was already in the room.

Rooster protruded a deck of cards a few minutes after Kael had finished his slice of bread. Kael cocked his head. He had heard of cards before, but he hadn't actually seen a deck until then. He was always too busy for trivial games like cards. Besides, he and his friends always found something better to do than sit around a table and play such games.

Rooster taught Kael as best as he could how to play a Farthuian game with the cards. It wasn't very fair. The game had to do with placing a higher-value card overtop of the opponent's and Kael always seemed to get the lowest cards. Or when he did get a decent card, Rooster always had something that would beat it. It was a game of strategy, Rooster claimed, but Kael couldn't see how. He won a few rounds but found it frustrating, so they soon gave up.

Kael thrust his cards on the ground, standing up and stretching his back. He walked to the window and peered outside. Scattered groups of the soldiers had stopped their training. Kael could only assume they were getting ready for supper. With a sigh, he decided to do the same.

Kael was about to remove his breastplate, but decided otherwise.

"You're going in a full set of armour?" Rooster scoffed. "They're going to think something's wrong."

Stifling a yawn, Kael shrugged. "I'll just tell them that I think wearing one's armour to a formal event is the proper attire. Considering the reason for the banquet, I think it's quite appropriate."

"Are you going right now? I don't think it'll be ready yet. I can still hear servants rushing around out in the halls. They're probably still getting things set up."

"Then let's go help," Kael responded, waving Rooster over. *Anything but more of your card games*, he added in his mind.

Shatterbreath angled her wings, banking towards the kingdom. It occurred to her that she didn't even know when the silly banquet would start, so she had decided to start circling the castle long before it would likely take place. She yawned, letting her limbs go limp as the thermals carried her. Waiting sure made her tired.

She dearly wanted to help Kael, but there was simply no way to do that. It was better to not let anybody know about their friendship. Right now, this was the best she could do. Circle the castle and do more of her favourite thing—waiting.

She scoured the castle's windows. She was a ways off, far enough to hopefully arouse no attention—although humans always became frightened when they even saw her. It wasn't like she was going to circle a town before attacking it. A rumble ran through her chest as she scoffed at the prospect. No, if she *were* to attack, they'd be dead already. Swoop in, breath fire, swoop out. Repeat. That's all it took.

Shatterbreath shook her head, causing the wind to whistle in her ears. She performed a lazy barrel roll. This is was idleness did to her. It made her mind wander.

Setting her sights back on the castle, she tried to find Kael in the mess of humans. Was he still wearing his armour? That would make things easier. Squinting, she angled close, feeling playful. She wondered how close she could get before...

A horn blared in alarm. Sighing, she backed off as a volley of arrows soared towards her. They weren't even close, but the message was all too clear. There was no room for a dragon in the human world. There never was.

When she looked back, much farther away this time, she heard Kael's whistle. It was hard to ignore. Tiny was leaning out on the battlements of the castle's walls. He wore a disapproving scowl. She let out a croak, amused. He was too far away to see however, and continued to frown. She knew he was telling her to back off.

Shatterbreath gained some altitude. She backed away from the city and caught a lazy thermal above the top of the nearest mountain. She started doing slow, tight circles, peering down. How long did banquets take? An hour? Four? Fifteen minutes? Hopefully the latter. However long, Shatterbreath would be ready.

She tensed her body, ready to zoom in if something—anything—went wrong.

Kael rubbed his face. What was that dragon doing? Why had she flown so close? Part of him believed it was pure accident, but he knew Shatterbreath better than that. She was probably teasing him again. It was all innocent, he supposed, but now wasn't the time. It had been a risk just to whistle at her. Someone could have seen their connection.

But they hadn't. So Kael shrugged it off. He turned on his heel and headed back inside. As soon as he had heard the warning horn, Kael had rushed outside, leaving Rooster to help the servants.

Kael opened the wooden door to the battlements, oriented himself, then strode through the castle's halls to the banquet hall. The banquet hall was located just underneath the king's throne room, square in the middle of the castle. As such, it took up the brunt of the building's middle section.

When he reached the doors, Kael cracked it open. The feast was nearly ready, although the food wasn't put out yet. He swung one of the decorated double-doors open and entered.

A huge, long table lined the room, providing enough seats for the king, his close servants, his highest generals and any noblemen friends he may have invited. All in all, it must have seated at least fifty. The room itself was tall and wide, with thick pillars spaced far apart that held up the rounded ceiling. The pillars were set about seven feet away from the walls, which gave plenty of room for servants to rush around and tend to the banquet. Yawning windows gave the room plenty of light, spaced so the sun would come in between the pillars.

As was tradition, everything was decorated in classic Fallenfeld style. The cloths that were draped against the walls and columns were sky blue, each adorned with a large version of their crest. Even the ceiling had a bird spreading its wings painted on it.

At the far end of the table, an ornate armchair sat. It was decorated with varying shades of blue and had the head of Fallenfeld's bird carved into each armrest. From the height of the backrest to the silver curving over its surfaces, Kael had no doubt it was the king's seat. Next to it must have been the advisor's chair. Kael cocked his head. It was a different style than the rest of the furniture. But he was too far away to tell exactly what made it unique.

Skirting just around the edge, Kael made his way to the far end of the table, running his hands over the backs of the seats. He stopped when he reached the end. Gently, he placed a hand down on the armrest of the advisor's chair. Whereas the king's seat was sharply angled and detailed with colour, the other chair was smooth and plain.

"It's nice, isn't it?" The voice behind Kael startled him. He jumped and pulled his hand away, as if the chair had suddenly burst on fire.

Kael nodded at Yseph. "Yes, very." The small man placed his palms on the armrest, sighing. Kael studied him. "But...if I may, why is it so different? It doesn't seem to fit the style of this room."

Yseph smiled sadly. "My father built this for me," he said after a moment's silence.

"He was a very good carpenter," Kael said politely. His thoughts were turned to Bunda. Her husband had always wanted to be a carpenter. He had only ever made two pieces of furniture...

"Yes, he was," Yseph said, clearing his throat. "I've had this touched up over the years, but I can still remember the day he gave it to me. It was his gift to me when I became the king's advisor. He was so proud." Yseph cleared his throat again. "And then there was a bandit raid..."

Kael's throat tightened. "I'm..."

Yseph waved his hand in dismissal. "Sorry? Don't be. Those bandits are nothing but animals. They should all be destroyed. I loved my father—and my mother. They took them both from me." Yseph's focussed on nothing in particular. "I visit their grave every night to give them... Ah, but never mind me. I ruin the spirit of the occasion." Just then, the double doors swung open. "It looks as though we're going to start soon. You may take your seat if you wish."

Kael nodded as King Henedral rushed in, his cape billowing behind him. He strutted around the table, chest out, a confident smile playing at his lips. He clapped Kael's shoulder and shook his hand.

"Ah, Kael! Let's get this feast on the way, shall we?"

Kael feigned a grin. "Yes, let's."

215

As generals and noblemen entered through the doors, Kael took his seat. After a minute or so, Rooster appeared beside him, looking flustered. Kael had forgotten he had left Rooster when they had been helping the servants get the meal prepared. They must have worked him hard.

Kael was relieved to see that the king's generals were all wearing their armour.

After several minutes, everybody found their seats. Kael was sitting on the king's right, at the front of the wide table, with Rooster sitting next to him. Across from Rooster, to the left of Yseph, there was an empty seat. The king took notice, but didn't seem concerned.

With a flourish of his robe, King Henedral stood, waving his arms. At once, the talkative guests were silent. "Welcome, welcome!" he announced with a booming voice. "I've called this banquet to celebrate the new friendship between our beautiful city, Fallenfeld, and this young man, Kael Rundown." Kael blushed. The king rubbed his hands together. "Now, let the feast begin!"

At once, servants began ferrying food from the kitchen, bursting through a door just behind Kael. Kael perked up, trying to see if any of them were carrying wine bottles on their tray.

A plate of food was placed at the front of the table. It was just bread. Kael frowned. Was their meal going to come in courses? He wasn't used to such a thing. Course meals were for the rich and he had never known anybody rich. Malaricus had nice things, but he didn't have *that* much money.

When a servant placed a glass down beside him, Kael immediately picked it up and peered inside. He sniffed it a few times, just to be sure.

King Henedral laughed. "It's just water, Rundown," he said, "but if it's stronger drink you seek, don't worry. That will come with the main course."

Kael nodded. He let out a sigh. There was still time left before... No matter, he might as well try to enjoy himself and the luxury of such a grand feast. Rooster was. He reached over and snatched half a loaf of bread.

Once Kael sated is hunger with a few buttered slices of bread, the servants took that away and brought him a strange dish. It looked like eggs mixed with cheese. Kael was hesitant at first and poked it with his fork, but once he did try it, he enjoyed it. It had a unique blend of taste.

The doors at the front of the room swung open. From the gold trimming his pauldrons and his multi-coloured cape bearing Fallenfeld's crest, Kael guessed he was the king's main general.

The man hustled to his chair, rosy in the face. Careful not to sit on the hilt of the sword, the man tucked in his cape and slumped into the chair. A servant placed a plate down in front of him and at once, he began to engorge.

The king watched him for a moment, amusement in his eyes. "Trouble, General Grodem?" he mused.

The general shook his head. "Everybody in the kingdom is skittish and our military is on high alert. That dragon that swooped by scared us all. We thought it was going to attack."

Kael hid a chuckle by taking a swig from his glass.

King Henedral frowned. "Yes, that was strange. There hasn't been a dragon here for ages. Do you think it will come back?"

General Grodem shook his head. "Who knows? Some claim the beast is circle above Mount Fell as we speak. It the brute was smart, it would stay away; I've ordered twenty ballistae to be set up. They were just finishing up when I left."

Kael choked on his water. He placed his glass down and coughed, pounding his hand against his chest to try and clear his throat. "What did you say?" he croaked.

General Grodem eyed him over his own glass. "If that dragon comes back, it'll get a pole skewered through its heart. Does that concern you?"

King Henedral, Yseph, the general and even Rooster turned to Kael to see what his answer would be. Luckily, none of the other nobles or generals were listening, so Kael was able to keep his composure in front of the small crowd.

217

"Uh, well, I have a fascination with dragons," Kael said quickly. "They're not as abundant as they used to be—I hear. It would be a shame to kill it."

General Grodem pounded his goblet on the table. "They should all be killed. The world is better without them. They burn down cities, kill hundreds of people and livestock and destroy anything near them just for entertainment. Tell me, Ambassador Rundown, how to they benefit the world? Would it truly be a shame to exterminate them?"

Kael shrugged. "I think dragons have a lot to give the world. There are probably many things we could learn from them."

The general squinted. "Such as?"

Kael hesitated. General Grodem was being nosy. Did they know about him and Shatterbreath? The general was trying to trick him into revealing something.

"I don't know," Kael said. "I just like them. It's nothing different than a person who has a pet mouse. Many people hate them, but to that person, it could be the greatest thing ever."

King Henedral laughed. "A pet mouse? What a silly comparison! Are you saying you have a pet dragon then? Ho, you're a joker indeed!"

Kael laughed as well, glad that the king wasn't as pushy as his general. General Grodem nodded at the king's laughter and lifted his glass.

"Forget we had this conversation then," he said politely.

Kael smiled. But he couldn't dismiss the general's earlier comment. They had set up defences against Shatterbreath. Even her tough hide wouldn't be able to stop a ballista.

There was a small period of time after the second course. The generals and nobles shared lighter conversations between each other. Kael could tell that the next course would be the main, and his heart dropped a notch. Soon they would serve drinks. Soon, he would see if the king trusted him. Soon, he would see if Rooster was correct or Shatterbreath.

Although Kael had just eaten some bread and a small plate of the egg dish, the smells that came with the servants out of the kitchen

218

made him salivate. Another plate was placed in front of him and a moment later, two servants came out carrying a massive platter with a whole roasted pig on it. Kael's eyes shot wide open. An *entire* pig? Just for them? That could last a family a week back in Vallenfend.

They placed the pig down in the middle of the table, putting other dishes down around it. There was no doubt this was the main course. The aroma wafting off the glistening pig was infatuating, but Kael's attention was turned towards the king. In his hand was a clear glass goblet, filled to the brim with an amber liquid.

Servants quickly gave similar goblets to everybody else in the room. Kael stared at his, feeling numb.

The king gave him a wink then stood up, grabbing everybody's attention. "Before we begin the main course, I'd like to propose a toast. Here, we have offered our finest ale on Kael's behalf." He held his goblet up high for all to see. Everybody in the room stood and held their goblets out as well. Suddenly, all eyes were turned on Kael. "Kael Rundown, you have the full support of Fallenfeld's army, as well as the honour of our respect."

"To Kael Rundown," Yseph declared, his eyes full of wisdom.

"To Kael!" was echoed through the room.

Kael stood up slowly, holding the goblet with weak arms. *Ale.* The frothy drink seemed so innocent in his fingers, taunting him with its intoxicating stench. He had a drink once, long ago. He knew he could tolerate the taste and stomach the alcohol, but he feared to bring the glass to his lips. *Was it poisoned?*

The room stayed silent. King Henedral watched him expectedly. Yseph's face was a mask. Rooster made a noise beside him, probably hinting that he should take a drink. Kael studied the table in front of him. He was delaying, searching in vain for some means of escape. All that was in front of him was his used cloth napkin and a crust of bread he hadn't finished.

Kael struggled to say something, but found his throat constricted. He swallowed and tried again. "I'm honoured, truly." The king's smile faltered. "But I don't suppose you have any wine?"

219

A susurrus ran through the banquet hall. The servants stopped hustling around, watching from the sides and even the cooks poked their heads through the door to see why everything had suddenly halted.

Yseph spoke up first. "Fallenfeld's ale is known throughout the land. You'll never have better. It considered a delicacy." There was a darkness brooding in his voice. "And an honour."

"Come now, Kael," King Henedral said, his tone disapproving. "Drink up and let us finish this feast. You said yourself you're in a hurry."

Kael lowered the glass. "I—I don't drink."

"But you requested wine?"

"Uh...yeah. I don't drink...anything strong b—but wine. Family rule."

The nobles started chattering among themselves. With shrugs, a few of them sat back down. King Henedral and his generals stayed standing. King Henedral placed his goblet back on the table. His hands were shaking. Kael could only assume it was out of anger.

"You would rather dishonour us?" he said gently. "After all the hospitality I gave you? After I agreed to help you?" His voice was rising. The chattering in the hall ceased. "Do you not trust us?" He was yelling now. "If you do not trust us, why should we trust you?"

Kael put his hands out defensively. For a moment, he considered just downing the ale in just a few gulps to sate their sudden anger. No, he couldn't take that chance. He started glancing out the window at the far side.

General Grodem drew the sword at his hip. He pointed a finger at Kael accusingly. "I knew it! He is a liar! He cannot drink our ale because the words he spoke were all lies."

Placing the goblet down, Kael shook his head. He drew his own sword, wishing he had his shield still. He had left it in his room because it would have been too cumbersome to bring to the dinner table. "That doesn't make sense."

"Then why have to drawn your sword?" Yseph called out. He had backed up behind the king, who had also drawn his sword.

Kael stood his ground. "Because you have drawn yours," he cried. "Listen, what I spoke was the truth! I just don't...want your ale."

"You seek our help," the king roared, "but you dishonour us by refusing the best drink we have to offer! Such..." He seemed lost for words in his fury. "*Disgrace* will cost you your life! Soldiers, kill him!"

Kael's heart sank. With that last order, he had lost Fallenfeld.

The room erupted in noise. The generals drew their swords, some of more clumsily than others. They spilled their dishes on the ground, shattering the plates and goblets. The nobles seemed to just realize what was happening and started screaming and running to the door.

As a wave of soldiers surged at him, they bumped the table. Kael stumbled backwards and his goblet of ale spilled over his breastplate and down his neck, soaking his chest and tunic. Careful not to get any near his face, Kael quickly picked himself up.

Time slowed as Kael blocked an incoming blade with the flat of his own. Over the angered men, Kael's attention turned towards the window. Ducking under another blade, Kael scooped up his glass and hurled it at the window across from him in one fluid moment. The window shattered, sending coloured glass raining down on Yseph, who had hid near the wall. Kael quickly put his fingers to his lips and whistled.

A crack of thunder echoed in reply. All the men in the room turned to the open window in confusion. Kael knew better. It was no storm.

Taking advantage of the man's distraction, Kael leapt forward and slammed the pommel of his sword into the nearest general's gut. The man doubled over and Kael weaved past him and around the swinging sword of the only general wearing a helmet, all while time had slowed in his perception. Kael elbowed another man in the side of the head and sprang up onto the table.

Kael proceeded to kick plates and glasses at the generals, trying to bide his time. General Grodem's sword came close to Kael's shins and he shoved the roasted pig at the man's face with his foot. The

221

cooked beast toppled the general right over, opening a path straight to the window.

Just then, there was another roar from outside. Shatterbreath was close! Kael avoided two swords as they slashed at his feet and then hopped forward, taking advantage of the empty space between the table and the window.

A massive man moved to intercept his path. Keeping his momentum, he tackled top-speed into the man's gut—having no other choice—and wrapped his arms around the man's trunk-like midsection.

Together, they toppled out of the convenient waist-high window. The tree-trunk man fell over the ledge with a startled holler. Kael managed to get himself upright and vaulted himself off the window's edge, straight towards a rushing blue shape.

The moment Shatterbreath heard Kael's whistle, she rocketed towards the castle, letting loose a roar to let him know she was on her way. As she neared the building, something launched past her. She hesitated, craning her neck to see what it was. Her heart fell. *Ballista.* She hated those things.

A horrible *whoosh* was the only warning she received as another spear-like projectile rushed towards her. She banked to avoid it, but more only came. She cursed herself for venturing so close to the castle before.

One ballista clipped her side. She yelped, more startled than hurt. She was going fast and the majority of the projectiles were missing, but they had set up many and it was impossible to avoid them all.

Shatterbreath growled and set her sights on Kael, who was fighting his way through a battalion of soldiers. Her safety didn't matter. She needed to get him out as fast as she could. If she didn't go fast enough, the soldiers would get to him before she did. That wouldn't do.

The castle was closer now. She grunted and brought her wings forward, cupping the air. Just as she did, a ballista tore through the membrane of her wing. It couldn't have been more inconvenient timing for her. The massive rush of air in her wing forced the small hole wider in her wing until it started to rip entirely. The membrane of her wing split open at about halfway, all the way to the edge, spilling blood to the streets below.

With such a big hole in her wing, Shatterbreath faltered. The tear was too great; the rest of her wing wouldn't suffice to keep her up.

Shatterbreath lurched forward, desperate to use what momentum she had left to keep her in the air. She slammed into the castle wall, but bent her limbs to compensate. A moment later, she pushed off as hard as she could, aiming up as to gain some altitude. Her right wing flapped uselessly and she spun through the air involuntarily. As she did, she spotted a small shape soaring towards her. Belly pointing towards the heavens, she reached up and snatched Kael out of the air as gently as she could with her left paw.

Still spinning slowly, she brought Kael in close. A blinding pain suddenly erupted in her shoulder. Her entire arm went limp and she lost her grip on Kael. His frightened yelp was so piercing. It caused her breath to come up shallow and the spines along her back bristled in terror.

She watched as he bounced off her thigh. She thought right then he would surely fall to his death, but he managed to plunge his sword into her tail just before he left her body. The sting of the sword was a small price to pay.

Shatterbreath was back upright. She pointed her muzzle straight forward and concentrated on trying to compensate for her torn wing.

A ballista struck her tail.

Whipping her head around, Shatterbreath witnessed in horror as the force of the ballista wrenched Kael from her tail. There was nothing she could do as he fell towards the earth at an arch. She kept going straight—there was nothing else she could do.

With a plume of dust, Kael struck something down below. Not a second later, he was gone from Shatterbreath's sight.

"Kael!" she roared. "Kael!"

Then she lost control.

Kael's sword slipped from his grasp as he fell towards the streets of Fallenfeld. The sword seemed to float away as time slowed to a crawl. Slow as dripping molasses, Kael blinked, feeling wind rushing in his face and in between the pieces of his armour. His hands were out and he was falling bottom-first towards the ground.

Somewhere in the back of his mind, he wondered, *would drinking the ale have been a better idea?* Shatterbreath raced away and he could numbly hear her scream something. The noise was distorted due to the wind screaming in his ears.

Then, only a few feet before Kael landed, everything returned to normal.

Kael crashed square into the middle of an awning sheltering a massive merchant hut. He tore straight through it and broke through a crossbeam supporting the booms keeping up the awning. Then, he landed in the hut itself.

Kael coughed. There were stars in his eyes and darkness fringed his vision. He was dimly aware of what had happened and could only sense that he had just survived a great fall. He coughed. He was surrounded by choking dust that blocked out everything except what was directly in front of him.

He tried to stir, but something crunched inside of him. He groaned and closed his eyes for a moment. It felt like a rib or two was cracked. He wiped his upper lip, aware that his nose was bleeding. Collecting himself, he sat up and gazed around, feeling quite dazed.

He was slumped sitting in a crater of carpets and broken pots. He looked up, rubbing his head. The world was spinning before his eyes, but he could see a pillar of light coming from above through a rugged hole torn in the ceiling. Had he done that?

Kael stood up but had to grab onto a cracked beam to keep himself upright. He groaned and struggled to stay conscious as blood rushed to his head. With the rush came the memories of what had just happened. His heart leapt as he recalled it all. He had jumped from the window onto Shatterbreath...the rest was mostly a blur. He stood up straight, brow slanted in concern. *Shatterbreath...*

Kael groaned and slowly climbed out of the wreckage he had made. When he exited the pile, he saw the rest of the hut was no better. It was large, but the extent of the damage created by his rough landing had destroyed most of it. Debris was scattered into the street, the roof was in shambles and almost all the pottery for sale was now broken.

A merchant with a shocked face stood only a few feet away from Kael, his arms reaching towards his ruined shop. When he saw Kael emerge, he became furious.

"Where'd you come from?" He let out an uncouth slur of insults. "What happened? Wh—what have you done to my shop?!"

There was a small group of women watching, their eyes wide. They must have been about his age. Kael avoided their gazes as they stared in disbelief at him, as if he had just fallen out of the heavens. Well, he practically had. Maybe they had a reason to stare.

Kael rubbed the back of his neck and a cloud of dust escaped his hair. How could he explain? He couldn't. "Uh...sorry?" That was all he could come up with. His mind was still groggy.

"Sorry?" the man cried, throwing his arms into the air. His black beard ruffled as he yelled. "Sorry? What...what about my shop? What about my goods? What—what—what is that sound?"

Kael listened for a moment. Bells had begun to ring. Off in the distance, he could hear men's frantic voices. They sounded furious.

"Sorry," Kael said again, spinning around. He bolted the other direction.

"Hey, what? Wait! Stop!"

Before the merchant could say anything more, Kael was gone. He sprinted partway down the street and spotted something. Without

225

breaking stride, he leaned over and snatched the handle of his sword, which had stuck blade-first into a bundle of hay.

Kael flew around a corner, nearly barrelling into a group of men talking among themselves. He squeezed through them, with a barrage of curses in reply. He took some wild turns, ducking into back alleys and weaving through the crowds. In a matter of no time, he had become lost. But it was a small price to pay. The guards hadn't even spotted him.

A dozen or so turns later, Kael stopped. He propped himself up against a straw wall in a back alley, clutching his chest. He coughed, tasting blood and residual dust in his mouth. Wheezing, Kael slid down the wall until he was resting on his buttocks. He closed his eyes and silently wailed.

He had been so close. So close to having another city join his cause.

But only moments ago, the very same people he had become friends with had tried to kill him. And now they were hunting him. And for what? Ale. Because he had refused the ale.

Kael gathered his wits. Suddenly, he was angry. He was furious. He began to tremble, hardly able to constrain himself. He smacked his palm against the wall supporting his back as hard as he could, which made an unsatisfactory *thunk*. *Ale? ALE!* This was all over something as trivial as a drink! Outrageous, obscene!

But then again...

Kael took a deep breath, calming himself. The odour of human waste made him crinkle his nostrils. He shuffled where he sat. He was probably sitting in a gutter right then. Kael whipped his head as he heard a loud noise from the streets. A few soldiers rushed by, disturbing the reeking air around Kael, but they didn't see him.

He relaxed as they passed by. A new odour caught his attention. He sniffed the inside of his breastplate. Ugh! There was still some ale on his tunic that hadn't dried. With a sneer, he picked at something near his neck. He pulled out a soggy piece of crust. Somehow, the last bit of bread he had left on his table had gotten caught in between his armour and his neck.

Kael stared at the piece of bread, saturated in the ale. Was it truly poisoned? Was everything he had done all in vain? Was Rooster correct, or Shatterbreath? But more importantly, *had King Henedral ever even trusted him?* The man could have been playing him the whole time.

Kael shook his head. He would never know. He was about to throw it away when a shuffle caught his attention. Out of the corner of his eye, he spotted a small, grey shape. He had nearly missed in it the shadows, but he knew what it was. A mouse.

He forced himself absolutely still, hugging one knee closer to his chest. Carefully, he placed the soggy piece of bread down a few feet away from himself. Then, he waited quietly for the mouse to return.

Cautiously, the mouse poked its head through a crack at the base of the wall. Its whiskers twitched as it sniffed the air. It considered Kael for a moment. Kael held his breath. The mouse came out of its hole and scuttle towards the crust. Kael let his breath out, careful not to disturb the little creature.

It picked up the crust with its forelegs and began munching away, sitting on its haunches in the filth of the alleyway. Kael watched it intently, the rest of the world melting away. The mouse swooned. Kael's heart jumped.

The mouse dropped the piece of crust. It fell on its side and curled up with not so much as a squeak. Kael stirred, but it didn't. He leaned over and poked it, which he ordinarily wouldn't have even considered. It didn't move. It didn't breath. It was dead. *Poisoned.*

Kael's stomach sank into his feet. He stared at the dead mouse, unable to tear his eyes away. The owner of the house Kael was leaning on would have one less rodent to deal with, but to Kael, it was a deeper revelation. It solidified what he had feared most. It was relieving in a way, but at the same time, dark and ominous.

Shatterbreath had been right.

Kael looked up, fury burning in his eyes. Rooster had been wrong. His fingers tightened around the grip of his sword.

Rooster.

Chapter 22

"Son, wait!" Korjan called.

Tooran flinched and lowered his dagger. Zeptus sneered and clawed at Tooran's wrist, but to no avail. "Father?" Tooran said, brow furrowing. "You finally caught up. Just in time to watch this liar's death."

"No, you can't kill him!" Korjan cried.

Tooran's face twisted. "What? Why not?"

Korjan stepped around Zeptus's ornate desk. Torches lined the walls, bathing the exquisite room in an uncomfortable light which cast eerie shadows over Tooran, Faerd, Bruce and the king's royal advisor. "Because, he is not the threat! King Morrindale is the true plotter! Zeptus is merely a pawn."

Tooran's eyes were full of question, but he merely squeezed Zeptus's neck tighter. "No, Zeptus has a weave over words like none other, I will not let him corrupt your mind to."

"What," Korjan asked, "are you talking about?"

"Zeptus told us the same thing, but I know better. I've seen how he can manipulate people with his voice. He has a...*power,* Korjan, a magic that I can't explain."

The king's advisor tried to speak, but Tooran shook him. Zeptus's purple eyes were wide in fright and his flat, greasy hair was in mess. His purple robes were wrinkled and his silver diadem had fallen off at some point.

"Quiet, you," Tooran snarled. "I will not let your deceitful voice speak again!"

Korjan gave his son a shove. "Let go of him!"

"No!" Tooran shouted. "I have watched for too long as this man corrupted our city and killed our men! I have worked *alongside* him to do so. I followed his orders like a faithful hound, well aware of his foul influence, but unable to disobey. I was a fool, Korjan."

Korjan grimaced. His own son calling him by name hurt Korjan in a way he had never been hurt before. "Tooran," he said softly, "listen to me."

Tooran winced.

"Son." Korjan gently took the dagger from Tooran's hand. "Let him go. Let me see what he has to say."

Tooran's face contorted. His chest was rising and falling heavily and he looked about the room, conflicted. He relaxed his grip, letting Zeptus take a haggard breath. "Fine," he declared. "Let him speak. Let him fill your mind with lies. But I will kill him if tries to fool you too."

Tooran backed away from Zeptus. The king's advisor fell to his knees, clutching his throat. His lip twisted in a snarl and he glared at Tooran for a moment before bowing his head towards the floor, sucking in air.

Korjan took a deep breath, drinking in the rich smell of Zeptus's study. Fear clung to the air. "Speak," he ordered at Zeptus. "Malaricus has told me these things. He told me you've been trying to help us all this time. That you've been...trying to help Kael."

"You're son is very wise," Zeptus croaked. Korjan cleared his throat, irked by Zeptus's scratchy voice. "It is true; I have a control over people like none other. It is my blessing and my curse."

"Explain."

Zeptus laughed uneasily. He stood up, legs wobbling. "It would be a long discussion."

Korjan looked him in the eyes. Purple. The blacksmith shook his head. "And what about helping Kael? Is that true as well?"

Standing erect, Zeptus nodded his head, his jaws working. "The first time that young man came to this castle, I ordered my men *not* to kill him. I've seen others who have tried to uncover our plot. They all died. There was something more to that boy, however. I knew it from the first moment I met him."

Tooran spun around. "That was you who gave that order to spare him?"

Zeptus nodded, folding his arms behind his back. "Yes. That was me."

229

Tooran placed a palm to his forehead. He blushed and walked to the other end of the room.

Zeptus watched him mirthlessly. He took a deep breath. "Despite what it may appear, I have no vendetta against Kael Rundown. Neither am I responsible for the tragedy that the king issued thirty years ago. In truth and in all honesty, this was all King Morrindale's idea. I have been nothing but the voice of his campaign. Unwilling, might I add."

"But you are still to blame!" Faerd roared, clenching his fists. "How can what you do be unwilling? You always have the choice whether or not to do something!"

"I would have chosen death," Zeptus shouted, "than follow the orders of that greedy, loathsome, vile man! Have you, ignorant boy, considered the full situation here? I am a slave! Yes, the dragon's blessing has given me power with words, but I am forced to obey the orders of those in higher power."

Faerd swallowed. His fists were still clenched, but he calmed down.

"Higher power?" Korjan echoed. "Dragon's blessing?"

Zeptus blinked. "Yes. But that is a discussion for another time."

"So you must obey anything the king orders?" Bruce wondered aloud. "That's..."

"Terrible." Zeptus finished the sentence for him. "I must obey the king and none other. Unless, of course, there is someone else who holds even more power than he. But as I see no other who could hold more power than a monarch, I am trapped under his control."

Tooran stepped forwards. "Then death will set you free."

Korjan put a hand to his son's chest. "No. I promised Malaricus Zeptus's blood would not be spilled."

Tooran flailed his arms. "Then what other option is there? Horan was injured and we killed several men to get where we are right now. I will not settle to simply leave him behind. This will solve no solution."

Everybody in the room went silent.

Korjan was the first to speak. "Then we take him with us."

"What?" Tooran barked.

"Pardon?" Zeptus asked.

Korjan shrugged. "We don't have much time, and as you said Tooran, we cannot let this all be for nothing. Zeptus, you can't continue to work as the voice of the king, either. Seeing as killing you would be a shame—"

"Shame?" Faerd laughed. "Ha!"

Korjan continued, ignoring his remark. "Then the only option left is to just...take you."

Zeptus scratched his chin. He opened his mouth to speak, but Tooran interrupted him.

"You don't get a say in the matter. We will vote on it. Who agrees with taking Zeptus prisoner? We will return with him to the cave where he will stay as our captive with us." Korjan and Bruce put up their hands. Tooran growled. "I wish to kill him now, and rid the world of one more pest. It comes down to you, Faerd. You have not voted. What's your decision?"

Faerd rubbed his gauntlets together. He scowled at Zeptus with his lone eye. He gently touched his eye patch, his face contorted as if he reliving the pain of when he had lost it. Korjan watched him closely.

"Let the liar live."

Tooran shoved Zeptus's desk onto its side with a growl. He yelled something unintelligible. "Fine! Bring him with us! He will surely kill us all!"

Tooran stormed out of the room and stood out in the hall, arms crossed, waiting.

Korjan nodded at Faerd. He then turned to Zeptus. "Please don't give us any trouble."

Zeptus sneered. Although he shared similar intentions as Korjan, it didn't make the man any more likable. "I will make it seem as though this is against my will," he rasped, "but truthfully, I am grateful to you. All of you. Th—thank you."

Tooran grumbled out in the hall, pulling a dagger from his sleeve to inspect it.

"What's this?" Bruce's voice piped up. Zeptus cocked his head at the boy. Bruce was pointing at a small clump of blue flowers that

231

had spilled onto the floor. They were lying on the ground beside some purple flowers, surrounded by the broken pieces of a vase Tooran had broken when he flipped Zeptus's desk.

The hubris man raised a thin eyebrow. "That is an extremely rare flower that grows in Icecrow feces." Bruce was about to pick up the flowers, but he stopped, frowning at it. "It was a gift, from the BlackHound Empire. How they got it, I have no idea."

"BlackHound?" Korjan asked.

"Please," Tooran snarled, "let's just get going, alright? It's a surprise the guards haven't come for us already."

Zeptus leaned over and picked up a flower, inspecting it. "Rare and amazing," he said, holding it up in the torchlight. "This remarkable flower can heal almost all wounds. It could fare important."

"Heals wounds?" Korjan asked. Zeptus nodded. "Bring that, we'll need it. Now, let's *go!*"

"Wait." Zeptus walked to one end of his room, putting the blue flower into his breast pocket. He pulled a cloth-covered helmet off the wall. "You used to be a member of the King's Elite, didn't you, *Tooran?* Put this on, and follow my orders. All of you *stay calm* and listen closely. It would be best if we avoided conflict as long as possible."

Tooran put the helmet on and without further delay the group headed into the halls, with Korjan walking tight behind Zeptus. It was hard for him to truly believe that Zeptus was willingly coming with them, let alone helping them to do so. This was all almost too much for him. They had come to kill Zeptus. Their mission had turned into so much more...

To Korjan's surprise, they didn't meet any guards on that level as they worked their way back to the stairwell. To his horror, neither did they find the bodies of the men he had knocked out or killed.

With Tooran in the lead and the rest close behind, it didn't take long for them to reach the stairwell, still unimpeded. Zeptus stopped them.

"Act as though you're my prisoners. Tooran, you're rejoining the King's Elite. Just for now," he said. "Unless a soldier attacks you directly, don't do anything unless I tell you to."

Tooran gestured down the hall. "There will be soldiers waiting for us at the bottom of the stairs. It is our favourite tactic to kill intruders."

Zeptus nodded. "I'm counting on it." He waved a hand down the stairs. "After you."

They worked their way down the stairwell. As Korjan rounded the corner at the bottom, his heart fluttered as he saw that there were seven members of the King's Elite waiting for them. They had been ambushed, as Tooran had suggested.

Korjan's mind began racing, trying to think of a way to escape their situation. He held his breath. There were too many of them! He was about to draw one of his swords when Zeptus stepped forward.

"Evening, gentlemen," he said, raising an eyebrow and giving a small bow with his head.

The soldiers shifted their weight. "Lord Zeptus?" one of them asked. "There are intruders in the castle... Are... What's happening here?"

Zeptus calmly turned and looked at his captors for a moment, as if they were nothing more than his servants. "Why, these are the intruders," he said with a sharp inhalation. "They intruded into my study, probably searching for treasure or the like. We are escorting them to the dungeons." Zeptus nodded at Tooran. "We have their complete compliance."

The soldiers were confused. "Really?" one of them asked, sceptical.

Zeptus scoffed. "Yes. They are under our control, but of course. I convinced them that life in the dungeons was better than no life at all. Seeing no other choice, they agreed to surrender."

The soldier hesitated for a moment. "That's—"

Zeptus cocked his head and scowled at the man. "What? You don't think I can take of myself? I am not useless."

Korjan could tell that the soldiers knew there was something more to Zeptus. But he could also tell they didn't fully understand what that might be. Zeptus himself had mentioned he had some kind of power... What could that mean?

Two of the soldiers took a step forward. "We will help you escort the prisoners."

If Zeptus was upset by this, he didn't show it. "Very well," he said with a nod.

Two shorter men detached themselves from the rest of the group. They came and stood beside Tooran, giving him a nod. Korjan's heart was racing again. Now that had two soldiers *escorting* them! How much more precarious could the situation get?

Without any further delay, the two soldiers and Tooran led the rest of the group through that level and to the stairs of the next. Faerd, Bruce and Korjan kept exchanging glances, as if to confirm to one another that this was all indeed happening.

Korjan sidled closer to Zeptus, making sure the two soldiers in front of them wouldn't notice.

"Could you convince someone to surrender to you," Korjan asked, "if the situation ever arose?"

Slowly and still facing forward, Zeptus nodded. "I could make you stab your own son, just with the power of my voice. In fact, I've done something like that before. How do you think the previous king died?"

Korjan hesitated. He stopped completely, stunned by the advisor's words. Faerd bumped into him from behind with a cough. Korjan jumped and started walking again.

The next set of stairs came and passed. Korjan caught his breath. He was getting tense again. How many levels were there? How long was their ploy going to work? *Were* they actually going to the dungeons? This could all be part of Zeptus's scheme. For all Korjan knew, he could have been telling the truth when he told the group of soldiers they were going to the dungeons. Perhaps he had been lying to Korjan's group. Zeptus had just said himself, he had that kind of power with his voice.

Either way, all Korjan could do was hope for the best. This mission of theirs was looking more and more colossally foolish with each passing minute.

There were more windows on that level, giving Korjan fleeting glimpses of outside. The sun was going to be up soon. He could just the faint glow over the rooftops of Vallenfend. He cursed silently.

"What are you doing?" a female voice called from behind. The voice was so sudden and alarming that Korjan flinched. Everybody whipped around except for Zeptus, who sighed before slowly spinning on his heel.

Zeptus smiled. There was calm, artificial reassurance in his eyes, as if he were about to tell a lie to a child. "Miss Morrindale," he said coolly, "you are up early this morning."

"Everybody is in a fuss," she said through a yawn. "It seems there has been another intrusion. Although I don't think daddy knows yet..."

"A false alarm," Zeptus cooed. "I have the culprits right here, we are taking them down to the dungeons where they belong. I'm sorry if we disturbed you, Princess. We shouldn't have marched passed your chambers. We'll be on our way."

"Just a moment," Janus Morrindale demanded, waving a finger. She scrutinized the lot and Korjan studied her right back.

Korjan had heard rumours about that girl. The king kept her locked indoors, as if afraid any contact with boys would poison her in some way. Korjan would expect such a child to cling to her doorway or hug herself tight, red in the face and too shy to utter a word, but strangely enough, she seemed quite the opposite. She had all but one leg out in the hallway and was leaning towards them, as if curious. She held an air of royalty and Korjan could tell she was spoiled rotten by her father. Ordinarily, she was the type of person the blacksmith would stress to avoid.

"Oh," the princess chirped. "He's not here." Her expression went blank for a moment and her smooth features relaxed. She quickly found herself again. "I thought perhaps that Kael had returned—returned for me."

Zeptus faltered. Korjan narrowed his eyes, confused. What had she just said?

"Excuse me, Miss?" Zeptus asked, recovering.

Janus blushed. She reminded Korjan so much of the king. "Kael Rundown. I met him in the castle. I've been thinking about him ever since. He's come back to see me once before, you know. Daddy doesn't like me knowing, but I do."

Zeptus narrowed his eyes. "I believe you're mistaken, Miss. Kael was here attempting to kill me."

Janus shook her head, her corn-coloured hair waving around. "Nope. He was here to see me. But Daddy's friends kicked him out before he could reach me." Her expression went vacant. "I just know he was here to see me..."

Korjan couldn't help but feel disgusted. He couldn't believe what the princess was saying. It was borderline delusional. He wondered if King Morrindale knew what he had turned his daughter into.

"Very well," Zeptus said. He obviously knew not to pick an argument with the princess. It would only cause more trouble. "If you have nothing else to say, we'll be on our way."

Janus tugged as the sleeve of her magenta nightgown. Her eyes lingered over the small group. To Korjan's relief, she only looked at him for a very fleeting moment. When she spotted Faerd though, her eyes lit up.

"Where'd you say you were taking these men?" she asked. Her voice adopted a formal tone, but there was something more hidden in her words.

"The dungeons," Zeptus croaked. "There will be no exceptions, Miss."

Janus frowned and bit her lip. "All of them? Can't you let the blonde one stay for a while with me? He seems nice; I'd like to...interrogate him."

"Miss Morrindale, he is a dangerous criminal!" Zeptus cried. "You cannot be serious."

Janus stomped her foot. It was an unimpressive display, but Korjan could hear the black-clad soldiers behind him shift their weight. "Let me have him for an hour, then you can have your way with him."

Zeptus only shook his head. "That's enough. We will be taking our leave now."

"Stop!" Janus yelled. Zeptus kept walking. Unsure at first, his soldiers started as well. "Daddy will know of this! He'll punish you again."

Again, Zeptus just shook his head. Korjan and Faerd followed, but Bruce looked noticeably distressed. He came up close to Zeptus. "Aren't you worried?" he asked. "She's going to the king! We'll be caught for sure."

Faerd gave him a nudge, a look of relief on his face. "What are you complaining about? I'd rather face the king himself and his army of secret soldiers than spend an hour with *her*."

Zeptus sniffed and put a finger to his lips, silencing them.

One more flight of stairs, and the party had reached the ground level. A wave of relief washed over Korjan. They were nearly out!

But when they strolled past the main entrance of the castle, Korjan's heart seized. He relaxed a moment later. What was he thinking? They wouldn't go out the front door. How foolish. Zeptus was probably leading them to another secret passageway. In which case, they would just knock out the guards and promptly escape.

Korjan's fear returned as they approached a dark, craggy part of the castle. They hesitated at the mouth of a yawning tunnel that stretched downwards, steep and foreboding. A fetid stench rose up out of the darkened staircase. The smell of corruption and rot.

Zeptus wheeled around to face the two King's Elite soldiers. Tooran took a step back. He eyed both of them for a moment before speaking. "Trudon and Rudoran, I am correct?"

The two soldiers nodded.

"Well then," Zeptus said calmly. He cleared his throat, which did little to soften his rough voice. "Trudon, would you be so kind as to kill Rudoran?"

Trudon and Rudoran both flinched. "Why?" Trudon asked. "What has he done to deserve this?"

237

Zeptus raised his eyebrows. "Why, he's been planning to slit our throats this entire time. Rudoran is in league with Kael Rundown and the dragon. He is a spy."

Rudoran put his hands out defensively. He tried to speak, but Zeptus cut him off.

"Silence! He's been manipulating us, trying to get us down to the dungeons so he could finish us off silently. I was only able to discover this as of recent." Zeptus hesitated. Whether to catch his breath or for effect, Korjan didn't know. The king's advisor's eyes gleamed in the faint light of the dying torch nearby. "His posture gives him away. He stands slightly slouched, as if already guilty of the terrible crime he was about to commit. And behold the way he squints at you, plotting your demise. Murder burns bright in his eyes. You must kill him before he kills us!"

Trudon's face was screwed up underneath his cloth faceguard. "Why?" he breathed. "What is your price? What was your reward for such treason?"

Rudoran stumbled to find words, but his mouth only opened and closed like a suffocating fish. Sweat was visible on his cheeks and he was shaking.

"Look at the fool. He cannot even think of a feasible lie to try and escape with." Zeptus drew close to Trudon. "Kill him now." His voice was low and snakelike. Korjan watched closely, as curious as he was terrified.

Trudon unsheathed a sword seemingly from thin air. He held the handle of the blade so tightly, his knuckles went white. His eyes flitted back and forth and he almost seemed to be whimpering.

Finally, he ran his partner through with the blade. Rudoran managed a gurgle before he fell to the ground dead.

Zeptus smiled down at the corpse. "Very good," he stated blandly. He patted Trudon on the back. Underneath his faceguard, Korjan could see the man grin sheepishly. "Now, Tooran, finish the job."

Trudon flinched. "Tooran? What?"

A knife burst from Trudon's throat. His eyes shot wide then rolled to the back of his head as he died. Tooran withdrew the knife and yanked his helmet off, a look of utter disgust spread across his face. "What was that?" he demanded, short of breath. "I could have just killed them both in a heartbeat."

Zeptus could only shrug. "Rather than explaining my ability, I thought I'd show you. That was a poorly woven story I came up with. With more time and information, I could make anybody do whatever I wanted. Be thankful I wish you no harm."

"Why are we at the dungeons?" Korjan asked, stepping away from one of the bodies. Blood was pooling on the floor.

Zeptus gestured down the stairwell. "Come. We must rescue a prisoner. I imagine his escape would be beneficial to Kael."

With a billow of his cloak, Zeptus started down the stairs. Korjan frowned at his son and sighed. "Is Zeptus our hostage, or are we his?"

Tooran couldn't say. Korjan could see it disturbed him. "Faerd, Bruce, stick close and watch our backs."

They descended into the dungeons of the castle. There was a heavy iron door at the bottom which Zeptus bypassed by pulling a heavy key out of his pocket and twisting it in the keyhole. With an arduous groan, the door unlocked and then swung open.

At once, the sounds of suffering buffeted Korjan. And with it came a terrible concoction of nearly-intolerable stenches. They walked solemnly through the dungeons. Every cell seemed to be filled with an emaciated shell of what used to be a human being. Naked men and women moaned at them, staring with unblinking, sunken eyes as they passed. Those who still had enough energy reached out towards them, their skeletal hands clawing for the lives they used to own. The sight of the newcomers seemed to spur some while others just stayed where they were, making Korjan wonder if they were even alive at all. Dirt seemed to be everywhere, unavoidable, clinging to the inside of his lungs and painting his brown tunic a filthy gray.

Korjan rubbed his arm and shivered.

Suddenly, Faerd pushed past the blacksmith. He grabbed onto Zeptus's robe and spun him around. "How could you do this?" he shouted, tears in his eyes. He shook Zeptus's robe, which seemed to

239

have little effect to the man himself. Zeptus kept his composure as Faerd shook him again. *"How could you do this?!"* Faerd shouted again, nearly hysterical.

Zeptus wrapped his fingers around Faerd's wrist. When he spoke, it was slow and calm. "Understand; this was not what I wanted."

Faerd pulled him close, and swung him around, taking advantage of Zeptus's lost balance. He pushed the man against one of the cells. Zeptus banged his head against the bar of the cell and he winced in pain. Faerd twisted the breast of the advisor's robe with his gauntlets.

"How could you let this happen?" Faerd snarled. "These are good men and women left to rot! You—you left them in here like they were nothing...nothing more than filthy animals!"

Clenching his jaw, Zeptus met Faerd's fiery stare with his own. Faerd only pushed him harder into the bar. A thin man stirred inside the cell, fear in his eyes, but otherwise stayed far away from the bars.

Faerd seemed to deflate. Slowly, he slumped to his knees, his hands running down Zeptus's robe. He grabbed a handful of cloth at Zeptus's knees, staring at the ground, tears streaking down his cheeks.

"You tried to put Mrs. Stockwin in here," he whispered. "You tried to put me in here. You...tried to put Laura in here... How could you?"

Korjan pushed Zeptus away from Faerd and beckoned Tooran and Bruce over. "Bruce, comfort Faerd for a moment. Let's get that prisoner and get out of here."

Zeptus nodded. "Follow me."

Leaving Bruce kneeling beside Faerd, Zeptus opened yet another door at the far side of the dungeons. Tooran and Korjan followed him through.

"Kael stayed in that cell for a time," Zeptus said, pointing to a cell on their left.

"Yes," Tooran said. "I helped him escape."

Zeptus paused, and listened for a moment. Korjan stayed deathly still and held his breath. Sobs and the ghostly wailing of the emaciated prisoners echoed from behind. Through the three or four windows in the dungeons, Korjan could hear dogs barking and roosters crowing. Other than that, nothing. Was there something Zeptus could hear that he couldn't?

Shaking his head, Zeptus kneeled in front of a cell at the far end of the room. It was the only cell that was fully enclosed, with only a small viewing window to look through. Korjan espied a few chests lining the circular end of the hallway, but he paid no more attention to them.

Zeptus peered through the portal. He protruded a key from his pocket and hastily opened the door. The cell had no windows, so it was dark. But even in the darkness, Korjan could see a thin shape slumped up in the corner. When they walked inside the cell, the frail figure lifted his head.

Korjan bent over. He didn't venture any closer. He squinted. The man's skin was...brown.

"Who are you?" he asked the emaciated man.

The prisoner didn't answer, so Zeptus spoke for him. "He is from the BlackHound Empire."

"Was," the limp form wheezed. The man shuffled, struggling to stand up. All he could do was bring himself into a sitting position on his wooden bed. "But I am no more. Have you come to kill me at last?"

"No," Zeptus said flatly. "We have come to set you free. You're coming with us. We know somebody who will want to meet you."

"Is it Commander Coar'saliz?" the prisoner wheezed. "Is he here yet? You are letting me out to die by his hand, aren't you?"

Zeptus shook his head. "You could say he's the leader of a resistance. And these are members of that resistance. They are here to assist our escape."

The prisoner perked up. He found enough energy to stand, but he still had to lean against a wall. Korjan quickly sized up the man. Although he was severely malnourished, he stood straight and proud, regarding them with calculating, war-hardened eyes. He had obviously been a general or leader back in his prime. Scars formed X's across his bare chest and across his shoulders, symbols of the

241

whippings and ill-treatment prisoners were subjected to. Korjan marvelled at the colour of his skin. He had seen very tanned people before, but never skin as dark as his.

"Resistance you say? Hope is not lost. But why have you come to help me? As I recall, you are the one who threw me in this place to begin with." His proud military posture faltered. He hunched over and coughed. "Why have you switched beaks, so to speak?"

"I am the reason you still breathe," Zeptus replied, emotionless. "Like you, I am a prisoner, although my bars are intangible."

"Korjan, Tooran!" Faerd's voice sounded strange echoing through the dungeons. "Trouble!" An audible smack came a second later. "Come now!"

Tooran rushed out of the cell and disappeared to the right. Zeptus for once looked dumbstruck. Korjan stepped towards the prisoner. "Whether you like it or not, you're coming with us. We have no more time for talk."

As easy as picking up an infant, Korjan scooped the prisoner into his arms. The man was so thin, he seemed to weigh next to nothing. With him in his arms, Korjan kicked opened the door to the main dungeon.

Faerd and Bruce stood at ready against a handful of King's Elite and—Korjan's nearly swallowed his tongue when he realized who it was—the *king* himself.

"Uh oh," was all Korjan could manage to say.

Gently, he placed the prisoner down in the corner where the cells met the doorway to the other room. Then he pulled out his broadsword, holding it at the ready. He was aware of Zeptus strolling up beside him.

The king was red in the face. Surrounded by four of his Elite, his fists were clenched like an angry child. "Zeptus, what is this about?" he demanded, short of breath. "Janus informed me you were up to no good."

Korjan swore under his breath. *Janus,* that spoiled—

"I'm leaving, Basal. I'm finished with this—with you. I've had enough."

242

"You're mine, Zeptus!" the king spat. "You are my servant! You cannot leave!"

"Watch us," Zeptus spat. Korjan glanced over his shoulder. Zeptus's scowl was poisonous.

That only made the king even angry. Fuming now, he pointed his finger towards his advisor. The four assassins around him twitched, eager to attack, but remained standing where they were. "You *will* listen to me! Zeptus, I order you as King, stop this folly at once."

Korjan heard Zeptus shuffle behind him.

King Morrindale smile greedily. "That's right. You can't ignore an order, can you? You never have been. Zeptus, obey my orders. Kill these—"

Whump. Korjan whipped around, confused. Zeptus had slumped to the ground. Tooran stepped over his unconscious form and notched an arrow to his bow, pulling so hard that the bow itself quivered as if about to break. There was a strange green orb—no larger than a plum—tied to the tip of the arrow.

"Stop!" Tooran demanded. "Don't move! Not a muscle or I'll kill you all! I wouldn't even think twice"

Two assassins moved in front of King Morrindale and the other two took a step forward. The king cringed in fear. "Stop, you fools! This is no idle threat. But then... Would you dare it, Traitor?" The king's voice was taunting. "If that thing detonated, it would surely kill everyone in this room."

"It would be a small price to pay," was Tooran's reply.

Korjan shifted his weight, unsure what the king was so worried about. It just looked like a simple globe to him. What was the threat? Almost all the prisoners were at their bars now, yelling. They were so loud Korjan struggled to hear what his son said next.

"Now," Tooran said, his voice quavering, "back up slowly. Give us some room. You will let us escape. No trouble, please, or I'll kill you, Basal."

King Morrindale put up his hands. "Please," he said, his void suddenly calm. "Let me leave in peace. I have nothing to do with this. Just let me return to my daughter. It is all Zeptus's doing."

"Liar! Even if that were true, the world would benefit from such a corrupted fool's death. But still," Tooran paused to catch his breath, "I will let you go. Leave!"

Hands up in a defensive stance, King Morrindale inched his way back to the stairs. He turned to climb them, but hesitated, narrowing his eyes. "He's bluffing. Keep Zeptus alive. Kill the rest—including the prisoner." Then, he ran up the stairs as fast as his pudgy body would allow.

Tooran cursed and lowered his bow. He *had* been bluffing.

The four assassins jumped to attack. Faerd engaged one at once, blocking an incoming attack with his thick gauntlets. Bruce stepped back as a shorter assassin locked blades with him. Deciding it wouldn't be the best to use, Korjan sheathed his broadsword and pulled out his two smaller swords. He parried a lunge that had been aimed at Bruce and started to fight the two remaining King's Elite.

The sound of metal striking metal resounded over the moaning of the prisoners. Korjan and Faerd could hold their own, but Bruce was faltering. Korjan couldn't help but wonder where Tooran had gone.

He parried both of his opponent's swords at once and whipped around to see Tooran snap the lock off of a cell door with the tip of his dagger. It swung open and the prisoner inside rushed out. The emaciated women threw herself at the nearest assassin dressed in black, screaming and batting her fists at the man. This proved to be no more than a distraction, but Korjan was able to take advantage.

Blocking a blow, he delivered a slice of his own. His sword raked across the left side of the assassin's chest, opening a deep wound. He groaned and collapsed.

Before the other assassin Korjan was fighting could attack again, Korjan kicked him hard in the stomach, sending him reeling. Korjan quickly sheathed his two swords and pulled out his broadsword once again. Instead of attacking his foe, Korjan sheered the lock off another cell door with one clean swipe.

Tooran had run to the other side of the room by then, seeing Korjan understand what he was trying to do. In a matter of seconds, Tooran had broken three cells open while Korjan had opened two.

The prisoners rushed at the remaining three King's Elite with total disregard for their own safety. The three members of the King's Elite backed off, trying to keep the swarm of angry prisoners away from them. They slashed wildly, but Korjan and Tooran released prisoners faster than the assassins could kill them. Not after long, the prisoners managed to get within the arc of the assassins' swings. Once they did, they overwhelmed the men, pushing them up against a wall and beating them savagely.

Korjan picked up their new dark-skinned companion in his arms. With a look of disgust, Tooran hefted Zeptus to his feet. He shook the man, but Zeptus was out cold. "Faerd," Tooran barked, "can you take him?"

Faerd crinkled his nose. "Really? Me?"

"Now, Faerd."

Not too gently, Tooran threw Zeptus over Faerd's shoulders. The boy shifted him for a moment, then nodded.

Without any hesitation, their group set towards the stairs.

The prisoners took notice and ran ahead of them, cheering. They sprinted up the stairs ahead of Korjan's group. Tooran didn't even have the chance to stop them. They would serve to distract any guards that might intercept Korjan, but he worried they would attract many others.

Leaving the three unconscious King's Elite behind and following the small mob of prisoners, Korjan quickly climbed the stairs. There were more guards waiting at the top. Korjan was relieved to find that they were only young men in blue tunics. Most of them, when the mob approached, dropped their weapons and ran. Those who didn't were quickly overwhelmed by the freed prisoners.

Korjan, Tooran, Faerd and Bruce skirted around the fighting.

"What's the plan, Tooran?" Bruce yelled out. Some of the prisoners had broken away from the fighting and were now following them. "Where do go now?"

Tooran kept up his pace. "I didn't account for so much...obviousness. Right now, the safest way is to escape through the training grounds."

"Training grounds?" Bruce echoed. "Where they *train* the *soldiers?* That's safe?"

"There's a secret passage," he said, slowing his pace. They had turned into a long, tall hallway. A main lobby by the looks of it. "Here, this way."

Two large doors were beset in the marble wall, looking forbidding. Tooran placed a palm on the door, pausing.

"Once we escape, split up and get to the scholar's as fast as you can. We'll regroup there and then get ourselves back to the cave as fast as we..."

He trailed off as he opened the door. The sun poured in, but Korjan's eyes quickly adjusted. His jaw dropped. A handful of mounted cavalry were positioned within several metres of the door. On the back of each horse was member of the King's Elite, wearing shiny black plate mail. When they spotted them standing in the doorway, they raised their maces, axes, swords or flails above their heads and charged.

Tooran and Bruce pulled the doors shut. Once they were closed, Tooran slid a wooden beam across the door, locking it. Not a moment later, the tip of a sword protruded through the wood with a violent wrenching sound.

"Oh, this is just getting better," Tooran cried. He backed away from the door and frowned. Korjan could almost hear the calculations running through his mind. "Aright, follow me. I think I know another way out!"

He motioned for them to follow then sprinted through a long hallway, one which Korjan guessed ran along the inside of the castle walls. He skidded to a halt at a corner, so sharply, Korjan nearly bumped into him.

He notched the arrow he had been carefully carrying, the same one with the small green orb strapped to the tip. He pulled back the string and leaned around the corner. Then, he let it fly and covered himself.

A moment later, there was an explosion.

The shockwave struck Korjan, deafening him. Smoking debris bounce off the walls, landing near his feet. The hallways were instantly filled with thick, black smog.

Korjan was aware Tooran was saying something, but his ears were still ringing. He strained to hear, but couldn't understand. At last, Tooran made a motion with his arm and sprinted towards where the explosion had just originated.

Korjan followed him, rounding the corner. The morning light poured through a massive opening in the wall, blow apart by whatever Tooran had strapped to the tip of his arrow. Korjan stepped through the smoke and over the knee-high lower section that still remained, gawking at the sheer power of what that tiny orb had done.

But they were outside, so Korjan quickly shook his stupor. As far as Korjan could tell, they were at the east side of the castle. The brown-skinned prisoner in Korjan's arms shielded his eyes from the sun, gasping.

"The sun," he said dreamily. "I haven't seen it in ages."

It was then Korjan realized how long he had been locked up.

A prisoner rushed past, jumping in the air. He stopped and shook Tooran's hand. "Thank you!" he said, smiling from cheek to cheek. "Thank you so very much! You've set us free!"

Several other prisoners were dancing in a similar fashion. Tooran looked lost. "Uh, sure." Korjan cocked his head. Tooran had probably never been thanked before.

With a nod, Tooran was off. The five or six other prisoners who had escaped followed suit. Korjan himself ran into the streets, sticking to the alleyways. He weaved around, avoiding any main roads and taking care to keep himself quiet. A few times, the brown-skinned man in his arms whimpered as Korjan rounded tight corners, but otherwise kept quiet.

Korjan could hear the sounds of frantic soldiers off in the distance, back at the castle. He was taking pains to avoid attention, but in truth, he wasn't worried about being intercepted by any guards or Elite. Korjan doubted the king would send his Elite after them. After thirty-so years of keeping his secret task force secret, he wasn't going to just send them searching in the streets.

After what seemed an hour, Korjan made it back to the Royal Athenaeum undaunted. He was relieved when he did too. Even though the man weighed so little, having to carry him for so long had taken its toll on his arms. It didn't help his already hurt shoulder either.

Korjan cast a glance around the area then quickly ascended the stairs to Malaricus's study.

He pounded on the door, feeling his shoulder begin to seize. The door cracked open and the scholar peaked through. Without a word, he retreated back in and a moment later, the door opened wide.

Korjan hustled in and placed the prisoner down on an empty couch. He sighed in relief, clutching his sore shoulder.

"Who's that?" Malaricus asked.

Korjan placed a hand on the prisoner's chest. His eyes were closed and for a moment, Korjan thought he was dead. He was still breathing. Good. Korjan drew away and frowned.

"Have any of the others arrived yet?" Korjan asked.

Malaricus nodded. "Your friend, Bruce, came first. He's over there." Indeed, Bruce was lying down at the far end of the room, sleeping. "Faerd and Tooran are here as well. And...Zeptus."

Korjan turned back to the prisoner, placing the back of his hand on his forehead. "Yes, things didn't go according to plan."

"Well, obviously."

Korjan was aware of all the people staying in Malaricus's room. But there was something different. All the bedding in the room was gone from the floor and they were all dead silent, staring longingly at him. Korjan hesitated. He gave Malaricus a questioning look.

"What's happening here?" Korjan asked, worrying what the answer might be.

"Korjan..." Malaricus said softly.

"No. You can't possibly be thinking..." Korjan's anger spiked. "*We're* hardly surviving as it is, Malaricus! Don't you even dare consider..."

"These people are frightened," Malaricus sighed. "Vallenfend is getting more dangerous by the day. We need to get them out of here."

Korjan shook his head. "No. No, Malaricus. I have too much to deal with already. I can't ferry all these people up the mountain. Not today. Not in these circumstances."

"Korjan, you have to take us with you. We have to leave the city." Malaricus's voice quavered. He was on the verge of tears. "What we've been doing was risky enough, but now... You've stirred up trouble. They're going find us. It's only a matter of time now. The dragon's cave is the only safe place to go."

"No!" Korjan shouted. He glanced at the women and children in the room. A child started crying. "They're not coming with us. How can you possibly expect to support that many people, Malaricus? You're a smart man, think about this. You'd be condemning them. There's not nearly enough food."

Malaricus straightened his back. "They have a better chance up there than down here. We have enough food stored to survive for two, maybe three weeks. I'm sure we can figure something out by then."

Korjan scowled. "How will we get them out of the city?"

"I've bribed a woman at the eastern gate. She's met Kael as well, she believes him too. She's willing to let us out as long as we take her with us. We could go in small groups of people to begin with and then all meet at the base of the mountain. From there, we'll travel together in a big group."

Just then, a door opened up at the back of the room and Faerd stepped out. He beamed when he spotted Korjan and called out his name. Thankful for the distraction, Korjan walked over to him stiffly. He could feel the people's eyes boring into him. He knew that their lives could very well depend on his decision. He could sense they knew it as well. "Faerd, you're safe," he said, clasping Faerd's shoulder.

"Yeah, Horan's doing good as well. Malaricus and..." he lowered his voice, "*Zeptus* made a poultice from those flowers. He's going to live."

"Good." Korjan suddenly felt very tired. "Good. Is Tooran here? I need to speak with him. Watch the prisoner for a moment."

Faerd nodded and ushered Korjan through. Tooran stood as he entered, at once relieved. "Father, you're here at last. I was worried for a time..."

Korjan threw his arms around his son. He didn't know why. Tooran seemed just as surprised as Korjan. Perhaps if he was feeling energetic, Korjan would have thought of something to say about how proud he was. As it was, the only way he could sum up all his emotions was with a firm hug. *When was the last time he hugged his son?*

"I've never had a son," a harsh voice commented. Korjan released his son and gave Zeptus an awkward look. "I can't begin to imagine what it would be like to have him taken away. Nor likewise, to get him back. I—I am truly sorry that we took him away from you."

Korjan scrutinized him, jaw working. All at once, he noticed the bed taken up the majority of the room. Horan was lying in the middle of it, still unconscious. He turned back to face Zeptus.

Korjan tried to find the right words. He tried to think of a way to explain how he had misjudged Zeptus. He tried to put to words how grateful he was for Zeptus saving Horan's life. But he couldn't. All he could do was thrust out his hand. Zeptus considered Korjan and then tentatively took the blacksmith's hand.

"Thank you," Korjan whispered. "I forgive you."

It took several seconds, but Zeptus's hard features softened. It was as though there was warmth flowing from Korjan's hand into his body, melting away the frozen shell he was hiding behind. A sincere smile bent Zeptus's lips—the first occasion Korjan knew of that the man had genuinely smiled. It was right then that Korjan knew his decision to spare Zeptus's life had been just.

Korjan cleared his throat, releasing Zeptus's hand. "It seems we have a problem."

"What is it?" Tooran asked.

"You know about all the people just outside the door?"

Zeptus frowned. "Yes. I helped conceal them for this long. Without my continued efforts though, I'm afraid their detection is inevitable."

"Which is Malaricus's fears exactly." Korjan rubbed his temple. "I'm afraid you just answered a question I had, Zeptus."

The two men seemed to realize the same thing at once, but neither said a word, as if doing so would solidify the problem. Korjan put their fear to words. "We're going to have to move them. We're taking them with us."

Chapter 23

Kael stood atop a ledge protruding out over the forest. Through the thick canopy, he could see fragments of Fallenfeld glittering in the afternoon sun. He clenched his fists and looked past the city that had rejected him, towards the forested mountains across the way. He scoured the scenery, looking for any sign of Shatterbreath.

She had not been taken captive or killed by any of Fallenfeld's soldiers. He knew that for certain. As he had escaped, dodging patrols inside the city, he had heard neither word of Shatterbreath's capture nor demise. Something like that was impossible to ignore. Which meant only one thing. She had crashed-landed. Kael had seen the holes in her wings before he was bucked from her body.

A thin line of smoke curled up from the mountain across the way. Kael narrowed his eyes, pinpointing where it originated. It was the exact same Shatterbreath made mention of days earlier, where she had told him where she figured the bandits were hiding. *Could she have been taken by bandits?*

Kael sighed, feeling utterly hopeless. *Shatterbreath.*

A rustle emanated from the bushes nearby. Numb, Kael turned to it, expecting a deer or some other forest animal to emerge. He gritted his teeth as he realized it was none other than Rooster.

Kael drew his sword. "Rooster!" he barked, startling the boy. In four long strides, Kael had made it over to where Rooster was still clambering out of the bushes. Kael seized Rooster by the neck and hefted him out of the bushes, twisted and threw him into the middle of the clearing.

"You traitor!" Kael yelled. "You are the reason Shatterbreath is gone! You've killed her! You tried to kill me!" His voice went dark. "Now I'm going to kill you."

Jumping forward, Kael lashed his sword out at Rooster, who managed to scramble backwards, dodging the blade. Rooster stumbled to his feet as Kael slashed again. This time, Kael's sword was deflected by a familiar shield.

"No, Kael! I—ugh—I didn't know, honestly!" Rooster blocked two more attacks with Kael's own shield before he was able to draw his sword.

Kael gripped his blade with both hands. "You said you were never wrong! You said they didn't practice that tradition anymore. Rooster, I swear, I'll kill you. The ale was poisoned, you idiot! If I'd have listened to you, I'd be dead right now!"

Rooster grimaced, hiding behind Kael's shield, the tip of his sword resting in the dirt. "Believe me, I had no idea! Kael, you have to trust me."

"Trust you?" Kael roared. "Trust *you?* Why should I do that? You said the ale was fine, yet, it was not. It was poisoned, Rooster, just as Shatterbreath said it was." Kael's hands were shaking now. His hands were squeezing the handle so tight, he could feel a few knuckles crack. "Was this part of your plan the whole time? Hmm? Did your leaders tell you to follow me, just to kill me? Or did King Henedral hire you?"

"N—no..."

"Shut up!" Kael shuffled closer to Rooster. "Then why are you just fine, Rooster? Unscathed. Hmm, why would they just *let* you go? And you have my shield as well. Were you planning on stealing that as well? Did you come back here to make sure the poison had worked?"

"I was bringing it back to you! Kael, you have to believe me, I didn't intend for any of this!" Rooster crouched lower behind the shield, eyes wide and afraid. "I've wanted to help you all along. I swear, I thought they had abolished that custom. I—I had no idea."

With a cry, Kael lunged at Rooster. The sound created by the clash of their swords echoed through the forest, startling nearby birds. With Rooster holding onto his sword with only one hand, having the BlackHound shield in the other, Kael was able to overpower him and he twisted his sword, prying Rooster's from his grasp. Kael drove his shoulder into Rooster's gut and tackled him to the ground. The shield fell from his grasp as they both toppled to the soft earth.

Gauntlets off, Kael struck Rooster in the face. In a feral rage, unable to control himself, he beat Rooster until his knuckles split. At last, Rooster found strength to shove Kael to the side. Without injured ribs inhibiting him, Rooster was first to his feet.

He kicked Kael hard in the side. The blow to his chest was blinding. Kael gasped through a throat of blood, seeing nothing but stars. Kael's hatred towards Rooster was instantly replaced by throbbing pain that seemed to consume him front the inside out.

Time slowed as Kael turned his head. Through a veil of black and red, he was dimly aware of Rooster out in front of him, features warped and darkened by the setting sun. Rooster's foot was raised, ready to strike again. Kael turned his head away, as if refusing to watch would dull the pain to come. Something sparkled in the grass, a familiar shape lying down just beyond his reach; a miniature silver lion snarling towards the sky. Kael reached out towards the lion, coiling his body at the same time.

Time returned its normal pace.

Kael pushed away from Rooster, avoiding the kick aimed for his side. At the same time, he grasped his sword and then sprang to his feet, sending a stab of pain through his ribs. It was worth it. Kael thrust his sword at the young man's face, the tip coming to a stop partway into the young man's cheek.

Rooster stiffened, his face swollen and bloody. Reality was distorting before his eyes, but Kael was coherent enough to pull together his thoughts. "Rooster, Cleaud," he said, trying his best not to slur his words. "Get out of my sight."

Hesitating, Rooster shifted his weight. Kael pressed the tip of the sword harder against his cheek, which had already begun to bleed. Rooster cleared his throat. "Where am I supposed to go? I have no means of transportation."

Kael let his voice go dark. "I don't care. You betrayed me." He faltered, voice cracking. "You may have...killed Shatterbreath. You are responsible for all this. You have been nothing more than a thorn in my side. I never want to see your face again."

Rooster clenched his jaw. His eye that wasn't swollen avoided Kael's gaze. "I—I'm truly sorry for—"

"LEAVE!" Kael screamed. Rooster flinched. He paused for a few seconds longer, gathered up his sword and then wordlessly left.

Kael listened as Rooster headed down the mountain. He sighed, feeling pain course through him. He wanted nothing more than to sleep. His exodus from the castle and recent fight had left him weary and fatigued. If he lied down right then and there, he feared he would sleep for days. He would have gladly done so, but Shatterbreath didn't have days.

Kael turned his attention back towards the mountainside across the valley. Somehow, Kael knew Shatterbreath was still alive. *But for how much longer?*

He wanted to go find her right then, but he was lacking the energy. He would only succeed in getting himself killed if he ran into trouble while searching for Shatterbreath in his current state. Fighting Rooster hadn't helped his situation at all.

Clutching his throbbing side, Kael placed his shield on the ground. He flopped onto his back, gazing at the darkening sky, head resting on the padding on the inside of his shield. Despite his fatigue, Kael couldn't fall asleep at first. He was too worried.

After an hour or so, he started to inspect his sword, picking at the scratches absently. The words *Noble, Strong* and *Proud* still gleamed with their precise beauty. For a time, Kael's eyes traced the lion designed into the hilt. He couldn't help but wonder who had owned the sword before him. Kael yawned. *Had he been a hero,* Kael wondered, *or just another young man sent to die?*

Thoughts conflicted, Kael drifted slowly to sleep.

As soon as dawn hit, Kael sprung awake. Gingerly, he pulled up his tunic. The area around his bruised ribs was a mottled blue and yellow. When he took a deep breath, he cringed. There was no doubt about it, he had a few cracked ribs, to say in the least. As he prepared to set off, girding up his armour, he resolved to do his best to ignore the pain. After all, wherever Shatterbreath was, Kael would bet that she was worse off than he was. A hole in the wing cannot be a comfortable thing.

The sun still hadn't warmed up the land by the time Kael made it to the bottom of the mountain. He watched Fallenfeld as he travelled along the edge of the mountains. The impossibility of his quest seemed greater now. Losing Fallenfeld had been a huge stumbling block. Losing Shatterbreath had been greater.

Kael's heart grieved. He hadn't felt this hopeless in ages.

Positive the line of smoke trailing from the forest was near where Shatterbreath claimed the bandits to be, Kael unsheathed his sword as he entered the forest. Eyes seemed to stare at him from every angle and he found himself spinning around often, searching for an unseen enemy. He was in bandit territory now.

After several hours, Kael was feeling even tenser. He could feel stress trying to choke him. He had no idea where he was. The trees on this mountain grew far apart, thin and tall, providing terrible cover. Whatever pains he took stifling his footsteps was lost sprinting from behind one trunk to the other. It wouldn't be hard to spot him approaching.

Furthermore, the trees' branches were wide and thick, as if hands that were trying to reach the other trees. It set forest in a strange twilight which Kael found extremely unnerving. Occasional beams of light poked through the canopy, lighting up the particles in the air. Kael walked through these often, flinching every time as he mistook whirling seeds for arrows.

Like Shatterbreath's mountain, this forest was very green, if more gently sloped. Moss seemed to cover everything on the ground and at any given moment, there were at least three small streams nearby. Kael brushed past the occasional fern, whose fronds hung heavy like horses' tails. Overall, the forest held an untamed, serene beauty which Kael found quite charming.

Something growled. Kael spun around, sword at the ready. He peered through the trees, scouring the underbrush. Was it a cougar, a bear, a bandit? The growl came again. Feeling stupid, Kael realized it was his own stomach.

Before Kael could try and solve his problem, a new noise disturbed his thoughts. Voices! Kael flung himself behind a large mushroom-covered log, pressing himself tight against the moss.

Calming his breath, he turned his head as to try and listened they came into earshot.

"Oi, the dragon killed Mick, did yeh hear about tha'?" one voice commented. Kael's heard jumped. Dragon. *Shatterbreath?* Who else could it be?

"Mick? Ah, foo. Who gives a lerk about tha' bloke? Probably got too close, anyway. Tol' him not to get too close." Kael studied their voices. They had a strange accent, which was unfamiliar to him. They talked fast as well, making it harder for Kael to interpret what they were saying.

"What do you think we're going to do with tha' beastie?" one of the men asked. Kael held his breath as the man stepped up closer to the other side of the log. Judging by their stench, Kael knew that the two men must have been bandits.

"I dunno," the other man replied. Kael coiled, preparing to strike. "I s'pose we're going to kill it. Tha' thing's more trouble than it's worth. Already killed Mick."

"Yeah, but he deserved it. You said you told him not to get too close. You know what I think we should do with it? We should—"

Kael sprung out of his hiding place. Before either bandit could do anything, Kael slashed at the nearest man's legs. The other bandit shuffled away, watching in horror as Kael climbed over the log. Kael stabbed the injured bandit through the heart and turned to the other.

The bandit, white in the face and trembling, pulled out a rusted falchion, swearing all the while. But despite the weapon, when Kael rushed at him, the bandit turned instead and began to run.

Kael chased after him. They weaved in between the trees, with Kael at an obvious disadvantage due to his armour. After a few minutes, the bandit was several yards ahead. Kael was beginning to worry when the bandit came to a complete stop, pursed his lips and whistled. Keeping his distance, Kael squinted at him, confused. *What had that accomplished.* A moment later, he received his answer in the form of an arrow. The projectile glanced off of his armour, and not a second later, Kael deflected another with his shield.

A hail of arrows erupted from the treetops. Kael bent low and ducked his head behind his shield as the arrows rushed at him. *Clink, clunk.* All the arrows deflected off his shield or otherwise missed. Kael chanced a peek.

There was a palisade up ahead, which seemed to have been hastily put together decades ago and then severely neglected. Most of the logs appeared to be rotten. Kael witnessed as at least a dozen or more bandits poured through a ramshackle gate set near the middle of the wall. Their clothes were brown and filthy, faces caked by dirt and weapons in less-than-ideal condition.

"Yar!" The first bandit descended on Kael, wielding nothing more than a dagger. He was fast, Kael had to admit, but with a kick and a backslash, the bandit was disposed of.

Kael sidestepped past a swinging flail, which made a *thunk* as it slammed into the ground. Kael cut him down as well, but only more bandits descended.

Fury escalating, Kael cut down the bandits as they approached him one by one. Eventually, they seemed to realize that they would have a better chance attacking all at once. It didn't matter. Time began to crawl as Kael engaged the enemies.

Kael deflected a hammer with his shield, ducked underneath a sword, and kicked the bandit holding the hammer. Whipping around, he cut two exposed throats and then bashed yet another bandit in the face. He was unstoppable as he weaved, parried and slashed in distorted time. No matter how fast they were or what weapon the bandits were using, they were no match for Kael. He could react to anything in less than a second. They were simply not quick enough.

In a matter of minutes, Kael had slain more than fifteen men. He stood surrounding by gore, panting, flustered. An archer up in a tree nearby shot an arrow at him, but Kael easily dodged it.

"Where is she?" Kael screamed, his own breath hot in his face as a gentle wind blew by. "You cowards, where is she?"

Another arrow sailed past, spurring Kael into action. He sprinted towards the gate set in the palisade. It began to close as he neared, but he dove inside, sliding on his stomach several feet before rolling over his shoulder back onto his feet. He slew the man at the gate before turning his attention towards the bandit encampment.

There were several dozen houses placed at no apparent order within the shoddy walls. The houses themselves were nothing more than shacks, with sinking, thatched roofs and in the same neglected, rotting condition as the palisade. Mud was everywhere, filling the camp with the overwhelming smell of earth. When Kael took a step, his boot stuck to the mud and he found it a growing task just to walk without stumbling. Even the walls of the shacks themselves seemed to be covered in mud—not just in between the cracks, but all over, as if the bandits had arbitrarily decided to just smear it all over their houses.

Drinking in the scene, Kael took a deep breath. There were already archers set up in near houses and bandits holding more shoddy weapons. Out of the entire camp, there was only one man riding a horse.

"Keep him here, brothers," the man on the horse yelled, raising a two-handed hammer. "Don't let the lerk get any further."

"I'll cut you all down!" Kael hollered in reply. "I swear I'll kill you all if you've hurt Shatterbreath in any way."

The bandit on the horse cocked his head. "Shatterbreath?"

With a cry, Kael rushed towards the group of bandits. It was reckless, but he was beyond the safety of himself. All he could think about was what the bandit had said earlier. *I s'pose we're going to kill it.* He needed to get to Shatterbreath before they finished her off. He didn't care how many bandits he would have to kill to do so.

The first three bandits fell without any trouble. They were so startled by Kael's bulrush; all they could do was stare in fright as he hacked them down. The rest of the bandits collected their wits and engaged Kael. These men were better trained, and there were more of them. Even with Kael's ability to slow time, he found it a struggle to keep ahead of their motley assortment of weapons. To make his situation worse, every once and a while, the man on the horse would sweep through, taking a swing at Kael with his huge hammer.

It was then Kael realized how bad of an idea this all was. His rescue mission was beginning to seem more like a suicide mission with every passing second.

The bandits began landing blows. A sword rebounded off Kael's armour here, a mace glanced him there. Kael winced every time, not only because it hurt, but because his beautiful set of armour was getting ruined. His shield was collecting dents and scratches as well, and indeed, the chips in his sword had already doubled.

Kael wasn't going to give up, however. He would fight until he saved Shatterbreath, or die trying.

The bandit on the horse swept through, narrowly missing Kael's head. Kael watched him in his peripherals. The bandit turned the horse around, brandished his hammer, and then charged forward. Kael panicked. This time, instead of sweeping past, the bandit was aiming straight for him! Thinking of no other solution, Kael readied his shield and lunged as the horse neared.

Kael struck the beast in its shoulder. The force of the blow sent knocked Kael off his feet and he tumbled backwards. The horse whinnied, lost its balanced, and then tripped. The bandit was bucked from its back. Unfortunately, he was better off than Kael.

As Kael looked up, the bandit was already rising to his feet. Kael tried to get up as well, but his body wouldn't obey. A spasm of pain lanced through his lower chest and he clawed through the mud, trying to find support. The bandits around him had stopped to watch as the man who had been on the horse walked over to Kael. His hair was dark, features hardened. Vengeance could be read upon his face.

Kael summed up his energy and stood up on his feet, which took a great deal of willpower. The black-haired bandit raised his hammer high above his head with both arms. Kael gasped and cowered behind his shield, placing his sword out in front of him, as if that would add an extra degree of protection.

With colossal force, the bandit brought down his hammer. The strike hit Kael harder than the charging horse. He felt bone crack in his shield arm and his sword, which had been pressed against his shield, shattered.

Kael slumped over backwards, the ringing of his breaking sword echoing through his ears. His left arm was numb for a moment or two, but seconds later, erupted in pain. The handle of Kael's broken sword fell uselessly away from him.

This was the end. Kael was defeated. He remained motionless, lying in the mud which oozed around him. He could feel blood flowing out of his nose, but he couldn't do anything about it. He had neither the energy nor willpower to move. The black-haired bandit moved into view, twisting the large hammer in his grip. He swung the hammer towards Kael's head.

"Oi, wait!" a voice called out. The hammer stopped a hand's breadth away. "Leave him."

Kael tried to move himself so he could see who his saviour was. He could hear the squishing of feet moving through mud and a shadow fell over him. As blackness crept over his vision, somebody leaned over him. Hands reached out towards him.

Kael passed out.

Chapter 24

Korjan leaned over the prisoner. Gently, he touched the man's dark skin, as if to confirm it was naturally that colour. He had never seen such a thing. The prisoner moaned in his sleep, his face contorting. In the background, children were crying. Their parents were trying to reassure them, but they didn't seem very convinced either.

Korjan did his best to drown them all out. He didn't want to face this undertaking quite yet. Instead, he turned to Malaricus, who was fiddling with a pack. "Would those blue flowers work to cure this man?"

Malaricus glanced at him and continued to fix his pack. "No. Unfortunately, the flowers work to cure disease and accelerate healing. This man is neither diseased nor injured. He suffers from malnourishment. We have to get him to eat some real food, and drink some water." Malaricus scanned over the people in his study. "But it seems that will have to wait. Korjan, we're all ready."

Korjan nodded. He gulped and then turned around. "Listen up," he said. It wasn't a necessary thing to say. Everyone was already listening; they seemed to have adopted him as their leader right away, even though it was Malaricus who had looked after them for all this time. "We're leaving, tonight. I'm not going to make this sound like an easy task. It will be dangerous. I can't ensure all of your survival. So stick close. Obey *everything* I say. Don't move until I say you can, don't speak until told to, don't even *look* somewhere I don't want you to."

Eyes were going wide. Jaw working, Korjan hesitated to drink in their expressions. He continued. "The most dangerous part will be exiting the city. You will be split into three groups, led by Bruce, Faerd and I. Once we're outside the gates, we will regroup. I cannot stress enough that we have to be absolutely silent. If anybody *unfriendly* notices us, it could spell death for you all. Splitting into three smaller groups rather than one large one is more discreet, but with only one escort, harder to defend. Try not to get noticed."

Malaricus nudged Korjan. "What of Tooran and Zeptus? You're not leaving them behind, are you? I doubt these people will be happy with Zeptus mingling with them. And there's also Horan and the prisoner to deal with..."

"Tooran is going to follow behind us with Zeptus," Korjan whispered. "We'll figure out what do with him once we're up there. You still have that donkey, right?"

Malaricus hesitated. "Yes, I keep her near the eastern gate."

"We'll put Horan on there to start, and then switch him for the prisoner as we go. I'll carry one of them until we stop and make a stretcher."

Admiration gleamed in Malaricus's eyes. "You're a good man, Korjan."

Korjan bit his lip. "I'll feel better once we're all up the mountain. I swear, Malaricus, I'll get you back for all this one day."

Malaricus chuckled. "Sure."

Casting him a fleeting smile, Korjan clapped his hands together. He wasn't sure about the whole ordeal yet. There were too many things that could go wrong. Still, he couldn't leave all the people there to die by the king's soldiers. Malaricus was right, they had a better chance of survival climbing up the mountain than staying still.

It didn't take long to separate the people into three groups. As it worked out, Bruce and Faerd were put in charge of two families, and Korjan three. Bruce was given the smallest family, and two of the four men that were there.

After Korjan gave him some instruction, Bruce left Malaricus's study. Korjan watched the boy through the window as he led the families through the streets. Morning was just breaking, so it was going to be harder to avoid guards without the cover of night. Hopefully, if the women and their children stayed calm, the whole precession would look like nothing more than a large family going out for an early-morning picnic.

Korjan let out a slow breath, trying not to show how nervous he was. His heart was pounding in his ears, so loud, he could barely hear himself as he directed Faerd's group to leave. Malaricus was leaving with Faerd, but he paused at the doorway, tears rimming his wise eyes.

"I never thought I'd have to leave this place," he said with a sniff, "especially under such circumstances. Oh, I hope King Murderdale gets what he deserves."

"Don't worry," Faerd grunted. "He will. Come on, Malaricus, let's go. See you in the forest, Korjan."

Then, it was just Korjan's group left. He eyed them over. His thoughts were turned to the women he had left up in Shatterbreath's cave. It was then he realized, these people shared the same cause as him. They believed in Kael. They were family. It hadn't been his keenest interest to escort them before, but now, he felt a great drive to keep them safe.

"It's our turn," Korjan said, scooping Horan up in his arms. "You there, he said, pointing to the other man in the group. "What's your name?"

The man cleared his throat. "Uh, Dresda."

Korjan sized him up. The man, perhaps in his late twenties, stood straight, but slouched his shoulders, telling Korjan that he was a disciplined man, but not necessarily confident. Underneath his slender brow, his eyes darted around the room, pausing to match Korjan's gaze for fleeting moments at a time. His chestnut hair was cut short and wavy and a beard covered the forefront of his face. He was the kind of man that would diligently follow orders. Korjan liked him already.

"Pick up this man and carry him. Stay close to me," Korjan ordered.

Dresda nodded. "Of course." He shuffled over to the prisoner, but hesitated. "His skin's brown..." A few children rushed over to see what he was talking about. "Won't this attract attention?"

"Wrap a blanket around him," Korjan said sharply. "We have to get going."

"Okay." Dresda nodded at a young woman. She looked to be his age. By his sheepish grin as he addressed her, it wasn't hard for Korjan to deduce that Dresda liked her. "Could you give me a hand, Laindy?"

Laindy seemed less impressed with him than he was with her. Korjan rolled his eyes. *Young love.* After a few minutes, Dresda and Laindy had wrapped the prisoner in a blanket, so that only his face was showing. The disguise was poor, but Korjan was confident that the blanket would draw less attention than an emaciated, brown skinned man from another continent.

Without further delay, Korjan led his three families out of the Royal Athenaeum. There were a few citizens meandering out on the streets. None of them paid any attention to Korjan's group, which was making its way along the edge of the street, heads down, arms tucked close to their bodies.

Korjan didn't have to tell the people he led to stay silent. They knew how precarious the situation was. They took the most direct route to the eastern gate, while still giving the castle a wide berth.

At one point, a lady came up to the group. She started chatting excitedly to one of the mothers Korjan was leading, remarking on how long it had been since they'd last seen each other and where she had been. Despite how clear the mother was letting the other woman know she did not want to talk, the lady kept rambling on.

They couldn't spare the delay, so Korjan approached the chatty lady. "Go away," he grumbled, sparing the formality.

"Who do you think you are?" the lady gasped. "Don't you know who I am? I'm Berenson's wife! You have no right to talk to me like that, peasant."

Korjan wracked his brain. Where was that name from? Berenson was one of Vallenfend's richest merchants. "Excuse me, Miss, I had no idea. Go away, *now.*"

The lady put a hand to her chest. "Why I never! I don't know who you are or why in the world Netelia would be following you...but nobody speaks to me like that! Oh, I'll have the guards after you! *They'll* teach a heathen like you some manners!"

Korjan leaned in close, which wasn't necessarily easy with Horan in his arms. "Let them try. Group, move on." Korjan turned his back on Berenson's wife, leaving her flustered. He caught a glance of Netelia, whose face had gone bright red. She shrugged at

Berenson's wife and then followed Korjan and the group as they walked on.

This only made the lady angrier. "Ooo, I'll show you all! Guards!" she screamed. "Guards!"

Korjan cursed and broke out in a dash, motioning for the rest of the group to follow. He had been hoping Berenson's wife was bluffing. Evidently, she *was* snuck-up enough to call the guards over something as trivial as this.

Her voice disappeared through the din as Korjan and the rest entered an open area. It was a clothes market by the looks of it, one which Korjan didn't recognize—he didn't often go to this side of the kingdom. He scanned the area as women hustled about the market, carrying bundles of clothing and trying to keep their children behaved.

"Stick close," Korjan ordered over his shoulder. "If you fall behind, we're not stopping to wait for you."

Korjan shouldered his way through the market, causing more than a few women to drop their bundles. He received many angry shouts and one woman even tried to hit him, but he did his best to ignore it all. Dresda was beside him the whole time, wincing and repositioning the prisoner in his arms.

"K—Korjan, right?" he yelled over the sound of the market.

"Yes?"

"I don't mean to be a bother, but, he's getting heavy." Dresda nodded at the wrapped up man in his arms. "I don't think I can hold him for much longer."

Yelling from behind interrupted the conversation. To Korjan's horror, soldiers had entered the market. He ducked down, but it was too late, they had already spotted him. The crowd, which had been busy before, was now thrumming. Women and children alike started screaming, trying to escape the market as fast as they could, which was also impeding the soldiers' progress.

Through the chaos, Korjan spotted a cart resting beside pillar. He pointed at it. "Dresda, there!"

Korjan shoved his way through until they had reached the modest handcart. Gently, he placed Horan down on the blue clothes that filled the inside and then helped Dresda do the same with the prisoner. "Get out of here as fast as you can," he told Dresda. "I'll fend them off and catch up later. Don't worry about me."

Dresda grunted as somebody ran between him and Korjan. "But what about you?" he asked, eyes wide. "I'm not brave. I—I can't lead these people!"

Korjan placed a hand on the man's shoulder. "Yes you can. They're your family, you must protect them."

Dresda seemed unconvinced. Before he could say anything else, somebody screamed. Korjan heard a shuffle behind and whipped around in time to parry an attack aimed for his head. He struck the soldier across the face, knocking the man to the ground. With a kick, the soldier was unconscious.

"Go!" Korjan screamed, drawing one of his thin blades. He watched out of the corner of his eye as Dresda hefted the handcart then joined the group as they followed the last of the fleeing crowd out the back exit.

With them out of harm's way, Korjan turned his full attention to the guards. There were six of them in total, with all of them being female except for two soldiers wearing blue tunics. The men were young and frightened, just like any other recruited soldier Korjan had ever met, but the women were more experienced. They were the long-term guards, and already, Korjan could tell they knew how to use a sword.

All at once, the female guards rushed at Korjan. He blocked three blades and swept under another two, tripping a soldier in blue as he did. The sound of battle quickly replaced the din of chaos that had filled the marketplace moments earlier. Korjan blocked, parried and dodged ever attack the six guards threw at him, but he was beginning to lose. A sword glanced his tunic here, another narrowly missed his leg there. He was slowing down, and his hurt shoulder was doing little to help.

Korjan deflected a blade and stepped back, conscious that the guards were trying to surround him. With his other hand, he hurled one of his swords at a soldier in blue to his side. The blade did little harm, but it let Korjan work his way further back, so that all the soldiers were once again in front of him. It also gave him enough time to draw his broadsword.

Every soldier put out their sword to block Korjan's wide swing. His blade missed the first three guards, but clipped the fourth, whose weapon slipped from his grip. Stopping short, Korjan twisted his grip and brought the blade back in a savage diagonal backslash. With a cry, the guard fell down, a wide gash spread across her chest. The wound was serious but hopefully non-lethal.

The best chance Korjan had to survive would try and pick the soldiers off one by one. He moved in close to a soldier who was standing slightly off to the side. Korjan hesitated as he saw the fear spread across his face. He realized right then, this boy was no different than Tooran. *Taken by force.* Moved by compassion, Korjan strike him with the pommel of his sword, knocking him out but not killing him.

Korjan held his blade against his back, successfully blocking an attack from behind. He spun around on his heel, catching a guard in the side with his sword. That guard too fell down writhing. Korjan watched with little amusement. He wasn't sure if that one would survive. But with his options so limited, there wasn't much else he could have done. Steeling himself, Korjan brandished his sword and faced the remaining three guards.

The fright in their eyes was all too evident. The soldier in blue started to shake as he glanced down at his fallen comrade. Without a word, the boy threw his sword to the side with a sob and sprinted out of the marketplace, leaving only two more guards remaining. Judging by their similar light hair and features, Korjan guessed they were related in some way.

One of the guards dropped their sword and put their arms forward. "Wait," she said, "Stop! We don't want to fight you."

The other guard also put down her weapon. "We meant no harm, really. My name is Jenfer, and this is Wendla. We want to come with you. Please, can we come too?"

Taken aback, Korjan stood up straight. "How do I know I can trust you?"

The first woman who had spoken, Jenfer, shook her head. "I'm sick of the king, I'm sick of his advisor. I sick of all the lies. I had to walk past the Athenaeum on the way to my patrol area. I could see what was happening up there, but I didn't turn them in. I wondering was when they would be leaving. When I saw Malaricus leave, I got my answer. Please, we believe in Kael too. Take us with you."

Korjan considered her words. It was because of her all those people were even alive. If any other person had been patrolling that area... If they would have alerted the king... "It's the least I can do," Korjan said. "Stick close and stay quiet, and you may come along."

"Really?" Wendla exclaimed. "Truly? Oh, thank you sir! Finally, we can be free of King Murderdale and that loathsome Zeptus! Thank you, thank you!"

Korjan gritted his teeth as he sheathed his sword. *Not entirely.*

Korjan instructed the two women to pick up their weapons. After gathering his equipment together as well, he and the guards exited the now-bloody marketplace. The streets outside were quiet.

"We must make haste," Jenfer said behind Korjan. She stepped out ahead and peered around a corner. "Where are we going?"

"Eastern gate," Korjan replied.

"More guards will be arriving shortly. I will go on ahead a few streets to make sure all is clear. I'll let you know if anything is wrong."

Korjan nodded. "Keep within sight if you can. I'm not waiting if one of you gets lost."

Jenfer. "I understand." With that, looking to and fro, she led on.

As they moved away from the marketplace, the streets became busier. It seemed that not everybody knew about the incident yet. Korjan could only imagine the gossip that would be going around the next day. It would create quite a stir.

With the Jenfer leading ahead, their flight from the marketplace went smoothly. There were a few instances when soldiers rushed past, but by the time they reached Korjan, he and the Wendla would hide first, having been alerted by Jenfer up front. It was a brilliant strategy, one which Korjan wished he could have employed to begin with. He couldn't help but to wonder how well Dresda had escorted their group.

Several minutes passed by until Korjan and the two women had reached the gate. They crept up to it from the side, trying to do their best not to be seen. They were nearly out, but they had to keep up their caution.

There was a female guard up ahead, with long brown hair. She shifted her weight uneasily, glancing around. This was definitely the woman they were supposed to meet. She espied Korjan as he approached, but did not greet him. Ever so slightly, she turned her head and at her side, waved her hand. The gesture was small, but the message clear.

Korjan halted at once. One of the women behind him bumped into him.

"Oof! Hey, what's the holdup?" Jenfer whispered. Korjan scanned the gate and surrounding area. He couldn't see anything.

"I don't know," Korjan said softly, still surveying the scene. "Something's wrong."

"There's nothing here!" Wendla said. "We're nearly there, let's just go."

"No," Korjan hissed. She went anyway. "Stop!"

It was too late. Wendla walked straight up to the gate. Korjan could clearly read the agony across soldier's face guarding it.

Something suddenly sprang from the gate above. Before Wendla could register what it was, it descended on her. With a scream, she crumpled to the ground as the dark figure landed on her. Rising up, a man clad in black pulled a blade from her chest. Jenfer screamed.

"Wendla, no!"

Korjan drew his double axes as two more King's Elite sprang down from the wall. Drawing their weapons as well, they stood posed beside the first assassin. Korjan cursed. *How many of these guys were there?*

"You killed my sister!" Jenfer cried. "You monsters! I'll kill you all!"

Jenfer rushed towards them, waving her sword out in front of her as if to cut them down like wheat. It was too late for Korjan to stop her, so instead, he hurled one of his axes. As the first black-clad assassin reared to smite Jenfer, the axe struck him in the chest. His swing went wild and he missed. At full speed, Jenfer tackled into him, sword first.

Korjan charged towards them, throwing his remaining axe. One of the assassins took notice and sidestepped the weapon, which whirled passed him harmlessly. He broke off to engage Korjan as his comrade attacked Jenfer.

Korjan pulled out his two smaller swords just as the black-clad man reached him. They locked blades for a heartbeat, then broke off. As Korjan fought the man, he could see Jenfer also fighting in his peripheral vision. The guard that had been at the gate had joined in as well. It was hard to tell, but it seemed as though the two women were doing well against the King's Elite assassin.

Pulling his full attention back to his opponent, Korjan doubled his efforts. The assassin was having difficulty blocking both of Korjan's blades. Korjan took advantage, kicking him the chest. With the soldier reeling, Korjan moved in for the killing strike. He lunged with his right arm, but the soldier managed to recover in time to pin the sword with his own. Before the assassin could do anything else, Korjan raised his other arm to finish him off.

Suddenly, his shoulder seized. Korjan faltered. The assassin pried free of Korjan's hold and slashed him across the chest. The blade glanced off Korjan's breastplate. But not a moment later, a brilliant pain erupted in his face as the assassin struck him with a heavy gauntlet. Korjan stumbled back, dazed. He was aware of something warm under his nose and stars danced across his vision.

Another flash of pain cracked across his cheek, then the other. The assassin punched Korjan once more in the chest then delivered a spinning kick to his stomach, knocking him off his feet. As he glanced sideways, he noticed Jenfer wasn't faring well either. She and the guard were struggling to keep the soldier attacking them at bay.

"Go!" Korjan roared. "To the forest, it's safe there. Leave me!"

The man clad in black cocked his head and moved slowly towards Korjan. Gulping, Korjan attempted to stand. To his side,

Jenfer and the gate guard attacked their foe at once. The attack failed, but proved effective to open a chance of escape. The two women turned and sprinted out the gates, leaving Korjan alone. The assassin had reached him by then. Before Korjan could attack, the assassin kicked him in his hurt soldier. Korjan dropped both swords, clutching his injury.

When he opened his eyes, the first thing he saw was a fist racing towards him, and then stars as it collided with his cheek. The force of the blow knocked Korjan unconscious. The assassin rubbed his fist. "Ah, at last, we have you." He crouched down low beside Korjan. "Death will not be a luxury you taste quite yet. The king will want a *word* with you first. Leave the women be and help me take him to the dungeons."

"Aye," the other Elite said.

Together, they picked up Korjan and carried him away.

Chapter 25

The first thing Kael was aware of was pain. Throbbing pain. He moaned as with each heartbeat, there seemed to come a greater pressure to the inside of his skull. He cursed when he rolled his eyes underneath their lids. Even his eyeballs hurt. His body ached. Kael was so stiff, he could barely even move his fingers without wincing. His arm, it seemed, was the worst. Despite the cast he discovered he was wearing, it felt as though his forearm had been trampled.

The next thing he felt was urgency. Wait! Where was he? What happened? The last thing he could remember was...fighting...a hammer...somebody's voice. Kael shifted where he lay. There was a wool blanket over him and he seemed to be resting on a hay mattress. Carefully, Kael opened his eyes a crack. It took a few seconds for his eyes to adjust, but eventually, the inside of a small wooden shack presented itself to him. Light poured in through an open doorway to one side of the room and squeezed through the scattered cracks in the walls. Beside him, his sword was sheathed and lying on a squat cabinet. Kael shifted some more to get a better look at the rest of the room.

"Oi, he lives!" a cheery voice exclaimed. "You give me a scare for a time ther, son."

Kael shot wide awake. He pushed himself upright in his bed, which only succeeded in giving him a splitting headache. Pressing his hands against his head as if to keep it from bursting, Kael forced himself to stay calm. The man who had just spoken was sitting on a chair nailed together by branches. He smirked at Kael, arms folded against his bare, dirt-stained chest. A tattered vest was draped around his shoulders, as brown and worn out as his baggy pants. His hair was cut poorly, with sections varying in length. Through his carefree, passive expression, Kael could detect wisdom. His smile broadened, exemplifying his dominant lower lip.

"More than that, you give me men a scare too. Quite the fighter yer are."

Kael clenched his jaw, placing both hands behind him to support himself. "What? Where am I? Who are you?"

The dirty man squinted, leaning further back on his precarious chair. "M'name's Tomn. And you, sonny, are in bandit territory."

Kael gasped and reached out for his sword. When he pulled it free of the sheath, he was shocked to find only half a blade came out. Then he remembered. His sword had shattered. Kael's spirits sank. He twisted the handle in his grip. *Noble, Strong, Proud.* Not anymore. He let the handle fall to the floor.

"Ah, yeah, sorry 'bout that," Tomn said. "But considering what you did you my people, it's a small compensation."

Kael frowned. "What do you want with me?"

Tomn smiled and clasped his hands together, leaning forward on his chair. "Ah, you're straightforward. I like yer. All's I want is some questions answered. Is that too much ter ask fer?"

"I'd rather die than fraternize with bandits," Kael spat.

Tomn laughed heartedly. "Ho, ernt yah ther blitty, yah lerk!"

Kael cocked his head. The bandit's accent was so thick, it was nearly impossible to understand what he was saying.

"Bandits?" Tomn scoffed. "That's all yeh see us by? So judgmental, tsk, tsk."

"It is because of *you* I was refused by Fallenfeld. It was because of you Shatterbreath is dead."

Tomn scratched his chin thoughtfully. "Fallenfeld, eh? Shatterbreath, huh? Tell me, what were yer doin' in Fallenfeld?"

Kael flopped down in his bed and stared at the ceiling. "It doesn't matter anymore."

"Well, of course it does!" Tomn rose from his chair and stood beside Kael. "If you tell me what yer were doing in Fallenfeld and why they done kick you out, I'll tell yeh about Shatterbreath."

Kael shot a wary look at him. "What did you say?"

"I'm taking that dragon's name is Shatterbreath," Tomn said, raising a brow. "And seeing how yah came in, all raged up, I bet that beastie means sommat to you. Now, like I politely asked before, let's talk."

"Is Shatterbreath okay? Is she hurt? Where is she?! Let me see her!"

Tomn placed a hand on Kael's chest and shoved him into bed. "Listen, sonny," he said darkly. "I'll let yeh see her. Explain to me first, why so many of my men had to die."

Kael hesitated. "*Your* men?"

The bandit chuckled. "Aye. You was talkin' ter the king of bandits and yeh didn't even know it. Why did Fallenfeld kick you out?"

Kael rose into a sitting position. "I'm not really sure. I think mostly because they're worried about bandit attacks."

Tomn frowned. "Ther always worried. Why would they kick yer out fer that?"

"I needed their help..." Kael trailed off, wondering if telling the bandit king about his quest was a good idea. "To defend against and invading empire from overseas. But because joining the fight would leave them defenceless to...your *people*, they didn't think it was a good idea."

"That's it?"

"Well, I don't think they trusted or believed me either. I don't know. Let me see Shatterbreath now."

"An invading empire yer say? Ernt tha' the blitty then... I'm sorry if we caused this on yer—what getting kicked out en' all."

An apology? Kael was the one who had just killed several of Tomn's men. *He* should be giving an apology. "Uh..."

"But to let yer know, our raids are only necessary. We don't want to steal. What we take what we need, only because ther's no other way."

Kael considered Tomn for a moment. Despite his grungy appearance, Kael could tell he was a sincere person. And, despite the circumstance, he believed Tomn. "Explain."

A faint smile played on Tomn's lips. "Can yer walk? Then come with me."

Warily, Kael got up out of his bed. He was sore all over, so it became quite the task. Once on his feet, he carefully touched the splint on his left arm. His heart sank. Nothing more than a stick

275

wrapped by gray cloth, it stood as a symbol. Kael wouldn't be fighting for a while.

Wordlessly, Kael followed Tomn out the door to the small hut. Daylight greeted him and, after his eyes adjusted, so did a dismal sight. The muddy bandit village stood before Kael, as brown and bleak as ever. Over to the right, down what seemed to be the main road to the village, Kael could see a procession of people. Tomn directed Kael towards it, setting off at a leisurely pace.

"You see, son, we were here first. A thousand years ago, our ancestors lived in this valley. Then, those accursed people down ther came and took our land." His face fell grave. "Those lerks kicked us out without giving us a chance! They took our land, our crops, our animals, everthing—leaving us with nothin'. Ever since, fer hundreds of years, we've stayed in this forest. We can't farm, we don't know how to build and we don't know medicine. We're barely staying alive! You think we want to live stealing everything? No."

They arrived at the back of the congregation of people. Men, women and dirt-caked children all stood, staring towards something at the far side of the village.

Kael turned to Tomn. "I'm sorry for your troubles," he said. "I—I seemed to have seriously misjudged you." They were walking through the crowds, who divided to let Tomn through. Kael caught the looks of children. They were sobbing, but when he passed, they stopped and instead stared up at him in fright, cowering near their mothers. They were afraid of him.

Tomn shook his head. "Aye, most do."

Right then, they reached the end of the crowd. When Kael discovered what they were congregating for, shivers ran the length of his spine. A huge weight seemed to press down on his heart. Kael sank to his knees. *This was his fault.*

They were standing in front of a graveyard. Headstones made from thick branches marked several freshly-dug graves. Crying at the base of fresh graves were the wives and children of the deceased. They were the families of those he killed.

"Now yeh see," Tomn said softly, crouching beside Kael, "who we really are. We're not animals. We're not heathens. Yet, we are divided and treated as such."

"I'm sorry," Kael said between his hands. "So sorry..."

"I don't blame you. We're used to death. These families will carry on."

A boom of thunder broke the gloomy silence, drowning out the crying of the mourning families and echoing long after through the forest. Not thunder. *Shatterbreath.* Kael lifted his head. She was near.

"Come," Tomn said, hefted Kael to his feet by the scruff of his tunic, "I'll take yeh to yer beastie."

Kael walked through the crowd with his head down. He had killed many people, yet the Tomn was being so hospitable. Yseph couldn't have been any more incorrect about the bandits.

Another sharp roar emanated through the forest. Definitely Shatterbreath. Kael laughed at hearing her voice. She was angry.

"Looks like Beastie's woken up again," Tomn commented. "For our sake, let's not keep yer from her any longer..."

The left the confines of the haggard village wall, following a faint trail leading up the mountain. Kael's heart was beginning to thrum. Shatterbreath was alive! He was going to see her! But as much as he was excited, he couldn't help but to feel a great degree of sorrow and regret. Tomn was willingly bringing Kael to Shatterbreath, without any trouble at all. Conflict Kael had created could have been avoided. The men Kael killed, his sword breaking...it was all unnecessary.

The next roar was significantly louder. She was close. So close, in fact, Kael could see a burst of flame soar high above the canopy a second after the roar dissipated.

"Shatterbreath!" Kael shouted. "Shatterbreath!"

Disregarding how sore his was, Kael broke out in a sprint towards where he believed Shatterbreath was. Behind, he could hear Tomn shout something. There was no time for that, he needed to be with her right away. He couldn't wait any longer. He had to see Shatterbreath's face, hear her voice.

277

Weaving through the trees, Kael kept calling her name, scanning the forest as he ran. Another roar rippled through the forest, shaking the trees themselves. The sound bounced in all directions and it was impossible to determine its source.

Kael wiped the sweat from his brow, spinning around trying to find out where she was. A snarl came and Kael set off in that direction. After running for a minute or so, Kael had to stop. He placed a hand against a tree to support himself as he caught his breath. He inhaled, running his hand along the trunk of the tree. He grimaced as his hand brushed against something course.

Leaning close, Kael inspected the tree. There was a crack running up its length. When he looked up, he discovered the tree was leaning completely over, broken by some unknown force.

Kael walked around it, frowning. He stumbled as his foot fell away into nothing. There was a massive gouge in the ground! Stepping into it, Kael took a deep breath—smoke and ash. Indeed, as Kael ventured further along, the earth was scorched and the gnarled trees blackened. This must have been created when Shatterbreath crashed. The gouge worried Kael. It was massive, with trees uprooted or otherwise mangled. There was no way Shatterbreath could have escaped such a crash landing unharmed.

A growl emanated from nearby. Kael sighed. *At least she was alive.*

Kael ran along the gouge. The mountainside, which had been relatively flat, sloped upwards into a gentle roll. Shatterbreath's frustrated growling coupled with the yelling of men's voices and rattling chains could be heard over the lip. When Kael reached the top of the small hill, he felt both relief and despair.

Shatterbreath was lying awkwardly in the middle of a low ravine, limbs sprawled, neck craned and tail thrashing. The river itself ran into Shatterbreath's body, pooling around her midsection and eventually flowing past her chest, resuming its path on the other side. Thick chains imbedded into the surrounding landscape held her more or less pinned to the ground, which she was doing her best to fight herself free from. Her muzzle was bound with leather rope and her wings wrapped closed as well. But despite the restraints, as Kael stood watching, she managed to open her mouth wide enough to spew a jet of flame.

The flame rushed eagerly to consume a bandit who had been standing nearby. Three other men jumped out of the way, springing to their feet seconds later to grab hold of the ropes lassoed onto Shatterbreath's horns. They were doing their best to direct her head away from another group of bandits which were trying to move in closer to her with little success. Even as Kael watched, her unrestrained tail managed to swat away several bandits which had moved too close.

Though the scene was hectic and dangerous, all Kael could focus on were Shatterbreath's eyes. Her pupils were dilated, half hidden by the wrinkles of her snarling muzzle. Feral anger burned in her emerald eyes, purely animal rage. It was the same ferocity Shatterbreath had displayed when they had been caught in the Ripwind cloud. It scared Kael. This was not the Shatterbreath he knew.

Kael worked his way down the ravine's low edge. As he did, a few of the bandits trying to control the enraged dragon noticed him. They stopped whatever they were doing and backed away from both Kael and Shatterbreath.

Kael was only a few feet away from Shatterbreath's head before he stopped. He watched her as she fought some more, cocking his head. Now that he was closer, he could see why her wings were bound tight. Blood was dripping down her wings and from where he stood, he could see the red of where her membrane was torn. Also, he could see the other injuries she had sustained as well. Minor cuts ran the length of her body, but there were others that were more significant. There was a long gash across her face, which began just above the edge of her lip, ran across her prominent cheek and ended at the top of her jaw. As Shatterbreath continued to writhe, Kael could what appeared to be a wide hole stabbed into her tail where a ballista had struck her.

Kael moved his gaze from her injuries to her eyes. Cautiously he stepped closer to her, putting out both hands. "Shatterbreath," he said softly. She continued to thrash.

279

As long as Kael had known the dragon, she had always been a controlled storm, a tame fury. Now, her full instincts had taken over. She had never been so unfamiliar, so threatening to him since the first time they had met. Like the first time they had met, Kael was afraid of her.

"Let her go!" Kael called out to the bandits holding the ropes tied to her horns. "Let her go."

After sharing worried expressions with each other, the bandits released the rope. Undeterred, Shatterbreath swung her great head around to view each person surrounding her in turn. Lastly, her eyes fell on Kael, where they lingered.

Kael took another step towards her. "Shatterbreath," he cooed. "It's me, Kael."

The dragon cocked her head and huffed, sending tendrils of smoke trailing from her nostrils. A throaty growl escaped her bound muzzle.

A tear formed in Kael's eyes. *She didn't recognize him.* "Shatterbreath!" he tried again. "It's me! You know me! Kael, Kael Rundown."

Shatterbreath narrowed her eyes. Kael caught his breath. She recognized him. All at once, realization came flooding over Shatterbreath. Her pupils returned to normal and her body relaxed. Shatterbreath lowered her head until it was nearly resting on the ground.

She forced the restraint on her muzzle wide enough to say one thing: "Tiny..."

Kael knew at once he had his friend back.

Kael closed the distance between them and wrapped both arms around the side of her face in a comforted hug. Shatterbreath closed her eyes and nuzzled him right back, humming loudly and sending vibrations through Kael's body. There they stayed for what seemed like hours. The ravine seemed to melt away. All their troubles disappeared. The pain Kael felt, the agony he had experienced for her loss all vanished. For a time, it was just him and her.

Kael pulled the bands off of her muzzle. "Tiny, Kael..." she sobbed A great, pearly tear rolled down her cheek. "I thought I'd lost you. I thought I'd lost everything..."

"I'm here, Shatterbreath. I'm fine." He gave a shaky chuckle. *"You* lost everything? What about me? I nearly killed myself trying to find you! I thought you were dead."

Shatterbreath rumbled as well, her equivalent to a laugh. "What a *shame* that would have been. I hope at least that idiot Rooster died when you came looking for me."

Kael let her go and stared into her eye. "No, he's gone. Shatterbreath, you were right. The ale was poisoned. I gave that traitor a beating before I sent him away."

Shatterbreath shuffled underneath the chains. "Good. Fine. I hated that scrawny morsel. You really should learn to listen to me."

"I know." Kael turned to the nearest bandit. "Get these chains off."

The bandit pursed his lips. "I'm not sure if that's a good idea. I have to ask the bossman. Oi, Frebbor, you s'pose we should—"

"No." A tall man walked into view from the far side of Shatterbreath. It was the same thick bandit that had been riding the horse. Still in his grip was the two-handed hammer. "I don't trust this lerk. That beastie's still dangerous, keep it locked up."

Just then, Tomn came strolling over the edge of the ravine. "He may be a lerk," he said, arms clasped behind his back. "But he's the only one who can calm ther beastie. Do what he says."

The tall bandit frowned. "Do what he says? Tomn, what the blitty you on about? Tha's a dangerous animal!"

"You going against me orders, Frebbor? A dangerous animal tha' may be, but our friend here is its friend."

Frebbor threw his hands up in the air. "Oh, its *friend*, why, excures me, Tomn! I had no idear." The thick bandit walked off, grumbling something incoherent.

Tomn nodded at a group of bandits watching. On his cue, they ran over to the anchors. It took three bandits to pull out on anchor, but after only a few minutes, the chains wrapped over Shatterbreath went slack. With a pause to scrutinize the surrounding bandits,

281

Shatterbreath cautiously raised herself off the ground. Water dripped from her underbelly as she stretched her limbs, eyes still darting about the ravine.

She huffed, sending a humid wave of air over Kael.

"Foo, your breath stinks!" Kael said, pinching his nose.

"Yours would too if you spent three days stuck in a chilly river," Shatterbreath snapped back. "Kael, what's happening? Why are these filthy creatures suddenly so friendly?"

Kael rubbed her shoulder, careful to avoid touching the slashes covering it. "We shared a...misunderstanding. These *bandits,*" Kael paused, catching Tomn's eye, "are the more welcoming that Fallenfeld. They mean us no harm."

"Aye, we mean nobody no harm." Tomn moved closer to Shatterbreath, who growled. "Especially not you, Beastie. We was only trying to help yer. Like I said, young..."

"Kael, Kael Rundown."

"Aye, Kael. Like I said, we may not know much about medicine, but we do know how ter stitch a wound. And you, Beastie, are covered with wounds. We only wanted ter help you."

Shatterbreath grumbled. "You..." She sighed. "I appreciate your want to help, stinky man, but nobody touches me. Only Kael."

Kael frowned and shook his head. "You're so stubborn, Shatterbreath," he muttered. "Fine, let's fix you up then."

Tomn put out a finger. "I'll bring supplies at once. Ah, but if we could...assist yah? Yer arm is hurt. That's a long job yer got doing it alone."

Shatterbreath growled. She inhaled, eyeing Tomn. "Very well. *Assist* and nothing more." Stiffly, Shatterbreath walked a few paces until she was out of the river. Then, with a rumbling sigh, she slumped to the ground, lying on her side. "Tell me, Kael, the details concerning your fight with that stupid bird, Rooster."

Kael couldn't help but to laugh. *There's the Shatterbreath I know.* "Of course." He climbed up Shatterbreath's foreleg and into his usual nook in between his shoulders. "Well, I was waiting up on the mountain for you..."

When Tomn had said it was a long job to do alone, he was not making an understatement. Indeed, even with the bandits assisting, it took several days to patch up all of Shatterbreath's wounds—her tail alone took a whole day. Despite the grimness of his task, it was relieving to spend so much time with Shatterbreath. After nearly losing her, it was wonderful to be near her, to hear her voice and breathe in her familiar aroma.

Though his bruises faded away, every so often an irregular movement would trigger a spasm of pain, reminding Kael how close he had skirmished with death.

With Shatterbreath flightless for a time, they were forced to spend their time in the bandit's forest. When he wasn't with Shatterbreath in the low ravine, Kael would return to the encampment to talk with Tomn. They would discuss the history of the bandits as well as Fallenfeld and Kael did his best to educate the man concerning blacksmithing, medicine and what little he knew about architecture. Kael was always impressed by how much they were able to learn from each other at the end of each conversation. Through his mingling with his bandits, he was proud to have a full grasp of their heavy accent.

After a week, however, Kael and Shatterbreath were both getting anxious. One evening, Kael slid off Shatterbreath's back to pace in front of her, fingering the handle of the mace Tomn had given him as a temporary replacement for his sword.

"I concluded," Kael began, "that Fallenfeld was an utter failure."

Smoke spurted out of Shatterbreath's nostrils as she cocked her head. "Really now?"

"However, I'm having second thoughts."

Shatterbreath rose to her feet. "You can't be serious." Careful of her wounds, Shatterbreath shuffled over to the river. "They'll kill you faster than a snake can strike. You didn't survive their deceitful test just to return and die."

"No, you're right, I'm not going back there." Kael stopped his pacing. "Not to the city anyway. The graveyard though, that's another story."

Shatterbreath paused, lifting her muzzle out of the river to huff in Kael's direction. Water dripped from her chin, splashing back into the river. "The graveyard? What will that accomplish?" She resumed lapping up the river water.

"Yseph, the king's advisor, visits his parent's grave each night. I want to talk to him about these bandits. I need to at least tell him they aren't a threat. Maybe, just maybe, I can convince Fallenfeld after all." Kael snapped his fingers. "In fact, I'm positive I can."

Tip of her snout still underwater, Shatterbreath sighed, causing the river to both bubble and steam. "Not to be pessimistic, Tiny, but how exactly are you going to convince them *now*? They've already tried to kill you over distrust."

"Well, without the threat of bandit raids, I'd think they'd be much more inclined to assist. Especially if the bandits are fighting against the BlackHound Empire as well."

Shatterbreath snorted, reared her head out of the water and coughed. Kael yelped and jumped away as a burst of flame escaped her jaws as she did. "Ahem, what?"

Kael's head was spinning with the prospect. He held a hand to his temple, as if the idea might leave if he let go. "I'll be right back, I must talk with Tomn."

Leaving Shatterbreath no less confused, Kael sprinted out of the ravine and back to the bandit camp. His sides screamed at him in protest, but Kael was too excited to notice. In a flourish, he sprung up the three steps to Tomn's ramshackle hut and threw open the door.

"Tomn, Tomn," Kael gasped. "We have to talk."

Tomn and Frebbor were the only ones occupying the room. They seemed to have been playing a game of cards before Kael interrupted. They exchanged glances before Tomn spoke. "Aye, Kael. What's happening?"

"Did I ever tell you why I went into Fallenfeld to begin with?"

"Aye, sonny." Tomn scratched his chin. "Yer said you was trying to convince them to help yer fight some invader or sommat."

"Exactly. I was wondering..." Kael tented his fingers, watching Tomn closely. "I was wondering if you wanted to join my cause."

For once, Tomn was speechless. It took several seconds before he found his voice. "Yeh mean us bandits...help yer? Fight against an invading force. Just like tha? That's quite a bit to digerst, don't yer think?"

"Well?"

Frebbor cut in. "Well? *Well,* we're not much of a fighting force to begin with." He named the ways on his fingers. "We'd be leaving ourselves vulnerable to Fallenfeld attack. We don't have enough supplies to support a war *and* a movement of our people that large would catch Fallenfeld's attention. Yer asking us to kill ourselves. And fer what?"

Kael scowled at him. Tomn shook his head. "I has to agree with Frebbor here, sonny. What's in it fer us? Yeah, I get it, saving our land n' such. No, we're a dying people, Kael. I'm afraid fighting in a war will only kill us faster. If yeh can promise me some way to...secure a better future fer us, by all means, we'll help yeh out."

Kael thought for a moment. *What made the bandits a dying people?* Fallenfeld hated them... No, they had no industry, no wealth. *No money.*

A solution dawned on Kael. "Let's say I know a way to get you a lifetime's worth of gold. Fifty lifetimes' worth of gold. What say you then?"

Tomn laughed and rubbed his nose. "Why, I'd say yeh were a bit blitty in the head! Tha's a lot of gold." Tomn stopped laughing as Kael's expression remained serious. He leaned forward. "But, out of curiosity..."

"I can quadruple that amount. Vallenfend has the biggest store of gold I've ever seen. It's all secret too. Help us, and I promise it's all yours."

Tomn's eyebrows shot up. Even Frebbor, who kept a hidden grudge towards Kael, was spurred by the prospect. Blinking several times, Tomn opened his mouth. No words came out at first. He swallowed and tried again.

"Yah telling me...you'd give us all tha?"

"Yes. I promise you as well that I'll find a way to train your men before they fight."

285

Frebbor nudged Tomn. "Do yer know what we could do with all tha' gold?"

"Yeah." Tomn nodded. "Kael, if yer serious, this could change everthing. With that much gold...we could buy a city! Why, we wouldn't have to live in the forest no more! We could *buy* a city."

"Or just build a new one," Kael suggested. "So, Tomn, are you with me?"

Tomn stood up, a huge grin spread across his lips. He thrust out his hand. "Aye, Kael. Consider the bandits yer ally. We'll back yeh up to ther end."

Kael took Tomn's hand. Fallenfeld may have been a disaster, but through that failure came an unsuspected ally. Through that failure, came two possible successes.

"Now, if you'd excuse me," Kael said with a short bow, "I have an advisor to talk to."

Tomn's smile doubled. "I'll let yeh to it."

"You're letting them keep all the gold?" Shatterbreath scoffed. "That's very..."

"Generous?"

"Not exactly." Shatterbreath jumped down off of a massive boulder, jarring Kael. "The other army you've recruited, the others you may still recruit—don't you think they'll demand some sort of payment? Even if they *are* fighting to save this continent. When they see the amount of gold you hand over to bandits, I'm sure they'll be a tad *upset.*"

Kael winced and clutched his ribs. "Hmm. Not many people know about that stockpile of gold. I was planning—somehow—to give the gold to the bandits secretly so to avoid any jealousy. As a reward, everybody else can have the spoils of war. I'm sure there will be a lot of goods left over once it's over."

Shatterbreath huffed, and a couple seconds later, Kael felt her hot breath wash over him. He was on her back and she was running down the mountain in the dead of night. Trees whizzed by, each one *whooshing* as it did. "I'm not sure about this idea... Or even the situation as a whole! I hope you're right."

"When have I ever been wrong?" Kael joked. Shatterbreath craned her neck to give him a look. "Sush, we're on Fallenfeld ground now."

Shatterbreath couldn't fly yet, so she was forced to run to the graveyard. Kael had faith that they wouldn't be detected by any patrols outside the city. His faith was renewed as Shatterbreath began running through the fields. As Kael had quickly learned about her when they first met, she was a master at stealth. So silent was she, Kael wouldn't have been surprised if they were moving through cotton and not grass. She muffled her footsteps so well; all he heard was the occasional rustle of her body in the wheat fields and the rushing of her breath.

With her speed, it was only a matter of moments before they were closing in on the graveyard. It was set outside Fallenfeld, closer to the western mountains than the city itself. A thick spiked fence bordered the entire thing with only one entrance guarded by several soldiers, protecting it from grave robbers. The fence did little to deter Shatterbreath and in one mighty bound she jumped clear over it, landing in between a row of tombs, crouching low.

Kael slid off her back, walked across the row and peered around the corner of a tomb. A long aisle of similar sarcophagi lined up for as far as he could see. The grid, coupled with the darkness would prove well to hide him.

"What's the plan, Tiny?" Shatterbreath whispered.

Kael took a deep breath. The mellow night was doing its best to cover the dusty smell of the graveyard, but the latter was too powerful, too permanent. Kael hated cemeteries. "Yseph told me he visits his parents' graves each night. Stick close; when he comes, I need you to eliminate the guards. I need to talk with him alone—well, without any other humans anyway."

A shuffle squeezed its way through the tombs to reach Kael's ears. A second later, the creaking of a worn metal gate.

"What should I do with the guards?"

Kael frowned into the darkness. "That's up to you."

There came the sound of scales sliding against stone and when Kael looked back, Shatterbreath had already disappeared. He shook

287

his head, amazed at how fast and quiet she was. Then, taking a deep breath, Kael wove into the grid of tombs himself.

It wasn't hard for Kael to figure out the pattern to the graveyard. At the back, furthest away from the gates, were where the richer people were buried—bigger tombs, more elaborately carved structures. The closer Kael moved to the front, the smaller the tombs became, until the tombs disappeared entirely, replaced instead by headstones.

Kael made his way along the outside edge of the graveyard, finding a spot along the spiked wall where he could see the entrance.

Now, he had to wait.

After only an hour or so, Kael perked up as the front gates swung open. Protected by two bodyguards, Yseph walked in, holding a bouquet of daffodils. Yseph paused inside and looked around, acting jittery. The frail man shook his head and continued onward.

As Kael moved to follow them, a thick fog rolled in. Shatterbreath was giving them cover. *Clever.* But as much as it helped it, it also proved to be a detriment. It became more difficult for Kael to follow and he was forced to get closer. Even still, he managed to stick close enough to watch as Shatterbreath pounced.

With nothing more than a shuffle, she scooped a bodyguard with her tail and slunk into the darkness. What she did with the man, Kael had no idea. He didn't want to think about it. Nor did he want to know what Yseph must have been feeling to discover one of his bodyguards had vanished.

Yseph began to shake. His remaining bodyguard whipped around several times, looking for his missing comrade. Kael hugged closer to the headstone he was hiding behind.

"Where did he go?" the bodyguard asked. "W—was he taken by a..."

"Ghost?" Yseph scoffed, collecting his wits. "Nonsense. There are no such things as ghosts. All these years I've been going here, and I've never seen any such thing." Kael could distinctly hear Shatterbreath let out a low rumble. Yseph winced. "At any rate, let us return with haste. One moment please."

Kael watched Yseph bend down in front of what must have been his parents' grave. The advisor placed the flowers down in front of the headstone and bowed his head in silent prayer. A blue shape moved through the mist, descending on the remaining bodyguard. Kael made his move as well, clearing the distance between him and the row of graves in front of Yseph in a few long strides.

In one graceful movement, Shatterbreath dispatched the last bodyguard. With a growl and a muffled cry, she had the bodyguard in her paws. With a *crack,* Yseph was now alone.

The advisor stood up in a heartbeat, facing where he bodyguard had stood only seconds before. Kael snuck right up behind him. Trembling, hands out, back crooked, Yseph backed up. Straight into Kael. Before the thin man could even gasp, Kael wrapped his elbow around his neck and clasped a hand over his mouth.

"Don't struggle," Kael hissed. He dragged Yseph deeper into the cemetery by his neck. When he thought he was a safe distance from the gate guards, he relaxed his grip. "Don't yell, don't fight. Just...listen."

"Rundown," Yseph spat. "A thousand curses on you!"

"A thousand curses?" Kael echoed. "On *me?* I should be the one cursing you and *you* should be thanking me."

Yseph remained cautious. "Why in the world would I thank you?"

"For solving your bandit problem, of course."

"Ha," Yseph grumbled. "Kill me or release me, but please, don't feed me lies."

"I'm not lying. I found the bandit encampment, I spoke with their leader. We have come to an...agreement. They are no longer a threat to Fallenfeld."

Yseph considered him for a moment. "King Henedral was right, we were wise to mistrust you."

"Mistrust *me?* I wasn't the one who poisoned *your* drink."

Yseph shot him a confused look.

"That's right," Kael said, "I knew the ale was poisoned. Without even telling me why, you tried to kill me."

"We had our reasons."

"Enlighten me."

Yseph sighed. "You are young, the situation you described seemed...preposterous. The king didn't trust you. In short, he saw you as a fool."

Kael forced himself to stay calm. "A fool? I don't care if you believe what I told you and your king, but believe this: the bandits are no longer a threat to you. Tomorrow the bandits will leave a sign."

Yseph squinted at Kael through the darkness. "What will the sign be, so I may know it when I spot it?"

"Daffodils," Kael said with a smirk.

Yseph took a shuddering breath. "I do not believe you. The bandits are animals. They cannot be reasoned with."

Kael took two steps back. "Just you wait. You'll see I was telling the truth all along. Consider yourself lucky I need your help. Have a pleasant night, Yseph. Give my regards to your parents." Kael turned to leave.

"Rundown," Yseph called out.

"Yes?"

"Unless you really are a fool, don't *ever* return to Fallenfeld."

Kael frowned and walked into the fog. Not long after Yseph disappeared from view, Kael could detect Shatterbreath's musky odour. Altogether, she appeared, scrutinizing him with one emerald eye.

"Well, how did that go?"

Kael was quick to climb aboard her back. "Rather...well."

Chapter 26

Five days. Five days they were gone! It was bad enough they had to leave in the first place, but to be gone for *five* days? Laura swore, if he didn't have a good reason, she'd punch Faerd as hard as she could.

Assuming he *did* come back.

As Laura stood, leaning against the wall of the cave's mouth, gazing down into the eternal fog of the mountain, she couldn't help but to wonder what was taking them so long. In the back of her mind, a small voice was telling her they were dead or that they had been captured. As much as she didn't want to believe it, the voice was probably correct. The mission they had left on was suicidal.

She had told them not to go. Why hadn't they listened to her?

Laura's mother came out of the cave. Wordlessly, Mrs. Stockwin wrapped an arm around Laura. For several minutes they stood there, staring down the mountain. Helena was still back inside the cave. She hadn't left or even moved much since Korjan had left. She only sat still. Maybe she was praying for them.

"What if they don't come back?" Laura's mother asked. "What if it's just us stuck up here?" She was on the verge of tears.

Laura felt nothing. "We're strong," Laura replied. "We'll survive."

"For how long?"

"For as long as it takes. We can do this. We can endure." The words felt hollow, empty. They were nothing but a lie.

"Do you think they actually did it?" Laura's mother said, perking up. "Did they manage to kill Zeptus?"

Laura frowned. *"Could* they do it?"

"We couldn't," a voice chimed in from nowhere. Laura spun around, just as Tooran seemed to fall down from nowhere.

"Tooran!" Laura shouted, throwing her arms around the man. He was firm with muscle. "You're back! Wh—where are the others?"

Mrs. Stockwin hugged him as well. "And where in the world did you come from?"

Tooran laughed. "I was up on that ledge above the cave—for quite some time now. The others should be coming shortly, with some...guests."

"What do you mean, guests?" Laura's mother asked.

Tooran hesitated. "Ah, it's a long story. Faerd and the others should be here shortly to explain what happened. For now, though, I have something else to tell you."

Laura and her mother exchanged glances. "What is it, Tooran?" Laura said cautiously, "what did you mean when you said, 'we couldn't'?"

Tooran took a deep breath. "We couldn't kill Zeptus."

"I knew your mission would fail. You should have listened to me."

"No, it didn't fail," Tooran retorted. "We made it to Zeptus's chambers. I was about to deliver the finishing strike, when Father stopped me. We had the chance to kill Zeptus, but we didn't. I know it's hard to digest, but he's not the evil man we all thought he was! He...he's merely the king's pawn. Well, was."

"Was?" Laura's mother echoed. "Tooran, what have you done?"

Sighing, Tooran continued. "We couldn't kill him. We couldn't spill innocent blood. I've done that enough. We couldn't leave him there either. So..."

Laura shook her head. "You didn't... Oh no."

The look on Tooran's face confirmed what Laura feared. "We took him with us. He's up on the mountain right now, alone."

Laura's mother's face went red. "You brought him *here?!* Tooran, how could you? It's bad enough that you refused to kill him, but you brought him here?! That man is responsible for my boys' deaths!" She pounded his chest, enraged. Tooran stood firm, face blank. "How could you? Take me to him! I'll do what you cowards couldn't. I'll kill him myself."

"That clarifies one thing," Tooran said calmly, lip twitching. "Zeptus can't stay with us."

"What are you going to do with him?" Laura asked.

Tooran scratched his chin. "I'll stay with him at the top of the mountain for now. Hopefully we'll be able to introduce him to everybody else with time.

Talking from down the mountain caught Laura's attention. She stepped up to the edge and listened. She could hear several unfamiliar voices.

"Tooran, what did you mean by 'everybody else'?" By the time Laura turned around, Tooran was already gone. Laura looked to her mother for an explanation, but she only shrugged.

Laura stepped down from the cave ledge. She focussed on the trees, trying to see anybody through the forest. She held her breath as she saw something move in between the trees, distinctly human. *Please,* she silently begged, *let it be him. Please...*

Laura's heart leapt as none other than Faerd strolled out of the forest, a stern look on his features as always. When he spotted Laura, he stopped and the expression melted away. Without further hesitation, Laura ran to him. Faerd embraced her in a tight hug.

"I told you I'd come back," Faerd said to her.

Laura let go of him. "No you didn't."

"Yeah, well..."

"Is the coast clear?" a voice interrupted from the trees.

"Yes," Faerd yelled back. "Come on up."

After some shuffling in the bushes, women and children began to emerge from the trees, with Malaricus among them, leading a donkey. Laura quickly recognized Horan resting on its back. Bruce was also among the few men that emerged. But, Laura noted. No Korjan.

"What happened?" Laura asked.

"Laura! Mrs. Stockwin!" Malaricus cried. "What a pleasure it is to see you all once again." The scholar put his hand to his chest. "Especially after the recent circumstances."

"Malaricus, Faerd, who are these people?" Laura's mother asked.

"Friends, family. They believe in Ka—" Malaricus stopped short as he spotted Laura's venomous gaze. "They are fed up with King Morrindale's scheming. If they'd had stayed in Vallenfend, I fear they would have all perished." Malaricus hesitated when he noticed Helena approaching. "Ah, Helena... How are you?"

Helena spotted his cautious attitude at once. She scanned over the tired faces. "Where's Korjan?"

Laura clenched her jaw. *She had told them not to leave.*

Faerd looked at his toes, similarly, Malaricus avoided Helena's gaze.

The only sound that penetrated the mountainside was the supple blowing of the wind through the trees. At last, Malaricus broke down. "He's gone," the scholar sputtered. "He...fell behind."

"You didn't wait for him?" Helena's voice was oddly calm.

"He fought bravely!" a woman from the back cried. She was wearing leather armour—a gate guard if Laura remembered correctly. "He gave himself to save us. B—but I don't think they killed him, no. They captured him. He's probably in the dungeons right now."

Helena seemed to deflate. As her shoulders sagged, the lustre in her eyes seemed to fade. "I understand."

"I told you all you shouldn't have gone," Laura spat. "Now look what you've done. Korjan's gone, Horan's hurt and now *these* people? Malaricus, didn't you pause to think how we're going to take care of all of them? We can hardly take care of ourselves!"

Malaricus put up his hands. "Laura, please calm down. They would have died if they stayed."

"They're going to die here! You haven't *saved* them Malaricus, you've only doomed them to slow death by starvation instead of death by the sword!" Laura stopped herself. The children. They looked so terrified, clinging to their mothers' skirts. Laura took a deep breath. Mollified, she spoke softer. "How long do you plan to stay up here?"

Malaricus seemed so old right then. Old, tired and frail. He sighed, eyelids fluttering. "Don't worry, dear, we'll figure out something. For now, I'm afraid there's no other answer."

"Fine," Laura said in a toneless voice, "I suppose, for *now,* our family has grown."

Faerd grinned. He spread his arms out wide, facing the crowd. "Welcome home, *family.*"

The people followed Faerd up the hill and into the cave. Laura stayed rooted to the spot, feeling conflicted. Her emotions seemed to be doing battle within her chest, with her heart as the battlefield. *How much longer could she take this?*

Laura glanced over at Helena, who was also standing still, blank-faced, numb.

After several minutes, Laura started on her way back up the hill. Helena stopped her, placing a hand on her shoulder.

"Laura, you told them it was a bad idea," Helena said slowly. "You were right. Korjan..."

"Will be fine. I usually enjoy being correct, Helena, but not today." Laura nudged free. "Keep praying, Helena."

Laura stopped when she reached the cave's ledge. She looked out over the edge, jaws set, brow slanted in frustration. A break in the fog revealed the landscape far below. Vallenfend was drenched in the shadow of an enormous storm cloud looming overhead. *Storm's coming.*

Sighing, Laura considered the situation. *Or has it already arrived?*

Chapter 27

Shatterbreath studied Kael as he examined her wing. Tiny sighed, running his fingers along the tear that kept her land-bound. She flexed the same wing, pushing the membrane against his body. He grunted in reply.

"Hold still," he complained, shifting his weight as he stood on her back. "How am I supposed to inspect this when you keep moving?"

Shatterbreath huffed, sending a plume of smoke spiralling above her head. "Maybe if you'd hurry up..."

"Please, Shatterbreath," Kael snapped. The look he gave her was not frustration, but sadness. "This is serious. Your wing may never heal. You waited too long to have this tear stitched up, it's not mending. If we can't fix it...you may never fly again."

The gravity of the situation struck Shatterbreath to her core. Never had one lone statement done that to her. Shivers ran over her spines as she considered Kael's words. *Never fly again.* What was a dragon without flight? What was the mighty huntress without her most valuable tool? Would she truly never take to the skies again? Already, she missed the wind flowing over her serpentine body. Already, she missed the cool breeze beating against her muzzle. Already, she missed the serene feeling of catching a lazy thermal and simply floating there for hours. *What was a dragon without flight?*

"What can you do," she sputtered, hardly able to control her voice, "to fix it?"

Kael sighed again. "I don't know. It may yet still heal. It's too early to tell. I stitched it closed, but either side of the membrane had already begun to scab. Unless I find a substitute, you can't fly on those stitches. They'll rip and you'd be no better off."

Raw emotion was flooding through Shatterbreath. She struggled to keep in constrained, but it was too much. Before she could stop herself, she had already filled her lungs. She opened her great maw wide and bellowed. She released her entire breath in one piercing, resonating note. Shrill and sorrowful, it echoed through the forest long after she had closed her mouth. It sounded nothing of thunder. It was weak, it was pained.

Kael doubled over, clutching his ears. He yelled something, but Shatterbreath couldn't hear over her sorrow. When her howl subsided, he stood back up, rubbing his ears.

"Wow, that hurt... Shatterbreath, listen to me," he placed his hands on either side of her muzzle, just below her nostrils. *"Listen. I will do everything I can to fix this. I promise you, you will fly again."*

Although Shatterbreath was shaking, she went still as she gazed into his brown eyes. She could feel her body relax and the scales on her body smooth back down. Wordlessly, she nodded.

"S—stay here. I will be back."

Shatterbreath nodded. As soon as the boy left, she let her body go limp. She rolled completely over onto her side, legs sprawled, head resting on the ground. Out of the corner of her eye, she could see the faint outline of her wing. Tears welled up in her still-open eye.

Would she ever fly again?

Kael ran through the bandit village, searching for nothing in particular. *How does one go about mending a ripped wing?* After fetching Tomn, the two went from building to building, searching for anything that could prove useful. After a while, they had found several sheets of leather, a dozen yards of wire, and other trinkets that caught Kael's attention. Unfortunately, that's all the bandits seemed to own. Shiny trinkets and otherwise useless items that were obviously stolen. The biggest find, however, came when a bandit family offered him a gold rung.

Kael weighed the small loop in his hand, shaped almost like a horseshoe, both the length and the width of his finger. It looked as though it was meant to support a curtain of some kind. It was sturdy, crafted entirely from polished brass.

"This will do," Kael declared, throwing the rung to Tomn, who placed it in the wheelbarrow. "How many more to you have?"

After Kael had collected eight rungs, he left the building and started back to Shatterbreath. So many ideas ran through his head, with the brass rungs occurring most often. By the time he reached her, he figured he had come up with a good solution.

Shatterbreath lifted her head as Kael approached. She remained silent, but her expression was all too clear. *Save me,* he eyes seemed to say.

Kael tipped the wheelbarrow, spilling the contents in front of Shatterbreath.

"What're yeh going to do?" Tomn asked. "I don't know much about healing ter begin with, but fixing a ripped wing?"

Shatterbreath began nosing through the things Kael and Tomn had collected. "It's a long-shot, I know. We'll figure something out." Kael kicked the tangle of wire out of the way, bent over and picked up one of the rungs. He considered it for a moment. "I think this might be all we need."

Shatterbreath sniffed the rung. "Are you sure? How will that little thing help?"

Kael collected a few more and put them around his arm. "Just trust me. Could you bring your wing down here? This time, hold still."

Kael took hold of the edge of Shatterbreath's wing and held the rung up to the tear. He frowned at took it away; it was too round. He tried to bend it to make it flatter, but was surprised to find he couldn't. After hitting it with a rock a few times to make the ends of the rung bend inwards and the whole thing relatively flat, he held it back up to her wing.

"This might work," Kael mumbled.

"What? What is it?"

"Aside from stitches, I once saw a larger wound closed shut with small metal tabs. I'm think they were stronger and would do better to hold the wound closed." Kael paused. "We could do the same with your wing by putting a bunch of these on to support the stitches you already have. It would double the strength and you could possibly fly. If your wing does mend with time, I could always remove them."

Shatterbreath considered him. "You only have eight though."

"I will make more. Tomn, do you have a smithy oven and a bellows?"

Tomn scratched his head. "Erm, what?"

Kael groaned. "I guess I'll just make one here. Shatterbreath, I'm going to need your fire. Tomn, I'm going to need metal. Small lengths of steel if possible. Also a hammer, and an anvil—I know you have one of those, I saw it before."

"Sure bet," Tomn said. "What's an anvil?"

Kael sighed. "I'll just come with you. Shatterbreath, you should come as well. Anvils are heavy."

Shatterbreath curled her nose. "Me? Go into the bandit's nest? I'd sooner eat a skunk then go in there!"

Kael shook his head. "You stubborn lizard."

Smoke escaped Shatterbreath's mouth as she spoke. "Watch your tongue, hatchling." After a throaty growl, she sighed. "Fine. I'll come. I'll get your thing and then hurry back here."

"Sounds good. Let's go." Without further hesitation, Kael started back on his way to the bandit village. Shatterbreath hefted herself back onto her feet and tentatively followed. Kael smiled; Shatterbreath hated not getting her way. And right now, she was furious. She kept huffing, scratching their ground and knocking down the occasional tree with her tail as they walked. Tomn seemed less amused than Kael, wincing and glancing over his shoulder whenever Shatterbreath made a noise.

When the time came to enter the actual village, Kael stopped, expecting Shatterbreath to be tentative. He was wrong. She walked straight over him and *through* part of the bandit wall without hesitation. Debris scattered around her legs, she peered back at Kael with a smug dragon grin.

"Where's your thing?" she asked.

"There *was* a gate, Beastie," Tomn said with a frown.

Kael realized that by then, half the village was already watching them. Blushing, he hit Shatterbreath in the leg with his borrowed mace, cursing under his breath. "This way."

Kael directed Shatterbreath over to the hut where he had seen the anvil earlier. "Wait here," he said, waving a hand, "and I'll drag it outside. From there, you can—hey, what are doing?"

Shatterbreath craned her neck over the hut and then quite literally, shoved her head through the roof of the hut. The roof caved in around her, burying every part of her head except for the tip of her right horn. Tail swinging, she fished around the wreckage of the hut, creating quite the tumult. By then, the owner of the hut had already run out, screaming. Kael buried his face in his hand, doing his best to ignore the owner's gaze as well as Tomn's.

Shatterbreath twitched and then brought out her head. The thatching of the roof rained down around her as she proudly lifted out the anvil between her teeth.

"Here's your thing," she said, shaking off debris and slamming the heavy chunk of metal down at Kael's feet. "Let's go. Fix me up."

Kael glowered at her. "Take it back to the ravine. I'll be there in a few minutes."

Shatterbreath scooped up the anvil and sauntered away. Kael watched her go, feeling vibrations in his feet from her weight. *Stubborn lizard.*

"I'm sorry for that," Kael said to the hut owner. "Really... Uh, is there anything I can...?"

"Nah," Tomn interjected as the hut owner put up a finger to say something. "He'll be fine. We won't be staying here much longer anyway. Anything else yer need, Kael?"

"Yes. I need a hammer and a few iron bars—a metal spear handle, anything like that. I—I think I saw a hammer in your house. Do you mind?"

The hut owner, shoulders sagged, blinked a few times, then nodded at Kael. "It's all yers."

Kael nodded apologetically, then went inside the hut. After a few minutes of rummaging, he managed to find the hammer and even a

300

few metal bars. When he exited, Tomn was waiting for him, holding several spears. Kael took those from him with one arm, holding the hammer and bars with the other.

"You've been nothing but help," Kael said to him, "despite how Shatterbreath has...damaged your villager and inhabitants. I...I cannot express my gratitude."

Tomn placed a hand on Kael's shoulders, wearing a soft grin. "Sonny, yeh may have saved me people. I should be thanking *you.*"

Kael smiled. "You're a good man, Tomn. I promise you, you're people will be rewarded for their patience. Now, if you would excuse me, I have a grumpy dragon to attend to."

Kael grimaced as Shatterbreath slammed the anvil into the ground. Seeing her hefting such a heavy piece of metal was discerning. It reminded Kael of her immense strength. In a distant way, it brought back memories of when he had borrowed her strength. *That had been fun.*

Kael adjusted the anvil where it was sitting in the ravine. It was the hardest spot of ground they had found. "Usually," Kael wheezed through a cloud of upturned dust, "the anvil is fastened to the floor of the shop. It makes it sturdier—better for working the weapon."

Shatterbreath blinked slowly. "You should save this for later, I haven't had a good night's rest in days! You'd put me asleep right away."

Kael scowled at her. "In this case, though, it'll have to do. I'm just making small pieces anyway. I don't need the support." He put one of the bars on the anvil and lightly tapped it with his hammer. "Why were you so destructive earlier anyway?"

"I don't like being bossed around." Shatterbreath came in close, showing her teeth. "I don't know if you remember our *deal,* Tiny, but I said I'd spare you only if I thought you were still useful." Her emerald eyes twinkled, but showed no friendliness. "This still stands. I won't tolerate *you* ordering *me* around."

Kael considered for a moment. "You really mean that?"

She squinted at him, amused. "One fell lick," she purred, sticking out her tongue, "and I'd be done with you, remember?" She yawned. "No more orders."

Kael sighed. He wanted to blame her complaints on her stubbornness, but he had to remember his place. He owed his life to her. He owed more than that. "You're right," he said after a long pause. "I shouldn't boss you around. You're in charge, I'm the servant. If I can't give you orders though, how am I supposed to heat up this metal?"

Shatterbreath raised a brow, humming. She shifted to rest her upper body on her elbows. "I'm open to suggestions," she said slyly.

"Can you heat this up? Not enough to melt it, just to make it malleable."

Kael turned his head as Shatterbreath blew her fire onto the bar he was holding. His leather gloves he borrowed weren't exactly made for blacksmith use, but they held up against the heat. Shatterbreath closed her maw, ceasing the fire.

While the bar was still hot, Kael began pounding on it, sending tiny sparks skidding across the anvil. Out of habit, he began moulding it like a sword, smooth, flat and long—but he quickly caught himself. No matter how long it had been since he had last made a weapon, the memory was still there. He paused, staring at the reddened metal. *Korjan.*

Shatterbreath stirred. "Is something amiss? Do you require more heat?"

Kael shook his head. Shatterbreath shut her mouth, disappointed. "It's just... I miss my friends."

"Hmm."

"Sorry, I'll continue." Kael was aware of Shatterbreath's gaze lingering on him. He set back to work, doing his best to ignore her.

By the time he had finished with the bar of metal, he had made it long and thin, so that it matched the brass rung he had flattened, but even flatter. Then, after Shatterbreath warmed it up again, he used a spearhead as a chisel to cut the bar into five separate pieces. Each piece was the length of his hand, but after he bent the corners perpendicular to the middle, like a square 'U', they were then the length of his index finger. Just like the rung.

Kael placed the prepared pieces to the side and hefted one of the brass rungs which he had already shaped. He motioned at Shatterbreath and she stretched out her wing for him to see. Kael placed the rung on the anvil and took hold of the edge of her membrane in both hands.

Kael's heart was beginning to thrum in his chest. *This is going to be difficult,* he thought grimly. "Shatterbreath, are you ready?"

Shatterbreath watched him apprehensively. All sorts of emotions seemed to be spread across her face. Her eyes were hopeful, but her features were taut—jaw clenched, lips raised, brow furrowed. Kael could feel a twitch in her wing, perhaps from her subconscious desire to pull away. She may not have understood what he was doing, but she knew all too well what was going to come next. It was going to hurt.

"A—are you sure there's no other way?"

Kael shook his head.

"What if the rip does heal? Won't this create holes in my wings?"

"It won't be hard to remove these tabs. If the occasion rises, I'll take them out and stitch the remaining gaps closed. With a tear as big as you've got, there's a very high probability it will rip back open. I'd rather take a chance with smaller holes than what you've got. Shatterbreath, this is the best option. Heat this up."

Shatterbreath's breathes were accelerating. "Very well," she said. Warily, she blew fire on the brass rung. "Get on with it."

Nodding, Kael rested Shatterbreath's wing on top of the anvil so that the outermost edge of the rip was in the middle. In one hand, he gripped the hot rung, in the other, the hammer. He planted one foot firmly on the ground and the other up on Shatterbreath's wing.

Kael placed the tips of the rung against her membrane. "On the count of three, okay?"

Shatterbreath's face scrunched up. "Okay."

"One."

Kael drove the rung through her wing.

303

Chapter 28

Shatterbreath leapt up onto a massive boulder overlooking the Fallenfeld valley. She stuck her snout into the wind, feeling the breath of the living earth. She closed her eyes, drinking in the moment. A deep inhalation revealed the many smells of late summer; the wheat far in the distance, the overpowering radiation of the forest surrounding and somewhere, the musky foretelling of prey.

Kael sat on her back. Instead of absorbing the joy of the moment, Shatterbreath could feel his legs gripping tight. The salty scent of his nervous body permeated the air around him, making its way to Shatterbreath's nostrils.

She sniffed, amused. "What's the matter, Tiny? Frightened?"

Kael shivered on her back. Whether from the chilly breeze that rolled through or nervousness, she couldn't pinpoint. "Yes. No. Maybe. Don't you think you should wait at least a day to let the tabs set?"

Shatterbreath flexed her wings on either side of her. She glanced to her left. The twenty-two tabs set in her wing twinkled in the morning light. With the flattened bronze rungs spaced two iron clasps apart, all the tiny metal pieces gave Shatterbreath's wing a charming uniqueness she wouldn't be quick to admit she admired.

Those tabs had kept her up all night. She wasn't used to them. They tickled, they clinked against stones and they still hurt. Shatterbreath craned her neck and growled. "These things better be worth it," she grumbled back at Kael.

He adjusted the sword sheath at his hip, unclasping the hilt from the sheath and clamping it firmly shut again. Even though the sword inside was broken, he insisted on carrying it. Shatterbreath had found this annoying. He was too sentimental. Leaving the bandits had been quite the ordeal too. Shatterbreath had been almost overjoyed to leave their stinking village, Kael had been less enthusiastic. He actually *liked* them! How deplorable.

"You're telling me? Putting those tabs on had been a nightmare!" He reached backwards to tug on the straps holding his pack to her spines. "Give me a moment to make sure everything is sec—"

"I'll give you to the count of three. One..."

Shatterbreath leapt off the rock, making Kael yelp. She pulled into a loose nosedive, wary of Kael's warning that she couldn't put too much stress on her wings. Before she could pick up a satisfying amount of speed, she pulled out and levelled off.

Shatterbreath felt a poke in her shoulder. Kael had smacked her with his borrowed mace. She rumbled. "Was that supposed to hurt?"

"That wasn't funny."

Shatterbreath angled her wings. "Your things seem to be working."

Kael leaned over. "Indeed they are. Just remember, keep it simple. They are mostly for precaution. If having to rely on them can be avoided, I would prefer—"

"Yeah, yeah. Cautious as a hatchling, slow as a stork, I understand." Fallenfeld was underneath them now. Shatterbreath beat her wings, aiming to put some distance between the city and herself. A thermal assisted her. For a moment, she considered regurgitating her last meal on top of the castle. She decided against it. "Where next, Tiny?"

For a time, Kael remained silent. Shatterbreath found it infectious, and she too went silent, letting the wind carry her into infinity. Oh, how good it felt to be off the ground. How good it felt to be free! She felt as though she had been chained up underground for years on end, and now released back into the world. Though tricky manoeuvring was out of the question, just to be up in the air again was ecstasy.

"Where next," Kael echoed. At once, she understood his silence. He was thinking again; brooding about his home and his friends. "You tell me."

Shatterbreath frowned. "What?"

"I promised you a day to just us. No kingdoms, no people, no BlackHound. Just you and me."

Clenching her jaw, Shatterbreath took a deep breath through her teeth. "Time is slipping by. Any day now and they might arrive. We spent enough time in the bandits' camp already."

"I know."

"We don't have time to spare then!"

"I know." Shatterbreath felt Kael stretch out on her back. "I made a promise that I intend to keep. This has all been for me, and you've been nothing but faithful and helpful—despite all that's happened to you." Kael sighed. "I need to pay you back. Besides, I need a day off too."

Shatterbreath cocked her head. Was he serious? When he had made that promise to her those many moons ago, she had dismissed it in her mind. There was too much to do, no time to fit a day like that in. His voice...he *had* been serious. He could hide his emotion, but not quite well enough to hide his true intention. He was being sincere.

Her spirits lifted even further. Suddenly, all seemed well in the world.

"So," Kael called out, "where to?"

Shatterbreath shook her neck playfully. "I know a place." She pointed her body back west and pumped her wings, picking up speed. What she had in mind wasn't necessarily close, in fact, they would be backtracking a fair distance; a place roughly in between Fallenfeld and the northern tip of the Arnoth mountain range, southeast of her old cave. Somehow, Shatterbreath knew that Kael wouldn't mind.

The flying was slow, levelled and extremely monotonous, but Shatterbreath loved every moment. After being told she would never fly again, being up in the air with the one who saved her wing was all she could ever ask for. She kept her peace, perfectly content. Kael remained quiet as well.

It only seemed like minutes, but before Shatterbreath knew it, a familiar mountain range rolled into view. It was late evening already by the time Shatterbreath started her descent into a wide valley cut deep into the mountains.

The hillside surrounding were so thick with life, the mountainside seemed to be covered in teal fire as a breeze flowed through the valley, shaking the dense foliage. A medium-sized lake ran the length of the valley, shimmering crystalline hues of sage and turquoise. The pure scent of untamed forest came at Shatterbreath from all angles, mixed together with the refreshing hint of clean water and fish.

"What is this place?" Kael asked reverently.

Shatterbreath flew directly above the lake, with the mountains far to either side. "This is where my father and I would go for fish," she said, surveying the land. "It is a lustrous place where no human has ever been. It is inaccessible except for creatures with wings. You are the first person to ever set eyes on this place."

"I am honoured then."

Shatterbreath nodded and swept down closer to the river. Inches from the surface she glided, turning with the valley as it snaked along. Fish jumped here and there, sometimes getting close enough that Shatterbreath could take a snap at them. She dared herself to go closer, letting her wingtips graze the mirror-like surface of the lake. Her talons she dragged through the water as well, creating an arc of water that sprayed up and over her shoulder.

"Ah, watch it there!" Kael cried. "You're spraying me!"

Shatterbreath craned her neck to see. He wasn't even wet.

"Oh, relax. It's just water!"

"Yeah," Kael whined, "but it's cold. Be careful now, you shouldn't get your wing wet."

Shatterbreath snorted, sending smoke trailing. "The water's cold, is it?" Just in spite of him, she leaned forward and dunked her head under the water for a second. The water rushed over her head and shoulders to run over her back. Kael screamed as he was drenched.

Opening her mouth, Shatterbreath bellowed in laughter. Kael wiped the water from his face and cursed, which only made Shatterbreath laugh harder. He made a sound that resembled a growl and then quickly removed his sword sheath and mace, tying them both to his pack.

"Oh yeah?" he said once he had finished. He stood up, making Shatterbreath raise a brow in interest. "Take this!"

Kael dove from Shatterbreath's back, straight onto her good wing. His body landing on the membrane caused her wing to dip just enough to make it hit the water. When it did, Shatterbreath tumbled head-over-tail through the lake. Somehow, she managed to keep her stitched wing up and out of the water.

Once Shatterbreath stopped tumbling, she shot her head out of the water and released a jet of flame high into the air. Kael was treading water several yards away, having trouble because now he was the one laughing.

"You silly hatchling," she spat, paddling over to him. Despite how sore she was from the crash already, she couldn't help but to chuckled as well. "I'll get you for that!"

Kael splashed at her. "Oh yeah, how?"

Shatterbreath cocked her head. "Like this." She spun around and brought her tail up from under Kael. Before he realized what she was doing, she flicked him high up into the air. Flapping her wings twice, she was out of the water and airborne. She caught Kael in the air, then twisted so that her back was facing the surface. She cupped Kael in tight and tucked her good wing tight against her body. Just before they hit the water, Shatterbreath had the satisfaction of hearing Kael scream.

They struck the water like a rock, making a gigantic splash. As the water swirled in around them, Kael slipped from Shatterbreath's grip. Wing still safe out of the water, Shatterbreath waited a heartbeat before emerging. Not a second later, Kael did as well, coughing.

"Alright," he wheezed. "You win."

Shatterbreath waded over to Kael and let him climb up onto her back, where he sprawled, still coughing.

Shatterbreath floated there for a moment, letting the chill of the water tingle her limbs. She felt Kael shivering on her back, so she paddled over to the shore. After collecting his things from her back, he walked onto the beach.

"Aw, now my equipment is wet," he said flatly. "Thanks."

Shatterbreath rested down on the beach, so that only her neck and wings were out of the water. Her tail gently swayed, creating currents around her body. "Whose fault is that?"

Kael frowned. "This time, I blame you."

He took out his sword and stared at it for a few seconds before unclasping the handle. He pulled it free, revealing the broken blade. He put his thumb over the top of the sheath and flipped it over. Water poured out of it.

"What will you do with it?" Shatterbreath asked. "It's useless to you, yet you carry it around as if it's still good."

"I don't know," Kael sighed. "It was truly a fine sword. It felt like...like it was meant for me." He leaned back, pushing his fingers into the fine pale brown sand.

"You have a mace now. Or you can always get a new sword."

Kael nodded. "I suppose so."

He continued to admire the handle of his broken sword a while longer until he proceeded to lie out everything from his pack to dry. He pulled out the armour first, which he also stared at for a time. Shatterbreath rolled her eyes. His suite of armour had many dents and scratches on it now and had all but lost its charming blue lustre. The same was with his shield. By the time he had laid out everything, half an hour had easily passed. It gave Shatterbreath satisfaction to see that his can of spice was ruined.

The sun was going down by then. Wordlessly, Shatterbreath stood up and shook herself, sending water droplets everywhere. Kael winced and blocked his face, but didn't complain. Once she was relatively dry, she paced over and sat down on her haunches beside Kael.

There they stayed, watching as the sun set at the far end of the valley. Rays of brilliant orange shot into the valley, lighting up the lake and making it seem as if it was molten metal. Haunting cries from wild birds echoed through the valley and still the sounds of jumping fish could be heard.

Shatterbreath could remember this lake from her youth so perfectly. The smells, the sights, the sounds...they had all remained the same for over a thousand years. She remembered sitting on the same beach with her father—she had even been sitting in the same posture. She could almost still hear the sound of his heavy breathing, slow and strong. But clearer than that, she remembered sitting on that beach with her mate. The touch of his muzzle against hers as they sat alone for days, the sight of his golden eyes set on hers...

A touch against her leg interrupted Shatterbreath's thoughts. She blinked and the memories were gone. Kael was leaning against her.

"Shatterbreath?" he mumbled.

Shatterbreath took a deep breath. "Yes, Tiny?"

"I—I've been thinking about home... About my friends. "I'm worried about them."

The sun was nearly down. The valley was submerged in a twilight Shatterbreath found troublesome for her eyes. She squinted. "I'm sure they're fine."

Kael perked up, pushing away from her leg. "How can you be sure? What if they're in danger? What if the King's Elite are after them? I—I've been having dreams that they're in trouble. I need to make sure they're okay."

Shatterbreath hummed, trying to calm him down. "I'm sure," she grunted as she stood up, "that they're fine." With a *whump*, she flopped down on her belly behind Kael. He leaned back against her, this time against her foreleg.

"I'm not so sure. I know there isn't much time, but Shatterbreath, we have to go back. I *have* to see them."

Shatterbreath wanted to retort, but she knew Kael wouldn't be persuaded. She nudged him with her muzzle, humming. "Very well."

He patted her. "Thank you."

"Tomorrow we leave."

Kael nodded in agreement. "Yes. Tomorrow, we return to Vallenfend."

Not long after the sun's glow subsided on the horizon, Kael fell asleep on the sand. Shatterbreath, however, could not sleep. The ghosts of her memories plagued her in the night. The valley was filled with them.

Chapter 29

Gently, Laura patted a wet cloth against the prisoner's forehead. He grumbled, but stayed asleep. He had drifted in and out of consciousness for the last four days. Every time he did wake up, Tooran, Faerd and her would gather round to try and get him to eat or drink something. He wasn't doing too well, but Malaricus was positive that his health had improved.

But why he was important, Laura could not understand. Everybody in the cave seemed to be certain he belonged to another continent from across the seas, and that he had once led a rebellion against a terrible empire which... *Blah, blah.* It was all nonsense.

Laura glanced over her shoulder, where Tooran was teaching the refugees how to use the weapons they had found in the cave. He was training them to fight—training them for war. Laura would practise too. She understood the need to defend herself if it came to it, but she thought it was foolish to prepare for a battle. Sometime along the way, their motley family had coined the name *Kael's Army* for themselves. It was then she decided not to train with the rest of them. Faerd learned how to use a sword under Tooran's tutorship, then taught Laura later in private.

Over the sound of footsteps and the occasional grainy scratch of metal, the continuous downpour of rain could distinctly be heard. It had been raining since Faerd and the others had come back! Without relent either—just their luck.

Faerd broke off from the lesson and came over to Laura. He knelt down beside her, frowning. "How's he doing?" he asked.

"Same as always," Laura replied. "He just lies here, looking pained."

"Hmm."

The prisoner winced and brought a hand to his neck. Whether he was dreaming or had an itch, Laura couldn't tell. She reached out and touched the back of his hand, amazed.

"Do—do you think he's—"

"From another land?"

"No," Laura snapped. "Diseased, sick...I don't know. His skin can't be naturally brown, can it?"

Faerd shrugged. "I think that's just how they are over there—where he's from, I mean."

A flash of lightning lit of the cave for a split second. A moment later, it was followed by the boom of thunder.

"At least we won't have to worry about forest fires," Laura chimed, "everything's going to be too wet to burn. Hey, including our firewood! Swell."

She caught Faerd's disappointed look before he turned away. Instantly, she regretted her snide comment. She hated that look, and lately, he had been given it often.

There came one more boom of thunder, *then* a flash of lightning. Laura shot to her feet, staring at the mouth of the cave. "That's not right," she mumbled, "thunder *follows* lightning."

Faerd gave her an unsure look. On cue, the rumbling of thunder filled the cave again. It was low and distant this time and judging from the lightning strike, it was fit. But the first boom...

More thunder. This time, it was sharp, crackling and laced with steel. Laura winced. If the others in the cave hadn't noticed the first irregularity, they did now. Everybody stopped what they were doing and moved to the back of the cave. Tooran snatched a torch off the wall and threw a blanket over it, snuffing it out. After a sharp order, others did the same to the rest. By then, the rocks in the ceiling had ceased to glow and after the last torched died, the only remaining light came from the mouth of the cave.

It wasn't enough.

Somehow, Mrs. Stockwin found her Laura in the throng of terrified bodies. She hugged her daughter tight. Nobody uttered a word, but Laura knew they were all thinking the same thing.

The dragon.

Another crack of thunder penetrated the darkness. It started off like before, sharp and painful, but reduced to a guttural rumbling and then cut off in a snarl. The light far off at the mouth of the cave disappeared. *Disappeared.* Something had moved in front of it.

Laura held her breath, listening for something, *anything.* Nothing. Only the sound of the terrified people around her broke the choking silence.

A smell met Laura's nostrils. Smoke, ash, and something altogether unfamiliar.

"Intruders!" a powerful female voice rang out. It was impossible to determine where it came from. "How *dare* you use my cave as your shelter?"

A faint light appeared in the cave, floating several feet above the ground. Slowly it grew brighter to reveal an upper and lower row of teeth. The orange light was set *inside* that pair of jaws. The mouth reared back and opened wide, releasing a jet of flame that arced above the refugees' heads. Several women, including Mrs. Stockwin, screamed. Everybody flinched and ducked to avoid the searing flame. Not only did the flame light up the room, it also seemed to rejuvenate the stones, causing them to glow once again.

The rest of the beast was revealed with the burst of light. Laura was right. Wings flared, teeth bared, claws outstretched, tail thrashing, it was mighty Shatterbreath.

"Filthy creatures," the dragon roared. "You will die for your intrusion! When will your kind understand? *Keep out of my cave!"*

It reared up high, opening its maw wide. Fire brimmed in its throat. *This is it.* After everything, this is how Laura was going to die. It was going to burn them all and there was nothing any of them could do about it.

Just as the dragon was about to release its fire, it grimaced. Slamming back down on all fours, it closed its mouth and flapped its wings once, and then took a few paces back.

"Stop, stop!" someone yelled. Laura gasped. She knew that voice!

The dragon bent down and a form slid off of its back, clinking as it did. The form stood up straight, paused for a moment under the shadow of the massive dragon and then strolled towards the group of refugees.

The person moved into the light of the glowing stones. Laura's heart leapt in her chest. She had thought he had given up on them.

She thought he had died. She thought...he was gone forever. There, standing in a dented suite of armour, wearing a smirk was the single reason for all of Laura's problems.

Kael Rundown.

Kael couldn't believe it. The last thing he had been expecting was to see his friends gathered in Shatterbreath's cave—as well as a sizeable group of people he didn't know. His surprise and joy were so overwhelming, for a time all he could do was smile at them. Their expressions were priceless. Then, altogether, the spell seemed to break and the throng rushed towards him. Before they reached him, however, Shatterbreath reared up on her hinds legs.

"Back!" she roared. "Get back!"

"Shatterbreath, they are friends," Kael said putting out his palms to try and calm her.

"I don't care. I want them out. This is not their cave to occupy, they are not allowed here." She landed on all fours and crouched low like an agitated dog. "You hear that? *Get out!* This is my cave—and Kael's."

"Well," Kael jutted in, "my cave is their cave. I say they stay."

Shatterbreath whipped her head to scowl at him with one great eye. *"Tiny..."* she hissed.

"We'll talk later. Go catch dinner." Kael gestured towards the opening. "Weren't you saying earlier how much you missed the game on this mountain?"

Shatterbreath huffed and snapped her jaws. She considered him for a moment longer, and then whipped around. Before sulking off, she nudged playfully with her tail. Kael grinned. She was upset that he had talked back to her again, but she'd forgive him.

Kael addressed the crowd. "Uh," he mumbled. "Hi?"

"It's him!" somebody shouted.

"Kael Rundown!"

"He's come to save us!"

Altogether, the crowd closed in on him. Kael was overwhelmed as people he didn't even know began hugging him, some of the women even giving him kisses on the cheek. Unsure at first, he began hugging them back, too relieved to care whether or not they were strangers. After hugging at least five different people, he found somebody he recognized in the crowd.

"Bunda!" Kael shouted. The butcher embraced him so hard, she squeezed the air out of his lungs and caused his still-injured ribs to ache. "It's good to see you too," he wheezed, "but I'm feeling a tad...delicate right now. Could you please...?"

Bunda held Kael at an arm's length away. The relief quickly passed from her face, replaced instead by a scowl. "Where in the world have *you* been? I've lost many a night's rest worrying about you, boy! Quite the trouble you got us into..."

Kael's heart was warmed by hearing her voice again, but his smile faltered. "Trouble? What kind of trouble? Bunda, why is everyone up here?"

Before she could answer, Mrs Stockwin appeared through the crowd, which was beginning to disperse. Kael hugged her and after a few more strangers talked to him, he found Helena as well. Helena was worse for wear. Her hair was even wilder than before and she seemed to be lacking energy. She smiled at Kael through sad eyes and shook his hand, but did not hug him as the others had.

His biggest surprise when came when two young men approached him. "Hey, Kael!" the taller one shouted. "Remember me?"

Kael squinted. "Ha... No."

"It's me, Bruce Nendara! I'll duelled you in the castle training grounds."

Altogether, the memory washed into his mind. Kael flinched. "Whoa! I remember you now! You..." Kael was stumped. The fact that somebody he had fleetingly met several months ago was now safe and sound in Shatterbreath's cave was baffling. Just as baffling was the fact that the twin, Horan, was standing beside him.

The crowd as beginning to back away now, giving Kael some more room. He was rocked to one side, nearly losing his balance, as Faerd practically tackled into him with a great bear hug. It took several seconds to pry him off. Once he had, Kael clasped his shoulder

Kael opened his mouth to say something, but faltered when he spotted the eye patch. "Faerd? Oh my... Wh—what happened to you?"

"You did," Laura hissed.

Kael gasped as he spotted his best friend. He stepped towards her, arms out wide to embrace her, but she stepped away. Kael hesitated. "What's wrong? What did I do?"

"You left us, Kael," Laura snapped. "Left us without a moment's hesitation. Left us to fend for ourselves. We've barely survived."

Kael's heart grieved by the tone of her voice. The times had not been nice to her. Her face was darker than he remembered, her eyes void of the cheeriness he once new. As she stood there, arms crossed, brow slanted, Kael knew at once she was no longer the girl he had reluctantly left behind.

"Laura," Kael said softly. "I'm back now. Everything's okay." He tried to hug her again, but she only backed away further. He wanted things to be the way they had been before. He wanted her to embrace him back and forget whatever troubles they had run into. For a moment, it seemed as though she wished for the same thing.

Laura pushed him away with both arms. "Get away from me."

"Laura, please," Kael pleaded, moving closer. "I—I'm sorry, I had no idea."

"Get away!"

Kael was forced away by a sharp blow to his jaw. He reeled for a moment, wincing. After the stars stopped dancing in his vision, he could see Faerd standing between him and Laura.

"She said to get away," Faerd spat. "You listen to her."

Kael glanced back at the throng. He suddenly felt so conscious, so aware of their watching eyes. Nobody said a word. Kael wiped blood from his lips. He stood up as tall as he could, clenching his fists.

"Faerd, what are you doing?"

"I told Laura I'd protect her," he replied through his teeth, "and I *will*. Even if that means from you."

Kael was about to retort when he noticed how Laura shied behind Faerd. Faerd glanced over his shoulder at her, concern deep in his uncovered eye. At once, Kael understood. He exhaled, and as he did, it felt like he was deflating.

"I don't understand," Kael said, feeling lost, "what happened here. Would *somebody* please tell me? Where did all of you come from? Why are you even up here in the cave anyway?"

"Well then, I'm going to need this," Bunda declared as she threw a blanket to the ground. "It's a long story. First though, I think *we* deserve an explanation, Kael." She sat down on the blanket with a grunt. "I swear, boy, if you don't have a good reason, I'm going to make mincemeat out of you."

Kael winced, well aware Bunda could very well carry through with her threat. "It is indeed going to be a long night." He sat down. "For all of you...newcomers, I'll start from the beginning. I'll explain how this all started and why our city—no continent—is in grave danger. It started when..."

Chapter 30

The air up on top of Shatterbreath's mountain was so refreshing, so cool. Coupled with the chilly rain, it sent shivers up Kael's spine, reminding him he was still alive. The last few hours had seemed so surreal as he recalled his story—right from the beginning. It was like reliving a terrible nightmare. Then again, any memories Kael had of before his enlistment seemed distant and faded, indeed like a dream.

For a time, he wasn't sure what was real anymore.

A great *whoosh* was followed by a heavy grunt and finally, the sound of rocks crumbling under Shatterbreath's colossal body as she touched down nearby. The dragon shook, shedding a great deal of water from her body, although the torrential downpour soon replaced it anyway.

With a grumble, she slumped down beside Kael, clutching a dead buck in her claws. Before engorging on her fresh kill, she considered Kael.

"What vexes you, Tiny?" She stretched her neck and ruffled his wet hair with a warm exhalation. "I thought you'd be happy to see your friends."

Kael clenched a handful of earth. "It's all my fault, Shatterbreath. They were chased out of Vallenfend because they were my friends. They nearly died several times over because of me. Faerd *lost his eye* because of me. We shouldn't have left. I should have stayed and protected them."

Shatterbreath crunched a bone. "Probably."

"Now they're stuck up here for good, forced to live in—no offence—a dragon's cave. Hardly enough food, uncomfortable bedding, constantly worried about Vallenfend attack. Terrible living conditions."

"They are."

He stood up. "How can you be so callous?" Kael yelled. "Do you honestly not care about them? Huh? They are *my* friends, Shatterbreath. Don't you care about me?"

Shatterbreath stopped feasting. Blood dripped from her chin, assisted by the rain. "If you haven't guessed, Tiny, I hate people. Haven't you stopped to consider *me?* You think I can just strut into a bandit village and be fine. You think you can summon me to a city for no reason other than to have some slack-jawed inbred *gawk* at me. You *expect* me to be absolutely tolerant with humans staying in *my* cave—which I've defended from your kind for a thousand years. I care about you, Kael. You are the only person I care about."

Kael's knees went weak and he sat back down. "I—I'm sorry."

Shatterbreath snorted, a flame spurting from her jaw and temporarily lighting up the mountaintop. "I'm not angry." She resumed her feast.

The rain was diminishing. Kael stared up at the gray sky.

"You're friends will be fine," Shatterbreath muttered.

"How can you be so sure?"

She flicked away the antlers. "I brought them a deer to feast on. They will survive for at least a week longer."

"That was a nice thing to do." Kael pondered her words for a moment. *Very nice.* Bearing in mind her recent confession, it wasn't something Shatterbreath would even have considered if it wasn't for Kael. All the trouble she had gone through, all for him. Kael had believed Laura would have stayed by his side through any trial. He was wrong.

Somewhere, deep down, Kael had been hoping, wishing, that Laura would take him back when he saw her again. He had dreamed that they would become partners for life. Now, that dream was broken and impossible.

Torn, Kael glanced over at Shatterbreath. Her emerald eyes glimmered back at him. Kael smiled at her. Shatterbreath hadn't left him—despite all the trouble they had put each other through. He doubted she would ever give up on him.

Shatterbreath was a true friend.

"Thank you," Kael whispered.

"For what?"

He placed a hand against her warm shoulder and smiled. "For sparing my life, for helping me on my quest ever-faithfully. For being my friend who's always there for me. For...everything."

Shatterbreath hummed and nuzzled him with her snout. "You humans are so sentimental." She paused. "In your case, though, I don't mind."

"Kael!"

Kael sighed and stood up. He scanned the mountaintop. Before long, Tooran and Malaricus appeared through the haze, followed closely by another figure. As soon as Kael recognized who it was, he dashed towards them, fists clenched.

"Zeptus!" he hollered. "What is he doing here?!"

Tooran grabbed Kael before he could get to Zeptus. "Stop, Kael! Control yourself!" Tooran demanded.

The ground rumbled as Shatterbreath bounded towards the four men. Shatterbreath reared up and took a deep breath. Tooran gasped up at the dragon and pushed Kael and himself away from Zeptus. Malaricus, however, moved towards him.

"No!" Malaricus yelled up at Shatterbreath. "Mighty dragon, he is no harm!"

Shatterbreath held her breath, eying the scholar. "He won't be much longer. Stand aside or I'll burn you too, old man. I don't care if you *did* help me before."

"You can't, you can't," Malaricus pleaded. "He is no threat, I swear. Don't you remember? I told you that day you took me to help Kael! I tried, at least, to tell you. I—I don't know if you were listening... But, ah, that doesn't matter. You can't kill him, he's innocent."

Kael broke free of Tooran's grasp and seized Zeptus by the front of his purple robe. He swung the thin man around, sending him off his feet and sprawling to the ground, away from Malaricus. Before anybody could do anything else, Shatterbreath placed a paw on Zeptus's chest and leaned in close, her muzzle only inches away from his face.

Zeptus's face went even paler.

321

Although it wasn't pouring anymore, there was still enough rain to run down Shatterbreath's face and trip off the tip of her chin one at a time. With every drop that fell from her face onto his, Zeptus flinched. Either of his hands clutched a talon and he squirmed under her paw to no avail.

Shatterbreath bared her teeth. "Tell me," she rumbled, "why I shouldn't crush him right now."

Malaricus approached her carefully, arms outstretched. "He is but a pawn, mighty dragon, of the King's will. He has been controlled and manipulated for decades, forced to act as the king's spokesperson."

"He is the one who manipulates, I've seen it myself," Kael said. "Crush him now."

"Let me explain," Zeptus croaked under Shatterbreath's paw. "Grand Shatterbreath, I am but a slave to the very magic that grants me my ability to control people." Shatterbreath exhaled, letting her warm breath wash over Zeptus. He squinted, but continued. "For you see, I am a descendant of the Favoured Ones."

"We realized this," Kael growled. "Kill him."

Shatterbreath's tail was thrashing faster now. "Explain," she purred.

"Though I have silver tongue, I am forced through my blessing to haplessly obey the highest authority—which in this case, is King Morrindale. Whether I like it or not, I am under his complete control."

"If you disobey?"

"Alas," Zeptus sighed, "such a thing is impossible. My free agency is like a locked door in my mind. It is clearly there in front of me, but without the key, no force on earth can open that latch. Simply put, I cannot disobey."

Shatterbreath twitched. She frowned and, reluctantly at first, removed her paw from his chest.

"What are you doing?" Kael demanded. "You *believe* him?"

"Yes," Shatterbreath said resolutely. She studied Zeptus. "Time has warped his bloodline's gift beyond anything I would have expected. It seems not only does the gift dilute, but change as well. In your case, Purple Eyes, a huge detriment."

Zeptus stood up and brushed himself off. The rain had stopped entirely by then. "Yes. I have been plagued by this curse for my entire life. Believe me; I never wanted any of this to happen. Kael Rundown, what has become of Vallenfend, the harm that befell your friends and the trouble I've put you through, I sincerely apologize for."

Kael was taken aback. He struggled to find his voice as he reflected Zeptus's words. *His friends...* "Tooran, what are we going to do about Korjan? How are we going to get him back? Is—is he even still alive?"

"Yes," Tooran said with a nod, "undoubtedly, the King's Elite would spare him for questioning."

Kael walked past Zeptus and closer to Tooran. "What about negotiation? Can we convince them to surrender him to us?"

"Doubtful," Tooran replied, tone flat. "You'd have to exchange something of *extreme* value to convince the king to trade. Considering the wealth of treasure he has already, I doubt you could find anything that would suffice."

"How about *someone* of value?" Shatterbreath suggested.

"Who?" Malaricus cried. "Who could we possibly trade? We'd be asking them to throw their life away! We certainly can't trade you, Kael."

Kael cradled his chin, deep in thought. "Shatterbreath could get me out. I—I seemed to be blamed for all this anyway, this could be a chance to make up for my wrongs."

Tooran shook his head. "No, I am afraid to say it, but you are worth more than my father at this point. King Morrindale would likely decide to kill you on spot instead of throwing you in the dungeons to be saved by the dragon. *Especially* after we managed to break in and out of there already—and we're only human."

Shatterbreath rumbled, catching their attention. She nudged Zeptus with her muzzle, who grimaced. "What about him then?"

Tooran shook his head vigorously. "Not an option. Under the king's control, Zeptus is just too great of a threat. That's why we decided to assassinate him in the first place."

"If you don't mind, may I have an opinion on all—"

"Silence," Shatterbreath cut Zeptus off. He shut his mouth at once. She cocked her head. "What's this?" she cooed, "that was unusual. Turn around."

Zeptus did so, still wordless.

Shatterbreath shifted her weight, her tail dancing playfully. "How interesting..." She stood up and paced around the advisor a few times, eyeing him the whole time. "Bend over, touch your toes. Pick up that rock. Good, now, throw it." Zeptus did each thing in turn, body stiff and looking quite unamused.

"Interesting indeed," Kael stated as he watched. "Would you stop making him do stupid pet tricks? We're trying to be serious here."

"I'm always serious," Shatterbreath snapped. "Purple Eyes, explain to me more about your curse. Who are you forced to obey?"

"Whoever has the highest authority," Zeptus replied. "Who that exactly is, I'm not quite sure. Basal Morrindale is the king, so common sense dictates he holds the most power."

Shatterbreath's eyes narrowed. "Common sense is often wrong. Tell me, frail human, what if you are not in the presence of said 'highest authority'."

"His word is still mine to obey. King Morrindale commanded me to obey only his orders. That command is standing."

"Hmm," Shatterbreath purred. Kael was beginning to understand what she was getting at. "Then explain to me why *I* could command you?"

Zeptus faltered. He opened his mouth to counter, but stopped and only stared up at her, confused.

"I am one of the only surviving Elder Dragons, ancestral guardians of this land. There is *no* higher voice than mine." She leaned in close. "So you, pathetic creature, are under my control now. Your petty king's orders are worthless."

Zeptus winced as if physically struck. For a moment, his expression was conflicted, as if he didn't know whether to be relieved or afraid. His hands started to tremble.

"Which means..." Kael snapped his fingers. "Which means Zeptus is no longer King Morrindale's advantage! Malaricus, go fetch Mrs. Stockwin, Helena, Bunda, Faerd and Laura. We need a family discussion."

Malaricus hurried off. A shuffle caught Kael's attention. Zeptus had fallen to his knees. Kael thought for a moment it was because of his grief—Kael knew what it felt like to be under the control of a dragon. But when he looked again, Kael realized tears were streaming down Zeptus's face.

"At last," he sobbed, "at long last, I will be freed from King Morrindale's twisting control! No longer will I be the lone cause to so many innocents' deaths! No longer is the weight of his sin bearing down on my shoulders. Oh, thank you, thank you, mighty dragon!"

Shatterbreath stretched her wings and rolled her shoulders. "Do not forget, you are under *my* control. I could make you my official cleaner to polish my scales day in and day out. Or, if I so decide, I could kill you in an instant. I wouldn't regret it."

"Anything would be a better than to suffer the deaths of any more innocent youth. I would rather die by your might than the blades of the BlackHound Empire."

"The BlackHound Empire," Kael ventured, approaching Zeptus, "when will they arrive?"

Zeptus put a hand to his forehead and closed his eyes. "I've lost track of the days... Soon, Rundown," he said ominously, "soon."

"What is it Malaricus?" Bunda's angry voice echoed from across the mountaintop. "I need my sleep you know! This better be..." Her voice trailed off as she spotted Zeptus. Behind her, Helena, Laura and her mother stopped as well.

Zeptus stood up straight after wiping his eyes. Even under the circumstances, he strived to look as trimmed and imposing as he could. Kael had to admit, he was good at it.

The advisor nodded at the newcomers. "Good evening."

325

"Good evening?" Bunda roared. "GOOD EVENING? Oh, where's my cleaver? I'm going to cut out his throat and decorate the back of the cave with his lungs." She started to charge towards him. "You know what you've done to me? To my boys? To *us?* You are the lone..." She began to tremble, too enraged for words.

Mrs. Stockwin, Helena and Laura had all started yelling as well at Tooran and Malaricus, who did their best to keep them at bay. Kael couldn't understand what they were saying individually, but the message was quite clear. He had never heard any of them swear so much... His main focus, however, was Bunda.

Before the woman reached Zeptus, Shatterbreath blocked her with her tail. The butcher tried desperately to climb past, but to no avail. Zeptus folded his arms behind his back, expression blank.

"Control yourself," Shatterbreath growled, "or I will." She gave Bunda a shove with her tail, sprawling the butcher.

Bunda clambered back to her feet, breathing heavily in contempt towards Zeptus. She whipped away from him to face Kael. "Kael!" she roared. "Kael, why is that man still alive? You're too weak to kill him. Let me do it."

Kael grabbed Bunda's arms to restrain her. "Bunda, listen. Ah, *listen.*" Bunda stopped squirming. "Zeptus will be gone soon enough, and Korjan will be here instead."

Helena pushed past Tooran. "Korjan?" she gasped. "Tell me how we can get him back!"

"We're going to propose a trade to King Morrindale: Zeptus for Korjan," Kael explained. "Hopefully, he'll take the bait."

"Giving Zeptus back seems kind of redundant," Laura said cynically "if we lost Korjan bringing that man up here to begin with."

"He's..." Kael hesitated. "Zeptus is—is a good man. He's been controlled by the king this whole time. He's really meant well."

Mrs. Stockwin snorted. The other women looked sceptical as well.

"It's hard to believe, but Zeptus is cursed," Kael explained. "He's forced to obey whoever holds the highest authority. That person used to be King Morrindale, but now, Zeptus must obey Shatterbreath."

"No offense," Laura scoffed, "but a dragon holding more authority than a monarch? Isn't that a little...absurd?"

Shatterbreath hissed. "Obviously, it is beyond your comprehension, silly morsel."

"Enough." Kael put out his hands to stop them. If they got in an argument, Kael seriously doubted Laura would win. "In any case, Zeptus is no longer a threat. Returning him to the king would prove to be no detriment."

"Wait," Tooran interrupted, "would Morrindale fall for this trade in the first place? You made it clear that you were leaving on your own will, Zeptus."

Zeptus shook his head. "Basal will take me back. He still believes he has complete control over me."

"Then what are we waiting for?" Helena breathed. "Give the king his monster!"

"I figured we should have discussed it first before carrying through with this plan." Kael scanned the faces his of his friends. "Obviously enough, it's unanimous."

"Then it's back to the king with me," Zeptus sighed.

"Zeptus," Shatterbreath declared, "you have been imprisoned within the confines of your own ability. I am Shatterbreath, Elder Dragon. From henceforth, I release you of your chains. From now on, you will obey only your own will." Zeptus's face lit up. "If somebody gives you an order, you will carry through with it only on your own accord. No longer will your blessing be your curse. No longer will you be the pawn of others." She craned her neck to touch his forehead with the tip of her snout. "Unless the impossible situation arrives where one with higher authority says otherwise, I hereby give you the key to your agency. Unlock that door."

Tears were brimming in Zeptus's eyes once again. "Thank you," he whispered. "I will. I won't forget this, Grand Shatterbreath."

"Now to negotiate the terms of trade with King Murderdale..." Kael muttered.

"Kael!" Faerd came running up the mountainside. Kael was wondering where he had been. "Kael, the prisoner has awoken! You should come at once."

Kael nodded. He had heard mention of the BlackHound prisoner, but hadn't actually seen him yet. He was interested to see what the man would have to say. Kael quickly climbed aboard Shatterbreath's back. With two strong wing beats, she was airborne. She angled her wings and they soared into the mouth of her cave. She walked the rest of the distance to the back, where the crowd separated to let them through.

"We gave him some water," a woman told Kael. "He's doing better than he was, but speak gently, he's far from healthy."

"I understand." Kael squatted down beside the heap of blankets the prisoner was lying on. Shatterbreath's exhalations washed over him from behind as she sat on her haunches to watch as well. Kael studied the prisoner's skin, amazed. He had heard all the talk of how dark their skin was, but had never experienced it for himself. Vert's words came to mind.

Dark as midnight.

The prisoner groaned and turned his head to face Kael. His eyes were even darker. "You... You're the leader of this resistance, aren't you?"

"More or less," Kael replied. "If you can call it a resistance. What about you?"

The prisoner squinted. "I was also a leader of a resistance at one time, before my dignity was ripped from me. We knew that the BlackHound Empire was planning to conquer new lands. We did not want others to feel the sting of its evil, so we decided to brave the voyage here in order to warn you. You know of the BlackHound Empire, correct?"

Kael nodded.

"But when we arrived here, instead of being accepted with joy, we found the BlackHound Empire's influence was already strong. Our craft was destroyed and my men all slain. They spared only me."

"Tell me more of the Empire," Kael said. "I need to know what we're up against."

"The BlackHound Empire is a terrible thing." The prisoner coughed. "They're leader is a vile, corrupted tyrant who believes there is no room for imperfection. Many have died because they did not meet his self-described code of perfection. They have enslaved so many nations to help fuel their ongoing war machine. In their wake, the vast armies leave only bloodshed and scorched land. It is only a matter of time before our over-populated continent because almost uninhabitable. That is why the campaign was launched to conquer lands overseas."

"What will happen when they come here?"

"There is no room for your people. Everybody on this continent will either be destroyed or enslaved."

Kael clenched his jaw. *Just as he suspected.* "I have been working to gather reinforcements to battle the Empire's invasion. How many soldiers will arrive?"

The prisoner grimaced. "The invasion force is massive. In total, it represents almost a third of the entire army at the Empire's disposal."

"We have Shatterbreath, this dragon, to assist us as well," Kael countered.

The prisoner shook his head. "The BlackHound Empire's second-in-command, Commander Coar'saliz, is spearheading the operation. He is almost as ruthless and cunning as his master. He will have surely discovered a way to dispose of your dragon I'm afraid. Even in a strategic location such as this, it will not be easy to fend them off. To try would mean countless deaths."

"There will be countless more if we fail. We will stand and we will fight. To the last man."

The prisoner admired Kael with his faded eyes. "You are brave, young warrior. To you and yours, I wish the best of luck. Be warned however, more is at stake than you realize. With so much of its army away, the BlackHound Empire will not be as powerful in the Homeland. If news that the Empire's overseas campaign failed, it will give the resistance hope. The people may realize that the Empire can indeed be defeated. A loss so massive would spur them into action. This invasion is pivotal to the sake of *everything*. If they succeed, the BlackHound Empire may never die."

Why did Kael suddenly feel so much more burdened? "I understand."

The prisoner stirred. One thin arm snaked out of the blankets and seized Kael's hand with surprising strength. "Don't judge my people by the BlackHound Empire's influence alone," the prisoner pleaded. "Please. The men in the army do what they are ordered to, it is not their fault. My people aren't evil..." His hand went limp and the prisoner closed his eyes.

Kael held the prisoner's hand for a moment longer, conflicted. He felt weighed down, is if somebody had thrown a second suit of armour over him. Kael chewed his lip and at last, released the prisoner's hand to put a finger to the man's temple. He was still alive.

"Shatterbreath?" he said over his shoulder.

"We cannot tarry any longer here," the dragon rumbled. "We've wasted enough time. The more kingdoms we can visit before they come, the more likely we will acquire reinforcements."

"You're right," Kael said. Just then, Laura and the others entered the cave. Kael sighed. "I think I've seen enough of my friends for now anyway."

"You're leaving?" Faerd said from behind.

Kael turned around. The refugees were all watching him. "I am," Kael declared. "I—I am needed elsewhere."

Off to the side, Laura folded her arms.

"Then we will let you go," Tooran announced. "We can fend for ourselves, Kael. I am training these men and women to fight with the blade. No longer are we defenceless. Will we survive."

"Thank you Tooran. To you, all of you, my family, I wish you the best of luck."

Kael started towards the mouth of the cave. As he passed close by Tooran, he motioned for him to follow. "Come with me," Kael whispered, "and we'll get your father back before I leave."

As Kael walked on, people gave him farewells.

"Good luck, Kael," a woman said.

"May the gods bless your soul."

Kael looked to either side, scanning their faces. Such strong people were they, in body and spirit. It made his soul rejoice knowing that there were people that believed so whole-heartedly in him. It gave him hope that others would as well.

Before he exited the cave, Kael turned around to give his family one last look. *His family*. It had started off small, but oh how it had grown. No longer was it just he and his close friends. Family was more than that. Family was the beacon for everything Kael worked to achieve. Family was hope.

"Take heart knowing," a woman began, "that *Kael's Army* is here for you."

Kael only had eyes for Laura. She scowled at him and turned away. Faerd tried to comfort her, but she only moved further away.

"Thank you, and...farewell. I will return with reinforcements, I promise." Kael raised a hand. "Together, we will crush the BlackHound Empire! Together..." He made a fist. "We will secure a future. Together, we will save this land."

Shatterbreath roared in agreement.

With that, Kael climbed aboard Shatterbreath. Gingerly, Tooran followed.

"To the top of the mountain," Kael announced.

With a hop and a spring, Shatterbreath was airborne. In less than ten seconds, she landed heavily on the mountaintop. Zeptus was waiting for them.

Zeptus fingered a gold coin in his fingers. A gold piece he had *borrowed* from the treasure room. Described on its surface was the BlackHound Empire's hound insignia. He flipped it over in his fingers, brooding.

Freedom. Absolute, unconditional freedom. He could do whatever he wanted. *Whatever he wanted.* How relieved he was. Relieved and angered. The others, the ones who captured him, treated him as nothing more than an animal, acting as if his life was as precious as a chicken's. They stood there, deliberating his fate as if he wasn't even standing there!

He was forever indebted to the dragon for lifting his curse. But the others... He had no tie with them. What would be their fate? Zeptus squeezed the foreign coin between his fingers. He decided to leave their future up to chance. He flicked the coin into the air. As he did, the dragon crested the mountaintop.

Zeptus caught the coin and studied which side it landed on. He frowned at it as the dragon landed nearby. Was he happy with the trade they were initiating? Absolutely not. Could he do anything about it? Absolutely not.

Then, he thought, *I will bide my time.*

Tooran jumped down from the dragon and strutted over to Zeptus.

As always.

Chapter 31

There came a rap on the iron bars. Korjan lifted his head. "Oi, you're a lucky one," his cell guard croaked. "We're letting you out."

Korjan sniffed. "To kill me?"

"To release you."

Korjan wearily stood up. Fatigued as he was, he still stood taller and straighter than his guard. "I doubt it." But as the guard protruded a set of keys and unlocked the door, Korjan had second thoughts.

"Like I said," the guard rasped as he seized Korjan's arm. "You're a lucky one. Someone's come with Zeptus as their hostage. They're trading him for you." As the guard led Korjan through the nearly-empty dungeon, he smacked his forehead. "Imagine that! Why would *anybody* trade Lord Zeptus for *you?* Huh, I didn't even know he was missing!"

Korjan smirked. "Imagine that," he echoed.

The chains to the cuffs wrapped around Korjan's arms jingled as they walked up the stairs. At the top, more guards were waiting. King's Elite guards as well. It seemed the king had increased his security all around after Korjan's escapade through the castle. Korjan's guard pulled a letter out of his pocket and showed it the only man not wearing a cloth over his face.

"King's orders—it's urgent," Korjan's guard announced.

The soldier sneered. "Yeah, I've heard. I think there's something peculiar about this." The soldier grabbed Korjan's cuff chain and lifted it to eye-level. "Your lot burst in here and take Zeptus—just to give him back. What are you planning?"

Korjan shrugged. "I wish I knew."

The soldier backhanded him. "Tell me, knave!" he spat.

"Oi, don't do that!" The King's Elite soldier turned his fiery gaze from Korjan to his guard. Korjan's guard cleared his throat. "Kael Rundown's demanded this man to be left unharmed."

"Kael Rundown?" the soldier echoed. Korjan caught his breath. "Kael...with the dragon, Kael?"

Korjan's guard nodded.

"So he's back," Korjan wondered aloud.

The soldier brought Korjan closer, still holding tight to the chain connecting his wrists. Breath hot in Korjan's face, he uttered, "He left?"

Korjan grimaced.

The soldier scrutinized him a few minutes more. "Fine, take him away," he said at last, releasing the chain.

With a nod, the guard continued on his way, Korjan in tow. The view of the inside of the castle was fleeting, but it brought Korjan some satisfaction to see that hallway Tooran had blown open was closed. Within minutes, they exited the castle.

Just outside, there was a small procession waiting to escort them. There were several guards garbed in blue, as well as the king himself, looking fatter than usual sitting atop a war charger. But, Korjan noted, no King's Elite soldiers.

Without a second glance, King Morrindale set off, closely followed by his entourage. Accompanied by another man, Korjan's guard shoved him along. People in the streets of Vallenfend stopped whatever they were doing to gawk at the procession. Almost everybody had seen the king at least once before at one of his public meetings, but not like what he was doing.

In fact, some of the women thought they could take advantage of the situation. A group of them—Korjan couldn't quite see how many—charged the procession. They battered against the line of soldiers in blue, waving pots or steak knives, trying to get at the king.

The skirmish ended as fast as it began.

For it seemed, as soon as the women collided with the soldiers, they collapsed. Korjan clearly witnessed as a soldier in blue removed a throwing knife from a woman's chest before pushing her body aside.

People screamed and backed away from the procession, but Korjan's eyes were to the roofs. Those knives had not come from ground forces. No, somewhere out there were members of the King's Elite. King Morrindale wouldn't compromise his safety by trusting regular soldiers alone.

Without any further incident, the procession arrived at the front gate.

King Morrindale stopped and whipped around. A crowd had gathered behind them, eager to see what the king was up to. They murmured amongst themselves, pointing fingers at Korjan.

The king frowned and leaned over. "Once we're through the gate," he whispered to the nearest soldier, "lock it. I don't want anybody getting out...or *in.*"

"Understood."

"As for Zeptus..." King Morrindale threw an unreadable look at Korjan. "Have him brought through one of the secret entrances. He's not missing, remember? Concerning Kael..." Korjan couldn't hear him as he lowered his voice.

The soldier nodded his head and after King Morrindale had finished whispering to him, made a gesture to the gatekeepers up on the wall. With a groan, the gates swung open, revealing the fields outside—and something Korjan would always remember.

Kael stood several yards outside the city wall, one hand resting a dagger near Zeptus's neck. He was garbed in a blue-tinted set of armour, bathed in the light of midday, looking like the gods' messenger. A mace hung at his hip—odd, considering he was clutching the handle of his sheathed sword with his other hand.

King Morrindale's frown intensified. As did the murmuring behind him. With a flick of his finger, the procession quickly marched outside and the gates slammed closed behind them. Korjan could only imagine the talk that would be circulating through the city the next day.

"Kael Rundown," King Morrindale called out. "What a pleasure it is to see you."

"Where's Korjan?" Kael called out.

The soldiers divided to give a full view of the blacksmith. "He's here," the king assured. "Safe and sound, just like we negotiated. Now, give back my advisor and you can have your scum back."

"At the same time," Kael said. "No tricks now."

The king smiled like a demon. "Tricks? Me? Please, who do you take me for?"

Kael sneered, but didn't say a word. He released Zeptus and gave the man a shove. Cautiously, the advisor took a few steps.

"Let him go," King Morrindale ordered. On cue, Korjan was released as well.

Korjan hesitated, hardly believing what was happening. Was it a dream? It seemed too impossibly good to be true. Kael Rundown had personally come back to rescue him?

Dream or not, Korjan stumbled towards Kael, too grateful to be sceptical. Kael's expression softened as Korjan neared. Zeptus, on the other hand, raised his brow as they passed each other. Ever so slightly, Korjan nodded back.

Three-quarters of the way to Kael, a thought struck Korjan. *The King's Elite.* They had been following the king and him during their journey to the gate. There was no way they wouldn't be watching then. Which meant Kael was in grave danger.

Korjan broke into a sprint. "Kael!" he yelled. "Kael, run! It's a trap!"

The king cursed from behind. Korjan could distinctly hear him yell a command: "Attack."

Korjan dove to the ground just in time. Several objects whizzed past, sinking into the earth around him. Kael had drawn his shield before the throwing knives struck him. Four knives stuck in his shield, another two into his greaves and one in his pauldron.

"To me!" Kael yelled to Korjan.

Before another volley of knives came, Korjan shuffled to get behind Kael. As he did, he felt a blade sink into the back of his thigh. Ignoring both the pain in his leg and lack of energy, Korjan stood up.

"Are you alright?" Kael asked.

"Don't worry about me," Korjan grunted, turning his attention to the attackers. The king and Zeptus had already disappeared, replaced by several members of the King's Elite. Archers appeared at the top of the wall as well as the assassins encircled.

"Can you fight?" Kael whispered.

Korjan scanned the attackers. "Not this many."

"I'm not in the best fighting condition either." On cue, Kael clutched his chest with his free hand. They both ducked as a volley of arrows flew at them. "All we need is a minute or so, hold on, Korjan."

Without further explanation, Kael put his fingers to his lips and whistled. After that, he handed Korjan a mace and pulled a knife out of his pocket for himself.

The soldiers attacked.

Adrenaline pumped through Korjan, filling him with strength. He blocked an attack with the shaft of the mace, pushed the soldier's blade away and carried through with a blow to the man's shoulder. Bone cracked under the weapon.

More soldiers replaced him. Korjan deflected several blows at once, but fighting with a blunt weapon was not his forte. Before long, it was evident that Kael and Korjan were losing. Kael had managed to get a better weapon—an axe—but there were too many soldiers. Plus, every so often, an arrow would narrowly miss either of them, reminding Korjan of the archers positioned up on the wall.

A strong attack caught Korjan off-guard. The soldier attacking took advantage and went in for a killing lunge. Before he could strike, an arrow buried itself in the man's chest, who promptly fell to the ground, dead.

Confused, Korjan turned his attention to the top of the wall. One of the archers lowered his bow and gave Korjan a mock solute. A moment later, the same archer tore his face mask off and kicked the archer next to him from the wall. Korjan gasped. It was Tooran!

Still, even with Tooran eliminating the archers up on the wall, Korjan's lack of energy was catching up with him. He was slowing down, and Kael too, was fighting with less vigour.

Salvation came with a roar. The enormous blue dragon came swooping in to tear away at the throng of soldiers. Korjan turned uncertainly to Kael, who had already begun moving towards the dragon. Korjan followed his lead.

A ballista whizzed past overhead, narrowly missing the dragon. Shatterbreath hissed and pointed her muzzle towards the source—a ballista station positioned at a corner of the wall. Kael stopped her.

"First priority!" he yelled, pointing at Korjan. "Tooran will take care of that. Kill everyone here, protect him!"

"Understood," Shatterbreath rumbled in reply. Before Korjan could even protest, she picked him up by the scruff of his tunic and placed him less-than-gently in between her shoulders.

The knife wound in Korjan's thigh was bleeding profusely. The loss of blood was working against him, making the scene blurred and even more confusing. For a time, he watched from between two massive wings as Kael and the dragon worked in perfect harmony. He attacked from the ground to eliminate soldiers holding longer weapons such as halberds and spears while she defended him. At one point, Kael dove into a roll while at the same time, she swiped perfectly above his head, decapitating a soldier.

Tooran, on the other hand, had already made his way to the ballista. The two women operating the machine didn't stand a chance against Tooran. Korjan watched his son proudly before the blackness in his vision overwhelmed him.

"Don't worry," a strong warm voice reassured. It took a moment, but Korjan realized it was the dragon's. "We have you."

Korjan passed out.

Korjan fluttered into consciousness, slowly becoming aware of voices around him. When he opened his eyes, he was happy to find Helena staring down at him. He was relieved to discover himself lying on the floor of Shatterbreath's cave; anything was better than the castle's dungeons.

Korjan reached up and touched her face. She didn't mind his rough hands.

"Helena," he mumbled. "Wha—what happened?"

"You risked your own life to save our family. You shouldn't have. It was dangerous and reckless. You could have been killed! Lucky for you they just captured you instead." Her expression softened. "But you're back now. I guess I'll forgive you."

"They demanded me to tell them everything I knew or else they'd torture me," Korjan said.

"And?"

"I've never been much of a talker."

"You're back now," Helena cooed. She squeezed his hand. "Nothing else matters."

Korjan turned his head. He could see the rest of the women and few men they had managed to smuggle out of the city sleeping nearby. Dresda was among them, leaning against a wall close to Korjan, also asleep. Korjan beamed at him. He had done well.

"Helena," Korjan ventured, "what happened? How did I get here? I remember...fighting. But it couldn't be possible, it must have been a dream."

Helena shook her head. "Tooran saved you. Tooran, Kael and the dragon."

A stab of pain shot up his leg, reminding Korjan of the battle. "Where is he now?"

"Tooran is sleeping."

"No," Korjan said. "Where is Kael Rundown?"

"He left. I think it's kind of rude of him to just leave us once again without telling us where he's going or when he'll be back. On top of that—"

Korjan let Helena rant on. She was just venting some anger, nothing more. He let his head fall back to his pillow and shifted his injured leg. Kael was gone, once again on his quest. Korjan smiled. He understood that Kael had to hurry. There was no time to look after him as he recuperated. Kael was busy enough saving Vallenfend.

He would have it no other way.

Chapter 32

With all the soldiers down, Kael hesitated. Korjan was safe on Shatterbreath's back, but he was bleeding from the leg. He needed medical help at once. But now was a perfect time to make a stand. The defences from the southernmost part of the wall were non-existent and reinforcements would take a long time to arrive if they dared to come.

"Land up on the wall," Kael demanded as he hopped aboard Shatterbreath.

With two great flaps they were both on the wall, overlooking Vallenfend. To Kael's surprise and relief, there was already a large crowd gathered in front of the gate. The king must have made a scene to get there to begin with.

Kael made a gesture and Tooran scrambled onto Shatterbreath's back to assist his father. Kael paced along the wall, scanning the crowd who was staring up at him expectedly. Shatterbreath growled and repositioned herself.

Kael took a deep breath. "Men and women of Vallenfend!" he cried. "I am Kael Rundown." A susurrus made him pause. "I have come back to deliver a message. Your king is a fiend and a liar. He sends your men off to die for the sake of greed."

"He lies!" a woman shouted. "You tried to feed us the same story as before, liar!"

"You're affiliated with the dragon!" another woman yelled. "Zeptus was correct! You can't be trusted."

"Fools," Shatterbreath hissed. The crowd went silent. "Are you so blinded by untruths that you cannot see the plot laid out around you? You follow orders like sheep, yet not know the real reason why. Would you let your children so die in vain? I should just kill you all now."

That gave Kael an idea. He already tried convincing them of the BlackHound Empire. Maybe it was time to convince them of something else.

"Your children," Kael ventured. "How long have our men been dwindling? How long has King Morrindale demanded every able-bodied man must go to eventually die? But not all young men have gone to fight. No, some have stayed."

Nobody said a word. If the crowd was silent because they feared Shatterbreath or if they were genuinely interested, Kael couldn't tell.

"King Morrindale has chosen the strongest young men to stay—to become members of his own secret task force!"

Whispers dotted the crowd.

"I speak the truth." Kael walked over to where Tooran had killed one of the archers. "See for yourself." He hefted the body up to show the crowd.

The crowd was thrumming now. Arguments soon broke out among them. Kael clenched his jaw, praying for them to believe him.

"It is true!" Tooran declared. He stepped down from Shatterbreath and onto the wall's top. "I used to be a member of what is known as the King's Elite. As Kael said, we were specifically chosen and secretly trained from young ages to become the ultimate warriors. Quick, silent and powerful, we carried through with the king's orders with all obedience. I myself have been on countless missions to silence those who speak against the king and quell any doubters among your populace."

The majority of the crowd had fallen silent. Kael could see so many shocked faces out there. One woman turned around near the front to face the crowd.

"The king has been keeping our boys for his own selfish purposes all this time," she shouted, "to use against his own people? He's going against this own conscription. He's going against his own law! We've all had friends disappear over the years. Now I understand why! The king *killed* them! With our own boys!"

"He's a tyrant!"

"Down with King Murderdale!"

"I will refuse to let any more of my boys turn into one of *them*."

"We've done all we can here," Shatterbreath grunted. "Let's leave at once."

Kael and Tooran clambered onto her back. She gave one last scowl at the roaring crowd, then took off, aiming at once to the top of her mountain. In a matter of minutes, they had landed on the foggy mountaintop. Before they disembarked, Tooran placed a hand on Kael's shoulder.

"My eternal thanks," he said, "for saving my father. For...ultimately saving me."

Kael nodded. "Stay safe, Tooran. We'll win this yet. Protect our family well."

"With all my strength." Tooran climbed off Shatterbreath, Korjan cradled in his arms. "And to you, might dragon, fly well."

Shatterbreath studied him. "An unfamiliar farewell...but I like it. Keep strong, warrior."

Kael double-checked to make sure everything he needed was still strapped to Shatterbreath's back. He patted her back and with a roar, she took off, leaving behind her mountain, and his family.

He wasn't grieved, however. He'd be seeing them again soon enough.

End of Book Two.